BY PLUCK
and
BY FAITH

The Odyssey of an Irish-American family

Lansing Bergeron

outskirts
press

Outskirts Press, Inc.
http://www.outskirtspress.com

ISBN: 978-1-9772-0022-8

PRINTED IN THE UNITED STATES OF AMERICA

This book was completed on Valentine's Day, 2018 and Is dedicated to Patricia, my loving wife, a woman of extraordinary compassion and unwavering dedication to her family, and the "last Brett standing". This is my Valentine's Day gift to you. It is also dedicated to all the lineal and non lineal Brett descendants who carry the DNA of John and Mary Brett.

PROLOGUE

There are three deaths. The first is when the body ceases to function. The second is when the body is consigned to the grave. The third is at that moment, sometime in the future, when your name is spoken for the last time.

David Eagleman

Pluck (Noun) *Cambridge Dictionary*
  >Bravery and a strong desire to succeed
  >Spirited and determined courage

Pluck (noun) *Merriam-Webster*
  >Courageous readiness to fight or continue against odds: dogged resolution

Faith (noun) *Oxford English Dictionary*
  >Complete trust or confidence in someone or something
  >Intellectual assent and trust

I am not, nor do I pretend to be, a professional writer. I simply have a story to share that I believe to be worthy and potentially entertaining and compelling. The story is loosely based upon the life and times of a family of Irish immigrants surnamed Brett; and the word *loosely* is an important qualification. Delving into archives up to one hundred years old is no easy task, especially if the exercise pertains to an "average" family with little historical reference. Anecdotes, rumor and legends, from necessity, must be given more credence than they deserve, and some details might very well be pure fiction. Be advised therefore, that this is not an historical family biography, but simply an unbridled attempt to create a narrative that relates the facts as closely as possible, while also producing a work that is enjoyable to read. If you, dear reader, should happen to be among the remaining descendants of the family and take offense or umbrage from some of the references, get over it. You would not be doing justice to your heritage. There is also historical reference woven throughout the book, to provide context and a perspective of the particular time, but the majority is from memory, and although I'm a history buff, and attempted to provide accuracy, it should not be assumed to be exact. I simply didn't want to take the time to research and verify accuracy, thereby disturbing my flow of creativity. My memory isn't what it once was. Besides, it was added purely for period flavor and interest, and although the Brett family had direct involvement, as some of the history was being made, some embellishment is likely and by design and only intended to make for more interesting reading.

With that disclaimer offered however, I did try to adhere as closely to fact, imperfect memory aside, as possible, with only a judicious application of creative license.

And finally, regarding creative license; I invoked more of it during the early part of this saga, and less after I became personally involved as part of the family and could relate experiences as more of a first person narrative. You will undoubtedly notice that the writing style of the composition changes abruptly at the point of my introduction into the story.

The impetus and inspiration for authoring this chronicle of the Brett family occurred quite serendipitously. My wife, Patricia, and I had transported the cremains of her brother, Charlie Brett, to St. Peter's Cemetery in Danbury, Connecticut for interment in the family plot, and while there, perform a little maintenance and light landscaping; planting flowers, removing grass incursion, edging and trimming around the various markers and headstones that were laid flat on the ground. Even though this was a perpetual care cemetery, we generally attended to site beautification whenever we visited. After most had been cleaned up nicely, leaving only the border of the large vertical granite family marker to be edged and the surface perimeter of the smaller marble headstone of the family patriarch, John James Brett, to be cleared- the latter being almost 60% obscured by trailing grass. As I edged the perimeter and cleared the surface of John Brett's stone, I noticed that the date of his passing was precisely 100 years, to the day, earlier. I was astounded by the coincidence. We had just placed the last of John and Mary's descendants, with the surname Brett, at rest next to his paternal grandmother and grandfather. An exact century had separated the two events and the reunion of souls had occurred. As I knelt there in deep contemplation, Patricia approached and knelt beside me. I asked her what she knew of her grandfather, John, and she replied; "Very little. He died thirty years before I was born. Relatives had always said that he was a good man, hard working and loving, with a big heart, jovial personality and a certain feisty pluck about him." She concluded by saying; "I only know for sure that they emigrated from Ireland in the late 1800's with virtually nothing". John Brett did indeed sound as though he embodied the spirit of pluck and faith and I was intrigued and wanted to know more about this man: An Irish immigrant hatter who had lived hard and died young. A man who had fathered seven children and had many more grandchildren. What had motivated him to journey to America? How did they get to Danbury, in southwestern Connecticut? What was their early life in this country like? What had caused him to die at such a young age? How did Mary survive, raising all those children after his passing? There was much to discover and I sensed that it would be a story worth telling. I vowed that his name had yet to be spoken for the last time, and as he spiritually communicated with me from the grave, I decided that he deserved to have his story told after 100 years of virtual silence. Taking that first step of commitment, I began my personal journey of discovery, and in the process, weave part of my own story into that of the Brett family and it became sublimely cathartic.

Part One

The Genesis of a
New American Family

1

THE DECISION

"You've taken leave of your senses John Brett!" she shouted, as he walked away, along the short, winding path leading to the broken, cobblestone street; now even more treacherous than usual, with potholes half filled with muddy water that had accumulated after a long, cold, two day rainy spell. He cast up his hand dismissively without speaking and because it was dusk and darkening quickly, he picked up his pace. Louder, she shouted; "What are you running away from?" He paused for a moment, turned and replied; "I'm not running away from anything." "I'm running toward something". "Something much greater than we could ever have here." She could sense his resolve and deciding that discretion was the better part of valor and knowing that the discussion was over, for the time being, she more quietly said; " Be careful on your journey home John." " I'll see you in the morning".

They always met on Sunday mornings before Mass at their church. John was born in 1864 and had just turned 24 years of age, while Mary, the object of his affection, was 7 years younger and about to turn 18. They were devout Catholics and had actually met a few years earlier at a church social. They had been courting for a little over a year since that time. Matchmaking was common during that era, especially among those with property or affluence. The matchmaking protocol was generally the prerogative of the parents but in the case of John Brett and Mary Walsh, both fathers had passed away and the mothers were somewhat ambivalent, completely absorbed with the challenges of maintaining and surviving in a single parent environment. Obviously, property and affluence didn't enter into the equation. So, the relationship between John and Mary took on a life of its own, without any guidance, assistance or intervention from their respective mothers.

Although it was legal to wed at 14 (sometimes as young as 12) for Irish females and 16 for males, the average age was 20, and the majority of females were in fact, married by that age.

John, at 24, had been preoccupied with helping support his beloved mother and younger siblings, and now that those siblings were old enough to strike out on their own and fend for themselves, he felt the freedom to engage in courtship. His responsibilities had been enormous and he had handled them well, and now, although he still felt a compelling responsibility toward his mother, for the first time he felt as though he had taken control of his life.

He felt a palpable excitement and determination to chart a new course and create a direction that might ultimately produce better opportunity and a better life. He had been prudent and frugal and although the majority of his income as a Thatcher, building and repairing thatched roofs, had been spent on maintaining his family's survival, he managed to save a small "nest egg" to be invested in a fresh start. At 24 years of age, he was ready to embark on an epic life journey. He had heard many anecdotes, tales and stories about young men emigrating from Ireland to America and achieving success, prosperity and happiness and could think of no reason why he shouldn't make an attempt to do the same.

He was determined to take the leap of faith and, in his mind, he possessed the courage and pluck to do it. He would book his voyage for April, a short 6 months away, and embark upon a new life journey. He would take his mother with him and deeply wanted to include Mary, as his bride. It was a bit of an oblique proposal of marriage, with the caveat being her agreement begin their married lives together in a new country, but he was determined to make the trip, with her or without her.

She loved John, and assumed at this stage of the blossoming of their relationship, that they would one day marry, but she wasn't convinced that leaving Ireland and beginning over in America was something she wanted to do. When John had issued an ultimatum of sorts, the previous evening, she was simultaneously angry and anxious. She was strong willed and usually in control and didn't appreciate having a decision of that magnitude made without her direct input. Unlike John, the perennial optimist, she had heard less than inspiring anecdotes and tales about the life of newly arrived Irish immigrants in America. Tales of discrimination, gangs, isolated ghettos where destitute, desperate, largely illiterate, mostly Catholic and poorly skilled Irish, many of whom had language deficiencies (many spoke Gaelic- Gaeilge or with an accent so thick it made them hard to understand) were common but largely ignored by John. John's optimistic confidence was tempered by Mary's sense of foreboding and risk. They had visions of prospective life in the United States that were in exact juxtaposition. But so were their respective personalities, so it was to be expected.

When they approached at the steps of the church that morning, they paused and stood facing each other for a minute or two without speaking a word. Mary then turned toward the front entrance steps of the church, firmly grasped John's hand and slipping comfortably back into her "take control" posture, led him to their favorite pew, still not speaking a word. John smiled to himself and breathed a sigh of relief. He sensed that Mary had made her decision, would accept his proposal and they would make the journey together as husband and wife.

With a wry smile, he leaned over and whispered in her ear; "I love you". She turned to him, smiled and winked. As they sat, hands folded and deep in contemplation, he leaned over and whispered in her ear again; "shall I speak with Father O'Malley about setting a wedding date after mass?" Again she smiled and simply said: "yes".

2

MAKING PLANS

Mary thought of herself as a strong woman; as a woman in control of her emotions, with a pragmatic and practical outlook on life. She was as attractive, robust and healthy as she was headstrong and determined. She had no shortage of distant admirers and potential suitors but her normally quiet and introspective demeanor, considerable intellect and very direct manner of speaking made her appear to be a better business partner than romantic conquest. Therefore, she might have intimidated many of those prospective suitors and had few "boyfriends" before John. John however, had, for some undefined reason, ignited a spark and although she wouldn't readily admit it to him, she would follow him to the ends of the earth. Perhaps he was her polar opposite; impetuous, outgoing, social and slightly opinionated- Fun loving and fond of occasionally spending raucous evenings at the local pub, yet driven toward improving his circumstance. The fact that he was handsome and feisty might have held some allure as well. John was small of stature, about 5' 7" tall and 145 pounds, but strong for his size and more than willing to engage in hard work. And rather than being intimidated by her sometimes stern and brooding nature, he saw it as an asset- as someone who could not only satisfy his romantic interests, but as someone who would be a great helpmate and partner; as someone who could help him achieve his dreams. He was smart enough to recognize his weaknesses and saw her as a way to add great strength to their potential relationship as husband and wife.

But Mary was slightly unhappy with herself lately, usually taking pride in being in control and steady, and she now found herself emotionally conflicted. Shifting between manic, joyful and exuberant when thinking about their upcoming wedding, to pensive, stoic and anxious when considering their journey, leaving family and friends behind and of the uncertainties starting life over in America would bring.

Things had improved significantly in Ireland since the Great Potato Famine of 1845-52 but in 1879 another "mini-famine" occurred and although there were few deaths resulting from it, there was great hunger and economic upheaval. Now, here it was eight years later and improvement hadn't been enough to restore economic stability and comfortable, secure living conditions, especially within their socio-economic class.

In spite of the horror stories and anecdotes regarding Trans-Atlantic travel of years gone by, with starvation, disease and deplorable conditions on the Conra-long (Coffin Ships) running rampant- when upwards of 30% of the passengers (many unscrupulous owners carrying two to three times the number of passengers designated) perished during the voyage and many more died shortly after arrival in Quebec, Canada or in the United States, travel to the new world to begin anew had a strong appeal.

Those severely over crowded vessels, disease ridden, without adequate food or water supplies, without proper sanitary conditions and with little regard for the safety and welfare of the desperate and already sick and malnourished passengers- where the death rate along the journey was so high that sharks would follow to ships to consume the bodies unceremoniously thrown overboard- were now replaced by steamships and much better conditions. During the days of the Famine, people had little choice and faced sure death if they remained in Ireland so they chanced the dangerous voyage.

Many had been "evicted" from their small plot of land by landowners or mortgage holders and, completely impoverished by the famine, had nowhere to go. Sometimes, just to get them easily from the land, they were offered free transport and promised money and food upon arrival in Canada or America (which of course, never materialized). Back then, the voyage could take from 40 days to 3 months depending upon the skill of the Captain and Crew and the weather. These ships were crowded with not only displaced and destitute Irish but with many from the "Highland Clearances" as well, their stories not unlike the Irish. With the government specified bare minimum of supplies being well below the actual amount necessary for survival, many ships ignored those "bare minimums" and didn't acknowledge the law at all, exacerbating an already dire circumstance. Therefore many already ill and severely malnourished became afflicted with typhus, which proliferated, reaching epidemic proportions, and therefore many of the passengers who were fortunate enough to survive the voyage were held in quarantine and passed away in make shift hospitals on Grosse Island after arriving in Quebec. Many were shipped to Canada rather than the United States due to the cost of restrictions imposed at U.S. ports. Because it was cheaper to send them to Canada, it received many more during the mid 1800's. For the most part, costly U.S. restrictions were imposed to discourage Irish Catholics from coming into the predominately Protestant (from Puritan roots) United States.

Fortunately for John and Mary, that had all changed significantly, and passage by Steamer in 1888 was relatively safe and not terribly uncomfortable. With that said, there were 144 Steamers lost (counting all classes) between 1838 and 1879 during Trans-Atlantic trade. One half of those were wreaked, 24 just disappeared without a trace, 10 were burned, 8 sunk in collisions and 3 were sunk by ice (icebergs). Between 1882 and 1890, 36 were damaged by ice in the North Atlantic.

So, in spite of the improvements, Mary was still somewhat apprehensive and frightened about the voyage. It would be her first time on a ship. The vast majority of the passengers would be Steerage, with far fewer First and Second Class Cabins provided for the affluent passengers. Steerage passengers would be assigned to the lower deck in much more crowded conditions but ample basic provisions would be provided. Unfortunately, the bottom section had poor ventilation and greater movement and swaying causing the potential for a solid 10 to 14 days of sea sickness.

Then, upon arrival, if one were to dock in New York, the First Class and Second Class passengers would pass through customs on the ship, with the prevailing attitude among authorities being that if one could afford an upgrade to a cabin, there was less likelihood that they'd be bringing in disease or would become a burden on the state due to economic necessity. On the other hand, the Steerage passengers would be required to transfer to New York Inspection Station at Castle Garden (Castle Clinton) for an inspection that could take 3 to 5 hours (Ellis Island didn't open until 1892). If they appeared to be in good health and had offered an ultimate destination in the U.S., they were sent on their way.

Decades before, immigrants weren't greeted by Utopia, but rather discovered a fairly difficult existence and assimilation, encountering prejudice and discrimination due to language (many spoke Gaeilge or "Gaelic", or spoke English with an accent so heavy that they were difficult to understand), religious differences (Catholics were distrusted and unwanted), illiteracy and lack of marketable skills.

Gangs were created, factions formed, underground economies developed and ethnic ghettos popped up along the eastern seaboard. The Irish tended to "stick with their own kind" but now, moving into 1890, assimilation was moving ahead and conditions for the Irish in the "New World" were improving but still daunting.

Much depended upon where one chose to establish roots. Arrival at Boston or New York was just a starting place for some, although many decided to make their life right there. John had an acquaintance who had made the journey a few years earlier and had created a life in New York. He had become loosely affiliated with and peripherally involved with a New York Irish Gang called "The Plug Uglies". He claimed it helped him "network" and get established but was vague on exactly how that had been facilitated and about the exact nature of his "employment". His correspondence offered a de Facto invitation that held little appeal to John. He had heard many tales of the brutal conflict (albeit possibly exaggerated for effect) between The "Dead Rabbits", The "Plug Uglies", The "Bowery Boys", The "Short Tails", The "Slaughter Houses" and the "Swamp Angels" (the fabled 'Gangs of New York") and decided that he wanted no part of that lifestyle. In addition, He and Mary were not "city people" and he wanted a more simple and wholesome environment for his new family. He would need to determine whether he wanted to set sail for New York or Boston and where to locate after their arrival. Being unsure, and having yet to decide, he chose a location midway between the two. He selected Connecticut as their ultimate destination and began to research in earnest, seeking potential employers and housing accommodations.

Mary delegated that responsibility to him while she prepared for their wedding, which would be a simple, low key affair with only family and the closest of friends. It would simultaneously function as a wedding ceremony and a "send off party" and would obviously be emotional and bittersweet. Her mood swings upset her sense of balance and control but by now she was committed and determined to embrace this great adventure with gusto.

Then, one morning a week prior to their wedding, as she carefully selected the items to pack in their steamer trunks, and as she was in the throes of deciding what held enough importance to be taken half way around the world to begin a new life and what did not, it hit her like an epiphany: This is their destiny- it was fate. It was meant to be and she embraced the concept whole heartedly and with an enthusiasm that she had yet to experience. She would not simply acquiesce to the notion but embrace it and take ownership of it as though it were her own. It was time to once again take control.

3

WESTWARD

By 1870 more than half of the immigrants into the United States were Irish. And, by 1899, Connecticut had one of the highest percentages of foreign-born residents in the nation. By the late 1880's, a strong, thriving enclave of Irish people had developed in the Fourth Ward of Danbury, CT and John had established correspondence with a family that had "planted roots" there about five years earlier. They were formerly from a small town near where John and Mary now lived. It was through them that John learned of opportunities within the Hatting Industry. The plan was coming together and he felt a stronger sense of direction.

Irish weddings had a reputation for being somewhat raucous and even bawdy and their's was no different. The frivolity and festivities were tempered though, by the knowledge that they would soon embark on a monumental journey and would be leaving friends and family behind; with the exception however, of John's mother Ann (or sometimes Anna), who would accompany them to America. The emotions ran strong, the liquor flowed and the celebration continued into the wee hours of the morning. There were "best wishes" for a long and healthy marriage, a safe journey, great success in the new country and lots of children. The newlyweds even remarked to some that when and if success in America had been achieved, they could happily assist in helping them plan a westward move as well. They somewhat disingenuously said that they would travel back to visit Ireland frequently and perhaps even "subsidize" efforts of family members wanting to some day make the same journey. However, most knew, deep inside, that it was only talk and intended to mitigate the sadness of a probable final good bye.

John, with his young wife and his mother, departed from Liverpool, England in early April of 1888. They boarded a ship called The Berlin and "set sail" for New York.

Their shared accommodation was steerage category on a lower deck. The room was small, dark and lacked ventilation, but it had two beds, a wash stand and some adequate lighting.

Sharing the room with John's mother would be somewhat awkward for the newlyweds and any thoughts of expression of "romantic physical affection" would be placed on hold until the end of the voyage. There was a lower deck promenade where they could get away alone and although it certainly wouldn't provide for a release of "sexual tension", they could at least have some private time to hold hands and whisper some romantic words to each other, dream of the future, fantasize about their new life in America and enjoy each other's presence. Both John and Mary, having been raised in religious Catholic homes, weren't very approving of public displays of affection anyway and were always conscious of their image of "respectability".

Their mutual inhibitions had yet to be overcome and although their marriage had been consummated through sexual intercourse multiple times, John had yet to see Mary fully naked. That wasn't all that unusual for the very conservative traditions of the culture of the day, and to some extent, it might make the circumstance of the trip easier to tolerate.

Once they had settled into the room, and had gone to the dining area for a simple meal, Ann went back to the room, leaving John and Mary to meander along the lower deck. The drone of the engines was softened by the whooshing sound of the screws (propellers) turning the water and the splash of the ship's wake. They were now three hours from port, the seas were very calm and the moon shone brightly, reflecting off the ripples of the tiny waves, light beams dancing from wave cap to wave cap as though choreographed by the Ocean Goddess, Aphrodite herself.

If physical romance was out of the question, this "spiritual romantic interlude" made up for it. It was a peaceful moment, offering a brief respite from the manic planning and preparation taking place for months before. It was a chance for contemplation and imagination. As they leaned over the deck and gazed toward the ship's bow, the huge expanse of ocean that lie ahead was a metaphorical representation of the life ahead- a "clean slate", fraught with uncertainty and risk but with potential and promise as well. Opportunity would abound and they were convinced that with their work ethic, deep faith in God and themselves, determination and pluck, they would create a successful and prosperous new life for themselves and for their offspring. They were simultaneously anxious and nervous while optimistic and excited, and they couldn't wait for the week long voyage to come to a conclusion so they can start their new life. They knew that there would be some discrimination and anti-immigrant attitudes to be encountered, some anti-Catholic sentiment and preconceived notions regarding Irish being "pugnacious drunkards and ignorant dolts with weird religious traditions", but within the relative safety of a closely knit community and the confidence that they had the necessary talent to facilitate assimilation, they were sure that life would be good.

It was sure to be better than life in Ireland for people of their station in society. After multiple agricultural catastrophes and much political and religious unrest, life in Ireland had become very difficult; so much so that starting over with virtually nothing was an opened door that was extremely appealing.

Unfortunately, starting on day two of the voyage, the weather turned, seas became rough, a deep chill was constantly in the air and seasickness became a common occurrence. It became so bad for Ann that she remained in her bunk most of the time and John feared that she would become dehydrated and very ill. They were all quite miserable for the remainder of the trip, but both John and Mary saw it as another metaphor for the almost certain difficulties that they would face in the future, ever confident that after the storm, the sun would rise, as it always does, and that they'd be stronger for having met the challenge.

When the city of New York became visible on the western horizon, cheers could be heard all over the ship and John, Mary and Ann quickly, and with great excitement and anticipation, began to prepare to disembark.

4

UNCERTAINTY

After the arduous task of clearing immigration, recovering their luggage and belongings, securing transport to Grand Central Depot and finally boarding their train for the Brewster, NY train station, where they would change trains for Danbury, they could finally relax for a few hours and collect their thoughts. Grand Central Depot had been built by railroad tycoon, Cornelius Vanderbilt in 1871. (it wouldn't become Grand Central Station until it was demolished in 1899 and rebuilt). John remarked that had they arrived in America eighteen years earlier, it would have been considerably more difficult and time consuming to travel from New York to Danbury. Ann, while only 48 years old, was rather frail and small of stature, having survived the great famine during her youthful formative years, and it appeared that malnutrition had impeded her growth. She stood four feet, ten inches tall and weighed just over one hundred pounds. She was feisty and determined to be strong and supportive of her son and daughter-in-law, but she tired easily and would occasionally suffer from bouts of melancholy and pensive apprehension. This was one of those times, and it was in stark contrast to the manic and excited mood of John and Mary.

As Ann dozed, then fell into a deep sleep, lulled by the

rhythmic motion and drone of the train, John and Mary reviewed plans for their next phase of the journey and refined the strategy. Once they arrived in Danbury, they would arrange for livery service to transport them and their possessions to a boarding house discovered while perusing some various Chamber of Commerce type information on the town that had been provided by the local hat factories. Hatting had reached its height during the 1880's and thirty plus factories employed thousands of workers as Danbury became the number one producer of hats in the country. Unfettered growth fueled additional demand for workers and John seized that opportunity to provide a badly needed starting point for their new life. And, there was so much more that enticed them: Main Street, while still mostly dirt, was now being paved in granite, flagstone sidewalks had been installed, sewers were installed, the Danbury Hospital was recently established and opened, (along with a school for nursing), a police department organized, a new horse railway created and electric arc lights had arrived. Another big plus for them was that St Peter's Catholic Church had been established around 1870 and the parochial school opened in 1885.

The created plan was; once settled in at the boarding house and taking the weekend to acclimate to their new surroundings, John would make a bee-line, first thing on Monday morning, to the Beckerle & Co. hat factory on the banks of the Still River at the northeast end of Liberty Street, with whom he had engaged in correspondence regarding employment. They had simply responded by writing; "Just come to the employment office once you arrive", and although that wasn't an official job offer, John felt confident that he could secure a position. Always the optimist.

Finally, as they neared the station in Brewster, they became very quiet and absorbed in personal thoughts. After a few minutes, Mary turned to John and said; I'll admit to you John, that I'm nervous and a bit frightened". "This is all new to us, and although I know we have prepared as well as we could, the future is still a complete mystery". He smiled, leaned closer and looking straight into her eyes replied; "That's what makes it so exciting!"

They changed trains in Brewster, NY and boarded the next train on the spur line to Danbury. They overheard other passengers remark about the snow covering much of the landscape and, being completely unfamiliar with the climate of the northeast section of the United States, were relieved to discover that it was quite unusual to still have snow cover linger into late April. The recent 'Blizzard of Eighty-eight" had been massive, the largest on record, and temperatures hadn't yet warmed enough to melt it all. That day however, was a balmy 68 degrees and delightfully sunny. With weather like that, it wouldn't be long before the ground was clear, buds would open, flowers would sprout and spring would arrive in full bloom, and as a matter of fact, the jonquils and daffodils were already in full bloom, peaking through the remaining snow cover and tree buds were fat and ready to burst open.

As they arrived in Danbury, they were greeted by a sign that read: 'Danbury Crowns Them All' circling the image of a Derby (Bowler) hat with the words, "Hat City USA" below. John saw it as an omen and was even more inspired to secure employment in the Hatting industry. Mary too, had been encouraged by it and once they secured a livery to transport them, Ann, and their belongings to the boarding house on Elm Street, they began speculating about the nature of the job, the hours and the wage, none of which had been discussed during correspondence.

The accommodations were small and rather austere, consisting of but two rooms. John and Mary would have one as a bedroom and Ann would sleep in the living space. There were a total of twenty occupants, including John, Mary and Ann. As basic and simple as the flat might have been, they all found it comfortable and satisfactory, for the short term. The boarding house had a dining room and a parlor as common areas where guests could gather and socialize. That opportunity to socialize would provide interaction with some locals (although most were transient) and during conversations, they could glean a great deal of information about the area. They might also make some friends and develop a circle of support and advice.

Their plan was to have John seek employment at Beckerle and Co., or if necessary, one of the other hat factories, while Mary would attempt to find work as a housekeeper or in textiles, clothing manufacture or food processing.

Only approximately five percent of women worked outside the home and most jobs available were considered to be an extension of home work. Mary was strong, healthy and determined and they had mutually decided that they would defer having children until they had become "established" and more secure. Ann would stay at home and tend to household chores. Mary was ambitious and felt confident that she could secure a satisfactory position and could contribute to creation of a secure foundation in their newly adopted hometown. They were realists and understood that John's hours would be long and demanding, requiring six day work weeks, ten hour days and the Hatting industry, like manufacturing in general, was fraught with risk. In America, on average, thirty-five thousand workers died and five-hundred thousand were injured per year in industrial accidents- and there was no workman's Comp.

There was a deliberate separation between owners and employees and the shop foreman had complete authority over unskilled workers and to some extent skilled workers too. That included hiring and firing authority and even setting wages. Some were downright dictatorial. With all that to be considered, the wage was only, on average for factory labor, one dollar and fifty cents per day, or nine dollars per week (in comparison, machinists earned about fifteen dollars per week and carpenters earned about nineteen dollars).

When the required annual income to "make ends meet" was approximately six-hundred dollars and the average factory income was approximately four-hundred and sixty dollars, it became obvious to Mary that she'd need to contribute.

Almost one in eight people (ten million) lived below the poverty line by 1900. If there was any really good news in this scenario, it's that by spring, turnover rates were sometimes as high as two-hundred to three-hundred percent, which meant that John shouldn't have trouble finding employment, and once settled in and a steady weekly cash flow was established, he could consider other options, if necessary.

Mary, on the other hand, wasn't formally trained in any particular craft or skill and would need to find something based upon her work ethic, determination, ambition and personality. She was quiet and serious by nature and not prone to joking or levity- many people, having experienced great difficulty and loss in their lives tend to be that way. However, that's not to say that she had no sense of humor. It's just that when it was made manifest, it displayed in sarcastic wit or a "dry humor" more common among the English than the Irish. Another asset was her striking beauty. She had fair complexion and porcelain like skin, lovely features, light green eyes, auburn hair and was curvaceous. Appearance contributed to "charisma" and "charisma" can help one find employment.

In stark contrast, John was jovial, devil may care, generally lighthearted and the perennial optimist. He depended on Mary's pragmatism and practical planning ability and was well aware of his shortcomings. The juxtaposition actually strengthened their relationship, as he knew it would back when he rather obliquely asked her to be his bride.

The factory "whistle chorus" that sounded at seven AM on Monday morning, audible even within the confines of their boarding house, signaled the beginning of a challenging week.

5

RACING AGAINST THE CLOCK

There was a distinct sense of urgency. John and Mary (as well as Ann) knew that there would be no time to waste and that it was critical that an income must be generated very soon due to their rapidly depleting funds. As John dressed and groomed in preparation for his interview, Mary said; "Good luck John. I hope you said a prayer last night". She continued; "We'll soon be beggars if you don't get this job". The perennial optimist, he smiled and confidently said; "Where's your faith in me, woman?" "There's no question that I'll get this job".

As John arrived at the Beckerle Hat Factory (which had coincidentally just released ads and notices stating that they were hiring), searched out the employment office and identified himself as a job applicant, he was told to wait with a few other candidates while the foreman, a man named John Ellrod, was summoned. He learned from another man waiting with him that Ellrod was about thirty years of age and had been with Beckerle as foreman for about two years. He was also deeply involved with the volunteer 'Kohanza Hose Company' as a fireman. John was also told that Ellrod was a member of the nativist group "The Order of United American Mechanics (O.U.A.M), which was anti-Catholic, anti-immigrant and anti-Semitic. Nativist's feared competition from new foreign workers and concentrated on limiting immigration or even reversing it. Learning that information made the normally "happy go lucky" John, slightly on edge and his confidence waned perceptibly. John was seated at the far left end of a group of 6 chairs, arranged in a semi-circle. To his right, was a man named Patrick, with whom he had struck up a conversation and from whom he learned the information about the foreman. The remaining four sat stoically, for the most part, with just some occasional nervous fidgeting. The room was floored with wide planks, some beginning to loosen and raise slightly from their joists. It was hot and dusty and the sounds of production easily permeated the paper thin walls. The door leading to the adjacent factory had a window that was so obscured with production residue that only partial light and some occasional movement from shadow figures shone through.

John Ellrod entered unceremoniously, and glanced around the room without saying a word. Even without speaking, one could tell that he was gruff, stern, humorless and lacking in personality nuance.

Finally, he handed out some forms asking if they were all literate; then paused, and in an obviously condescending manner, said; "I mean can you read and write?" Most nodded in the affirmative, with the exception of a young, shabbily dressed man with a peach fuzz mustache who appeared to be about seventeen years of age, who responded by simply saying "some".

Ellrod muttered something indiscernible while casting a disdainful look at the young man. He then told the group to fill out the form, and turned quickly, as though he had forgotten to do something urgently needing his attention, and left the room. After about five minutes, he returned and collected the applications. After quickly perusing the forms, he asked a few cursory questions of each applicant while they remained assembled in a group. When he got to John, he asked how long he had been in the U.S. and about his work as a Thatch Roofer, probably more because it was a highly uncommon practice in the eastern United States and he was just curious, than it having any bearing on the prospective position.

They never had any private, individual time with Ellrod during the interview process but ultimately, they were all hired for one position or another. Three were hired as unskilled, dye room workers, one for the "back shop" as a Roughbody worker and John, due to his age (he was older than the other job seekers) and his work experience, was assigned to be an apprentice Blocker. He was pleased with that, simply because once he learned the skill and became a Journeyman Union Hatter, he would be one of the higher paid workers in the production end. What did not please him, however, was the fact that he would be working directly under John Ellrod. He was perfectly fine with being a subordinate and taking orders and direction from his supervisor, but he also demanded respect and dignity. He suspected that treating workers with respect and dignity was a component of his foreman's personality that was in short supply. Never the less, the job was his and he was elated. In his manic and hyper excited state, he virtually ran back to the boarding house, without taking time to wait for a livery service, anxious to give Mary and his mother, Ann, the good news.

Obviously, Mary and Ann were also elated. They breathed a collective sigh of relief now that the relative security of a job had been secured and that evening's conversation consisted of some longer term planning, and the good fortune of finding work reinforced their decision to emigrate as being the correct path for their lives. Neither John nor Mary were able to able to quickly fall asleep after retiring to bed and they engaged in at least an hour of "pillow talk" before finally dozing off. Topics were scattered and "all over the map" but after some discussion on one particular subject, one that had been addressed just a few days earlier and promptly dismissed and ignored by John, there was a lengthy pause, and then finally mutual agreement. The topic was family and children. Mary reiterated that she wanted to seek employment too. She wanted to create a much better life in America than they had experienced in Ireland and to reach the goal she had established in her own mind, a second, supplemental income would be necessary. John resisted at first, but he could quickly tell that he wasn't going to win this battle.

Mary was headstrong, stubborn and determined and she seldom lost an argument. Her proposition was unique, in that, only approximately four to five percent of married women worked outside the home. That's not to say that there wasn't competition for "woman's work" however. About forty percent of single women worked, along with about thirty percent of widowed or divorced women. In many cases, because lower income workers had great difficulty making ends meet, even children were sent to work.

By the turn of the century, in the year nineteen hundred, some one million, seven hundred thousand children were working (and to the delight of exploitative employers, they earned, on average, one third of what an adult worker would earn).

Mary told John that she had spoken to a gentleman at the store where she had gone to purchase some sundries, and during casual conversation, he mentioned that he knew of a physician's family, residing on Deer Hill Avenue, who needed a housekeeper.

This was a somewhat typical work offering for women, with most jobs being considered an extension of "home work". Jobs in food processing, textiles and clothing were common, as were jobs as domestics. She told John that she intended to apply for the job the next day. She rationalized that, with John's mother, Ann, at home and willing to attend to all the household chores, she would be free to engage in work outside the home. If she were able to secure the job, they would need to prioritize finding a place to establish living quarters equi-distant between The Beckerle Hat Factory and the Doctor's home on Deer Hill Avenue, thereby mitigating transportation challenges.

The following day, Mary did as promised and walked the two-plus miles to the home to meet with the wife of the doctor to apply for the position offered. Mary was awe inspired by the home and it seemed to epitomize all that she imagined life in America to be. But she was also a realist and knew full well that it was highly unlikely that she and John would ever achieve that level of success and prosperity. That didn't deter her from dreaming though, and she fantasized that perhaps their children might some day enjoy that level of affluence. Mary was personable, if not downright charismatic, and pro-jected an image of responsibility and strength. But as a new-comer to the country, she displayed less confidence than she might have while still in Ireland, and spoke with deference and humility when addressing her potential employer. While the conversation seemed to go reasonably well, Mary was ul-timately told that numerous individuals had applied and that a decision would be made after discussions had taken place with "the doctor" (She didn't refer to him as "her husband" or by his given name, but rather "the doctor", which Mary found quite odd and somewhat pompous and haughty). She said to "expect a message, one way or another" by the end of the week but Mary had a nagging feeling that she wasn't convincing enough and didn't emphasize her desire enough.

To Mary's great satisfaction and delight though, she re-ceived the offer of employment a full day before she was told to expect word. She had been concerned that she didn't inter-view well, and had been relentlessly critical of herself but the official offer provided vindication and eased her mind.

After suffering great depravation, poverty, loss and de-spair in Ireland, their lives now had hope and direction and the promise of a bright future. They were almost giddy with joyfulness and the excitement of creating a new life. But there was much to do and a lot of "settling in" to be done before a routine was permanently established and "roots" were firmly planted. The next six months would be non stop activity of assimilating and creating their new life.

They were ready to vacate the boarding house and heard of a tenement building with reasonably priced flats available in Danbury's fourth ward, where many Irish and some newly emigrated Italian people had moved, establishing an enclave of families with similar cultural backgrounds and socio-economic levels. That had great appeal but it would still be a few weeks before they were financially able to leave the boarding house and facilitate the more permanent move.

6

HALCYON DAYS PUNCTUATED WITH MANIC INTERLUDES

That summer was unseasonably hot and humid, something to which John and Mary had difficulty adjusting. As far north geographically as Danbury, Connecticut was, it still exhibited a climate that was quite different from that experienced by them while in Ireland. Ironically, the very hot summer followed a very cold and snowy winter, with the great "blizzard of eighty-eight" having just occurred in April. Compounding the irony was the fact that the previous summer that preceded that cold, snowy winter had been very hot as well.

John's working conditions had exacerbated the stiflingly hot weather, adding to his discomfort and left him physically drained by the end of each shift. The hat factory was poorly ventilated, noisy and toxic. A process called 'Carroting', which involved washing animal furs in an orange solution of mercuric nitrate (generally matting together rabbit and/or beaver skins), applying heat, moisture and pressure was used to yield the product. The steam would rise to the ceiling, condensing and falling in droplets like toxic rain. Even the rubber aprons worn by many, couldn't provide protection, and combined with the high perspiration level due to the physically demanding work, most workers were in a constant state of overheated, damp discomfort. The workers mostly acknowledged and ignored the health risks and dangers associated with mercury exposure, and the need to work and lack of other skills trumped any concerns one might have regarding future debilitating ailments. They faced the evidence of the substantial risk every day as they worked side by side with other workers who had become afflicted with what had become known as "the Danbury shakes". One need not depend upon anecdotal stories and rumor when facing, first hand, the manifestations of the disease constantly. It was the life of a hatter when viewed in the cold light of harsh reality. The onset was gradual for some, depending upon exposure levels, but for others, it fairly quickly presented (within a year or two) with symptoms ranging from subtle to dramatic. Tremors would appear, getting progressively worse as time passed. Drooling, slight vertigo and subtle staggering, irritability and anger shifting into pathological shyness and eventually, debilitation.

To compound the risk further, the very same hot, steamy, poorly ventilated workrooms, where men toiled in such close proximity, also created a perfect environment for the transmission of tuberculosis. As a matter of fact, tuberculosis was the leading cause of death at that time.

The hat shop owners and top executives were all either in denial, or knew the truth associated with the dangerous working conditions, and aggressively down played the risk by claiming that the workers who exhibited the mercury poisoning symptoms were actually intoxicated or "had the flu".

But, in spite of the harsh conditions and associated health risks, mostly acknowledged and ignored by workers, and to some extent unions, the hat shops remained a thriving industrial juggernaut earning fortunes for the owners.

With over 4.5 million hats produced in 1880, ushering in the greatest decade of production for the industry, Danbury was known as the hat capitol of the world. Owners continued prospering and thriving and to some extent, in spite of the risks, long hours and hard work, laborers were doing reasonably well too, relatively speaking.

Many, if not most, were immigrants who suffered extreme depravation and hardship before coming to the Untied States, and were glad to have work and provide for their families, even if it was dangerous. By 1870 more than half of the immigrants were Irish, but that was changing, and German and Italian immigrants were now coming in large numbers. By 1899, Connecticut had one of the highest percentages of foreign born residents in the country. The population of Danbury had almost doubled (to about 19,000) during the previous decade and that population growth increasingly consisted of immigrants.

Labor Unions were also now becoming more involved and active in approaching management, demanding safer work conditions and better wages. Obviously that created some strife, disputes and tension between workers, factory owners and the labor unions. As labor, political, and ethnic conflict was beginning to play out, newspapers ran stories of labor unrest, strikes and violence around the country as well as in Danbury. John identified as a pro union democrat and began to become slightly more involved in union activity. But he was also a realist and tactician and kept his involvement, other than his membership, which was all but expected, discrete and as little noticed as possible. In addition, John had a visceral dislike for his foreman, John Ellrod, and the feeling was mutual. Ellrod tolerated John and for the most part, ignored him and let him do his work without interference, primarily because he was a hard worker and because he had learned his job well, was good at it and was a top producer. John tolerated Ellrod because he had to.

John had an outgoing, jovial personality and was well liked by his co-workers. He easily formed friendships and socialized multiple times during the week, after work, by patronizing a saloon near Liberty Street, on the banks of the Still River where the factory was located. As with the pubs back in Ireland, the saloons served as excellent places to kindle friendships, discuss work, politics or world events and to network. It was there that John received an invitation from an acquaintance to join the Wooster Hose Company Number 5, as a volunteer fire fighter.

It had been said that the fire brigades were highly politicized, sometimes violent, and frequently lacking in expertise, professionalism and could at times be irresponsible. John couldn't care less about the negative reputation and implication of some nefarious activities taking place within the brigades or by members. He simply wanted another venue for socializing and networking so he accepted the invitation and was promptly approved.

Back in April (around the time that John, Mary and Ann had arrived) a petition was put forward to create a charter for a City of Danbury and in July, the Charter Committee had their first meeting. The rapid growth of the area excited John and he was determined to explore all areas of opportunity.

One such opportunity occurred one evening while John was at his favorite saloon enjoying an ale or two with friends. A representative from another Hat Factory, called Deitrich Loewe, entered the bar and tacked a notice on the bulletin board. It simply read; "We are hiring- Apply at once". John realized that as long as John Ellrod was his foreman, he probably didn't have much chance of advancement at Beckerle, let alone job security. Now, eight months into his tenure, he felt that he was skilled and capable and felt confident that facilitating a change in employment would not only be easy, but the prudent thing to do.

With Mary's support and encouragement, he made the change that late November. As it turned out, it was also a slightly higher wage. But, that pleased Mary greatly. They had both set their sights on buying a house some day. They

were well focused and reasonably frugal and were already beginning to create some savings. The rent for their flat in the
tenement building was higher than the boarding house, but
provided a reasonable amount of space for three people living together. But it was noisy, drafty and quite run down and
when they decided to start their family and raise children, a
better home would be necessary.

They were also quite upset and frightened that December
after receiving the news about an arson attempt at their former boarding house on Elm St. The home's only entrance had
apparently been doused in kerosene and ignited placing the
twenty occupants in grave danger. Fortunately, the fire was
contained and extinguished quickly and no significant damage was done. Their thoughts were flooded with "what if"
scenarios and having been occupants of that building a few
short months earlier, gave them pause and created more than
a little anxiety. In addition, it had the effect of increasing their
resolve to one day move from the tenement building and buy
a home of their own. A private home where they could safely
raise their family and feel more secure.

With a great many suspicious fires occurring in town, the
local press began to ask; "Do we have an arsonist (Dubbed
The Fire Bug) in our midst?" There had been more than a
dozen fires of suspicious origin within the months of June
and July. The most frightening was an incendiary fire in July
at the house of the Street Railway's former superintendent,
where seven or eight men faced the risk of being burned alive.
The Hartford Courant called the fires "something like a reign
of terror".

There were also incidents of sabotage; one example being
a fire hose being rendered inoperable by the saboteur. The
community was on edge and suspicions were running rampant. Many thought the motives were political in nature, or
perhaps prejudicial. But, with all the allegations and suspicions, there was no single individual or group identified as the

main suspect. The "Firebug" brought fear to the citizenry and the crimes took prominence in local, and even state wide news reporting. But Danbury was a rapidly growing community, on the threshold of becoming an official town, and as such, the crime rate was growing proportionately with it. Stories of shooting, beatings, drowning's and poisoning were becoming more common, but John, Mary and Ann accepted it as the reality of a growing town and didn't let it get them down.

When the transition to Deitrich Loewe unfolded smoothly and almost seamlessly, John and Mary were both elated and quite honestly relieved. There is always anxiety and uncertainty when making a job change and they were pleased that move was going well. They were, after all, immigrants and as such, a wrong move or a mistake in judgement could prove disastrous and financially fatal. But John was obviously a risk taker and realized that without risk, gain would be minimalized.

Mary too, was content with her employment. She was held in high regard by the family for whom she worked, and although lacking in the people skills possessed by John, her serious yet cordial, no nonsense approach to accomplishing the task at hand, is exactly what the family wanted. She would obviously never be considered "a friend" nor would she ever be considered "like part of the family", nor did she want to be. "Everything in its proper place"; she would say. The cultural differences and wide gap in social status was far too significant, but as a business relationship, it was what both parties wanted and needed. Mary had few friends, although there were a few women in their neighborhood with whom she would occasionally have tea and chat. On those occasions, she would gossip effusively; almost gleefully, about her employers, awestruck by their extravagant lifestyle, and as a casual observer, taking cues on the "proper way to act in high society". Her friends, who worked in more mundane surroundings, hung on every word.

As a couple, their long work hours and physically

demanding work precluded any meaningful friendships with other couples because they were generally bone tired by the end of the week and just wanted to be together and spend time with Ann. However, there were two other couples (also Irish immigrants) that they had met during Sunday Mass at St. Peter's Church and they usually got together after services for some social interaction.

By the spring of 1889 their lives had developed a rhythm and flow and a welcome routine. They had quickly assimilated into American working class life and although they still had bouts of melancholy and home sickness, they now identified as Americans. Their correspondence with family in Ireland became less frequent and ties less binding. They were learning new customs and traditions and embraced a sense of permanence and patriotism.

Christmas celebrations were new to them and they adopted the holiday with childlike fervor. By 1890, John had become a fan of a relatively new sport: Professional Baseball. It resembled Cricket and it didn't take long for him to develop a good understanding of the rules. He even played recreationally on occasion. He became a fan of the New York Giants but, to John's disappointment, they unfortunately came in at sixth place (out of eight teams in their division-National League) that year. The 'Brooklyn Bridegrooms' won the NL pennant that year. In the American Association, the Louisville Colonels won the pennant. The World Series between the two resulted in a tie.

John also purchased a used bicycle and learned to ride it for transportation to and from work. For two people, one entering her twenties and him at mid twenties, they were learning a lot of new things and feeling as though life was an adventure. The experiences brought them closer together and their affection continued to grow. Mary respected John's sacrifice and devotion and he admired her beauty and unwavering support. In the bedroom, they were still somewhat inhibited and reserved, in keeping with their strict Catholic upbringing and social and moral conventions of the day. But that too was changing and as Mary transitioned from late teen years into womanhood, her passion increased and her desire to begin having children was getting hard to deny. In addition, the traditional Catholic method of birth control was abstinence and "the rhythm method", both impractical for any couple serious about actually controlling the time of arrival of children.

John insisted however, that she be patient, and that they must first be prepared to raise a family by having their own home and be financially well enough prepared, so that Mary could discontinue working and devote full attention to raising their children.

Ann entered into the equation too. She had been a great helpmate for Mary, taking almost full responsibility for household chores and virtually "mothering" both John and Mary. Ann also pitched in by taking in laundry, assuming that because she had already taken on that responsibility for the family, she might as well include laundry from some paying customers as well, thereby contributing further to the cause of home ownership.

To say that John was a devoted son would have been an understatement. He idolized his mother and she absolutely adored him. When John's father died during a cholera outbreak, he became the de facto and titular head of the family. Together, he and Ann, along with four siblings, watched John's father die a terrible death from the disease. To compound the tragedy, John's younger sister was also stricken and died, a mere five months later, leaving Ann deep in grief and profoundly despondent. Ann had endured enormous depravation and hardship during the famine and to have survived only to lose her husband at a very early age, and then a beloved daughter as well, was almost more than she could bear. John consoled her and assured her that he would take care of her and provide for her "as long as she lived".

He immediately stepped in and quickly squelched the uncertainty by working hard to provide support and strength for the family and continued to do so until his remaining siblings were grown and out of the home.

Ann grieved for a very long time but John comforted her and the other siblings with his positive attitude, sense of humor (he loved limericks and frequently entertained them with funny stories and sometimes even somewhat ribald humor) and without his efforts, the emotional and economic devastation would have extended far beyond their limits. Once the younger siblings were gone, John felt an enormous relief, as though an enormous weight had been lifted, it was only then that he let his mind wander off to thoughts of emigrating to America. However, he would keep his vow, and if in fact he sailed to the new country, he would bring Ann with him. As time passed, the love and affection between mother and son grew and an inseparable bond was formed. And being true to his promise, he insisted that Ann make the journey to America with them. Her appreciation for his loyalty and sacrifice was enormous and she loved her son more than life itself.

There were times, when the depth of affection caused some slight marital tension though. Mary simultaneously appreciated and resented Ann's taking on the role of matriarch. It obviously provided opportunity for her to engage in full time employment and lessened the load, but it also could be stifling when Ann would not only "mother" John, but Mary too. It had the effect of interfering with normal development of the husband and wife relationship. Mary, being rather headstrong and fond of control, subconsciously felt that her rightful position of matriarch had been usurped and minor arguments arose over trivial things like how to prepare certain favorite foods or methods for doing laundry or even the sometimes lack of "orderliness" in the house.

They never became shouting matches and were always respectful, but a tension was usually present. John always took on the role of peacemaker and deftly redirected or injected some levity to keep things relatively harmonious. He loved them both immensely and became frustrated when they bickered but was intuitive enough to realize that two headstrong women living within the same household could be challenging, but he wouldn't have it any other way.

And finally, with Mary feeling somewhat inhibited in outward demonstrations of affection toward her husband by having a constant third person"observer" within the relationship, and a growing level of sexual need, made manifest in her continual and almost obsessive references to beginning to have children, she began to promote the notion of moving to a larger residence so that she might create a bit more space between her and Ann and where she might begin to develop a greater sense of autonomy and privacy.

But, with all that said, they were a close, loving, harmonious family unit (at least as "harmonious" as three people living in close quarters can be) and shared common goals. And now, with Mary more overtly expressing a strong desire to start having children, Ann was beginning to embrace the notion of grandchildren too, and she became a common advocate. The test of wills was beginning to shift in Mary's favor with this new ally and John was beginning to accept the inevitable. He would reiterate the need for patience and "proper timing", but it now fell upon deaf ears.

And in reality, it had been somewhat miraculous that a pregnancy hadn't already occurred, with the most common form of birth control being "The Rhythm Method" promoted by the Catholic Church, and abstinence, which was becoming more and more difficult to exercise.

7

FIRST GENERATION
AMERICANS

Their first five years in America had passed quickly. John was content working in the hat shop and it appeared that he might have an opportunity to move into a foreman's position. Mary had changed jobs when the Doctor for whom she worked decided to merge with another practice in Norwalk and moved his family there. Her new position was very similar and actually only about a half mile from her previous one. Fortunately, the new employer's family was more down to earth and friendly and she fit in nicely and derived greater enjoyment from working for them. Life in America hadn't yet become all that they had hoped for, but it was pretty close. If Henry David Thoreau's assertion that "most men lead lives of quiet despair" was true, and I suspect that in 1893 it was indeed relatively accurate, it didn't apply to John. Danbury had become a city in 1889, with L. Legrand Hopkins elected as Mayor, with a huge celebration held on May 9, 1889, and the new city was growing and thriving; there were libraries, a good hospital, organized police department and fire department, electric light had been introduced; there were entertainment venues like the Great Danbury fair, Lake Kenosia (with construction of an amusement park set to open in 1895 that some claimed would rival Coney Island), various parks and social clubs. John, Mary and Ann loved their church, Saint Peter's, and were thrilled that it offered a parochial school to educate their children once they arrived. Main Street had been paved with granite, there were flagstone sidewalks, some sewers (other then the Still River!) electric arch lights and a horse railway. The "Fire Bug" threat had, for all intents and purposes, ended; although no one had ever been arrested and charged and definitively identified as the arsonist.

The Pinkerton Detective Agency had been hired to assist in the case and after an exhaustive, years long investigation, no ultimate suspect or conclusion had been provided. The "Gay Nineties" had begun as part of the "Gilded age" and with the "Progressive Era" in politics, a focus upon ending corruption in government and bringing forth greater equality (1890-1920). There was a pervasive optimism and merriment looking forward to the turn of the century. Popular music included Folk Music, Marches and Classical (with Jazz to gain popularity during the later part of the decade). An economic recession hadn't impacted hat production greatly and John's employment seemed secure.

When they read stories about the western part of the country, it seemed as though they were in a different world in Danbury, and they were generally happy to be removed from the more primitive environment. But a proliferation of those stories reinforced the vastness and diversity of America and almost provided a sense of invincibility: Stories of the Transcontinental Railway, cattle drives, gold discoveries, train robberies, notorious outlaws and "Indian" uprisings-Dime Novel heroes and villains. One horrific example was a newspaper story about the massacre of innocent Lakota Sioux men, women and children at Wounded Knee, in South Dakota in December of 1890 by the U.S. Cavalry.

They found it inconceivable that the new country they had

enthusiastically embraced could be responsible for such a hei-
nous and deplorable act. But as with most other Americans at
the time, they simply acknowledged, felt pangs of shame and
guilt and then promptly ignored it, consumed with the challenges of maintaining their own existence and distracted by
daily responsibilities. John and Mary (and Ann too) worked
very hard but they were thankful for the opportunity to do
so, and they all realized that had they remained in Ireland,
their lives would be probably have been fraught with great difficulty and despair.

The hard work paid off, and finally, when Mary confided
in Ann, and told her that she suspected that she was pregnant,
they were giddy with joy, and confident that, by the time the
child would arrive, they could seek out a larger place to call
home and, if kept modest, they were prepared to rent a bigger
house with room to raise a family. John, of course, had yet to
be informed or consulted, but within the matriarchal structure of this particular family, I doubt that any objection to
moving to a larger home, (and therefore paying higher rent),
that he might offer would gain traction.

It took over a week before Mary gained the courage to tell
John. She really wasn't sure why she felt such anxiety about
disclosing her "condition". Perhaps it was because their lives
had developed a consistent pattern and routine, with an ebb
and flow of daily and weekly activities that provided a sense
of security and expectation. This blessed event would change
everything. After John's shift at the factory, he had gone to the
Kohanza Hose Social Club. The social club had formed after
the city created a paid fire department and the services of a
couple of the volunteer departments were considered expend-
able and no longer necessary. Some volunteers were integrated into the paid department while others were just dismissed.
Clearly politics and rivalries were involved and tensions ran
high, and during the tumult, John had left Wooster Hose.
A short time later, he was invited to join the Kohanza group

(presumably because they approved of his "political leanings") and feeling a kinship and affinity, he was more than happy to accept the invitation.

When John arrived home, after his shift and a short visit to the social club, then to his favorite saloon, Mary immediately detected the smell of alcohol on his breath and, feeling somewhat irritated, had second thoughts about telling him the news. But she had waited long enough and couldn't contain herself any longer. Not only that, but Ann was pushing her to tell him soon, "or she would tell him herself" which Mary perceived as an idle threat but it encouraged her to have the conversation soon, never-the-less.

She escorted him to the kitchen table, where most of their meaningful, personal discussions took place. The kitchen was primarily a dedicated food preparation work space, with a farmhouse sink, iron handled pump for accessing water and a large wood stove. But due to the limited space in the flat, it served as the dining area as well.

There was a well used wooden table covered with a linen table cloth and some slightly rickety and mismatched wooden chairs. As austere as the surroundings were, it always provided a comfortable and relatively private spot to conduct those "substantive discussions", whether they be for making future plans or working out disagreements or just sharing some pithy gossip.

Mary poured them each a cup of tea into a pair of their better china cups (among the few that weren't chipped) which signaled to John that this wouldn't be simply sharing a bit of juicy gossip. "Pillow Talk" conversations were pretty much out of the question due to the fact that John was sound asleep within seconds of his head hitting the pillow and as many times as Mary had tried to share day's events or news or even personal fears and concerns with him, by the time she had finishing her initial comment, the only response was the sound of his snoring. But she understood the difficult and demanding conditions under which John worked and appreciated that he was usually completely fatigued by the time evening arrived.

As they sat quietly at the table, he could, in spite of his slightly inebriated state, sense that something significant was up. Without speaking, he gave her a puzzled look while she clasped his hands in hers. Her eyes were glistening and she exhibited a faint smile, paused and took a deep breath, and simply said; "We're expecting".

It took a moment for the news to register. Finally, he smiled, squeezed her hands tightly and replied: "Good". "It's time". He stood up, walked around to her side of the table, lifted her up and embraced her. The embrace lasted for a long time without any words being spoken. His head was spinning and it wasn't from the alcohol consumed earlier. There were plans to be made and directional changes to facilitate. He was happy but found it difficult to articulate his joy. They retired to bed, made love and slept soundly.

8

REDEFINED PRIORITIES

The long awaited, highly anticipated and welcome arrival of their beautiful daughter, Rosalind, whom they called 'Rose', occurred in 1893 which unfortunately coincided with the "Panic of Ninety-three". "Wouldn't ya know it"; Mary said. "Just when we think the time's proper ta bring a child into the world, the economy goes bad!" John replied; "We got no crystal ball, Mary", "All we can do pray fer guidance from above". This is God's gift to us and with his grace, we'll do just fine".

President Grover Cleveland, although considered to have been a good President and a man of honesty and integrity, had substantial difficulty in handling the great depression that followed the 'Panic' and it continued until about 1897. A huge strike also occurred in 1893 involving nineteen Hat Factories which further exacerbated the challenge of supporting a family, and the ensuing "lock out" lasted long enough to create substantial hardships. The economic depression thankfully ended in 1897 and in early 1898 Mary gave birth to another daughter, whom they named Anna. Two years later, a third daughter, named Mary, whom the called 'Shelly", was born. After having patiently waited before beginning to have children, once they started, they certainly didn't waste any time in producing offspring!

John was a doting, adoring and lenient father handing off the disciplinary responsibility to Mary and Anna. In spite of the challenges and concerns at work, and the growing tension between unions and employers, the physical toll the environment in the shop was beginning to take on his health, and the financial strain of raising a rapidly growing family, John was happy. He relished the time spent with his family and looked forward to their situation continuing to improve. They had rented the larger unit of a duplex house on Fairfield Avenue in the Fourth Ward where many other Irish families, as well as other immigrant families lived. As the family grew, they seized upon an opportunity to rent the other half of the house at a very reasonable additional rental amount, which would finally provide separate, private space for Ann; and to have ample bedrooms and living space for three children by combining the two units.

Ann lived primarily in #2 Fairfield Avenue and John, Mary and kids lived in #4 Fairfield Avenue. However, they treated it as though it were a single family home and everyone had free and easy access to both living quarters.

As the century turned, there was a nationwide optimism, tempered by a vague sense of anxiety. There was no denying that a cultural revolution was at hand, especially in the state of Connecticut, where one of the highest number, by percentage, of foreign born citizens in the entire country resided, and Danbury was a representative microcosm.

The 'melting pot" created an amalgamation of various cultures, and continuing immigration, along with assimilation, provided the catalyst that yielded a uniquely different and purely American cultural fusion. It was wonderful to behold. It was a time of relative prosperity, more available leisure time and growing trend toward materialism. Some within the middle class were even beginning to enjoy some short vacation time.

John and Mary thanked God that they had taken the leap

of faith twelve years earlier, mustered up the courage to take a risk and begin their lives anew in America. They had faced their fears head on and were now reaping the rewards of hard work, determination and sacrifice. Life was good. It could certainly be better, but it was good, never-the-less.

On the New Year's Eve of December 31st, 1899, for the first time in their lives, John and Mary went out to ring in the new year, and the new century. While Ann was watching the children, they gathered with a few friends at the Groveland Hotel, at 275 Main Street, for the celebration. They couldn't really afford it, but Mary, who was seldom very outgoing and social, and always frugal, was oddly insistent, which John found somewhat perplexing and out of character. As the evening wore on, and the festivities were beginning to come to a close, Mary took advantage of an opportunity to whisper something in John's ear while their friends were distracted by a piano playing vocalist. She gave John the news that she was once again pregnant. Child number four was on the way. With the family growing at such a rapid rate, John found the news rather daunting, but at the same time, he desperately wanted a son. Perhaps this time would be the charm.

John James Brett, Jr. was born in the autumn of that year. He was a nine pound, four ounce baby but Mary was only in labor for a short time and easily delivered a strong, healthy green eyed baby with lots of black hair, and the Midwife and all others present during delivery remarked how he so closely resembled his father. John was elated and beside himself with joy and pride. He loved his daughters dearly, but greatly wanted a son. He was thrilled that his boy would be able to take advantage of all that America had to offer and looked forward to raising him in this "land of opportunity". What he didn't know, was that his son would face many challenges before being able to take advantage of those opportunities.

9

THE GATHERING STORM

The world was changing rapidly when the new century arrived. The United States was being considered a military power after the resounding defeat of the Spanish in the short duration conflict and decisive victory in the Spanish-American War. Cuban Rebels had been fighting for independence from Spain since 1895 and by 1898, with American public opinion overwhelmingly supporting the rebels, the Battleship U.S.S Maine was sent to Havana Harbor. On February 15th of that year, the Maine was sunk after a mysterious explosion, which was then attributed to the Spanish Military. War was officially declared in April and for all intents and purposes, ended in July; with The Treaty of Paris being signed in December, bringing it to an official close with the granting of Independence to Cuba and ceding Guan and Puerto Rico to the United States.

John greatly admired Theodore Roosevelt, who rose to fame during the war, especially during the Battle of San Juan Hill, where Roosevelt was given credit for valor and bravery along with his Rough Rider's of the '1st United States Volunteer Calvary'. In truth, most of the intense fighting was done by the 'Buffalo Soldiers', a regiment of African-American soldiers whom had earned some fame and notoriety of their own during the Indian Wars (the name "Buffalo Soldiers" was actually given to them by the Indians). They earned five 'Medals of Honor' during the battle of San Juan Hill.

United States Naval prowess had manifested during the war as well and contributed decisively to the victorious outcome.

John had quickly become a patriot and displayed an obvious pride and affection for his adopted country. Both he and Mary, and Ann too, missed Ireland. They missed the beauty of the land, the culture and family, but in dominant juxtaposition was their love for America. They had become Americans first, and were pleased and proud that their growing family would be raised and live their lives in this land of opportunity.

John read the newspaper cover to cover and tried to be well informed on politics, world events and cultural trends. He would also go to the public library when he had available time, in an attempt to broaden his knowledge. As a father, he felt it necessary, so that he might provide well informed guidance, direction and insight to his children.

They faithfully attended St. Peter's Church and fully intended to send their children to Catholic School, where he felt that they would not only receive a vastly better education than he did, but also become grounded with a strict religious foundation. The library provided entertainment, when little else was available. There was some limited theater, Vaudeville and outdoor band concerts, but they were "few and far between". To entertain the children at home, they read to them and had purchased a second hand piano.

Ann had somewhat learned to play, and it became a favorite form of family time. The "Brownie Box Camera" had been introduced in 1900 too, and they were "saving up" to buy one. There were various parks available and during warm late spring, summer and early autumn months they could picnic and frolic with the kids.

And then there was the perennially anticipated Danbury State Fair, which during some years, was their top entertainment venue. There was innovation in food items too- the ice cream cone had been invented by an Italian immigrant in New York (although it has also been credited to a Syrian immigrant who offered it at the St. Louis World's Fair in 1904), and the Hamburger Sandwich was created and offered to customers of 'Louis' Lunch' in New Haven, CT and both items could now be obtained at the Danbury Fair.

If it sounds as though their lives had become almost idyllic, that might be a stretch, but from their perspective, life at home wasn't too far from it. Work, on the other hand, had become fraught with tension. There was constant bickering amongst workers, and union representatives were antagonizing owners and management, and owners were pushing back at union "intrusion and meddling", resulting threats and saber rattling on both sides. To compound John's anxiety and stress, he was beginning to detect a subtle tremor in his hands and occasionally his upper lip. He saw co-workers with full blown, or close to full, manifestations of "Danbury Shakes" every day (a result of the exposure to mercury) and didn't need a professional diagnosis to realize that he might be at risk of the disease progressing rapidly if he didn't take some precautionary measures. At only thirty-eight years of age, the math wasn't in his favor. He had seen men his age experience early onset and rapid deterioration and others a much slower progression and he knew he was "rolling the dice" but he prayed that he'd be one of the more fortunate of the many victims. Unfortunately, at this point in his life, Hatting was what he knew, he was good at his job, D. E. Loewe paid him relatively well, as a skilled 'Blocker' and he had few, if any, other options. He had a family that depended on him, who needed the security, support and economic safety that his income provided, and this was where he must stay.

But a defining moment occurred in 1901, that would change their circumstance dramatically and irrevocably alter their lives; more than any event since the trip to America thirteen years earlier.

John was very well liked by his co-workers. He had a good sense of humor, a friendly, outgoing personality, a sense of perennial optimism and attractive, charismatic countenance. At times, the life of the party, albeit always reserved and proper when outside the saloon, favorite pub or the Kohanza Hose Social Club.

He was also a person of deep faith, as were Mary and Ann. He was firmly convinced that God had guided him to this place in his life and trusted in further guidance moving forward. He prayed daily and attended church with his family every week. He was devout but he wasn't overly pious. He knew that he wasn't perfect and had some nagging guilt regarding certain aspects of his behavior, and if at times he was loath to admit it, Mary would readily remind him. That too, didn't bother him and he would simply respond by saying; "that, my Love, is why I'm beholdin to spend twenty minutes in the confessional with Father Kennedy each week and yur only spendin three".

But John's top priority was his family and as "socially adroit" as he could have been, he chose to spend the majority of his leisure time with them. As a matter of fact, although he had many casual friends, he had absolutely no very close friends. Whether that would become an asset or a liability in the ensuing few years, remained to be seen.

On April 22nd in 1901, D. E. Loewe, John's employer, became only the third Hat Factory in Danbury to formally declare that they were an "Open Shop". They had been pressured to unionize by the United Hatters Of North America (UHU) but Loewe rejected them, insisting that his workers were fairly treated and well paid and had no grievances. His non-union workers were free to join the union if they chose, but saw no benefit. Essentially, "open shop" meant that the workers were not required to join the union and had freedom of choice to join, or not to join. They had functioned this way since reopening after resolution of the lock out of 1893. This outraged the

UHU, who had organized seventy of the eighty-two hat firms. The union was also busy trying to organize Henry H. Roelofs & Co. and therefore didn't officially respond to the declaration until June of the following year when seventeen union workers at Loewe were ordered by the union to go to work at another hat shop where personnel shortages were being experienced. They complied, but ultimately returned to Loewe, stating that work conditions were not as congenial as they were at Loewe. When H. H. Roelofs & Co. acquiesced and surrendered, the union refocused on Loewe. On July 25th of 1902, all of union workers walked out of Loewe. The next day, on the 26th, all but a small number on non-union men left as well, after being told that victory was all but assured and if they remained, they would have their names crossed off the employee list when the union won (as had been done to "hold outs" at Roelofs & Co.). It was suggested that no one would buy Loewe hats after union representatives "went on the road" to discourage purchase of their product without the 'Union Made' Label. Most of the workers were men of integrity and didn't want to strike before completing their unfinished work, so the union agreed and said that it shouldn't take more than a few days to finish up and after that they had to leave.

John was a union man and a supportive member. He recognized the need for their representation of workers and the benefit of their involvement as their "agent" and he supported recognizing the UHU as the worker's bargaining representative. Safety within the plant was lax, exposure to toxic materials posed great health risks, wages could stand some improvement and workers could be terminated at will and without just cause.

Conditions needed some improvement but as stated by Loewe, and agreed upon by most workers, employees were indeed treated fairly, by industry standards, and wages were as good as any other shop paid, perhaps slightly better. Therefore the declaration was greeted by workers with mixed emotion.

John was hoping beyond hope that an amicable agreement could be arrived upon and when the American Federation of Labor (AFL) offered to assist and support the UHU, his optimism rose. With that added clout, pressure might be brought to bear, and what John thought to be unthinkable, a long term strike and subsequent cessation of income, might possibly be avoided. With a wife, mother and four children at home to support, it MUST be avoided.

Between the time of the declaration and "shit hitting the fan" moment, tension within the factory had been running high. There were arguments and heated discussions, expressions of fear and high anxiety and everyone was on edge. John had tried to stay out of conversations and remained stoic and focused on his work, but his mind was racing. He hadn't quite plunged into a panic, but had considered the consequences of long term unemployment and it clearly upset him.

During the time provided to the men to finish up unfinished work, the company remained steadfast and union unyielding and after a few days without compromise or resolution, the union ordered the men out, calling for a strike. To further ensure that all workers complied, threats, veiled and otherwise, of physical violence were made and threats of social ostracism were implied and inferred. It had come to the worst possible scenario.

When John arrived home a sat down with Mary and Ann to deliver the bad news, they both wept and could barely contain their anxious fear. Mary's hands were shaking as she asked John what he intended to do. "How will we pay the rent and feed the children"; she asked. John stared at the floor, shook his head and said; "I don't know yet". "I'll think on it tonight".

After a sleepless night, he still hadn't decided. Seven year old Rose, was getting ready for school and Anna and Shelly were playing together while Ann was feeding the baby. Mary had prepared breakfast for John, as she always did, but said little as they sat together having their morning tea. She never asked him what decision he had made, but simply kissed him and smiled as he left for work. By the time he arrived, he still wasn't sure what to do. Would he fall in with the rank and file and walk the line, or should he place an unfettered continuation of income and seamless support of his family as top priority? He paused for a few moments, walked up to the picket line, paused again, not really hearing what was being said, or more accurately shouted, then walked briskly to the entrance and immediately went to his station. He was one of only eight men who had decided not to join the strike and continue working. Seven of them were not union members. John was the only union member to cross the line. He felt that his family had to come first. Having experienced depravation, acute hunger, abject poverty and despair in Ireland, he would not permit his children to have that experience, or anything close to it, here in the United States of America! His resolve was unyielding and he knew there could be "hell to pay".

Management called an impromptu meeting with the "group of eight", to be held in the vestibule, which separated the entrance from the production facilities, warehouse and offices and, albeit limited in size, it would have no problem accommodating that small group of "loyalists" (management's term- which was decidedly a misnomer, in that their motivation had little to do with loyalty). It took about twenty minutes for the owner and top management to arrive and address the few men assembled there. Their executive offices were intentionally located quite far from the actual production area, which could easily explain the delay, but one couldn't help but notice that they were accompanied by a few unfamiliar faces. Based upon their burly appearance and serious and authoritarian demeanor, John assumed that they had been contracted as body guards. As that thought crossed his mind, he couldn't help but wonder if he too, might be in potential physical danger.

The men were given a cursory "thank you" and informed

that preparations had been made for alternate workers to fill the place of striking workers, in anticipation of this occasion. They were then dismissed and told to go to their respective stations and function was efficiently as possible until "replacement workers" (Scabs) would fill in and production returned to "normal levels".

The scabs and strike breakers were a tough lot. They were prepared to be accosted in the streets and at the gates of the shop and were ready to engage in self defense and force when necessary; and even sometimes when it wasn't all that necessary. They were usually either strong and relatively fearless and/or just in desperate need of work and therefore willing to place themselves at risk. But either way, they weren't that difficult for shop owners to find.

They were subjected to the union member's visceral anger and hatred that frequently went well beyond passive hostility, jeers, catcalls, epithets and the occasional thrown object, to include manifestations of rage through physical violence and beat downs.

10

A MURDER OF CROWS

Intensifying John's feeling of pressure and anxiety, while simultaneously providing great joy, was the arrival of their fifth child, James Henry Brett, in late Autumn of that year. They were thrilled to have another son, but the burden of raising and supporting this large and growing family was weighing heavily on his mind. The potential for violence during a labor strike was common knowledge and only ten years earlier, in July of 1892, a silver miner's strike in Coeur d'Alene, Idaho saw thirty men killed during a fight between union and non-union workers, requiring President Harrison to send in troops to restore order. Thus far, the Loewe strike had been relatively peaceful and "orderly" but John had lost friends, was voted out of the Kohanza Hose Social Club and ostracized at his saloon and pub hang outs.

Much was changing on the national front as well. The Philippine- American War ended and just a year earlier, Leon Czolgosz, a former steel worker and an avowed anarchist shot President McKinley at the Pan American Exposition in Buffalo, NY and he died eight days later. As tragic as that was, John was pleased that Teddy Roosevelt, whom he admired greatly, had become president. Although John was a democrat, he wasn't steadfastly loyal to one party or the other and liked the image of Roosevelt that had been created by the press and in particular, magazines. An anecdote regarding a bear hunting trip to Mississippi, where Teddy Roosevelt was the only member of that hunting party not to shoot a bear, involved one of his assistants actually capturing a bear and tying it to a tree and inviting Roosevelt to shoot it. He declined, saying that it would be categorically un-sportsman like. Shortly thereafter, a political cartoonist lampooned him with a cartoon depicting Roosevelt releasing the bear, which inspired a stuffed toy maker to create "Teddy's Bear" which gained great commercial popularity. John and Mary were seeking one to purchase as a Christmas gift for the children and checked at the recently opened local Woolworth's and Sears stores to no avail. Interestingly, strikers didn't appear to be pinched for money and retail business remained good, which might have explained the difficulty finding the item, or perhaps the trendy item just hadn't reached smaller markets yet.

If John, and to some extent Mary, were made to feel like social pariahs, they were okay with that and with their income flow continuing unabated (even though a boycott of Loewe's product was having a negative effect on business), they felt that they had made the right decision.

One unexpected benefit in the production downturn was that John was able to enjoy the rare occasion of some time off and on one unseasonably warm late autumn Saturday, during a time frequently referred to as "Indian Summer", he was surprised with just such an opportunity. He and Mary packed an impromptu picnic lunch and they walked with daughter Rose to a local park to enjoy some quiet time and the warm sunshine, while Ann assumed responsibility, as she usually did, for watching after the other children.

It provided a nice respite and a way to ignore the difficulties at work, the passive hostility (and frequently verbally abusive epithets) of some of their old friends and the nagging feeling that, even though all was going reasonably well under the circumstances, a dark, cold and ominous fog was slowly building over their lives.

They arrived at their favorite spot, where the long afternoon shadows, and prismatic effect of the autumn sun, shining through the wispy cirrus clouds, presented with dappled patches of golden light upon the grass lawn, seeming to cast an ethereal glow on the world. The grassy hollow was sparsely punctuated by the occasional rock cluster and some young saplings of numerous varieties. It was there that they spread their blanket and set their basket. Beyond, was a densely forested area, appearing to be mid way between the Pine-Oak cycle; Balsams, hemlocks, spruce presented on the coniferous side of the equation, evenly mixed with young oaks and maples on the other.

The net result was the delightfully co-mingled scents of pungently fragrant evergreens in subtle juxtaposition to the drying, recently fallen leaves, and faint aroma of the decaying leaf matter in an underlying composting layer from the accumulation of the previous year's release. There was a palpable therapeutic effect on their emotion, contributing to the subtle euphoria of the experience. The hollow recess in the otherwise flat topography tended to collect an inch or two thickness of pine needles, gently transported to the area by the autumn breeze, and softly resting beneath their cotton blanket. As they sat quietly, they could hear the breeze caressing the tallest blades of grass, as the rye, perennial fescue and tall wheat grass would sigh and whisper, as though faintly singing with pleasured gratitude, happy to have been gracefully animated with dance-like movement, and indebted to the wind for the motion assist. When the breeze would cease, the tall grass seemed to reach worshipfully toward the warm sun and the vivid blue sky. It was one of the most enjoyable afternoons that they had spent together in a very long time. They became lost in the moment and it provided merciful relief from the uncertainty that the future held.

When he returned to work, early the following Monday morning, the euphoria created by the pleasantries of the week-end soon dissipated. A co-worker who had been exhibiting symptoms of "Hatter's Disease", on that morning presented with much more severe and obviously debilitating symptoms. The trembling and shakes were grossly exaggerated that day. He tended to stagger and stumble while walking and when John approached him to ask if he was okay, he noticed profuse sweating and a pronounced redness in his fingers and cheeks. Rather than respond, he shyly turned away, facing the floor and said nothing, as though frightened and confused by the question and approach. John alerted the foreman who sent the man home. The foreman was quite familiar with workers exhibiting symptoms, and whether it be denial or avoidance, he would usually attribute it to "drunkenness" or "severe flu", as those in management had been taught to do, and send the worker home. A great many other long time workers had also developed some symptoms, frequently mild, but witnessing the effect of long term exposure was a sobering experience. Like many others, John couldn't help but notice a continuation of those still slight personal manifestations of exposure, with occasional shakiness and trembling of his own, but tried his best to ignore and take whatever precautions he could. But this time, the observation caused a distinct rush of fear.

That same day, another reinforcement of the reality of his strike breaker status was provided when he learned that Mr. Loewe had obtained an injunction against the UHU and AFL, claiming that they were interfering with his business through the boycott of goods. And, held as culpable as the unions, were the striking workers themselves. If upheld by the courts, that could mean liens upon homes and attached bank accounts.

Obviously, this would exacerbate and escalate already high tension levels and animosity between striking union members and those currently working at Loewe.

The troubling observation of health risk potential,

combined with the business news, that Monday morning, had delivered a "one, two punch" that seemed to expose his work life again to that cold light of harsh reality, and the normally happy-go-lucky John was admittedly despondent.

John realized though, that Dietrich Loewe wasn't being vindictive, he was merely trying to save his business. He had gone from showing a strong profit to a substantial loss in one short year as a result of the boycott, and he was a fighter.

D. E. Loewe was born the son of a prominent farmer in Germany. He studied at an agricultural college and technical institute but cut his studies short due to an illness. After recovery, he emigrated to New York in 1870 and briefly worked as a laborer and a clerk. In 1871 he moved to Danbury and spent three years learning hat making (while filling in as a house painter during slack times). He was clearly ambitious and hard working. In 1876 he was promoted to foreman at one of the top hat factories in town, but quickly left to expand his skills by learning 'finishing'.

He learned his craft well and was, once again, promoted to foreman. In May of 1879, he and two partners opened their own factory with a small nest egg that they had managed to save. He was living the American Dream. By 1896 he had created a very successful brand and business and had developed a substantial base of retail accounts. He had even opened his own retail location is New York City. He was well known and respected for his philanthropy and had even represented Danbury's Fourth Ward serving on the City Council.

But respected or not, the adversarial position between Loewe and the striking union workers, town's union members in general, and many union supporters in the area was causing great animus, and to some extent hostility.

Thus far, John had avoided any major conflict and although he had engaged in some elevated rhetoric and verbal sparring with some of his now former friends, it never went beyond that. He feared that this injunction might ramp things up a notch though. On the other hand, he no longer associated with former work friends who participated in the walkout and strike (by mutual decision), and because they had made it clear that he wasn't welcome at the old haunts, meaning saloon and pubs, and he therefore ceased frequenting those establishments, he really didn't expect this news to have any tangible effect, other than to further malign his reputation as a traitor to the "cause" and a scab.

Being outgoing, social and charismatic were helpful traits when one's life is turned upside down by events and due to circumstances beyond your control, and old friends needed to be replaced with new ones.

Many of the "replacement workers" tended to be a rough lot and were crude, braggadocios and vulgar. Some expected physical violence to be possible, if not likely, and were more than willing to face it head on. Others though, were more like John and simply wanted to earn an honest living and provide for their families and wanted to be left alone while they did it. It was with the later group that John had formed some new friendships and he hoped that when the chaos of the strike came to an ultimate conclusion, they would be retained as permanent employees.

During the spring of 1903, John was offered a promotion to the position of foreman. He was elated and began to feel that his hard work, attention to detail and perfecting his craft, and yes, even loyalty to the company and refusal to join the strikers, had paid off. He was pleased to have attained this milestone just before reaching his fortieth birthday.

He was congratulated by some of his fellow workers and shop friends and the suggestion was made that they stop by their favorite saloon after their shift to celebrate. John was anxious to get home and share the news with Mary, Ann and the children and at first, refused, but he acquiesced after considering that these guys would now be working under him and he wanted to use the occasion to enlist their support and backing- plus, it had been a while since he had enjoyed a few beers after work and he found the notion quite appealing.

When the shift ended, John and four of his recently made friends gathered their lunch pails and coats and decided to walk to a rather ramshackle establishment called 'The Dusty Derby'. The bar was only a few blocks away from the factory, an area commonly targeted by many entrepreneurial types seeking to match demographics with potential. Many drinking establishments tended to cluster around shops, factories and various places of employment to provide easy access to a likely group of 'Blue Collar' patrons. The owner was a German immigrant named Ernst Weber who tended bar, ran the business and to some extent, even did his own cleaning and maintenance. He was a little gruff and snarky, but had a good sense of humor and was honest, and generally well liked. He was a very large and burly man; over six feet, two inches, and weighing over two hundred, twenty-five pounds during a time when the average male height was five feet, eight inches and weight was around one hundred fifty pounds. Like John, he sported a handlebar mustache and spoke with a booming voice. Beards had fallen out of fashion and moustaches were "in". Changes in men's fashion are slow to evolve but the popularity of Teddy Roosevelt and promotion of "The Strenuous Ideal", emphasizing masculinity and muscularity, had caused the shift from the Frock Suit to the Sack Suit, from beards to moustaches, or completely clean shaven and wearing shorter hair, sometimes parted in the center. John liked to think of himself as dapper and enthusiastically embraced the trend.

There were few patrons in the bar when the group of friends entered. Generally, there was an equal mix of Irish, German and Italian working class men and all seemed to like Ernst well. Most called him "Ernie", which he hated, but the more he protested, the more it became entrenched.

No one meant disrespect and it was more a term of endearment. John hadn't stopped in for quite some time and he sorely missed the days of lively conversation, the smell of smoke and spilled beer and sound of raucous laughter. He always enjoyed the opportunity to discuss politics with his peers, sometimes spreading political propaganda, airing common grievances, and gaining varying perspectives on local news and events. In his mind, this was the best place to use as a means of grassroots communication.

The interior had sawdust covering the floor, some said "to soak up the blood should a fight break out" but it was actually for a more practical purpose- absorbing the tobacco juice from an errant, mis-directed launch of excess chewing tobacco effluent toward the spittoon. Recently, Weber had installed a sheet metal trough extending along the entire bottom of the bar to replace the spittoons. A slow but steady flow of water from a spigot kept the trough flushed. Perhaps he was attempting to add an element of "class" and refinement to a decidedly un classy place. Rumor had it that more than one inebriated patron had relieved himself without ever leaving the bar!

Ernst greeted them with; "Velcome boys!", then directed his greeting to John and said; "Ya, Brett!" "Long time, no see". They ambled over to a large wooden table and ordered pints of Barnum Ale, produced by the Hartman Brewing Company in Bridgeport, which was the Dusty Derby's best selling draught beer, and especially popular with Hatters.

Since the strike began, the ambiance wasn't quite as jovial and cordial as it had been prior. Alcohol can bring out repressed emotions during times of economic stress, especially when that stress is caused by a labor dispute and subsequent strike, and old friends can easily feel betrayed when a "disloyal" co-worker doesn't adhere to the strict code of behavior established by pontificating union leaders, and worse yet, rejects an order to strike as John did. Independent thinking was frowned upon. And, people tend to line up on either side, whether they are directly involved or not. Union Workers

stick with other Union Workers, even if they weren't associated with that particular striking union or with the specific
company involved, and that conflict of sentiment had an effect on the atmosphere in the bar.

The four of five other patrons glanced at John and the other Loewe employees as they entered the bar, briefly distracted
from conversation and their drinks. One acknowledged with a
casual nod and the others returned to conversation, ignoring
them.

After a couple of pints of ale, the mood lightened demon-
strably and John was starting to feel somewhat melancholy,
thinking back to other occasions enjoyed years earlier at this
very same establishment. Much had changed since his early
days as an apprentice hatter, but this place never seemed to
change at all. John found that comforting.

By the time they ordered a third round, two men from the
Beckerle Factory, whom John remembered from his short
time spent there, entered, but they were simply old acquaintances, not friends. As a polite social reflex, and without really
thinking much of it, both John and Luca Lozza (pronounced:
Lowt-za), one of his companions, gave a courteous nod toward
the door, as an acknowledgement of their arrival.

The men both stopped, as though surprised, turned and
looked at each other, paused briefly until one of them tapped
the other on the arm and motioned with his head toward the
bar. The bar was long, almost the entire length of the room,
and well worn from years of use without any attention to re-
finishing. There were no barstools, so if one were to drink at
the bar it was standing; but there was a brass foot rail just in
front of the long trough spittoon. They ordered a boilermaker
and as Ernst was drawing the beer from the tap, one of the
men exclaimed loudly enough for everyone in the bar to hear;
" Ernie!- It stinks in here!" "It smells like someone shit in the
corner!" Ernst replied: "Whudda ya talkin' about?" "This place
smells like a rose garden".

He was a little slow on the uptake, but after a few seconds he realized that it was an antagonistic comment directed toward John and his companions. Ernst then dismissed the remarks with a flip of his hand and went back to pouring the beer. The other man chimed in and said; "You're wrong Barney". "It's not shit that ya smell, it's scabs". At that point Ernst said; Don't be startin trouble or ya can leave right now!" Luca turned to John and the other companions and, in his thick Italian accent said; "ignore deez ass holes" and they went back to their conversation.

The men at the bar finished their first round and ordered another, then Barney, the guy who had made the initial comment, turned to face John's group.

He leaned back on his elbows, resting against the bar and just stared at them without making a comment.

The guy was clearly looking to start trouble and although John wanted to avoid it at all cost, he certainly wasn't going to back down from these two agitators. He also realized that there were only two of them, and counting John himself, five at their table. In addition, the four companions were accustomed to violence directed at "strike breakers" and well prepared to face hostility head on. Finally, DJ, one of the more muscular and aggressive members of John's group, had enough and shouted; "What are YOU staring at, ass hole!" "Scabs- the lowest form of humanity"; was the reply. DJ's retort was simply; "Go ta hell". At that point Ernst walked over to the two guys standing at the bar and firmly and with authority said; "Are you gonna shut up or are ya gonna leave?" The guy the turned around and remained quiet.

Knowing of the potential for disturbances and escalating work related arguments, the town had assigned more police officers and patrolmen to the areas where strikes were taking place. Ernst mentioned to the unruly patrons that it probably wouldn't take him long to summon a policeman should the need arise. During the following ten to fifteen minutes things appeared to be settling down and the verbal altercation had, for all intents and purposes, ended.

Then the guy named Barney finished his beer and left and the second guy remained at the bar.

A few minutes later, Barney returned with three companions of his own. Ernst exhibited a look of consternation as he mumbled; "Here come da flock of Crows". The analogy wasn't a bad one at that. Crows arrive in noisy groups and can be obnoxious and disrupt the peace.

Having run his establishment for well over a decade, Ernst was well acquainted with "disruption".

He had also become well versed in conflict resolution, knowing that the negative impact of such disturbances can create unwanted challenges toward his marketing efforts, such as they were. Business reputations were, to a large extent, based upon the behavior of the clientele and one's ability to foster a civilized and convivial environment. He could plainly see that this verbal confrontation and underlying animus existing between the two groups, could easily erupt into a full fledged brawl. So could the few patrons seated to the rear of the saloon, just past John and his group. When they noticed the rabble-rousers enter, they promptly placed money on the table to pay for the drinks they had consumed, and leaving their last round unfinished, got up and quickly left the establishment. Seeing that business go out the door tended to piss off Ernst slightly and exacerbate his already darkening mood. When DJ, Luca (who happened to be the most hot tempered of the group) and John stood to face Barney and the other three men, Ernst decided that it was time to be preemptive.

He reached under the bar and retrieved an axe handle that he kept on hand as a "peace keeper". He also carried a firearm, but had never brandished it, or had occasion to, always depending solely on his homemade "persuader" to quash brewing trouble. The gun was kept strictly for protection against serious crime, such as a robbery, and Ernst's intimidating size alone was apparently enough to cause a would be thief to re-consider and seek out a softer target, because an attempt had never been made.

The axe handle was pretty intimidating, in and of itself, and Ernst was quite proud of his creation- he even named it Brynhildr.

He had drilled a hole through the wider end, through which he had strung a short length of rope tied into a loop just large enough for him to slide his large hand through, and loop it around his wrist. That would help prevent it from being taken away by someone offering resistance to his "direction" during their "education" in proper bar room protocol and behavior. It was also stained in a dark oil finish resembling a rifle stock, which added to the intimidation factor. He had rarely used it but its presence alone was enough to maintain the calm. This, he decided, was a perfect time to test its powers again. As the four men crossed the threshold, he ceremoniously removed the axe handle from it's location, slide his hand through the loop and extended it straight out, as an extension of his arm, toward the entry door and the men entering, as though point-ing directly toward the door, and said: "OUT!" There were some murmurs of protest but they all knew of his steadfast re-solve in situations like these and quickly acquiesced and left. He followed them out and once outside, he took an additional measure to ensure tranquility by removing a police whistle from his pocket and sounding it loudly. Other than yelling, it was the only way to summon a policeman. If one happened to be within close proximity, it could be very effective. If not, a person would need to handle a situation on their own. The "strike zone" had been designated as an area where potential illegal activity might occur, so a higher presence of patrolmen was in effect. Within a minute or two, one arrived and after being briefed by Ernst, chastised the men who were still loi-tering outside the saloon and sent them on their way with an admonition.

Relieved to have avoided a physical altercation, John and his friends ordered one more round, joked about the confrontation, speculated about who would have won, had it come to blows, and continued to bond. But John was anxious to get home to family and share the news (and relate the events at the saloon too); and news of that importance shouldn't be shared while one was feeling the effects of a few too many pints, so he finished quickly, paid his tab and left for home while his companions remained for another round,....or more.

11

ENJOYING NORMALCY

By the year 1908, the Brett family was living the "American Dream"; or at least the American Dream as they defined it. They didn't achieve great fame or fortune by exercising a strong work ethic, exhibiting determination, thinking creatively, investing wisely, being frugal and spending conservatively, as a select few had done; but rather used those same traits and attributes to at least create a relatively secure lifestyle, and a small amount of savings and to provide adequately for their family. They hadn't become "rich" by any stretch of the imagination, but they were raising a large family, gainfully employed, adequately fed, clothed and sheltered and had a vision for greater achievement for their children. They were generally content. And, they were still very much in love- with each other, their family, and their adopted country. But to make ends meet and create a small amount of savings, John had to work twelve hour days and frequently six days per week.

The children were healthy and happy and getting a good education- the oldest three of them attending St. Peter's School, and young John had started in public school, with J. Henry set to begin classes with him next year; opting for public school for the boys primarily due to cost. Rose and Anna had learned to play piano, as did grandmother Ann who played "by ear" having never learned to read music as Rose and Anna had done. The family had purchased some popular sheet music and during times of family gatherings played old favorites such as 'In The Good Ol' Summertime', of which one million sheet music copies had been sold, 'By The Light Of The Silvery Moon', 'Sweet Adeline' and 'In The Shade Of The Old Apple Tree'. The family loved music, so much so, that they had taken some savings and purchased, as a Christmas gift for the entire family, a 'Victrola' manufactured by 'The Victor Talking Machine Company' in New Jersey. It was an extravagance that they really couldn't afford and probably the only time the normally thrifty and frugal couple would treat themselves and their family to something as lavish. With five or six turns of the crank handle both sides of a record could be enjoyed and with a new needle installed, the sound quality gave the impression that "the performer was in their living room". John was exceptionally fond of the famous tenor, Enrico Caruso and purchased 'Vesti La Giubba' from I Pagliacci, which became the first million selling record ever in the United States.

Music and reading were the primary forms of entertainment, although John didn't read all that well. Sometimes, the oldest girls would read to the family from books on loan from the library, but they owned a few as well and John particularly liked 'The Red Badge of Courage', The Virginian and the 'Adventures of Sherlock Holmes' which Rose read to him over and over. The girls were proficient in needle crafts and young John liked playing baseball.

On warm Sunday afternoons, after Mass, they would sometimes play croquet in their back yard. They had purchased a horse, albeit an older horse beyond its prime at twenty when bought, but John was convinced that with proper diet, proper hoof and dental care, it would serve them for another ten years. John had also purchased an inexpensive buggy that needed major repairs, and within four dedicated Sunday afternoons of laborious restoration, had it functioning well, which made trips into "town" much easier.

As they tasted prosperity, they longed for additional material items, which tended to keep them motivated. As a foreman with tenure, John had pretty much peaked in income potential, and with their family growing, Mary, along with grandmother Ann, needed to stay at home caring for the children. While feeling relatively secure, in reality, they had a tenuous grip on their financial security. With no income tax at that time, John took home a substantial amount of his pay check, but there was no Social Security, no Unemployment Benefits, and certainly no public housing for the aged or handicapped, so there was no one, or no thing, to depend upon in times of emergency. Due to that, and to the fact that Blue Collar kids found it difficult to scrape together enough money to leave the nest, many, if not most, stayed at home until their early thirties, contributing to household expenses while simultaneously saving for marriage and a life on their own. With that in mind, John had already began preparing both Rose, and his employer, for her to take a job at the same hat shop where John worked. Many women worked in various departments, but John had suggested that she attempt to secure a position as a "Trimmer", which was, in John's words, one of the "safer and cleaner" departments. With the changing culture, there were other jobs becoming available to young women too. With the invention of typewriters, many worked in offices, with a full one third of clerical workers and telephone operators now being women. In addition, eighty-five percent of teachers were now women. Only eight percent of students graduated High School but a higher percentage of High School Grads were female than were male. At college level however, a very small percentage of grads were women. Courtship for young ladies was more formal and structured with a distinct protocol. A gentleman caller would be entertained in the parlor or in warmer weather, on the front porch swing or rocking chairs, at the woman's home, sometimes even serenading with a banjo or guitar. At fifteen Rose was maturing quickly and John anticipated some male suitors showing up soon. John adored his children and it pained him to think of them leaving home to start a life on their own. But, he also knew that they had become a very tightly knit family and felt confident that when they did ultimately leave, they would remain close in proximity and relationship.

Just as Rose was reaching young woman status, another surprising event complicating their family dynamic occurred: Mary became unexpectedly pregnant, which led to the arrival of another child in June of 1908, when Walter Charles Brett, their sixth child and third son, was born.

At forty-three years of age, John considered himself to be well to the high end of desirable age for fatherhood, especially when a man's average life expectancy was only forty-nine years; but sometimes, when one throws caution to the wind, and engages in somewhat reckless expression of physical affection during a "fit of passion", the consequence, if not certain, is pretty predictable. And, being strict Catholics who had adhered to the "rhythm method" for birth control, not to have paid heed to Mary's "fertile times" was indeed risky. With that said, neither John nor Mary were troubled by the arrival of another mouth to feed, the added responsibility of an even larger family, or the prospect of raising children well into their late fifties or early sixties, but rather perceived this as yet another blessing from God.

They were pleased to be bringing another life into the world during exciting and rapidly changing times.

Within two years, Motor Cars were gradually becoming an accepted mode of transportation, after the introduction of the Ford Model 'T' in 1908, which put automobiles within reach of "common people". A substantial price drop a few years later, would indeed make the "Tin Lizzy" commonplace within middle class families.

Cars like the Rolls Royce Silver Ghost, depicted in magazines and newspapers, while certainly way beyond the reach of most people, added to the allure and cache of the new technology. Slowing growth though, was the fact that there were only one hundred and forty-four miles of paved roads in 1910 for the eight thousand cars owned by the population. Eight percent of households now had telephones, with the percentage being higher in the urban areas, resulting in the exponential increase in the ability to quickly and easily communicate with friends, neighbors, community services and emergency services and even city government agencies. While, on average, 95% of all births took place at home, with the growth of Danbury Hospital, that ratio was decreasing quickly. Interestingly though, only 10% of doctors had a college education (having gone only to "Medical Schools") so the Midwife, specifically trained to assist during child birth, was still the preferred option. With the continued influx of immigrants and due to the agrarian culture in many parts of the country requiring children to work in fields at an early age, as well as the common practice of employing child labor in industrialized cities, where desperate, impoverished families had no choice but to send their kids to work, the illiteracy rate still registered at 20%, but that too was improving quickly. Even cultural nuances in areas of hygiene were evolving. Average women generally only washed their hair monthly, commonly using egg yolk or borax or a combination of those ingredients. The majority of households didn't have bath tubs, and personal items such as deodorant and tooth paste weren't readily available as commercial products, but rather home formulated "recipes" were the norm.

In 1910, Danbury was a growing and thriving city with a population of over twenty thousand residents. It was a highly diverse and multicultural town with improved government services, better police and fire protection, more retail establishments and restaurants opening, more and better entertainment options and improved medical care. It was heavily 'blue collar' and industrialized but beginning to expand with high end residential sections and due to economic growth, more 'White Collar' and Professional jobs were being created. The Brett family too, was continuing to grow and thrive in 1910. Rose, now 17, had taken a job as a "Trimmer" in the same hat factory where John worked and her contribution to household expenses helped considerably. After a couple of years, the addition of another income contributed to the household significantly enough for John to approach The Union Savings Bank seeking a mortgage loan. Their current landlord had become quite aged and was seeking to liquidate his personal holdings to facilitate a more comfortable "retirement". He had previously told John that he would be willing to sell the property to them, if John and Mary ever became financially capable of making the purchase. That comment had triggered a more dedicated, determined and enthusiastic savings program, and precipitated John and Mary's dream of home ownership. Now, with Rose's contribution, it was close to becoming a reality. However, the banks required a down payment of 40% to 50% and only offered 5 to 7 year terms.

They really weren't surprised by that revelation; it was common practice, but using the bank to secure a mortgage was also fraught with risk. They could legally raise rates indiscriminately, they could arbitrarily reduce the term to 3 years and could foreclose after only two consecutive late payments. There were other places to go for loans- certain ethnic groups had formed their own loan associations (the Irish included) but they seemed to John as being less secure and he resisted sharing "private information", especially financial, with anyone. When casually discussing his "bank concerns" and subsequent hesitation to actually make the commitment with his landlord, he offered to finance John himself, if the 50% down payment could be provided. The conversation then became serious and a reasonable sale price was determined and agreed upon. The Brett family did indeed have enough in personal savings to come up with the down payment and in 1912 they purchased their home. The feeling of satisfaction was overwhelming for both John and Mary and they experienced an enormous sense of pride and accomplishment. Their hopefulness, dedication and work ethic had brought them farther in America than it ever could have in Ireland. And, a joyfulness and optimism pervaded the entire household and family. It was a happy time.

Their life was a long shot from perfect though. Work was still very demanding and exhausting, foreman position or not, and running the household was challenging for Mary. Preparing meals for six children and a husband, and cleaning up after them, was demanding, even though Ann helped.

Their icebox was small and needed a large ice block loaded every other day (delivered by the "Iceman" via horse and commercial buggy) and the drain pan needed emptying twice daily, Mary needed to venture out to the grocery, the butcher shop or fish market frequently due to very limited cold storage, there was baking to do and house cleaning; six children and a very "untidy husband" (in Mary's words) dramatically exacerbated the "normal" cleaning routine and with John's long hours, Mary and the older children assumed the responsibility of caring for the horse and outbuildings and yard. During summer months they tended a garden, which provided the only fresh vegetables they consumed during the year. For most of the year, they only had access to canned vegetables. They also had a chicken house with a few laying hens and Anna and Shelly gathered the eggs and tended the chickens. And then there was the outhouse! No one wanted the job of moving it to a new location when it reached practical capacity and it became necessary to dig a new hole (over five feet deep), cover over the old hole and relocate the outhouse to another spot. Certainly more than a one man operation! And the occasional requisite application of additional lime and wood ashes to reduce odor was never a fun job. There was a small can of the lime-wood ash mixture within the outhouse for sprinkling down the hole after each use, but about once per week, (especially with a large family) someone would need to go out and raise the long wooden seat, which was hinged at the back, and apply a heavy dose. All avoided that job. And then there was the coal furnace in the cellar. It was a stone cellar; dark, musty and damp and dirty from coal dust. The furnace needed to be kept burning during the long winter months and needed constant attention. They still used a wood stove for cooking and baking and even for heating bath water. They had a water pump bolted to the counter adjacent to the sink, but that was the only source of running water in the house. Electricity was becoming more prevalent but they still used kerosene lamps for lighting. Between those lamps and the wood stove, cleaning was a never ending chore. Their home was furnished and decorated nicely, albeit using second hand, but still solid and functional furniture and handmade decorator items. There were a few relatively nice Victorian chairs and a tattered love seat in the parlor but most of the other furnishings were basic and utilitarian. The Parlor was generally "off limits" to the younger children and John's tendency to roughhouse and engage in boisterous play with the children- "as though he were one of them!" was a comment shared by both Mary and Grandmother Ann. John loved his kids immensely and they completely adored him. One of his greatest pleasures in life was spending time with his family playing games, wrestling with the boys, reading to each other and sometimes just looking through the Sears Roebuck or Montgomery Ward mail order catalogs, fantasizing about items that they would someday like to have. There was now a "Five and Ten Cent Store" in town called Woolworth's and he would sometimes single out a particular child and walk to the store and purchase a small item for them, to reward for an accomplishment or exceptionally good behavior.

When one of the girls was chosen they would feel very special and loved the attention bestowed upon them by their father.

On the surface, John was a simple man with simple needs. But in reality, there was a complex depth of integrity, resolve and burning desire to craft an existence and environment that would nurture his children, display intense love and commitment to his wife and honor his loving mother. The pluck and faith required of a man who had the mettle and courage to walk away from a poor existence and build a new and better one, half way across the world, was also what gave him the strength and to some extent, cunning, to thrive as a new immigrant to America. Once settled, small, seemingly insignificant, yet necessary, acts of bravery, sacrifice and discipline became part of his, and their, daily routine- just as it was with thousands of other immigrants striving to build a better life, working in very difficult and frequently dangerous jobs, sacrificing to put food on the table and provide for their families and deal with the ostracization inflicted upon them from "mainstream" society. No single great acts of heroism to bring great praise or laudatory articles in newspapers, simply a steadfast determination, resignation and positive mindset. They were all unsung, every day heroes contributing to the fabric of 20th century American life. If Thoreau's assertion that "The mass of men lead lives of quiet desperation" contained an element of truth, it did not apply to John. He loved his life and gained great satisfaction from selflessly giving to his family. He maintained an unyielding optimism and happy, easy going persona in spite of the challenges and risks associated with his everyday life.

Though it wasn't an idyllic life, he and Mary were mutually content, deeply loved each other and their family and could see an even brighter future- if not for them, certainly for their children. Like any married couple, they occasionally argued and bickered; usually over methods of disciplining the kids

(Mary was the primary disciplinarian and John was considerably less than authoritarian), about John's perceived "untidiness", his occasional over indulgence when staying too long at the saloon with his friends or his frequent reluctance to complete certain chores around the house. Within this devoutly Catholic home, there was an avoidance of outward displays of affection between John and Mary, especially in front of the children and a certain propriety was always maintained but there was, never the less, a deep and abiding love between them.

Their affection toward each other, while around the children, and Grandmother Ann, was made manifest through a casual, cheerful lightheartedness, jesting and poking good natured fun at each other, and an unwavering display of mutual respect. In the privacy and sanctity of their bedroom, however, a physically passionate component of their relationship was able to be enjoyed, the obvious manifestation of which was their brood of six children! They had the good fortune of discovering a home sizable enough to provide adequate bedrooms for the children (although some of them shared), a single, private bedroom for Grandmother Ann (there were cribs in Ann's room so that she could care for the infants at night) and a private bedroom for John and Mary, that was located somewhat remotely from the others.

The fact that the house was a duplex, with units combined as one, ultimately provided the perfect floor plan for a large family. Toward the end of 1912, with Mary turning 42, and John at 47 years of age, they began to believe that they were approaching the end of child bearing age, and yet, during a warm, sultry evening in early September of that year, Mary became pregnant once again. She was either unsure or in denial, but she didn't disclose the news to John, and then the rest of the family, until December of that year. She obviously couldn't have known it at the time, but a fourth daughter, a seventh child, would arrive somewhat prematurely, in

May of 1913. With Rosalind at twenty, Ann at seventeen and Shelly at fifteen, help with baby care and raising the newborn would certainly be available, which would be a God send with Grandmother Anna set to reach seventy-three and becoming incapable of sharing the load due to simple age and some developing health problems.

While John's persona at home was affable, relaxed and easy going, his image at work was slightly different. He was a good foreman; well liked, admired and respected by those workers who reported to him but equally well liked and appreciated by his employer. He walked that fine line between the two, empathetic toward workers and respectful of them, while direct and expecting a "full measure" of work for income paid. He was tactful when discipline and redirection was needed, but clearly expected full and immediate compliance; and if he didn't get it, and got insubordination or vulgar resistance, he wouldn't hesitate to terminate and release the employee from service. It didn't take many of those occasions to develop a reputation as a strong, no nonsense foreman and it garnered the respect of employees and owners and top management alike.

His days were long, and while not as physically demanding as they had been twenty-plus years earlier, he still became thoroughly exhausted by week's end. Adding to his concerns, was the slow progression of symptoms of "Hatter's Disease". The tremors and trembling were more pronounced, sleep was fitful and a constant, nagging, though minor, cough was present. But his income was adequate, and he was held in such high regard by his employer that he was given a small, token, unscheduled raise in pay when he made the announcement that a seventh child was about to enter the Brett household. That news made Mary very happy, and even though Rosalind was contributing a majority of her own income toward household expenses, the thought of yet another mouth to feed, concerned her. In addition, their income and lifestyle, even with Rosalind's contribution, provided little opportunity for "personal extravagances" and this small increase in income just might allow for an occasional treat- a small reward for their impeccable work ethic, self sacrificing for their children, steadfast loyalty to John's employer and willing self denial of small material luxuries. Aside from spending time with his family, which provided enormous joy and satisfaction to John, he craved few other indulgences. He had a distinct fondness for beer and enjoyed time spent at the pub with some select friends, and on rare occasion, he would treat himself to a bottle of Irish Whiskey (which Mary and even Grandmother Anna enjoyed discretely sharing).

His only other vice, if one could consider fashionable apparel a "vice", was his proclivity for fine, fashionable clothing and he considered himself to be a man with some degree of sartorial aplomb. He obviously couldn't afford to indulge himself frequently and would therefore meticulously care for his "dress clothes", wearing them only to Sunday Mass and on very special occasions. Mary too, took pride in her appearance and enjoyed fashionable attire as well, although not to the extent that John did. Some of Mary's friends would refer to him as "Dapper John", which amused her and slightly embarrassed him. On any given Sunday, one might see them going to church; him wearing his favorite 'Norfolk Jacket' (a belted jacket with box pleats front and back) and either a Bowler hat or 'Newsboy Cap' while she would wear a calf length, conservatively colored skirt, known as a "War Crinoline"which had replaced the "Hobble Skirt" that had been in fashion a year or two earlier. The Hobble Skirt was tailored wide at the hips, full length and narrow at the ankles. The War Crinoline was a flared skirt and length was raised to the calf, rather than ankle length. As with most change in fashion direction, the trend began in Europe, then later, manufacturers in the United States. This one however, contained an element of practicality with the aesthetic; its impetus being conservation of material for the war effort.

The new skirt would usually be paired with a white blouse (called a shirtwaist) and shawl, and the children tagged along, well scrubbed and neatly attired. The girls were always perfectly behaved but the boys could become slightly "antsy" and borderline unruly so Rosalind and Ann, and sometimes even the very devout Shelly, would assume the responsibility for keeping them in line. Nothing can be more embarrassing and humiliating for a twelve and ten year old boy than to be publicly reprimanded and chastised by one's older sister!

Sunday was always a great family day. After services, they would return home, gather fresh eggs and prepare a sizable breakfast, all but Walter, the youngest (under seven, and yet to have received the sacrament of First Holy Communion) having fasted prior to receiving the Eucharist. John Junior would always want to help with the preparation, priding himself as "the best twelve year old biscuit maker on earth". After a while, his siblings began calling him "Cookie" which served a dual purpose: first, it provided a little good natured kidding and gentle mocking, and second, as the nickname stuck, it became a good way to avoid confusion, with two John's living in the same household. After breakfast they would listen to piano music, mostly performed by Rosalind, while they would sing along; the boys poorly, except for John Sr., who had a wonderful tenor voice, or they would read, view photographic stereo cards on their 'Stereoscope' (they kept a large basket of stereo cards in their parlor), play yard games during nice weather or take long family walks or picnics in the local park. During winter weather John Junior, Henry, Rosalind and Ann would ice skate, or if snow was present, go sledding. Shelly (young Mary) wasn't fond of the outdoors and spent her time in the house, reading, learning to play music or helping her mother and grandmother with chores.

When spring arrived, John, Jr. and Henry could always be found in the backyard playing catch and more often than not,

John Senior would join in, (they were all avid baseball fans) or sometimes they would organize an impromptu sand lot game with some neighborhood friends.

In early spring of 1913, Harriet Leonora Brett arrived prematurely. Mary's age might have had something to do with it but early arrival or not, the baby was relatively healthy for a "preemie" and after a few months of attentive care, she was as healthy as any newborn, albeit still only six and a half pounds.

The older girls were elated and the boys were generally ambivalent. John, Jr. was thirteen, Henry was eleven and Walter only five, and they were preoccupied with boyhood. The girls, on the other hand, were doting and "practicing at motherhood". Rosalind was especially conscientious and treated "Little Leona" (she was called "Leona" from birth) as though she were her own. It was a time of joy and after twenty-five years in America, life continued to be good for the Brett family.

12

THE YEAR NINETEEN-FIFTEEN

A s World War One was raging in Europe, John and Mary couldn't help but fear United States involvement, even though President Woodrow Wilson had taken a "non-intervention" position. "Cook", (or "Cookie", as they now all called John Junior) was fifteen and Henry was thirteen and if the war continued for very long, they might both be of fighting age; and based upon their glorified image of war and their youthful exuberance and naivete, they might be inclined to enlist. On May 7th, the RMS Lusitania was sunk by a German submarine killing 1,200 people, 128 of whom were Americans. Of course the act was condemned by the President, and a demand that submarine warfare against commercial vessels be ceased immediately was issued, but compliance for any length of time was doubtful. Later, between September 25th and October 14th, French and British soldiers fought an extended battle with German troops and sustained very heavy losses in France during the battle of Loos. John and Mary had good reason to be fearful.

One the home front, the severe recession of 1913 and 1914 had come to and end, but the sixteenth Amendment, providing for the federal government to levy taxes on income remained, and the previous two years of economic turmoil had placed a burden on the Brett family. At age nineteen, Ann had joined Rosalind in the workforce and Shelly was seventeen and one of the relatively small number of young women to remain in high school until graduation. "Cook" was becoming bored with school and began working part time after school as an apprentice plumber. At age thirteen, J. Henry was entering puberty and starting to develop his own unique personality. He had joined the Boy Scouts, which had formed a few years earlier, in 1910, but wasn't much of an outdoorsman and preferred comfort and ease over camping, hiking and crafts. He read voraciously, especially about successful businessmen and tycoons like; John D. Rockefeller of Standard Oil, Andrew Carnegie of Carnegie Steel Company, Samuel Sachs (Goldman, Sachs a & Co.), J.P. Morgan, Jay Gould and Cornelius Vanderbilt of Railroad fame, even Thomas Edison and Henry Ford. He took inspiration from them and their stories and was determined to achieve great success himself one day. Even at his young age, he clearly disliked the financial pressure and adapting to a more austere family budget that the recent recession had caused.

John's hours at the Hat Factory had been unpredictable and frequently shortened which was responsible for the income shortages. Rosalind too, had experienced cuts in hours and loss of any overtime work which further exacerbated the problem.

Fortunately, 1915 saw a return to more normal conditions. Normal that is, with the exception of Rosalind's serious romance with her new beau, William McAllister. He was handsome, level headed, conservative, ambitious and (importantly) Catholic and worked as a Revenue Collector.

Both John and Mary, as well as Grandmother Ann, considered him to be a great prospect for becoming a Son-in-Law and enthusiastically approved of the relationship. After a formal courtship of almost a year, with the family's blessing, they set the wedding date for early spring. The ceremony would be held at St. Peter's Church and the reception held at the family home on Fairfield Avenue.

They were a family of modest means, therefore the wedding would be devoid of any extravagance but while spending restraint would be exercised, unbridled enthusiasm, merriment and celebratory revelry would undoubtedly prevail (in true Irish tradition). It had also been decided that Rosalind and William would move in and set up housekeeping at the Brett family home, creating an even larger family. The change occurred smoothly with limited disruption and William was immediately welcomed by all.

There were some exciting things happening on the world events scene too. In January, Alexander Graham Bell successfully called his assistant Thomas Watson in San Francisco, CA inaugurating the first transcontinental phone service. It had been intended to take place earlier, in 1914, to coincide with the Panama-Pacific International Exposition which was to showcase the recently completed Panama Canal, and some tests were completed prior to January of 1915, but the official start was recorded as January twenty-fifth.

In the field of science and physics, Albert Einstein formulated his Theory of General Relativity and on the political front, the House Of Representatives rejected a proposal to give women the right to vote, which clearly angered all of the women in the Brett household, with the exception of Grandmother Ann, who though it "wasn't necessary because most women influenced their men anyway and his vote was cast for both of them". The other Brett women just collectively shook their heads in disbelief but were far too respectful and well mannered to object or criticize the assertion.

In the field of sports, a young, upstart baseball star with the Red Sox, named Babe Ruth hit his first home run while pitching 12 innings of a 13 inning game against the Yankees. The Red Sox lost four to three.

On the business front, the Raggedy Ann Doll was patented

and was a huge success, especially in the Brett household where they all kiddingly exclaimed that it should have been named Raggedy Shelly because it resembled her red hair and fondness for plaid in her clothing choices.

As the year came to a close, they all agreed that 1915 had been good to the Brett family. The wedding of Rose and William was a beautiful, fun filled and joyous affair and now that they resided at the Brett family home, paying rent and some expenses, financial concerns were greatly diminished. There was ample space and even with a new son-in-law joining the family dynamic, they were living in greater harmony than ever.

And, to make things even more exciting, albeit more complex, Rose announced that she had just become pregnant. That bit of news was sobering for John and Mary, realizing that when Rose's due date arrived, toward the end of summer 1916, they would have their three year old daughter, Leona, and a newborn grandchild living in the same house! That, they said to each other, would be like "going back to the old days". But never the less, they were thrilled with the news.

They were a close knit, loving family and all pitched in and took mutual responsibility for home maintenance, child rearing, cleaning and made a financial contribution. And while that was a great relief to John, the realization of having a child that wouldn't reach an age of independence for another thirteen to fifteen years would mean that he would be entering his late sixties before the responsibility of raising children was behind them. He wasn't sure if he'd be able to work that long.

As he approached the age of fifty-two, he had been working in the Hatting industry for almost twenty-eight years. His tremors were getting worse and although he hadn't been exposed nearly to the extent that many workers had, he recognized the symptoms of mercuric nitrate poisoning and knew that "The Danbury Shakes" which is what many called Hatter's Disease, was taking a toll. He was starting to experience breathing problems and some memory lapses and became concerned that if the progression continued, he might not be able to function in his position as Foreman. In addition, he was starting to experience mood swings. He had always been happy to the point of jovial, in spite of what hardships, difficulties or personal strife he encountered. He had always been the eternal optimist- positive, determined and fun to be around. But now, his gregarious and very outgoing nature could be replaced with short bouts of shyness and introversion. He could be uncharacteristically somber and even sullen, then swing back to his "old self". And, he was drinking more than usual. Not to the point of habitual intoxication, but occasionally getting too close.

Compounding his concern, was the shift from favored employee status, toward "persona non grata" with his employer. John was as empathetic as he was cheerful and optimistic. He cared for the plight of his fellow workers and when he saw so many afflicted with the frightening effects of mercury exposure, it troubled him and weighed heavily upon his conscience. His own symptoms provided further empathy and he had decided that he needed to become their advocate. He pleaded with management to act quickly to provide greater safety measures and at least acknowledge the problem. They were still, to a large extent, in denial. He spoke with fellow church goers, a few concerned journalists and even some politicians as they campaigned in his Fourth Ward hang outs. He was making waves and it wasn't appreciated. Finally, after some thoughtful introspection and realization that he would need his job for another fifteen years caused him to back off and remain silent for now. He would just do his job and hope for the best.

13

VIRTUAL METAMORPHOSIS

In 1916 the Model T Ford was selling for about $360.00, and after dinner one evening in the early spring, John, William and "Cook" adjourned to the front porch to enjoy an uncommonly warm late March evening; and John and William decided to light up a cigar while "Cook" eaves dropped and enjoyed the smell of second hand smoke. He had already begun smoking, and had quickly developed a preference for Fatima Brand cigarettes, but kept it a secret from his parents. William, on the other hand, knew he had acquired the habit after having spotted him smoking a short time ago, with a few of his friends, while he was out walking in the neighborhood, but never betrayed his confidence. They began discussing the possibility of purchasing a car for family transportation but came to the conclusion that, if they did, they would need the seven passenger Ford Town Car, which sold for $640.00, to accommodate the large family. They might have been able to scrape up enough of the $360.00 for the base model but it would be impractical, and the Town Car was beyond reach at this point in time. It was a fantasy conversation and while they all realized that they weren't yet ready to make the purchase, it provided a fun way to spend an evening and bond closer as the three oldest men of the family. It was, to use the French expression; "pour parler"- just for talk. "Cook" was pleased to be included and it made him feel important.

As the family grew and matured, and "Cook" and Henry were approaching manhood ("Cook" gainfully employed and Henry still in school), Rose had married and was expecting, Ann was in the work force and dating, Shelly was approaching high school graduation and John and Mary were aging; not to mention the addition of son-in-law William to the family circle, the relationship dynamic was changing considerably. Contributing further complexity to this evolving dynamic was Grandmother Anna's failing health. While in relatively good spirits, she was weak and tired easily and suffered from respiratory problems. Therefore, she did little to help with chores and provided much less assistance with the care of three year old Leona than she had as recently as the year before. The family meetings, while not "scheduled" as weekly discussions, as was somewhat customary in other Irish families, were impromptu, random and casual but usually taking place on a Saturday evening or during Sunday dinner. Years earlier, they were simply for the children to share the most meaningful events of the past week and for John and Mary to provide input, direction, wisdom and guidance and to briefly touch upon issues impacting the family, whether positive or negative.

They never shared anything of a serious nature that might cause angst, but felt that treating the children as important members of the family circle, whose informed knowledge of the trials and tribulations, as well as the joys and successes of everyday life, was a learning experience that would instill a sense of confidence and prepare them for the realities of the world. Now, however, the family meetings had become more adult and included political, financial and morality discussions, as well as sports and work banter, and as usual, the ever present good natured kidding and teasing.

And then there were the shared dreams and aspirations- talk of some day buying that automobile, or what

Shelly planned to do after graduation, or proposed names for William and Rose's first child, or even some "outrageous" behavior witnessed while down town Danbury, strolling or shopping. In addition, John now had some competition as family joke teller and limerick provider as William contributed some comedy (sometimes slightly ribald) offerings as well. But then, during that warm spring of 1916, the conversations took on a more ominous tone. On April 24th the Easter Uprising of Irish Republicans against British occupation began in Dublin. After twenty-eight years in the United States, the Brett family (and McAllister too) had essentially lost touch with their relatives in Ireland. It was unintentional, but the demands of building a life in America and the hectic nature of their lifestyle and work schedule didn't provide much time for correspondence. They wrote frequently at first but as time passed, the frequency diminished considerably. Never the less, they were concerned about their mother country and relatives who might be effected by the political turmoil. World War One was also a frequent and sobering topic. Germany and Austria-Hungary had notified the United States that they would assume the right to sink any armed merchant ship and the US promptly rejected that "right". Within the family, there seemed to be an even split regarding whether the United States should become involved or not.

The conversation on May seventh was exceptionally lively. The weather was near perfect and they had all walked to St Peter's Church for mass and then returned home to enjoy yard games and prepare Sunday dinner. An elderly Portuguese neighbor had recently butchered a large portion of his herd of rabbits and had generously given some to Grandmother Ann to prepare for dinner. Mary facetiously joked that; "He had an eye for her", (meaning amorous intentions). The beautiful weather combined with an exceptionally passionate and inspiring homily delivered by the priest had placed everyone in a good mood. This particular Sunday there had been a visiting priest, which was always a welcome occasion because their regular priest had a reputation for being rather boring. During dinner they spoke of the war and of the troubles in Ireland, but also more mundane topics such as Arthur Roth winning the Boston marathon with a time of two hours, twenty-seven minutes, and sixteen seconds (which all family members found to be amazing) and how much they enjoyed their new, recently purchased record, by Enrico Caruso, entitled 'O Solo Mio'. The frequency with which John played the recording received some criticism and sarcastic teasing from those younger family members who didn't share his enthusiasm for opera and classical music.

During that Sunday dinner, John also described an unusual dream that he had the night before. He had frequent dreams, many bordering on hallucinogenic and uncommonly vivid. While he wouldn't say it, he knew that it could possibly be an associated symptom of mercury exposure and 'Hatter's Disease". But this one wasn't frightening or disconcerting at all, but rather comforting and pleasant, albeit oddly melancholy and surreal. He had dreamt that he was sailing once again on the steamship 'The City of Berlin' which is the vessel that he, Mary and Ann had sailed upon when they first journeyed to America. In his dream, all passengers were sailing First Class because steerage class had been completely eliminated.

He was reclining on a lounge chair on the promenade of the upper deck watching an astoundingly beautiful sunset and listening to a musical ensemble, positioned somewhere out of sight and quietly playing some of his favorite Irish melodies. Both the sun and the moon were simultaneously visible on the horizon which he found remarkable, and he turned to comment to the only other passenger present, who was seated to his right. At first, he thought that he had been on deck alone, and was enjoying the solitude, but later noticed in his peripheral vision, that he had a companion. The "companion" was wearing a white terry cloth robe, with the ship's insignia embroidered on it, and a white Bowler Hat, tilted slightly, obscuring his face from view. Between them, attached to the hull and next to a port hole, was the famous Derby Hat neon sign, that greeted visitors at the Danbury Train Station as they arrived in town, that read: 'Danbury Crowns Them All'. It took a moment for his vision to focus in the red light cast by the neon sign, and after clarity returned, the individual straightened his hat, exposing his face, and John recognized his father as the person seated next to him. He slowly turned toward John and smiled. His father looked as he did when he was a very young man, not as he had near the end of his life. John wanted to speak to him but could think of nothing to say. But it was a comfortable silence, as though communication through spoken word was unnecessary and volumes had been communicated the instant they gazed at each other. He felt a loving contentment fill his body as they both returned their view to the setting sun and rising moon. They were seated on the port side of the ship and the calm seas were glass-like with a color-mixed reflection of blue from the light of the moon and orange from the light of the sun. The intensity of the glorious reflection created a swell of emotion and John spoke the name, Vincent Van Gogh. John's father then spoke aloud, repeating a quote from Van Gogh; "Love many things, for therein lies the true strength: and whosoever loves much, performs much, can accomplish much; and what is done in love is done well". John nodded in agreement as he gazed at the sun, beginning to dim, and the moon, gaining intensity, then turned to acknowledge but found the passenger had vanished. Then he awakened.

After listening to the description of his dream, all who were gathered around the table remained silent for a moment, letting the oddity of the dream sink in, then William chuckled and said; "we had better check the level in the Bushmill's (Irish Whiskey) bottle!" They all laughed and the conversation moved on to other topics.

14

BEING STRONG

"You never know how strong you are until
being strong is the only choice you have".

Cayla Mills

On the following Monday morning, the household was as manic as usual. Leona was being "fussy" and poorly behaved, "Cook" was looking frantically for a misplaced tool that would be necessary for a job scheduled for that day, Henry was running typically late for school and Shelly was doing her best to quiet Leona and help Walter get ready for his day at school. With the hectic and irregular schedules, the family seldom had breakfast together, but more typically in random fashion and "on the run"; but Mary always prepared breakfast for John and made something for him to take to work in his lunch pail. As John finished his morning tea, he said that the spring day was so beautiful that he planned to walk the entire distance to the factory. Most of the time he would only walk down Fairfield Avenue to South Street and wait for the trolley, but today, he would leave somewhat early and walk leisurely, enjoying the warm, sunny weather. He kissed her and the children as he left and said that he might need to work overtime tonight, so don't be surprised if he returned late.

Rose had gone on a part time schedule due to her pregnancy and today wasn't feeling well, so she went back to her bedroom to rest after William had left. By 10:00 AM everyone had left for work or school, the baby had been put down for a nap and Mary could finally take a breath and pour another cup of tea and relax. She was surprised by a knock on the door and when she answered it she was greeted by a local constable. She noticed two other officers standing out by the curb, all three exhibiting a very serious and stern countenance. She immediately felt a sense of dread; her heart began pounding and she felt a flush of heat engulf her body. He said; "Hello Ma'am; are you Mrs. John Brett?" She abruptly responded; "What's wrong!" He said; I'm afraid I have very bad news." Before he could continue, Rose had entered the room and joined Mary at her side. She had heard the knock on the door, and the uncommon occurrence of a visitor at that hour of the day sparked her curiosity. She was still slightly drowsy, having dozed off while resting after the early morning activities but awakened quickly as she too, felt a sense of foreboding, and she, almost shouting, interrupted saying; "What's wrong, Mother?" The Constable cleared his throat and repeated; "I have some very bad news- I regret to inform you that Mr. John Brett has passed away this morning".

Mary couldn't respond but gasped, then let out a guttural sound as though she had been punched in the stomach, then cried out as though in great pain. Her knees buckled and Rose and the Constable caught her before she fell to the floor. Rose began to wail while she and Mary embraced. The Constable expressed his deep sympathy while he ushered them to the sofa in the parlor, supporting their combined weight with his arm around their shoulder. Once they were seated, he explained that John had walked as far as the trolley stop and sat on the bench, telling another commuter that he felt ill and had a severe pain in his left shoulder. He continued by saying that he had intended to walk to work on this beautiful day, but now thought that he had better wait here for the trolley. Before he could say anything else, he collapsed. None of the other commuters knew anything about resuscitation and therefore could not render assistance.

By the time the horse drawn ambulance arrived, most present concurred that he had passed. When he arrived at the hospital, it was confirmed. He had suffered a severe, fatal heart attack.

He concluded by reiterating that he was deeply sorry to have given them this terrible news and provided his name and contact information should it be needed. He said; "If there is anything you need, please let me know"; but the offer was empty, and he knew full well that there was nothing he could do to help ease the pain and loss.

Rose was weeping uncontrollably and rocking back and forth on the sofa, but Mary, while still in shock, was more stoic. Her mind was spinning, and the flood of emotion caused by a profound sense of loss, sadness and grief was in direct contrast with her duty to help see her family through this devastating crisis, make appropriate funeral preparations, inform family and friends and consider ways to continue the family's ongoing support and welfare. While she was torn apart inside, she kept her emotions at bay, at least for now, while she took control of the tragic situation. She thought to herself; "This is a time for me to be strong."

As the family returned home from school and work, they were each informed, and as expected, they all took the news badly. They idolized their father and couldn't believe that their lives had been turned upside down in the blink of an eye. William tried to provide comfort, assurance and solace, as did "Cook", as the eldest, now thrust into the role of the new male "leader" of the family. Shelly took the news the hardest. She adored her father and was almost incoherent and hysterical in her expressions of grief. It was indeed a dark day within the Brett household and the void created by the loss of their beloved husband, father, son and father-in-law was palpable and devastating. He had been with them always, leaving their side only for work, and the house was experiencing a prevailing emptiness, gloom and sorrow without his presence.

Most affected, perhaps even more than Mary and Shelly, was Grandmother Ann. She almost worshiped John and loved him with an intensity that only a mother could muster. She could have never have imagined that he would "cross over into the dimension of heaven" before her. Her initial shock and disbelief were quickly replaced with depression and agonizing grief. She retreated to the confines of her room, refusing food and personal interaction.

Mary became a woman in complete control and her mission was to orchestrate a fitting tribute to "a fine, loving, courageous and self sacrificing man". She had been relieved to discover that due to the close proximity of the trolley stop to St. Peter's Church, somehow their priest had been notified and he arrived prior to the ambulance taking John to the hospital. Therefore, the Sacrament of Last Rites was administered, which provided some comfort to Mary.

In keeping with Irish tradition, she wanted the Wake (Slainte) to be held in their home. At that time, a home's parlor was frequently referred to as the "Death Room" because it was used for wakes and funerals in most homes of the day, especially suburban homes, and even though the custom began to change when a 1910 'Ladies Home Journal' article that exclaimed; "With the growing proliferation and of Funeral 'Parlors' and the evolving custom of home funerals shifting to 'Funeral Homes', the Death Room can now be called the Living Room!", Mary was insistent that John's tribute be held at their home. Another common practice, (albeit rapidly decreasing in popularity, inversely proportional with increase in the middle class activity of taking home photographs), was

"Memento Mori" which was a final, after death photograph, professionally taken.

The height of popularity was during the Victorian era. During that time, portrait photography was too expensive for average working class people, so money was saved for the last photo as a remembrance. When approached by a local photographer, Mary declined.

Many home parlors had a "Wake Table", which had a center plank, wide enough and long enough to accommodate a coffin, and two leaves which could be dropped to provide easy viewing when visitors arrived to pay respects. With the leaves raised, the table could be used for dining or whatever else the owner chose, but it was generally present in many homes with the specific purpose of providing display space for a coffin.

Mary estimated the time of John's death as closely as possible and stopped all clocks in the house at that exact time. They wouldn't be restarted until the funeral service was complete. She also opened all doors and windows when his body arrived home, "so that his soul could easily take wing", if it hadn't already. The family wasn't sure if she was being controlled by superstition or simply a desire to believe that his soul would have remained with his body until returned home so he could offer a "final good bye" in spirit. According to tradition, the bereaved would often times be too distraught to sleep, and it was considered bad luck to leave the body unattended, so they would sit and keep a vigil next to the body all night (hence the term "wake"). It was another example of a practice created for practical reasons, during times of yore, when body snatching and corpse robbing were common, evolving into a more superstitious practice during contemporary times. Mary was no exception and she spent the night at John's side, weeping, speaking words of love and listening for his unspoken guidance. As antiquated and superstitious as the custom might have been, the process provided a private opportunity to grieve that was at least partially cathartic and offered a modicum of comfort. She also prayed and placed his rosary beads around his folded hands and read some of John's favorite bible verses and passages.

John was well liked and many friends and co-workers attended his wake. He had made a few enemies along the way, especially during union squabbles, but all respected and appreciated his work ethic and enjoyed his outgoing, sometimes jubilant personality; and everyone admired his devotion to his family and to God; and he was a great role model for younger workers. It was a solemn affair but like most Irish wakes, there was lots of food and drink served to the mourners. The family seemed to hold up reasonably well, with the exception of Grandmother Ann. "Keening", defined as wailing, vocal expression of grief, most times inarticulate, and incoherent, was a common practice during "old country" Irish Wakes and sometime engaging in this somewhat extreme form of grieving can help the bereaved cope with their loss and recover more quickly. When Grandmother Ann entered the parlor and began "keening" it was heart breaking to watch and clearly upset baby Leona and some guests unfamiliar with ethnic behavioral oddities practiced by Irish, Italian and other cultures at funerals as a coping mechanism. She was given some latitude and time, but after a while was taken back to her room to grieve in private. It was a relief to those of a more reserved, frequently taciturn and sometimes stoic nature, whose Victorian and Puritan roots might have culturally discouraged such displays of raw emotion. They had come to pay respects, but hadn't expected to be exposed to such uncomfortable goings on.

Mr. Loewe, the factory owner, even stopped by to pay his respects as well as did a Forth Ward Councilman. Mary was pleased.

The funeral service was held at St. Peter's Church, after which everyone gathered at St. Peter's Cemetery, located in the Mill Plain district of Danbury for graveside comments and final prayers. The family had previously purchased a plot with nine spaces and John was the first to be interred there. It is at the southwest end of the cemetery boundary near Kenosia Avenue and Lake Kenosia, where John and Mary had spent many enjoyable spring and summer days. The uncommonly warm spring had given way to an Arctic plunge bringing very cool, rainy and windy weather into the area. Mary thought to herself that it was only fitting that the heavens grieved as well". Mary regretted being able to provide only a small marble stone to mark his grave, but with an uncertain financial future, she felt that his memory would be well preserved in the hearts of those who knew John, and that a large stone would be superfluous and impractical. She was resolved to someday soon, place a large Brett Family marker at the grave site. At the conclusion of the graveside service, no gathering of mourners took place at the family home. By that time, Mary and the family was too exhausted and emotionally distraught to welcome anyone into their home. While they were appreciative and very thankful for the tremendous outpouring of sympathy, condolences and prayers, they preferred to mourn only as immediate family.

Sadly, within four months, John's mother Ann, followed him to eternity. She had never recovered from the profound grief, continued to reject interaction with family members, refusing most food and weeping constantly.

As the profoundly deep and unrelenting mourning persisted, along with lack of sleep and proper nutrition, negatively impacted her immune system, she soon became ill with a severe flu, from which she couldn't recover, and it progressed into full blown pneumonia and within days she quietly passed in her sleep. While deeply saddened, the grief stricken family had little additional tolerance for further anguish and sorrow, and they all said that they were relieved that Ann's emotional pain had ended. They were convinced that she was happier to be with John in heaven. She was interred at John's side, in the family plot to the left of John. The right space was reserved for Mary.

John died a young man- at only fifty-two years of age. But he had accomplished much in his short life. He certainly didn't achieve fame, fortune or notoriety as defined by most people. But he was deeply loved by his family, he had created a new and better life for them and had facilitated the establishment of roots in a country where THEY might grow and prosper and some day enjoy the quintessential American dream. He taught them well, he loved them greatly and his legacy would continue through them and what they made of their lives. He wasn't all that unique. He was an immigrant like many thousands (and ultimately millions) of others whose self sacrifice provided a platform for his offspring- by working hard, and sometimes dying young, they could provide better opportunity so that their children might get more out of life. Sadly, many like John Brett have been forgotten by second, third and forth generations, and few take the time to reflect upon the sacrifice of their ancestors. But those ancestors have the satisfaction of gazing down upon their descendants, and taking pride and satisfaction in those whose lives are well lived and worthy of the sacrifice made so many generations earlier. The squandered lives, on the other hand, creates a blemish on their soul. The obligation of offspring and descendents is to honor the sacrifice of men and women like John and Mary Brett, and to live their lives to the fullest and not to squander the gift. We commonly think of heroes as those who perform some great act of courage and selflessness. Soldiers, police officers, firemen or just average citizens thrown into a situation that requires a great courageous act. But the "unsung heroes" like John Brett, who perform small, life long acts of courage, sacrifice, generosity and love are likewise worthy. They are the lesser heroes, who don't know it, and would dispute it if told that they were worthy of admiration and respect, and the humility only adds to the claim.

Part Two

The Generations

*Family is a Circle of Strength and Love...The family,
with every birth and every union, the circle grows;
our family is a circle of strength where every crisis
faced together makes the circle stronger.*

Harriet Morgan

15

A ROCK TO CLING TO IN THE STORM

Mary was a pillar of strength for the family. Their lives had been shaken, first by the loss of John, then the passing of Grandma Ann. The routine had been disrupted, the anxiety increased and the level of sadness, as the reality of life without their beloved father and husband, painfully becoming manifest in his absence during their daily routine, intensified. The responsibility for guidance, direction and affection, in the past, generously provided by John, now fell upon Mary, and she assumed the mantle without hesitation or reservation, in spite of her own profoundly intense grieving. She was their rock and kept them focused and positive, assuring them that "everything would be alright". She had known hardship and depravation in Ireland and was determined that her children would not be faced with that here in the United States. She would do whatever was necessary to keep them safe, secure, fed, sheltered and provided for. During the day, she was serious, determined and had a strong resolve to bring normalcy back into their lives and to figure out ways to preserve their financial security.

She displayed little overt emotion after the initial week or so after John's death, although she wore black for the entire balance of the year of 1916. As a widow, she suffered silently, holding emotion at bay, with her mission of helping the rest of the family cope with the loss taking top priority. She frequently thought of a Nathaniel Hawthorne quote: *"Time flies over us, but leaves its shadow behind"* and she constantly felt the shadow and spirit of John at her side. As each day ended and she retired to the privacy of her bedroom, she set aside that mantle of strength and determination, reached over to feel the emptiness of her bed, experiencing the painful loneliness of sleeping without John for the first time in almost thirty years, and wept quietly, crying herself to sleep each night. The nighttime was for grieving mightily so that the daytime could be spent focused on rebuilding their lives. And, it should be said that she pulled it off masterfully.

In the past, she had assumed the responsibility of disciplining the children when necessary, simply because she found it easier than John did. She was naturally more serious and somewhat uncomfortable with outward displays of affection, even toward her children. She was clearly a loving and nurturing mother, but more reserved, pragmatic and had higher expectations of orderliness and compliance with rules of behavior than John did. He, on the other hand, outwardly took things less seriously, keeping concerns and serious thoughts to himself. Always joking, kidding and teasing, he provided balance and juxtaposition to her stern oversight.

After John's passing, Mary actually became more unyielding and less tolerant of misbehavior, finding it virtually impossible to adopt John's more casual approach to child rearing. If she wanted to temper her somewhat autocratic style of parenting by integrating some of John's style, and soften her approach, she was unable. With that said, she also became intensely protective of her youngest children. A "Lioness" will protect her cubs, regardless the consequences, even death. Mary became the lioness and she monitored their activities and interactions with non family members closely, always prepared to come to their defense at the slightest indication of danger. As the family dynamic continued to change, Rose, as the eldest child, and now mother of her own children, also embraced Mary's style of maternal oversight. She was very much like her mother, not only in personality, but in stature and countenance. They were extremely close and the passing of John brought them even closer. It was almost as though Rose had become a clone of Mary and they jointly ran the household. There was a subtle shift into a distinctly matriarchal family unit (if it hadn't been already). John would have been not only okay with that arrangement, but would have enjoyed and appreciated it, respecting Mary and Rose's abilities in family leadership and motherhood and would have seen it as a compliment to his position as head of the family. William wasn't quite so accepting though. He wanted more control of the day to day application of household management and of parental discipline. Knowing it would be a losing battle, he held his tongue, but some tension was evident. To further exacerbate the rising tension level, "Cook", now well into seventeen years of age and working full time, felt the role of surrogate "head of the house" should have been assigned to him, now that his father was no longer here. William, believing himself to be certainly more qualified to assume that role, thought that Cook was brazenly showing disrespect when he ignored direction and was out of line and trying to usurp HIS authority. What was once a cordial, friendly and almost brotherly relationship had cooled significantly. But in reality, both William and Cook were well aware that it was really Mary and Rose who called the shots and any thoughts of changing that dynamic were simply an exercise in mental masturbation. Never the less, the tension was palpable and the cheerfulness that pervaded the home when John was alive was painfully absent. In spite of the tension, no words were ever spoken in anger, no arguments occurred and deference was always given to Mary and Rose. And, in their collective wisdom, Mary and Rose assigned the titular title of "head of household" to both William and Cook, just to stroke their male egos.

But life goes on, and 1917 was to become an eventful year. Young Ann had met and fallen in love with a man named Christopher Crowley. He was handsome, ambitious and charismatic and, as they had done with Rose, the entire family enthusiastically approved of the relationship. Mary was also convinced that he would be a good provider for Ann and would become a great "family man". A June wedding date was set and all happily welcomed him into the family. He and William became best of friends and usually hung out together when not working. Cook began spending less and less free time at home and developed a large circle of friends with whom he socialized when not at work.

He was also feeling the need for independence and was already starting to think about creating a small nest egg for a place of his own. However, with a sizable portion of his income going toward household expenses, he knew it would be a while before he could emancipate himself from the familial and social constraints of living at home. But with William's income increasing as he advanced at his job, thereby finding it possible to make an even greater contribution to household expenses, Cook hoped that his solo launch into the world beyond Fairfield Avenue might come sooner rather than later.

William and Rose, after the birth of Ruth, their first daughter, soon became pregnant again, toward the end of the year, and from necessity, took over an even larger portion of the house; and along with it, a much larger responsibility for household expenses. It was a de facto "deed transfer" (albeit, not legally executed) from Mary to them and along with it some blessed relief from the constant financial worry she experienced. The net result was a subconscious segue from Mary as owner of the house (and shouldering full responsibility) to Mary as "co-owner of the house" along with Rose and

William (sharing responsibility). While Cook was still contributing from his work as a plumber; no longer an apprentice and moving into a more specialized (and physically demanding) position as a Steam fitter, Henry was working delivering groceries and little Walter was working as a Newsboy, delivering and selling papers, their joint contributions provided some relative comfort and adequate funds to support the family reasonably well now that Rose and William had taken on the majority of household responsibility.

On the national front, after attempting to remain neutral and avoid becoming "entangled", on April 6th of 1917, the United States entered World War One. President Woodrow Wilson expected that a target number of one million volunteers would step up but when only 73,000 came forward, due to the considerable unpopularity of that war, the 'Selective Service Act' (Draft) was created. Cook would soon be 18 and therefore eligible to be drafted. Mary became concerned and petitioned the Selective Service Board, asking for an exemption for him due to his necessary contribution to the welfare and economic survival of the family after John's passing. The exemption was granted. Most pleased was nine year old Walter, who looked up to "Cookie", as he called him, as a father figure after the passing of John.

In spite of the exemption, it was a relief when the war ended and the specter of conscription no longer existed.

By 1920, William and Rose had three children: Ruth, Evelyn and Colin. Ann and Christopher Crowley had moved to Torrington, Connecticut where he took a job as a retailer.

Henry, being highly ambitious and committed to becoming successful, began taking classes at Danbury Normal School and some additional correspondence courses, and began considering a direction for a future vocation.

At age seven, Leona was closer in age to her nieces and nephews than to her siblings. She was treated like a little princess and already showing signs of being headstrong and independent. Shelly had completed training at Danbury Normal School, hoping to become a teacher, but upon completion of studies, took a position as a bookkeeper and secretary at a local business.

She had blossomed into a beautiful young woman; green eyed and red haired, taller than average (and certainly taller than most of her siblings) a statuesque figure and she exuded self confidence. She was also devoutly religious which helped her cope with the loss of her father. She adored him and took the loss harder than all other family members, other then Mary and Grandmother Ann. Now, four years after the fact, she still grieved and prayed for him each night. She was very active at St. Peter's Church and volunteered at St. Peter's School where she had received her grade school education.

She was bright, charming and extroverted, yet she didn't currently date anyone. She had platonic relationships, some developing into slightly more than that, but was celibate and committed to remain so until marriage and when suitors became overly aggressive or acted with impropriety they were quickly rejected. She had even briefly considered becoming a nun. Her Catholic faith was important to her and she was determined to remain chaste and virtuous until "Mr. Right" came along- something that wouldn't be easy as the "Roaring Twenties" were upon the horizon.

16

IF THE TWENTIES CAN ROAR, SHOULDN'T WE?

The 1920's might have "roared" in the big cities and among elites with leisure time and disposable income, but for the masses, the roar was more like a loud purr. Substantial social and cultural changes were indeed taking place, but were more subtle and gradual than portrayed in popular books and movies about the era. Some major events that helped precipitate cultural change were the passing of the 18th and 19th amendments. The passage of the 19th amendment was enthusiastically applauded by women in the Brett family and they all felt that it was too long in coming. They relished the "right to vote" and were elated that their voice would be heard.

The 18th amendment, on the other hand, wasn't well received at all. Irish culture found nothing offensive or wicked associated with the consumption of alcohol, especially beer. Drinking was commonplace at family functions and holiday celebrations, and was generally consumed at most family meals. It was a component of social activities as well and they wondered how they would circumvent this "silly and arbitrary" ruling.

The first influence of the "roaring twenties" made apparent

in the Brett family though, was through attire. If not full heart-edly adopting the "Flapper Style", clothing that hinted of it was embraced by the women in the family. Heavier use of "make up" and shorter dress and skirt lengths were accepted and while Mary, and to some extent even Rose, claimed that it exhibited the "look of a prostitute", they eventually desensitized and acquiesced, ultimately embracing the style themselves.

Women were moving into white collar jobs and house-work became easier with the invention of vacuum cleaners and washing machines. The electric refrigerator made food storage easier and more dependable and increased mealtime options.

The first radio station, KDKA in Pittsburgh, launched in 1920 and by 1923 there were five hundred stations, and by 1929, twelve million households had radios. Movies had quickly morphed from silent, black and white, to talking, color, full length feature presentations.

By the end of the decade, three fourths of the population had visited a movie theater every week.

And then there was the automobile and the freedom it represented. By 1929 there was one car for every five Americans. Along with the proliferation of the automobile, a plethora of associated businesses sprung up. Gas Stations, repair shops, motels, roadside diners and more. Cars were even available for purchase on credit!

It became an age of jazz and blues in music, and to flaunt prohibition, the Speakeasy became a ubiquitous feature on the social landscape.

If most of the family took these dramatic changes in stride, mitigating the social influence by retaining and tightly holding on to their conservative upbringing and roots, Cook and Henry, and to some extent even young Walter, who would be coming of age toward the end of the decade, took more unbri-dled advantage of the social changes and "roared" right along with the times.

With many "first generation" Americans, the cultural influence of growing up in an immigrant family had a profound effect upon their value system and perspective on life in the United States. While their parents adapted to assimilate, they, being native born, saw no need to adapt, but rather to contribute their hybrid perspective to general society as part of a social evolution, defining and facilitating "the melting pot affect". It was a hybrid cultural nuance.

In 1923, John, Jr. (Cookie) was 23 years of age and James Henry (Henry) was 21. They both had their late father's verve, optimism, good looks and lust for life, but only Cook displayed any of his mother's serious side and strict self discipline. They were both strong, vigorous, handsome and ambitious young men; Cook with a strong work ethic, determination and slightly aggressive demeanor, and Henry with a bon vivant, man about town, gregarious nature who enthusiastically embraced the increasing societal shift toward hedonism, materialism and excess that was pervading 1920's society.

Cook was dating one woman exclusively, but showed no urgency toward "tying the knot" and Henry was playing the field, dating multiple women. They both had active social lives and enjoyed frequenting speakeasies and dance halls, although Cook's profession as a Steam fitter left him quite exhausted by the end of a work day, which forced him to curtail many of his social activities. Henry, on the other hand, was working in sales and kept more socially active. Much of the time they socialized together, with a common circle of friends. The Volstead Act, contrary to its intention, actually precipitated higher levels of alcohol consumption, not lower. Feeling that "Prohibition" was an arbitrary, intrusive and a ridiculously misguided effort to legislate morality- and it focused on something that in their mind wasn't at all immoral, Cook and Henry (as well as most other family members) acknowledged the law but ignored it.

They certainly weren't alone in their opinion. Connecticut

was a state with a very high percentage of immigrants and first generation Americans raised in immigrant households, and many cultures accepted alcoholic beverages as normal part of every day life and felt that there was nothing inherently wrong with the moderate consumption of beer, wine or liquor.

As a matter of fact, in 1920, Connecticut and Rhode Island were the only two states whose lawmakers voted AGAINST ratifying the 18th amendment.

In addition to patronizing speakeasies, the Brett's made their own beer at home, and Cook and Henry were now considering building a small still in their old horse barn adjacent to the family home. They fantasized about creating an Irish Whiskey like that which had been so favored by their father. Not some rotgut, adulterated concoction sometimes found in the most sleazy, disreputable gin mills, mind you, but rather a fine whiskey that had been distilled with quality ingredients and ultimate care- something that could command a top price, if it were to ever be made available for consumption by non-family members.

They knew that there'd be risks, and that Mary and Rose had strongly discouraged it, as did their very conservative, pius and outspoken 25 year old sister Shelly, but thought that if planned carefully, properly camouflaged and discretion were strictly exercised, the risk could be minimized and the benefits substantial.

As Henry expounded on the plan and developed a strategy with Cook, it became increasingly clear that he not only wanted to produce some whiskey for their own consumption, but anticipated that select friends, perhaps even a speakeasy or two that they knew well, and maybe even a pharmacy or two (many took advantage of the "medicinal purpose" loophole in the law) might be potential paying customers for their 'bootleg' contraband product. Cook had suspected all along that Henry had ulterior motives but offered no resistance. He too, considered an opportunity to supplement their incomes with revenue coming from a "hobby venture" to be quite attractive. Obviously, they knew full well that the endeavor would be breaking the law, but they rationalized, claiming that "lots of people were doing it" and "why should organized gangs and career criminals be the only ones profiting from this government folly?" Speakeasies masquerading as restaurants and pharmacies (under the guise of providing alcohol for Doctor's "prescriptions") were profiting greatly too, so why not them? Youthful exuberance and a somewhat foolhardy sense of invincibility were firmly in control.

While the rest of the family might have disapproved, they also turned a "blind eye" to the boys flurry of activity during the set up process. They were already producing beer for family consumption, so this endeavor merely expanded an already risky activity; or at least that's how Mary, Rose and Shelly justified ignoring the leap into full blown whiskey production.

The boy's intention of selling "over production" to prospective outlets and potential consumers should have been obvious since day one, based upon the quantities of raw materials and distillation equipment.

They discretely purchased small amounts of kernel corn from many various vendors so as not to create suspicion, and purchased items to be converted to distillation equipment from hardware stores, farm supply stores and various catalogs to further avoid suspicion. Henry took charge of the procurement of the raw materials, such as the corn and champagne yeast, and Cook (his nickname taking on new meaning as a "cooker" of Moonshine), procured the mechanical items, mostly from Meeker's Hardware Store. In addition, Cook was the plumber- steam fitter, mechanically inclined and therefore well qualified to assemble the apparatus.

Meeker's had been in business since 1883 and the Brett's were regular customers and knew the proprietor well; well enough in fact, that even if the recent purchases seemed somewhat unusual and strange, no one would have questioned it.

When they asked Mary to launder some old burlap feed bags, within which they intended to soak their corn kernels to get them to sprout, she immediately knew that their "project" was under way, but she said nothing, as though they had just asked her to launder some soiled shirts. Henry had acquired over 100 pounds of corn, at which point they decided to begin their first batch. Within a few weeks they had produced a good quantity of Moonshine, and rather than purchase charred oak barrels to produce whiskey, they steeped some oak chips in it and within a few days had a palatable concoction worthy of testing.

They diluted and bottled it and having found it to be relatively pleasing and drinkable, offered it to some close friends, without disclosing its source. The positive response was an affirmation that they hoped for and confirmed that were on the right track, so they approached the owners of the few speakeasies that they patronized most, offering small "teaser" quantities of the product at prices too good to refuse. They also approached a local pharmacy, discretely offering an "unoaked" version for the creation of medicinal product. It was undiluted and the pharmacist could add ingredients to suit the (patients?) prescription.

They had heard that Walgreen's pharmacy, from Chicago, had experienced tremendous growth from the sale of such products, but Walgreen's officials denied it, saying that their success and growth was a result of their soda fountains and the popularity of their proprietary malted milkshake. Skeptical and perhaps even slightly cynical, Henry and Cook decided that the malted milkshake story was pure, unadulterated bullshit and concluded that pharmacies were a good target for the sale of their product. People wanted alcohol and would think of very creative ways to obtain (and sell) it.

Many pharmacies circumvented prohibition by purchasing alcohol stamped "Bottled in Bond" and mixing minor ingredients with it, or leaving it unadulterated, and attached a Doctor's prescription to the back of the bottle. Cook and Henry were hoping that they could entice a couple of local drug stores to surreptitiously purchase directly from them, if their quality and pricing offered higher profit potential.

The same concept would be applied to speakeasies- create a product with high quality and at attractive pricing, and carve out a niche that would provide a discrete way to supplement their incomes, while remaining small enough to go virtually unnoticed by the big time players from Hartford's East Side, who were largely responsible for trafficking booze from central Connecticut into Danbury. They had a lot of the businesses engaged in the restaurant subterfuge firmly in their grasp and many of the underground speakeasies and dance halls who had no interest in establishing the guise of a restaurant as well, who simply presented a clandestine venue for covert sale of alcoholic beverages, music and dancing. The Brett boys were well aware that the East Hartford connection could become very aggressive when it came to amateurs horning in on their distribution network, which meant that keeping their activity confined to the size of a "hobby with benefits" would be the most prudent thing to do. And there were others involved from Manhattan and Long Island who should be avoided at all cost as well. Becoming a thorn in the side of any who were heavily involved in the bootlegging business could result in an extended hospital stay or worse. Much of Danbury's liquor also came into town via ports on Long Island Sound, where Rum Runners would receive alcohol from large ocean steamers of European origin who remained outside U.S. territorial limits in safe zones. They would generally make stops in Bermuda or the Bahamas picking up cargo and then sail to the area three miles off shore called 'Rum Row'. There, they would off load into speed boats who would travel to the Long Island shore ports and meet with distribution crews. There was talk of increasing the off shore limit of territorial waters to 12 miles, from the current 3, and if passed, it might have an impact on that source. Those L. I. Sound Rum Runners had obvious ties to organized crime and Cook and Henry had absolutely no interest in pissing them off.

On the positive side, Cook and Henry were also well aware that the state, local and federal prohibition agents were concentrating on cleaning up Hartford's East Side, coming down hard on that area's bootleggers and speakeasies alike. That would essentially keep them somewhat distracted while Cook and Henry established a small but loyal clientele. They clearly had no aspirations of becoming like Al "Snorky" Capone (It was said that Capone's inner circle called him "Snorky", meaning elegant, rather than "Scarface" which he didn't like) and were both content with their day job but used the bootlegging business as more of an adjunct income generator.

In addition, they were both very social, popular within their small Fourth Ward Community and pretty well known. Their father had been very well liked and missed by many after his passing and he was fondly remembered by beat cops and politicians. The Irish Cops tended to be well integrated as part of the community and frequently did "favors" for fellow Irishmen should they be guilty of a minor infraction or petty crime. This close network of Irish brothers was something both Cook and Henry considered to be their ace in the hole.

Sure enough, in 1924 the territorial limits safe zone increased to 12 miles. This, combined with improvements in law enforcement techniques, surveillance and equipment, and a ramping of intensity of efforts by prohibition agents, curtailed the flow and increased demand for locally made product.

This provided the opportunity that Cook and Henry were waiting for and they began going beyond offering their "Shine" to friends, relatives and a few closely held secret speakeasies. But, discretion being the better part of valor, and Mary and Rose's constantly badgering and chastising them, and warning them to exercise strict constraint, caused a distinct hesitation and even trepidation. They were torn between the allure of easy money and a more glamorous lifestyle, and the potential for arrest, incarceration and fines, not to mention the destruction of their facade of propriety and civic righteousness that they currently enjoyed with day job employers and oblivious friends and acquaintances. Shame is a powerful force.

They ultimately exercised discipline and caution and expanded their customer base to include only a few more speakeasy locations and a slightly wider group of private citizen buyers. But even with judicious control of the sale of their homemade liquor, they were still able to augment their income nicely. John was earning about $58.00 per week as a steam fitter and Henry was earning about $45.00. Added to that was their bootlegging profits of $80.00 to $100.00 per week, split equally. They were on the cusp of crossing the line and entering the high risk danger zone. While the family enjoyed the extra income, concern was rising. It was reaching a point where it was no longer an innocent hobby taken to an extreme limit, and about ready to become a full blown criminal enterprise.

Toward the end of August, when Cook went to his regular barber shop, after work, he brought along a few mason jars of liquor, concealed in his lunch pail, to be sold to his personal barber, who was also a regular customer for Cook and Henry's liquor. The barber, an Italian guy named "Beppe" (nickname for Giuseppe) Rossi, quietly sold some bootleg booze from his shop, to a few trusted patrons, and also engaged in some clandestine illegal gambling.

However, he usually he reserved most of the Brett's booze, of which he was very fond, for his own consumption and resold the lower quality shine he purchased from other sources. He also sold some of his own homemade wine and sometimes traded a bottle of wine and a free haircut to Cook in return for the liquor. Bartering in its finest form. As "Beppe" finished cutting the hair of, and shaving, his current customer, the only one in the shop at the time, he seemed to intentionally take extra time sweeping up before motioning for Cook to enter the chair. The previous customer lingered a while, making small talk and cracking a final few one liner jokes before exiting the shop.

When it was finally empty of other customers his first words directly to Cook were; "do you remember your father's old friend Luca Lozza?" John replied; "Of course; but I haven't seen him but maybe once or twice since my father's funeral". Beppe then, in hushed tones (even though the shop was empty) confided in Cook that Luca had been another of his sources of bootleg liquor.

He said; "As a matter of fact, he had built a nice little business for himself and had become a major supplier for a lot of local speakeasies". Cook was somewhat surprised that word of Luca's "enterprise" hadn't gotten out and that he didn't have any idea that he had been competing with his father's old friend for the past few years.

He thought to himself; I guess that's a testament to the ability of his buyers to keep their sources close to the vest. "Beppe" continued; "Well they nabbed him!" "The cops arrested him last night and I hear that they got lots of evidence and witnesses who will testify- Also got 30 one gallon jugs of his whiskey." "He's probably goin' down for a while!". When Cook asked how he was discovered, Beppe just shook his head and shrugged. Cook said; "Well Beppe, ya just can't be too careful." "If you need some extra product to pick up for the shortfall, I can bring you some extra tomorrow". Beppe declined, saying that he was just going to sell less. The bust of one of his sources had apparently put the fear of God in him!

Although he made light of it, the conversation troubled Cook and clearly struck a responsive chord. He thought about Beppe's words all the way home and struggled through a sleepless night. He didn't have time to discuss it with Henry because he retired to bed well before Henry returned home from a night on the town. The following morning he was up and off to work long before Henry awakened. Again, Beppe's words haunted him all day and a lot of very consequential negative thoughts ran through him mind. He had never been as comfortable with their enterprise as Henry had been and this recent news became the tipping point. When he returned home from work that evening, he went directly to the rocker on the front porch and waited for Henry to arrive. In spite of this change in routine arousing curiosity, Mary intuitively remained silent and didn't disturb Cook. Henry's hours, as a salesperson, were erratic, but he usually got home shortly after Cook. He made a point of waiting for him to return that evening, so that he could greet him on the porch and have a private discussion before entering the house.

He sat on the porch, rocking and deeply pondering their dilemma for almost an hour, enjoying the warm, sultry, late summer evening and brilliant sunset while thoughtfully considering how to approach Henry with his proposal that they cut back significantly on the bootleg booze operation, and only make enough for family and close friend consumption- perhaps even discontinue it in entirety. He would share the conversation that he and Beppe had, and for good measure, he would share an anecdote he recently heard about another local amateur bootlegger, named "Red" Doyle, who had been badly beaten, allegedly by members of the East Hartford Connection, after he had gained too much penetration into the local speakeasy clientele. His main thrust would be that they were becoming gradually desensitized to the risks and that, in his opinion, it was time to reevaluate. He also hoped that, being the older and well respected big brother, his influence would have weight.

Finally, in addition to all else, their poor mother and sisters would breathe easier and little Leona and young Walter wouldn't be subjected to observing the ongoing negative influence of Cook and Henry's lawless reaction to prohibition- not to mention the devastating effect that having Cook and Henry getting arrested for bootlegging would have on the family, from an income as well as morale perspective.

The prospect of incarceration for Henry and Cook could be crippling and for them to survive on William's income alone would be very difficult (Shelly was making a small contribution as well; working as a bookkeeper and office manager, but not much).

In his left peripheral vision, Cook caught a glimpse of Henry as he jauntily walked up Fairfield Avenue from the trolley stop on South Street. Henry always had a spring in his step, and if he wasn't whistling or humming a tune, he commonly had a cigarette in his hand. In spite of the warm, humid and sultry late summer weather, Henry, always impeccably dressed, was wearing a recently popularized Seersucker Suit and a straw 'Boater' hat. Seersucker had typically been considered a "poor man's suit" but had recently become popular on college campuses as a form of "reverse snobbery" and was gaining strength as an acceptable summer option in men's fashion nationwide, especially in the south. Henry, always wanting to project an image of trendy and fashionable, took pride in being on the leading edge of the bell curve of men's fashion trends.

Cook nonchalantly waved, and Henry responded by shouting; "What are you doin' sitting outside in this heat, Cookie?" Cook replied; "Waitin' for you, pretty boy!" "Well then, ya better grab me a cool drink if you're expecting me to sit outside with the likes of you!" "Perfect"; Cook replied. "That's exactly what I want to talk to you about". Henry, now at the porch steps, exhibited a quizzical look and said; "You're looking serious". "You're not going to put me in a bad mood are ya?" Cook paused and said; "Sit down. Let's have a talk".

Cook shared what had been on his mind, his grave concerns, the anecdotes he had heard and finally, proposed that they discontinue their "enterprise", or at least the "commercial" portion of it, at once. He told Henry that he was out of it, no matter what Henry decided, but hoped that he would agree that it was time and the prudent thing to do, with all the potential harm an arrest could cause the family to endure.

He said that he believed that their father was watching from heaven and that he most likely wasn't very proud of their actions regarding the disregard of the laws of his beloved adopted country, no matter how seemingly misguided.

Henry said very little but seemed deep in thought. He enjoyed the lifestyle, accoutrements and trappings of a person with disposable income and liked the favors provided by some of their customers and friends "in the know". He also enjoyed the social popularity and prestige that someone with a little extra money can garner and, he was becoming quite the ladies man. He was clearly ambitious, and wanted success, prosperity and financial security, but he also had self confidence and a strong intellect and believed that he could achieve those things while pursuing his legal endeavor as well.

However, he wasn't ready to acquiesce without sleeping on it and taking time to think it through. Cook thought to himself, "I think he could go either way but I pray he sees the logic and good common sense in what I'm proposing and isn't blinded to it by the easy money". Their customers would miss their product but there were plenty of others recklessly engaged in the same business (most not nearly as cautious and discrete as Cook and Henry), who could readily fill the void created by their cessation of business.

Their customer's supply would likely seamlessly continue without hesitation or momentary lapse.

Thursday and Friday came and went. Henry had been taciturn and quite reticent, saying very little and keeping to himself most of the time. Cook usually worked on Saturday, at least in the morning, but Henry did not. Even though Henry was off that Saturday, he had awakened early and gotten out of bed before Cook left the house. Without so much as splashing a little water on his face or running a comb through his hair, he entered the kitchen where Cook, Mary, Rose and William were seated having coffee and finishing breakfast. He was still in his night clothes and looked very disheveled and his eyes were red (apparently from some excessive partying the night before), but cheerfully said; "Good mornin' fine family" and shuffled over to the stove and poured himself a cup. Making a loud dragging sound of wood on wood, he then slid a chair that had been placed in the corner over to the table, making a space for himself. He still wasn't very talkative but after his first sip of coffee he said; "Tell ya what, Cookie- If you meet me at 'Benny's Cave' (a restaurant/ speakeasy that they frequented and were fond of) for lunch, I'll buy!" Cook replied; "You're on; see you there around 12:30".

Cook arrived at the bar around 12:50 to find Henry already seated with a man and two women whom Cook didn't know. When Henry glanced up and noticed Cook entering the establishment, he quickly excused himself from his group, without identifying or introducing Cook, and motioned to him, pointing to a table in the corner, well away from other patrons. Henry carried his half consumed beverage with him to the new table, they sat facing the door, and before a word was spoken, the bartender brought over a beverage for Cook and placed it on the table. Henry smiled, motioning by nodding and tilting his head toward the drink and said; "I took the liberty of ordering you a double". "After all, we're celebrating our retirement from the liquor business!" Cook emitted a sigh of relief, returned the smile and said; " You're smarter than you look!" With a shout of "Cheers" and a clink of the glasses, their enterprise was closed.

17

FATHER FORGIVE ME, FOR I HAVE SINNED

No formal announcement to the family was made but everyone easily noticed that the level of activity had been reduced to a crawl. Cook and Henry still tinkered in the horse barn (which is the euphemism they used to explain hours spent distilling) but it was only for short periods of time now and for the sole purpose of creating spirits for family consumption. The family also couldn't help but notice that there were no unexplained trips into town carrying discretely packaged items that didn't return with the boys as they came home empty handed. The family had typically acknowledged and ignored their time spent at their "hobby" and generally turned a blind eye to their illicit activities. If family members were complacent, they were also conflicted with a sense of foreboding and anxiety. As much as they enjoyed seeing the boys prosper, improve their personal lifestyles and make larger contributions to the general family welfare, they breathed a collective sigh of relief after it become clear that Cook and Henry were now on the straight and narrow. Most relieved of all was Shelly. She was relieved because she loved her brothers and feared for their safety and reputation; but she was also relieved because she took pride in her family's image as God fearing, righteous and well respected among peers, and of their perception with the general public as having a high code of moral standards. She was comfortable that all of those virtues applied to her, and now she optimistically hoped that her wayward brothers would regain an aire of respectability, knowing that many within her social circle were aware of, or at least suspected, their illegal activity (although they would never speak of such things directly with Shelly). At times, they had embarrassed her with their reckless disregard for the law and for the family's reputation; she was constantly fearful that her friends would find out, but now she felt proud that they possessed the strength of character necessary to change course before it became too late. She was pleased, relieved and happy.

By 1928, "the reckless years", as she called the time when Cook and Henry engaged in bootlegging, were becoming a faded memory. Cook was doing very well as a steam fitter and had just taken on young Walter as an apprentice. Walt was a quick study and learning the trade faster and more proficiently than anyone with whom Cook had ever worked.

Henry was doing well selling insurance (for William's agency), William and Rose were thriving, with their family growing at a rapid rate; having babies one to two years apart, and Leona was a happy, headstrong 15 year old. Ann and Christopher Crowley were also raising a family and prospering up in Torrington, CT.

Shelly, on the other hand, felt frustrated and somewhat confused.

As she was rapidly approaching 30 years of age, she had yet to discover anyone with whom she felt worthy of a long term commitment and relationship. Her standards were extremely high. She had idolized and adored her father and held on to his memory with complete reverence. She wanted a husband to be in his image. She was an extremely attractive woman; somewhat tall, red haired, green eyed, alabaster skin with a few random freckles, and a curvaceous and rather voluptuous figure. Men were easily attracted to her, would flirt and ask her out on dates, but her outspoken manner, directness and her somewhat overbearing self confidence would quickly intimidate and turn off many of her admirers and suitors.

And if that weren't enough, she was deeply religious and proper and determined to remain a virgin until marriage. As a consequence, she was about to turn 30, her biological clock was ticking and there was absolutely no one whom she found appealing. Her dating usually involved two or three dates, then abruptly relegating the individual to platonic status and adding to her list of "just friends"- generally because they wanted to "move too quickly" and expected more than she was willing to give. To cope with the frustration and loneliness she immersed herself in work, then volunteering to work as a secretary at the church after her day job. She had a large circle of female friends and quite a few platonic male friends as well and kept socially active and generally happy, but was beginning to feel the urge to move out of the family home and venture out into the world on her own. Unfortunately, as deeply as she had yearned for independence, she wasn't financially able to do that quite yet. She was greatly valued and respected at her job, but didn't earn enough to support herself in that current position. She established a goal of saving enough to go out on her own by January of 1930, but wasn't sure where, or doing what for employment. She was ambitious, but saw little opportunity at her current position. It was a time of frustration and confusion. But she stayed focused and was approaching her goal when, the events of October of 1929 caused reason for pause. The Stock Market had shown considerable turmoil during the week leading up to Black Tuesday, October 29th, when the Market crashed. Rumors and media accounts of people jumping from Wall St. buildings (largely untrue) sensationalized the event further, inciting widespread panic. Economic concerns (and a multitude of other reasons) had caused an unprecedented sell off and the ensuing fear, anxiety and financial uncertainty that overwhelmed the populace also forced Shelly to reevaluate and postpone her emancipation and independence launch.

Danbury was primarily a Blue Collar town, with limited numbers of the population actively involved in purchasing stocks and speculating in the Stock market, and therefore it didn't see much immediate impact from the Great Depression, which was the spawn of the crash. However, there was a distinct cumulative effect that began to manifest significantly by 1932. By that year, unemployment figures approached 24% and Danbury too, was showing signs of severe economic hardship. The local carpenter's union met and voted themselves a $1.00 per day pay cut (to $8.00) and subsequently, at a 1933 meeting, voted another $.85 per day cut, to remain competitive and attract work. Cook's Steam fitters Union did a similar cut, but it wasn't enough to keep him working full time.

As a contract laborer, he would experience longer duration gaps between jobs. William kept his agency afloat but his income was reduced and Rose took a part-time job back at the hat shop, while Mary tended the Grandchildren. With a U.S. unemployment rate of almost 25%, obviously there were many out of work but some participated in day labor or odd jobs to make ends meet, others planted gardens and shared produce with those less fortunate, the federal government sent in 12,000 bags of flour to Danbury, which were distributed to the unemployed by the Red Cross, and those who had the where-with-all to raise chickens, shared the eggs. People generally tried to take care of each other and the less fortunate, which tended to somewhat mitigate the severity of the depression in Danbury. Never the less, times were difficult and trying.

People were commonly seen on street corners selling pencils and bread lines were typically in place at the Spring Street and Elm Street bakeries. Milk was a nickel a quart but, as low as it was, some vendors still had to sell it on credit, allowing well known patrons to run a tab.

Walter, still technically an apprentice steam fitter, had more difficulty than Cook finding work, so he took a job driving a bus. Those were hard times, but the family supported each other and became even closer. Mary would frequently share stories of the severe depravation experienced by people in Ireland during and after the great famine and tell stories of her youth, when the next meal was always in question. The stories helped place the hardships in perspective and as difficult as the times were, they always gave thanks for what they had and for the strength of their family unit. They had each always contributed to the household and the family in their own way and as best as possible, and the depression only served to reinforce that.

But life goes on and individuals need to pursue their own dreams and independence, and by 1936 Cook and his girlfriend, a woman named Bertha (always going by the nickname "Bertie") were seriously considering marriage. Even though the dynamic would change after Cook moved out to set up a home with Bertie, he promised that he would continue to help financially support his mother. Coinciding with that news, was an opportunity that became available to Shelly.

She was actually beginning to think that she just might be living at home indefinitely, but while reading the Sunday edition of the New York Herald Tribune, she discovered a help wanted ad for someone with her qualifications for a position as a Bookkeeper/ Secretary/ Office manager on Long Island, NY, to work at the Fresh Meadows Golf Course and Country Club. It had been where the 1930 PGA Championship and 1932 U.S. Open were held. Gene Sarazen, who was a former Pro at the course won the Open in 1932. Shelly, feeling confident and well qualified, as well as anxious for an opportunity to strike out on her own, applied. After being granted an interview, she arranged for transportation to Flushing, Queens

NY, via the ferry departing from Bridgeport and arriving in Port Jefferson, Long Island. That, in itself, was no easy task, considering that she needed to arrange transportation from Danbury to Bridgeport and from Port Jefferson to Fresh Meadows. She used it as an example of her organizational skills and management ability during her interview. She was at "the top of her game" and, in her mind, interviewed well.

Her credentials and experience were excellent, she presented a confident, self assured persona and all but made the assumption that the job would be hers.

After the interview, a week passed without word. Frustrated, she decided that she would contact the potential employer and demand to know why she hadn't been selected. But, on the 8th day, before she was able to facilitate contact, she received a written offer. She enthusiastically accepted, and with only a 30 day period before her official start date, she rapidly began making preparations. The first priority was to sit down with Mary, give all the details as they existed at that time, and reassure her that she was ready to venture out and live on her own and would remain in close contact with the family. Next, she would inform and reassure the rest of the family, exclaiming that "it would be great fun to have them come and visit her once she became established."

She viewed it as a great adventure, and was bubbling over with excitement. She had visited Manhattan on a few occasions with one or more of her siblings, but aside from that, had never ventured far from Connecticut.

Next on her agenda was locating living quarters. She discovered a reasonably priced efficiency apartment very close to the Golf Course and the landlord assured her that it was a very safe area, comfortable and that it was adequately furnished, so she took it sight unseen. During the interim, she randomly met with her closest friends to bid farewell, while promising to remain in touch. She also extended advanced invitations to them, reciting a litany of entertaining activities and appealing attractions that awaited their visit.

The 30 days flew by and before she knew it, it was time to move to Long Island. There were undeniably mixed emotions, with a slight sadness, melancholy and tinge of anxiety in juxtaposition to the elation, jubilation, optimism and excitement she felt, but her focus and determination were in control and her organizational skills were on full display.

Being six years past her original goal of independence by 1930, she had amassed a much larger nest egg than she had anticipated, and was able to easily "set up housekeeping" in her new abode, purchase some new work attire and decorate her new apartment with some personal touches. Like Connecticut, Long Island had high percentages of Irish and Italian immigrant families, both first, and second or third generation. Naturally confident and gregarious, she quickly made friends at work, at church and about her neighborhood. St. Peter's had been such a large and integral part of her life in Danbury, that finding a church in her new environment took on paramount importance and she found one that delighted her with friendly and spiritually inspired parishioners and a priest who was articulate, motivational and spiritually stimulating. He seemed more approachable; more welcoming, congenial and affable than other priests she had known. He too was somewhere in his mid thirties and she thought that his youthful countenance and demeanor might be responsible for his unique ability to relate to a wider range of parishioners of various ages and religious commitment.

He was also unique in his level of intellectualism and biblical knowledge. Rather than just clarify the gospel reading during his homily, he would create an intricate sermon that applied current circumstance and timely issues to gospel themes and circuitously meandered until bringing it to a surprise close with a revelation that left the congregation amazed, silent and deep in thought for many minutes as they contemplated his words. He was masterful. His appearance was unique as well. He had thick black hair, brilliantly blue eyes, perennially tanned complexion and was over six feet tall. She loved her new church and greatly admired her new pastor.

Shelly was creating the life she had hoped for and was content. She excelled at her job and became highly valued by her employer. She enjoyed meeting people of the social class who commonly joined Country Clubs and Golf Courses and liked the level of sophistication and affluence on display. The greater the exposure, the more she wanted to attain more of it herself.

She had settled into a comfortable lifestyle and enjoyed frequent visits from family and old friends and returned to Danbury often. Her existence in Long Island had taken on a life of its own, separate and distinct from her peripheral life tied to Danbury. She had become more socially active and enjoyed male companionship but still hadn't discovered "Mr. Right". But she was okay with that, deriving great satisfaction from her friendships, her work, her weekend trips into NYC via the train, or trips to Jones Beach and Coney Island with friends and the time she donated to her church as a volunteer secretary. As a matter of fact, she looked forward to the time spent at church volunteering more than any other aspect of her typical work week. She often stayed late and enjoyed long discussions with "Father Guy", which was the nickname and term of endearment assigned to Father Gaetano Monti by parishioners. He gave helpful and insightful advice and always brightened her day.

When the Strathmore Vanderbilt Country Club opened in nearby Manhasset, as the conceptual center of a community built by the famous Long Island developer, William Levitt, it had a 100 foot swimming pool, three clay tennis courts and a beautiful clubhouse. It became the talk of the area and the subdivision surrounding it highly desirable and they were seeking a top notch office manager to run the country club office with credentials similar to Shelly's. As they began their recruitment process, asking about individuals managing competitive clubs, the same name kept coming up: Shelly Brett. "If you want a direct, take charge, highly talented manager, she's your gal"; they said. When they made contact she was somewhat surprised but certainly amenable to having discussions. When she met with the recruiter, an immediate mutual bond of admiration was formed and at the end of an hour and a half long interview, he offered her the position on the spot. It included greater autonomy, higher salary and free living accommodations at the country club. It was an offer she couldn't refuse. It would cause minimal disruption, with Manhassett being very close to her current residence. Her friends would remain the same, her church would remain the same and her favorite hang outs would remain within close proximity. Excited, she called the family that night to announce the news (they now all had telephones).

She provided a two week notice to her current employer and began preparations for another chapter of her "adventure". But before she did anything else, she wanted to tell Father Guy. She looked forward to seeing him that evening when she went to the office adjacent to the rectory to complete a bookkeeping task and was brimming with excitement, filled with anticipation of his reaction. He was not only her priest, but had become a trusted friend and confidant, not just listening to her most personal and sensitive aspects of her life in the confessional, but during candid, personal conversations as well. She deeply wanted his approval and to have him share in her elation. She held great affection for him and wished that other men that she knew could be more like him. When she arrived at the church, only to discover that he was at the hospital ministering to a sick parishioner, her disappointment was profoundly palpable. She had difficulty concentrating on the bookkeeping tasks she had intended to complete and considered waiting as long as it took for him to return.

Then, thinking that it might appear unseemly and

inappropriate, she closed up the office and went home, feeling uncharacteristically sad.

The next day, during her lunch hour, she called the rectory and her elation quickly returned when he answered the phone. She said that she had some great exciting news that she wanted to share with him and asked if he was free for dinner this evening so she could tell him in person. She added; "It's cause for celebration and I'm buying dinner!" Intrigued, he replied; "How could I refuse an offer of a free dinner, Shelly?" "I can't wait to hear your news". Then, after a short pause, and recalling the many previous conversations they had regarding her determination to advance her personal situation and career, and sensing something life altering about to be announced, he continued; "I hope it doesn't mean that you'll be leaving the area though". "Oh, heavens no!"; she replied. "I'm far too content with my adopted home to leave it". "Well THAT'S a relief"; he responded.

With Shelly's assertion that "news of this importance deserved a special dinner venue", they mutually agreed to meet at the Manhassett train station and take the short 17 mile ride to Manhattan for dinner in the city. Shelly selected a restaurant location in midtown that she had recently discovered while on a weekend excursion with friends. She felt comfortable taking a taxi cab from the station to the restaurant, now that New York City's Board of Aldermen and Mayor Fiorello La Guardia had established the Haas Act, introducing a license and medallion system, thereby making taxi transportation more dependable and safer.

She had exercised restraint and refrained from giving him the news about the new position until they were seated at the restaurant. On the trip into NYC, their conversation covered many topics, as it typically did, ranging from politics, the looming specter of war and speculating about possible U.S. involvement, the economy, current "Pop Culture" and fashion trends, music and the inevitable segue into religion and spirituality. They usually agreed on most subjects, but when they didn't, there was frequently spirited debate and stimulating point, counter-point. They mutually found their discussions to be thoroughly engaging, intellectually challenging and enjoyable. They truly liked each other's company and had become very good friends.

Once seated at their table and wine had been ordered (he insisted on selecting and ordering the wine, and paying for it, knowing that she only drank occasionally and wasn't very knowledgeable of wine), she couldn't contain herself any longer and shared the news of her new position and the details about the increased salary, benefits of living accommodations and greater autonomy. She could clearly see that he was sincerely happy for her and relieved that she would be staying in the area. He reached over and squeezed her hand and offered congratulations. The lively conversation continued during dinner and as the amount of wine consumed increased, the nature of the conversation began shifting toward topics of a more personal nature. He inquired about her plans for the long term future, her desire to have her own family, her emotional and physical needs as a maturing woman and how these things fit with her spiritual reality and commitment. She felt comfortable discussing things with him that she wouldn't have discussed with any other man, including her father and brothers- for that matter, even her mother and sisters! Again, she thought to herself, why couldn't I meet a man like him who wasn't a PRIEST!

As dinner concluded and they made their way back to the train station, enjoying the after glow of a wonderful evening and the pleasant weather, conversation ebbed and a comfortable silence ensued. As they boarded the train they noticed that few passengers were on board, presumably due to the late hour and it being a week night. The rhythmic rocking of the train and clacking of the wheels on track provided a soothing ambiance. A short distance into the return trip home, she broached a subject that she would have never dreamed of discussing with him: celibacy. She said that she had an issue of great intimacy about which she would like some advice. She asked; "Father, (she always addressed him as Father or Father Guy, even though they had become close friends) is a woman of my age being foolish by remaining chaste and celibate?"

"I find myself with longing and desire, but repress those feelings, holding out for the right partner in marriage". "By church teaching, if it's wrong for an 18 year old woman to engage in sexual relations prior to marriage, is it equally wrong for a woman of 39?" He said; "I know of no distinction the church makes regarding age, but I find it unique and commendable that you adhere to such high personal moral standards." "Believe me, I have heard many confessions and I assure you that you are extremely unusual in that regard." He continued; "But that is an issue between you and God, and I believe that the answer is more likely to be found in prayer and contemplation than from another person facing the same temptation and conflict, and likely to rationalize the answer to conveniently suit their hunger- even if that person is a priest." She nodded indicating understanding and then asked; "Forgive me if I'm getting too personal and pushy, and I don't mean to shock you with this question, but you are a man committed to celibacy through church tenets and vows of the priesthood; how do YOU handle it?" He paused and sighed, as though deep in thought, and finally said; " If faced with the temptation of sin, and a lesser sin can provide an escape from the greater, commit the lesser."

She gazed at him quizzically, analyzing the response. He could see that she was confused by the response, so he added; "One can obtain temporary physical release without a partner, as a private act intended to provide respite from the tension of physical longing". She had feared shocking him with her question, but now it was she who experienced some degree of surprise and shock, and even embarrassment, by the answer. Fortunately, they were arriving at the station as he gave his response and the conversation ended quickly. They hugged when they parted company, as they always did, and he kissed her on the cheek and said that he would see her when she returned to the parish office in a couple of days to help create that week's newsletter. Their intimate conversation on the train had aroused her and the hug and kiss on the cheek exacerbated that arousal. She wasn't the sort of person who routinely hugged or showed public displays of affection, having been raised in a very conservative and reserved family, but understood that culturally, he was raised differently and had witnessed him showing affection to many other parishioners and on numerous occasions. A simple kiss on the cheek, or both cheeks, was a common Italian greeting and she never thought of it as anything more than that....until now. On her way home, and even after she arrived, she relived the evening in thought. She couldn't get Father Guy out of her mind and experienced an epiphany of sorts when she came to the conclusion that something she had feared was happening; she had fallen in love with him.

As she reclined in bed trying to read before retiring for the night, she was unable to concentrate on her book, so she extinguished the light and pulled up the blanket. Sleepless and conflicted, mind racing with feelings of guilt, shame, and how to emotionally extricate herself from this no win situation, she kept visualizing his face and hearing his words. She felt a longing and desire that was impossible to repress and thinking about his reference to a "private act" to reduce the sexual tension, she imagined him engaging in that private act while thinking of her. She then caressed her most sensitive erogenous areas while fantasizing about him and climaxed quickly. The release provided a restful night's sleep.

The manic activity and numerous preparations associated with the job change and move kept her distracted for the next few days. She had a friend who owned an automobile and together they moved some personal items to her new apartment. The country Club was beautiful and Manhassett was picturesque and pleasant. She was impressed by the architecture and opulence of the Strathmore Vanderbilt and the affluence of the area. But, in the midst of all the associated activity of preparing to move and getting some job training prior to the start date, she thought about Father Guy. Should she confess her true feelings toward him, knowing that it could go nowhere? Should she act as though nothing had changed and continue as friends, keeping her inner most feelings to herself? After much contemplation, she chose the latter; and actually considered reducing the amount of time she spent volunteering at the church. When she dropped by the church office, scheduled on Friday to help with the newsletter, she would make an effort to mask her feelings and engage in business as usual. To express her feelings would serve no purpose. He was a man of God and committed to the life of a priest- unmarried and celibate.

As she completed her tasks at work, she could think of nothing but him, and the anticipation caused nervousness and butterflies. There was no reason for nervousness and excitement other than the fantasy scenario she had created in her mind. He was kind, compassionate, understanding and seemed to intuitively read her emotions but had never once provided any indication that he shared her romantic feelings. She felt like some high school sophomore who had developed an obsessive adolescent crush on the star football player, knowing full well that he would never reciprocate, and she was embarrassed by her ridiculous fantasy. The improbability of their friendship going beyond platonic was obvious and that reality depressed her. She deeply wanted to continue seeing him but knew she had to get her emotions under control. He was a PRIEST, doing God's work, and she felt shame and guilt for even considering that a love relationship, including physical expression, might occur.

As she arrived at the church office she was greeted by the housekeeper, who had just exited the rectory and was headed over to the adjacent office to do a quick cleaning there. They exchanged a few pleasant words and brief area gossip, after which Shelly indicated to the housekeeper that she would tidy up after working on the bulletin and newsletter, so she wouldn't need to. The housekeeper thanked her and expressed appreciation, suggesting that she needed to get home as early as possible to prepare for her child's birthday party the next day. In parting, she turned and shouted; "Oh yes, Father Guy isn't home so be sure to lock up the office when you leave".

She couldn't believe it. He knew she would be coming to finish some bulletin entries and even said that he wanted to sit down with her to provide some direction on an important item for the weekly newsletter. She couldn't help but feel ignored and unimportant. She was saddened to tears. She knew she had to "get a grip". This was a categorically irrational emotional reaction!

She fumbled in her purse for her key, entered, and quickly accomplished the tasks that could be completed without his direct input, then lightly cleaned and organized the office, and left feeling profoundly disappointed. She knew that Saturday was his busiest day, with preparations for mass and completion of his Sunday homily and even if she returned to the office, under the guise of completing a few items, it would be unlikely that she would see him. It provided little solace knowing that she would she him at Sunday services and mass. He would be completely distracted by other parishioners, many of whom tried to monopolize him time.

She spent that Saturday alone, doing odd jobs around her apartment and running a few errands, her mind lost in thought.

When she arrived at church that Sunday, she sat in her usual pew, close to the front and at the center aisle; specifically chosen so that she could be close enough to create good eye contact with him and hear his words clearly. As always, she hung on every word and on this day he delivered an exceptionally poignant and thought provoking sermon, masterful in construction and eloquence. She loved his words and hearing him speak. His sermons would frequently evoke emotion and thought provoking introspection from parishioners, especially her. She always felt her heart swell with affection for him after his delivery. It was analogous to the emotion some might experience after hearing an extremely talented vocalist or musician perform in person during a concert.

As expected, upon exiting the church, she saw him positioned at the top of the large stone steps just past the massive wooden entry doors, shaking hands and greeting the laity with his typical wit and charm. She made an uneasy approach, navigating through a small circle of people engaged in conversation with him, overhearing a few of them praising his sermon, stating that it was even better than usual. As he thanked them for "their generous kind words", he noticed her, smiled, then briefly paused the conversation long enough to say; "Good morning, Shelly". "Can you call me on Monday?" "I have a few things I need help with in preparing for the Bishop's visit next week". "Of course!"; she replied. He then returned to continue conversing with the few parishioners circled around him.

During her lunch hour on Monday she called the rectory and his housekeeper answered. She said that Father Guy had been called away unexpectedly, but had anticipated her call during lunchtime so he left a message. The message simply was: Please stop by the office on Wednesday evening, after work, to assist in organizing and reconciling some accounting records and other bookkeeping issues that needed to be updated prior to the bishop's visit. He would be present to clarify some of the information. Shelly agreed and the housekeeper promised to relay her response as soon as Father Guy returned.

Shelly was disappointed that she wouldn't be able to

see him before Wednesday, but pleased that he needed her help. Tuesday and Wednesday dragged and when she finally punched the time clock at the end of the day on Wednesday, she was euphoric with excited anticipation of spending some time with him, even if it was only to assist with some office work. She had asked her friend, who had helped her move, if she could borrow her car so that she wouldn't be relying on erratic and frequently undependable taxi service.

Shelly wasn't a very good driver, even though she had learned to operate an automobile over eight years earlier when Henry offered to provide lessons in his car. She mastered it fairly quickly and easily but never owned a car of her own, and therefore never polished her skills. Never the less, her friend agreed, but cautioned her to drive slowly and carefully. Shelly replied that she ALWAYS drove slowly and carefully and not to worry. As friends, they were close enough to be able to recognize subtle changes in mood and her friend asked if she was okay. When Shelly said; "Why do you ask?", her friend said; "Because you're as giddy as a school girl". Shelly just shrugged and said that it was just a crazy day at work.

She stopped at a local diner for a quick bite to eat and wondered if Father Guy had eaten dinner yet and if she should call him to ask if she could bring him some take out, but decided not to.

She arrived at the parish office just before sunset. A recent rain had left a glistening reflection off the leaves and red berries of two large holly bushes planted at each side of the office entrance door. The evaporation of the moisture on the blacktop parking area created that familiar ionization smell frequently lingering in the air after a recent warm weather shower and the mist in the atmosphere produced a brilliant rainbow. Father Guy must have been expecting her, or just coincidentally noticed her arrival, because he exited his residence immediately and briskly walked to the office entrance to greet her with the usual hug and kiss on her cheek.

She had longed for that touch and it caused a warm flush to engulf her body. He mentioned that Father Daniel, a new Associate Priest who had recently been assigned to the parish due to its rapid growth, was taking care of some necessary preparations in advance of the Bishop's visit inside the (now shared) residence and he would assist her with the necessary office items that were important to have in order prior to the visit. They entered and illuminated the bank of lights over the desk, credenza and file cabinets but not the lights over the rear section of the office where a large conference table, circled by ten straight backed chairs, was positioned adjacent to a small relaxation area containing a large upholstered 'Art Deco' styled sofa, two matching arm chairs and a coffee table.

Shelly advanced directly toward the desk, opened the drawer and removed the accounting ledger, opening it and preparing to get to work. He slid one of the chairs from the conference table over to a place beside her and they immediately addressed all outstanding items. The conversation was matter of fact, task related and all business and within ninety minutes, they had completed the reconciliation and organization to his satisfaction. They breathed a collective sigh of relief; Father Guy saying that he felt comfortable that it would meet muster during the Bishop's inspection.

He thanked her profusely, stating that she provided an invaluable service to the parish and that he didn't know what they would do without her. She modestly responded; "It's nothing. I do it as much for you as I do for the church". He confided that he had been somewhat tense and anxious lately, primarily due to the rapid growth of the parish, the associated changes, the addition of the new associate priest and the Bishop's visit. He apologized if he had seemed remote, distracted and inattentive.

She nodded indicating understanding. He then suggested that they adjourn to the more comfortable seating area to relax, chat a while and enjoy a glass of wine before she had to leave. She said; "That would be wonderful- I've missed our talks". As he walked to the small pantry area to retrieve a couple of wine glasses and bottle of wine, and she walked over to the seating area, she became a combination of nervous, excited and fearful that she might say or do something that she would regret and would embarrass herself. She stood there without taking a seat, and when he returned with the wine she said; "I really should go". Surprised, he asked why and if she was okay. She simply responded by saying; "I should just go". Puzzled, he cocked his head slightly, as if in contemplation, paused, and said; "Okay. I'll walk you to the car- And thank you again for all you do and for being you!"

As they typically did when parting company, he embraced her and attempted to kiss her cheek. This time however, she turned her head to meet his lips with her's. The affectionate kiss on the cheek became much more. They held the kiss for a long time, passion growing in intensity during the duration. She finally pushed back slightly, cast her gaze at the floor and said in a whisper; "I'm sorry". He placed the upper edge of his forefinger under her chin and lifted her head so that she couldn't avoid looking directly into his face. He began to say something, but paused, remaining silent, then he initiated the next kiss. It was deep and passionate and a clear indication to both of them that a line had been crossed.

They side-stepped awkwardly toward the sofa while still locked in embrace and kiss. They sat on the couch becoming breathlessly engaged in an elevated, magnificent and sublime level of physical intimacy that had been denied to each of them for a very long time. He opened her blouse and caressed her gently while she swooned from the delightful physical contact. Due to her inexperience and naivete, she wasn't a very active participant, but welcomed his advances enthusiastically. The foreplay continued until the point of not return was reached and when he finally penetrated her gently, she experienced brief pain, but her heightened state of arousal provided ample lubrication and the intense pleasurable sensation mitigated the brief discomfort.

To her, he seemed more experienced and skillful than expected, in spite of his priestly vow of celibacy. But then again, she had nothing or no one with which to compare the experience. He climaxed rather quickly and remained inside of her, locked in embrace, while his state of excitement subsided. He gently caressed her, kissed her softly, but said nothing. She too, enjoyed the moment and remained silent, serenely content with the after glow and warmth of the first complete intimacy of her life. But she was also in fear. She feared that she had reached the precipice and was about to fall head over heals in love, and that it would become unrequited love because he was a priest first and a lover second, and due to that circumstance, nothing good could come from it.

When he rose from the sofa, he went to the restroom and returned with a towel that had been dampened on one end. She was completely unfamiliar with that level of intimacy and sensing her embarrassment, he turned away and walked back to sit at the desk which was out of view. When she was dressed and presentable she walked over to his chair and he stood to embrace her again and kissed her gently saying little more than; "call me tomorrow". "We can talk then after we have gotten our thoughts together". She smiled and left into the warm, sultry evening with her mind racing.

They did indeed speak the next day and many days thereafter. What had started as reckless and highly risky behavior during that first physical expression of deep affection; a moment of weakness, and yielding to a wave of unbridled passion and desire, fraught with danger and negative consequence, evolved into a years long relationship that both parties knew would have to be enjoyed with complete discretion, and acceptance of the fact that it would never go beyond the privacy of their secret meeting places. There were romantic dinners and weekend rendezvous far removed from their local area and prying eyes, long evening talks, intimate luncheon dates and frequent trysts at the church office. There were even a few times, when the associate priest was away and Guy had the entire rectory to himself, when she would spend the entire night. They truly loved each other, but accepted the circumstance and the reality of conducting a clandestine relationship. By exercising caution, discretion and talented "acting" while together during public gatherings or when together in public places, appearing to be merely good friends, the relationship lasted for years without anyone being suspicious (perhaps a few closest friends were, in fact, suspicious, but never had any conclusive evidence and it therefore never got any serious traction on the rumor mill) and the well constructed subterfuge was never exposed.

Their lives were mutually busy and career focused but they became a rock for each other, private times providing psychological rest and refreshment, a cathartic release and physical joy. They acknowledged the sinfulness of their behavior, and then ignored it, rationalizing that being in love can not be a sin even though it includes physical expression which contradicts the "unrealistic" vow of celibacy. They still engaged in frequent discussions of spirituality, church doctrine, defining God, morality and agreed that, in God's mercy, when considered in context, they could be forgiven for this relatively minor transgression when viewed within the scope and balance of good works done in the rest of their daily existence.

When the relationship "cooled", it cooled of natural causes. He was becoming well known as a dynamic, charismatic, highly admired and well respected priest and was designated to be transferred to a very prestigious and much larger parish in a rapidly growing, affluent section of the expanding area of Long Island. She was traveling more and taking frequent trips back to Danbury to visit family. Without actually ending, the time together became less and less frequent sometimes going a month between direct contact, but they always remained in each other's mind and the relationship continued in an intermittent fashion for decades.

18

SEEKING OPPORTUNITY

If the Great Depression had been actually a good time for Shelly; with abundant professional success, relative financial prosperity, a satisfying love relationship (though secret) and a feeling of being in control of her life, it wasn't quite the same for some of her siblings. Shelly not only survived the depression, she thrived. Her determination, faith, perennial optimism, self confidence, serendipitous love affair and "carpe diem" attitude had served her well.

While it hadn't become a time of poverty and despair for the rest of the Brett family, as it had for many less fortunate members of American society, it had become a time of challenging financial difficulty. With construction being intermittent at best, Cook was working fewer hours and the resulting loss of income prevented him from contributing very much toward the welfare of his mother. He and his girlfriend, Bertha (who was called "Bert" or "Bertie" by most friends and family) had married and purchased an old colonial styled farm house on rural Joe's Hill Road, in the Mill Plain district of town. It was an old house, built sometime around 1895, and seemed to frequently be in need of repair and maintenance. They were getting by and making ends meet, but had little left over at the end of the month to go toward supporting Mary, as he had done while he still lived at home.

With most of the steam fitting jobs going to men who had tenure and vast experience, younger laborers like Walt, found it difficult to obtain work, even though he was highly skilled and talented in his craft, and had been well trained by Cook and other Master Steam fitters whom had also collectively taken him under their wing. That meant he had become more of a drain on the family unit than a provider.

Tragedy also struck the McAllister side of the family when William had taken ill with a severe case of the flu, the symptoms of which mirrored the Spanish Flu of the widespread epidemic a couple of decades earlier. It had lingered longer than typically expected, weakening him to the point that he became susceptible to pneumonia. After three weeks of battling the flu, then the resulting pneumonia, he passed away, leaving Rose a widow, and seven children, four of whom still remained at home, without a father. William and Rose's daughter, 22 year old Ruth, had a job working as a dress shop clerk, so she was able to contribute, and Henry still resided at the family home and was doing well as a broker and insurance salesman, so he was now making the most significant contribution toward the family's support.

In addition, Leona had graduated near the top of her high school class and attended Danbury State Normal School (renamed Danbury State Teacher's College in 1937), receiving certification in teaching. She was working as a fifth grade teacher and still living at home.

Ann and Christopher Crowley had opened a retail furniture store in Torrington and now had two children, named Ann B. and James, and were financially extended too far to be of much assistance to the rest of the family on Fairfield Avenue.

Walter, feeling like he needed to seek out other opportunities (he had even taken up driving a bus part time), and experiencing a swell of patriotic pride, decided that joining the

Navy would provide a chance to see the world, use his skills, gain some excitement, serve his country and reduce the burden on his family.

With age thirty on the horizon, he was somewhat older than most recruits, but he was in extremely good physical condition, generally as a result of the very heavy labor performed by steam fitters. He was small of stature, about five feet, seven inches tall, and one hundred and forty pounds, but he was feisty, had good stamina and endurance and a "can do" attitude. He could be a bit of a wise ass and occasionally exhibited a sarcastic sense of humor but was also capable of respect and deference. He was accepted without hesitation.

After goodbyes to family and friends, many of whom tearfully expressing anxiety regarding the potential of war and enlistment placing him in harm's way, and a raucous going away party with Cook, Henry and a few other close friends, he was sent to Newport, Rhode Island for basic training.

He was expecting a "great adventure" but reality soon hit him head on when he found himself naked and cold in a large room filled with 100 other recruits. After receiving numerous shots, a buzz haircut and being told to remove shirt, pegged pants, underwear and any other possessions and box them up and ship them home, he began to wonder of he had screwed up and the great adventure would in actuality be little more than a degrading pain in the ass.

Navy Supply Clerks tossed uniforms, various and sundry other articles of clothing and gear that he would use during his enlistment time, at him with a smirk and a smug attitude. Little scrutiny regarding physical size was exercised by the Supply Clerks and many "Boots" (as the new enlisted men were called) ended up with inappropriately sized uniforms. Based on his smaller than average size, the odds of receiving items that were too large were pretty good, but he got lucky and while his uniform was larger than he would have selected for himself, it wasn't so large that he appeared lost in it.

He was then provided with a hammock with a mattress, two mattress covers (which the Supply Clerks called "fart sacks"), a pillow, two pillow covers, two blankets and a Sea Bag that was approximately 2 feet by 3 feet in size. The bag had metal grommets and a draw string rope with which to cinch it and hang from a rack. They were then told to stencil their name on the bag and other items. When traveling, his mattress, with sleeping gear rolled inside, would be rolled again in his hammock and secured to his Sea Bag. They also learned a designated method for folding and rolling clothing and personal items so that they would fit into the small space within the bag and avoid wrinkling.

They could then sling the bag over their shoulder and march off with all they owned. Finally, they were provided with their "bible": 'The Blue jacket's Manual' which outlined all they needed to know to become a sailor. It was then off to get "introduced" to the Chief Petty Officer assigned over the "Boots".

For a guy of much higher than average age for recruits, he handled basic training pretty well. The strenuous nature of his civilian job put him in better physical shape than many of the younger men and the only difficulty he had during basic training was passing the third class swim test. Ironically, he had joined the Navy without knowing how to swim- not at all! He feared the water and when family members offered to teach him as a young child, he wanted no part of it. He STILL wanted no part of it and dreaded having to qualify. As the time approached, he decided that, rather than awkwardly try remain afloat and humiliate himself in the process- or even worse, drown, he would need to think creatively and avoid the test completely. If he ended up overboard, for whatever reason, sometime in the future, he would worry about it then.

Boot Camp would only last for about six weeks and he just wanted to get through it and then, perhaps during some time while on leave he could practice swimming a little and learn while under much less pressure. Or maybe not. Either way, he was getting in a bit of a panic about it and simply had to come up with a solution. He had quickly formed a close friendship with another barracks mate (Company 19, 10th Regiment) and felt that he could be trusted. He confided his fear of the water and of swimming to him and offered to pay him to participate in a ruse, taking the test on his behalf, masquerading as Navy Recruit Brett. When the time came, Walt laid low and hoped for the best. The class was large enough and the instructor wasn't observant enough to notice, so, to Walt's great relief, they actually pulled it off. The six week duration of basic training seem to pass by rapidly and although 95% of the recruits were fit, well trained and ready to graduate, they were held an additional two weeks, simply because there really wasn't a pressing need for them at the time. Those extra two weeks seemed interminable and like they would never pass. There was a redundancy and lack of spirit and enthusiasm and a sense of "featherbedding". Finally, they were given leave before receiving their assignment and Walt was anxious to return home for a while and see his family.

Mary was filled with joy, seeing her son after what had been his longest absence from home, and she planned a large family gathering to celebrate. Everyone was elated to have him back home and many expressed concern over news stories regarding Hitler's radicalism and the growing threat of Fascism and, God forbid, the potential of war. Shelly traveled up to Danbury from Long Island and Father Guy actually accompanied her. It was common knowledge that they were very close friends and as unbelievable as it sounds, no one suspected that there was anything more to the relationship than that. To the family, it was inconceivable that the pious and devout Shelly, and a Catholic Priest could be engaging in anything more than a close friendship and mutual devotion to the church.

As a matter of fact, in spite of the torrid affair, Shelly had absolutely no hesitation or reservation in evangelizing,

proselytizing and becoming critical of certain behaviors exhibited, in spoken word and actions, by her male siblings. A
bit sanctimonious and hypocritical, to be sure.

Mary spared no expense (by her standards) in creating the
celebration. She spent days preparing a special meal, including
many of Walt's favorite items, and there was joy and laughter,
stimulating conversation and many words of affection, and
bonding together; the family hadn't seemed this strong and
jubilant since John was alive. Cook and Henry took Walt aside
during a lull in the celebratory revelry and suggested that the
three of them get together for a celebration of their own the
following Saturday evening. Walt enthusiastically agreed.

"Celebration of their own" was code and a common Brett
euphemism for carousing, drinking and socializing with available women. These days, however, for Cook it simply meant
an excuse to get out of the house and further bonding with his
brothers during a "boys night out". Since marrying Bertie, he
had become much more reserved and joined in primarily to
keep the others from getting themselves into trouble.

The following Saturday, Cook met Henry and Walt at
Pane's Restaurant (formerly known as Bennie Pane's Stone
Bar and Grill) where they planned to order a pizza, have a few
beers and reminisce about growing up in the family home on
Fairfield Avenue. Cook arrived first and sat at the bar waiting for his brothers to arrive. As he was making small talk
with the bartender, he noticed four women enter and recognized one as a friend and former classmate of Leona. He
smiled and greeted her with a wave and as her companions
were being seated at a table near the bar, she walked over to
the bar and engaged in a brief conversation with Cook. It was
pretty much the typical exchange of pleasantries and mean-
ingless banter; "long time, no see", "how have you been",
"you're looking well", "what's new with you", etc. and as her
friends were seated, she invited him to join them. He replied;
"I'd love to but I'm waiting for Walt and Henry to arrive". She

responded; "great, they can join us too!" He accepted the invitation and slid another table against theirs, and then a few additional chairs. She introduced Cook to her friends, told a little about how they knew each other, making reference to Leona. Within a few minutes, Henry and Walt arrived together and were somewhat surprised to discover Cook seated at a table with four women. Both being naturally self assured and in high spirits, they tended to swagger confidently as they approached the table before being invited, made a teasing remark about Cook having the male magnetism of actor Tyrone Power, and applauded his ability to "attract four stunningly beautiful women", and then without hesitation, introduced themselves and sat in the vacant chairs. Walt was instantly attracted to one of the women, named Betty Manacek. Her features were slightly more chiseled than soft and her resemblance was somewhere between Greta Garbo and Bette Davis. He thought to himself that she looked "Eastern European" but really wasn't sure what that meant.

He found her to be quite lovely and as their conversation progressed, he found her intelligent as well. She was conversant on many levels and friendly, while very reserved and difficult to "read".

He discovered that she had recently graduated from nursing school as an RN, and had been born in Czechoslovakia in 1912 when the area was still part of the Austro-Hungarian Empire that collapsed at the end of WWI. She and her mother had immigrated to Danbury when she was approximately six years of age and they lived with an Aunt (her mother's sister) near Lake Avenue. She was reticent and quiet without being shy and clearly didn't show emotion easily. Even her laughter was controlled. He attributed it to the fact that she had experienced life in war torn Europe during her earliest childhood years and as a nurse, had probably seen more than her share of sadness, and for those suspected reasons, kept her emotions in check. Never the less, he was infatuated, but he really couldn't tell how she felt about him.

The group ended up spending hours together that evening, ordering pizza and round after round of beer. Cook was the first to excuse himself and leave, stating that Bertie would divorce him if he stayed any longer. Then, two of the women claimed that they needed to head home as well, leaving Walt and Betty, and Henry and a woman named Doris, who also collectively arose from their table and adjourned to the bar. As closing time approached, and they were planing to leave, Walt asked Betty if he could see her again before he left for deployment and she agreed. He really wasn't sure how she'd respond but was pleased that she agreed.

They actually ended up having two dates before he was shipped out and he was beginning to believe that she might actually be fond of him after all (although there had been no intimacy). She asked him to correspond during his deployment and she would do the same. She took some time off from work to see him off as his leave ended and he was heading back to base and it was then that she passionately kissed him for the first time. He had gotten a kiss on the cheek after their dates, but this was a long, soulful kiss on the lips and clearly an indication that the relationship might develop into something more than just a casual, fleeting romance. What timing, he thought to himself. Just as he was leaving for his assignment, he felt the rush of a budding romance! For the first time, he felt some slight regret over his somewhat impetuous decision to enlist and the requirement to be away from home for extended periods, now that he had reason to want to remain home. Nothing I can do about it now, he thought, as he bid farewell to the family members gathered to see him off and gave a final kiss to Betty. I'll just make the best of it and hope that the next three and a half years pass quickly.

19

A THREAT AND
REALIZATION OF WAR

Reality is a bitch, Walt mumbled, as the stifling heat and deafening noise of the engine room numbed his senses. He had been assigned to the U.S.S. Dale, which had been designated as one of the Destroyers to patrol the east coast and Caribbean at the time. As a Machinist Mate, he had various possible assignments and duties but had been assigned to the Engine Room for this cruise. The U.S.S. Dale was a Farragut Class Destroyer and as much as he disliked being assigned to the Engine Room, the itinerary itself turned out to interesting and enjoyable. Before this, he hadn't traveled far from Danbury, but now, as the recruitment ads said; "he would see the world!" They sailed from Norfolk to the Dry Tortugas, Florida, Galveston, Texas and even escorted President Roosevelt on his trip to the Bahamas. Walt was an affable, good natured sort of a guy (unless someone really pissed him off) and he made friendships quickly. He adjusted well to life as a sailor and, as time went on, even began considering making a career out of it. However, he was corresponding with Betty at least twice per week, usually more, and they were becoming closer through written words than either of them would have expected. Their letters shared intimate details of their past lives, fears and ambitions, and common values. When he was home on leave, they spent virtually every waking minute together (at least when she wasn't working at the hospital) and were quickly becoming engaged in a passionate romance. As the romance developed, and when Walt feared that his long absences would strain the relationship, and perhaps even jeopardize it, he proposed marriage (in his mind, to ensure continuity of the relationship). Betty accepted without hesitation. On June 27th, 1939, they were married quietly at St. Peter's Rectory. The wedding was reserved and low key for a couple of reasons. First, Walt wanted it expeditiously scheduled before he left on his next deployment. In addition, Betty's family certainly didn't have the money for a large, lavish wedding. Tragically, Betty's mother had passed away shortly after arriving in the United States and Betty's older sister, Sue, had raised her (she still lived at the home of Sue and husband Rudy). But the most likely reason was that Irish Catholic families (as well as other ethnic Catholic groups, like Italians), frowned upon "mixed marriage" (referring to religion). It was important for them to ensure that any children resulting from the union would be raised Catholic.

Betty was Lutheran, and determined to remain so, but had no problem agreeing to a Catholic upbringing for any kids that they might have. Henry and Cook couldn't care less if she was Catholic or not, but Mary certainly did, as did Shelly. At first news of Walt's intentions, Mary vociferously expressed her displeasure, as did Shelly, but once they got to know Betty and learned that she was an RN, they acquiesced and came to accept her.

Shelly, in particular, didn't want to make too big a deal of it, considering that her long running affair with Father Guy was many times more egregious than mixing religious disciplines. As a matter of fact, she was becoming quite cognizant of the fact that some family members were recognizing a bit too much familiarity in behavior between Father Guy and Shelly and some even commented that "strange" and sometimes "smirking" looks were exchanged between them creating awkward moments and some further suspicion and speculation.

To criticize as vociferously as Mary, would be imprudent and just might elicit a "The Lady doth protest too much, methinks" (as quoted from Hamlet) from some of those harboring suspicions. Therefore Shelly assumed a 'discretion as the better part of valor' position and finally voiced her approval; but didn't attend the wedding.

Betty's close friend, Miss Winnifred Ginty was Maid of Honor and Henry was Walt's Best Man. Surprisingly, there were more of Betty's family present than Walt's.

They borrowed Henry's shiny, new 1939 Chevrolet Master Deluxe to Take a short Honeymoon trip to the Finger Lakes region of New York State and moved into their first apartment at #14 Fifth Avenue in Danbury, only a block or two from the High School at 181 White Street.

During their trip, they talked in great detail about their future and the likelihood of the United States becoming embroiled in a war. Betty cautiously suggested that it might be wise and prudent for a man, newly married, to consider rethinking his plans to remain in the Navy during such dangerous times, and proposed that he return to civilian life at the end of his "hitch". At first, Walt resisted, but after further discussion, reluctantly agreed to give it serious consideration. His next, and final deployment, took him to San Diego and a west coast patrol cruise to Alaska, but his mind was on his new wife and starting a family and home sickness hit him hard. In October of 1940 he was honorably discharged and returned to Danbury, hoping to return to his old profession as a Steam fitter.

Re-adjusting to civilian life and marriage took some time and he wasn't sure he had made the right decision. He worked as a bus driver for the Danbury Power and Transportation

Company, then for Henry, as an Insurance Salesman, then finally with a large construction firm in Waterbury. He was just going through life waiting for an epiphany.

Walt had a Navy buddy who was on the U.S.S. Greer during an incident that had occurred on September 4th, 1941. The Greer was a Wickes Class Destroyer that had been recommissioned on October 4th of 1939 as Flagship of Destroyer Division 61, had been patrolling the east coast and Caribbean and had joined the "Neutrality Patrol" in February of 1940.

A letter Walt had received from his friend did more to agitate him than President Roosevelt's 'Fireside Chat' broadcast to the American public, describing the incident and his "Shoot On Sight" order, which stated that a Nazi submarines' very presence in any waters that the United States deems vital for its defense constitutes an attack. By the account of Walt's friend, and all other accounts for that matter, the German Submarine, U-652, had deliberately fired a torpedo at the Greer (which was clearly flying the American Flag), followed by a second attack shortly thereafter. The Greer then pursued the Submarine ultimately dropping numerous depth charges.

America accused Germany of initiating the attack and Germany accused of the U.S. of initiating it. Either way, Walt saw it as further evidence that tensions were rapidly increasing and that we would soon be joining the war, and he quietly regretted not being able to militarily participate in the eradication of this growing threat from axis powers. Three months later, on December 7th, 1941, when the Japanese attacked Pearl harbor, Walt was, like most other Americans, outraged and fully supported a declaration of war, which occurred the following day during Roosevelt's 'Day Will live In Infamy' speech.

The war became Walt's primary topic of conversation, at work, socially and at home. He felt a strong patriotic duty and that he must do something to support the war effort. At almost 35 years of age, and as a married man, he didn't quite know how or what he could personally do, but the answer came quite serendipitously with the creation of the Navy Seabees in March of 1942. Their motto: Construimus Batuimus; "We build. We Fight; Can DO"- "The difficult we do now, the impossible takes a little longer", suited Walt perfectly. Having been through Naval Training and with extensive training in steam fitting and construction, this new branch was made to order. With the official declaration of war, civilian contractors were no longer viable- International law made it illegal for civilians to resist an attack, and as non military they would be classified as guerillas, which would subject them to immediate execution upon capture. Seabees would be skilled tradesman and workers who could, at a minute's notice, drop tools and pick up arms to defend themselves and their project. In April, Walt re-enlisted in the Seabees at the rank of Machinist Mate First Class. Because finances would be difficult, it was decided that Betty would move back in with her sister, Susan Engles, and Sue's husband, Rudy, for the duration of Walt's enlistment. In addition, they would try to diligently save money from both Betty's income, as a practicing nurse, and Walt's military pay, so that they might purchase a home at the end of his enlistment.

In May, Walt went to spend three weeks undergoing basic training at Camp Allen, Virginia, then to Davisville, Rhode Island and on to Quonset Point prior to being deployed to Newfoundland. He was officially back in the Navy and the Seabee's suited him perfectly. His deployment to Argentia Naval Air Station, Dominion of Newfoundland, to assist in construction of the base was something he found exciting and stimulating and a welcome change from his life in Connecticut.

As a married man, he had found the perfect balance of satisfying his need to fulfill his "patriotic obligation" (his words and perspective), while performing a valuable service through his construction skills, and at the same time, remaining out of harm's way (at least, relatively so). If a potential attack were to become imminent, there would be plenty of advance warning and strong defenses. He thoroughly enjoyed the camaraderie of like minded men of his age in the 17th and 28th Battalions, and the fellowship of the other Naval and Marine personnel stationed there. He was a "man's man" and the rather machismo environment suited him well. In spite of the fact that war was waging, or perhaps because he was, in some way, involved in it, he was the happiest he had been in his entire life. He was even once again beginning to entertain thoughts of making a career out of it. But more time and experience would be necessary before any very serious consideration could be given and it was still a little premature, to be sure.

At this stage of the conflict, there was no guaranteed victory and no assurance that his future deployments would be as close to home or as removed from the battle front. But if the truth be known, after all the flowery words regarding "patriotic obligation", performing valuable service, and camaraderie were spoken, and rationalizations complete, the mundane predictability of married life back home, and the monotony of the work a day world were quite simply something for which he was not yet ready. This welcome hiatus before the potential arrival of children and creating a family would become the impetus for a closer look at reality.

20

A WOMAN MARCHING TO THE BEAT OF A DIFFERENT DRUM

Leona was headstrong, liked being in control, was outspoken and would let no one, or no thing, stand in the way of her ambition. Having lost her father when she was just past the toddler stage, she was raised in what became a matriarchal family, headed by Mary and Rose. If there had been the pretense that it wasn't, it was a very superficial pretense, and everyone certainly knew exactly who was in control. At times the men were humored, but clearly the women called the shots on most important issues. As a result, Leona learned by example. She was exceptionally bright, probably the most intellectual member of the family, and a feminist before the term existed in common parlance. She graduated from St. Peter's School in 1926, where many of the Nuns took a special liking to her, and because she was such a voracious learner, and craved a broad scope of knowledge, they provided extra curricular coaching, guidance and teaching (the proverbial "teacher's pet") and she graduated at the top of her class.

At Danbury High School, she achieved comparable excellence and was universally popular, albeit, she seldom dated and when she did, the relationships were brief and decidedly casual. Her personality was somewhat like that of her sister, Shelly, only on steroids. She was high energy and direct and didn't mince words. While her personality might have been like Shelly's, her physical characteristics were not. She was somewhat short, slim and fit, had very curly strawberry blonde hair and fair skin, prone to freckles when she spent time outdoors and in the sun. In juxtaposition to Shelly's more voluptuous figure, Leona was muscular, in a thin, wiry sort of way. She was green eyed and had very pleasant facial features but seldom used much makeup, other than the very minimal and basic varieties.

She graduated from Danbury Teacher's College in 1934 and later studied at Yale University, New York University and The University of Connecticut. She served as President of the 'Danbury Teacher's College Forum' in 1934 and became quite prominent in the teaching community. She held teaching positions in Terryville and Southington before being assigned to the Danbury School System (at Main Street School). She took a job as a 'Method and Time Study Engineer' at the Remington Arms Plant in Bridgeport, CT after the start of the war and then, when the announcement of the formation of the Navy WAVES was made, she enlisted.

She made no immediate announcement to the family because she wanted no send off party, like they had done for Walt, or lengthy good byes, and wanted to get her personal things tidied up and in order without distraction. She would be reporting to the Midshipman's School at Smith College in Northampton, MA to begin her course of indoctrination in a mere two weeks and was focused on getting her personal affairs in order. Mary couldn't help but notice the flurry of activity and when she asked Leona what was going on, Leona matter of factly gave her the news. Walt, who was now at the rank of First Class Petty Officer, and home on leave, was the next to learn about her decision. She had always been close to Walt, being the two youngest of the seven siblings, but she now felt a special kinship, with their mutual enlistment in the Navy.

The WAVES, an acronym for Women Accepted for Volunteer Emergency Service (Women's Naval Reserve) could provide an opportunity for Leona to add some excitement to her life, meet new people, and maybe even learn new things and advance her career.

She was a bit of an iconoclast anyway, so no one was surprised at her decision, and family just took it in stride, comfortable that virtually all WAVES deployments and assignments were stateside, non combatant and therefore safe.

That August, of '42, she headed off to 'The U.S.S Northampton', which was the Nickname the recruits had given the U.S. Naval Reserve Midshipmen's School at Smith College (in Northampton, MA). After the two month training, she would be a Commissioned Officer, with the anticipated length of service being the duration of the war plus six months. Based upon her knowledge and experience, she had received indication that she would work as a cryptographer after training, which would need Top Security Clearance. She could be stationed in either Norfolk, VA or Washington, DC.

It was an arduous bus trip to Massachusetts from Danbury and a less than auspicious arrival at Smith. The bus in which Leona had been riding had a flat tire, requiring a long wait for the service truck to travel to their location and facilitate a repair, it was hot and muggy, the exhaust fumes were nauseating and they didn't stop for food along the way; and now, as they pulled into the college parking area, a severe thunderstorm began, with high winds and a deluge of rain. Never the less, Harriett Lenoria Brett was excited (she never liked her formal, given name and went by Leona or H. Leona Brett 90% of the time) and filled with exuberance and had an almost gleeful anticipation of what the next stage of her life as a Navy Officer would bring. This adventure would also signify her emancipation, full independence and freedom from parental and family oversight at the ripe old age of 28. Until now, she had been living in the family home, under the watchful eye of her mother, Mary, and older sister Rose; not to mention the fact that she was the "baby" sister to her male siblings and as such, they were particularly protective; especially John (Cook). She had an aire of sophistication, common to those women who were very well read and well educated, and sometimes even a somewhat haughty and slightly conceited demeanor; but in reality, under the facade, she was in many ways, naive and slightly insecure.

This experience, she thought to herself, just might provide some final pieces to the puzzle that was the enigmatic Leona Brett.

On the bus ride to Smith, she was seated next to a young woman named Ruby, who was originally from Mount Kisco, New York, but had moved to Stratford, CT during her high school years when her father took a job at Sikorsky Aircraft. As they chatted and got to know each other during the long bus ride, Leona took an almost immediate liking to her. While they seemed at first to be polar opposites, there was a commonality in self confidence and determination and a certain mutual "joie de vivre", although both had a decidedly different way of expressing it.

Ruby had enjoyed a privileged upbringing, living in an upscale suburban home, pampered by her doting parents; her Mechanical Engineer father and her glamorous, socially active mother (who had inherited a relatively sizable sum of money from a wealthy grandparent), and had sent Ruby to the best private schools.

However, she became somewhat rebellious and headstrong as a late teenager and young adult, decided that she didn't like the college environment at Albertus Magnus College, considered dropping out on numerous occasions and barely made it through; albeit, the strict liberal arts curriculum, which required four years of either Latin or Greek (she chose Latin) might now pay off in her new adventure as a Navy WAVES enlistee.

Obviously, the recruiting officer saw a good fit for someone with a background as an English Major with Latin proficiency, and considered her an individual who might be compatible as a cryptographer or in a communications capacity. But that really wasn't on her mind when she enlisted. She was simply seeking excitement, adventure, a change in environment and "to sow some wild oats". Where Leona was serious, patriotic, conservative and mission focused, Ruby was devil may care, extroverted, thrill seeking and, based upon their conversation, sexually uninhibited.

One common stereotype, inappropriately assigned (by some) to the women of this new branch of the military was that they were "fast women", looking for a man, and perhaps hoping to snag an officer and a gentleman. That might have been started by some of the resentful male members of the military (and/ or perhaps their spouses) who could now have their respective stateside duties fulfilled by these new WAVES recruits, freeing them up for deployment at the front. That was the last thing that many of them, (and their families), wanted, which could easily explain the less than enthusiastic reception many WAVES received, and the tendency to malign their character . Either that, or it was the product of some hopeful fantasizing by testosterone laden males anticipating working in close proximity with these newly enlisted young women and hoping for some easy "extra curricular" entertainment. Either way, it didn't apply to Leona at all, but might have quite easily applied to Ruby; although Leona felt pretty sure that it wasn't creation of a long term relationship that was on Ruby's mind but rather a more playing the field, sexually liberated experience that she preferred.

Leona recognized that she would need to fight for respect under those circumstances, while Ruby wasn't as concerned about garnering respect as she was with enjoying new experiences. Very different women to be sure, yet they quickly established an undeniable connection.

They stayed close, continuing to bond during the basic training and surprisingly, Ruby showed an ability to focus and learn quickly and her intellect became more obvious. Even the more tedious aspects, like studying the Blue Jackets Manual, she breezed through and Leona became even more enamored with the varying layers of Ruby's multi-faceted personality. As luck would have it, upon completion of their training, they were both given the rank of Ensign and assigned to the Naval Communications Annex located at Massachusetts and Nebraska Avenue in Washington, DC.

They were given temporary housing near West Potomac Park and were told to catch the bus at the Lincoln Memorial to travel to the annex until more permanent housing could be completed. Once settled in, they were given three days leave before being required to report for work.

They crammed in as much as they could during those three days- sightseeing, dining out (Ruby usually treated), went to a Washington Post sponsored Starlight Concert at Meridian Park and patronized quite a few bars. Leona was fond of cocktails and mixed drinks, especially Martinis, as was Ruby, which was another aspect of their commonality. Ruby also smoked, but Leona did not. Leona never picked up the smoking habit, nor did Mary or Shelly, even though other family members smoked heavily. Like their father, Cook and Henry (and Will McAllister) went through at least a pack per day, and Rose smoked as well, but only three or four cigarettes a day. Walt occasionally smoked cigarettes too, but much preferred cigars.

The women felt quite liberated, frequenting drinking establishments without male escorts, being military women and smoking in public, which was frowned upon by many other more reserved women. Even though she was a number of years younger, Ruby actually exerted a pretty strong influence on Leona. Her obvious charisma and free spirit were traits that Leona found impressive and appealing and she was quite attracted to her; not in a sexual sense necessarily, but their strong mutual affection for each other meant that, under certain circumstances, it couldn't be ruled out.

Patriotic satisfaction aside, the mundane monotony of the sometimes tedious routine left them frequently craving some after work excitement, but the long hours, occasional weekend or evening shifts and rigid discipline of the military environment, not to mention the strict rules assigned to WAVE Quarters 'D', left fewer options than they would have liked. After about six months of the enlistment term, they were jumping at each and every chance to enhance their respective individual, and mutual, social lives. Even the innocuous USO Hanger Style Dances and the common Dance "Mixers" were something that they looked forward to. On an unusually warm and sultry early spring evening, they spontaneously decided to attend one such mixer after overhearing another staff member mention it to an on duty officer.

Those dance mixers were usually mildly entertaining but seldom the exciting venue that they hoped for, but it would be a break in the routine and an opportunity to socialize with some new people.

This one happened to be well attended, the dance music selected was better than usual; with some of their favorite Big Band and Swing Music chosen for the play list, and Ruby had smuggled in a flask of white rum in her purse so she could discretely fortify their punch, which all contributed to it being a more enjoyable activity than they had originally anticipated. Ruby's technique for surreptitiously spiking their drink was perfected to an art form and her adroitly executed maneuver was never detected. She would reach down into her opened purse which was resting on the floor, carefully unscrew the cap of the flask, then raise the purse to the table, being very careful not to spill any of the flask contents, then, setting it in front of her with enough room to place her half filled beverage glass between her and the purse, reach in and retrieve a small mirror and lipstick. She would apply the lipstick, then while continuing to hold the mirror above the purse with her left hand to further obscure the view of the action taking place behind the purse, raise the flask with her right hand to just above the edge of the purse opening and tip it toward her, pouring the rum into her (or Leona's) glass. She was masterful!

The venue sure wasn't Rick's Cafe from Casablanca, but it was about as good as it gets for two WAVES looking for a diversion on short notice. Shortly after they arrived, two Naval Officers entered the club, their striking good looks catching Leona and Ruby's attention.

The two men began circulating, mixing and mingling immediately, seemingly on a mission to dance with every woman in attendance. Both were polished dancers and based on the reaction and facial expressions of their dance partners, quite engaging and captivating in conversation. Before long, they made it around to Leona and Ruby and politely asked them to dance.

As suspected, their dance moves could cause swooning and their "gift of gab" was obvious. Both Leona and Ruby were clearly infatuated and turned on the charm. It must have worked for both of them because the circulating stopped, they took seats at Leona and Ruby's table, and repeatedly danced together for the next solid hour, briefly changing partners with each other, but coming back to their original partner for extended dance sets. The men told of their wartime exploits, future ambitions and charmed the women with a plethora of complimentary words and flattery. As the contents of Ruby's flask, now being shared by four, reached its last few dregs, conversation became more lively, with jokes being told, oblique sexual innuendo and gratuitous adulation part of the dialog. During the next dance, Leona glanced over her shoulder to notice Ruby leaving the hall with her dance partner. When she returned to where they were seated, she discovered a note that simply read; "You'll need to return home by yourself". "Don't worry about me- I'll see you later". Conflicted, she wasn't sure if she was angry at her or happy for her; but she felt quite "on the spot" and slightly awkward being left alone with someone she barely knew.

Feeling nervous and uncomfortable, she suggested that it was getting late and that she needed to start thinking about returning to her quarters. He appeared to sense her discomfort and suggested that he escort her back to the housing facility, but she refused, thanking him for an enjoyable evening. He then asked for permission to call her and expressed a desire to see her again. She smiled and said; "Absolutely; I'd like that". She kissed him on the cheek before rising from her chair, then he arose with her, taking her arm and walked her to the door. Before parting company, he initiated a second kiss; this time on her lips, and said; "I'll call you tomorrow".

She smiled all the way back to the annex, reliving the evening in her thoughts. She also worried about Ruby and her somewhat reckless behavior but also knew her well enough to know that she could take care of herself.

21

KEEPING THE HOME
FIRES BURNING

Walt wasn't a particularly romantic kind of a guy. He had a strong sex drive but wasn't inclined to wine and dine, buy roses, whisper sweet nothings or cause Betty to swoon from his romantic musings; and he pretty much offered more direct and prosaic hints when in the mood for intimacy. When he came home on leave, the pent up desires were in control and Betty had learned to expect amorous advances immediately upon his arrival home, so she always strived to create ample alone time to help ease the tension by providing intimacy and re-bonding time after the extended absence. One such occasion was back in July, when he traveled home on leave from Newfoundland (when he had first heard the news of Leona's enlistment) and both were feeling a distinct rise in libido and anticipation as the long awaited rendezvous time approached. She was living with her sister Sue, and brother-in-law Rudy, and they both clearly understood the situation and therefore graciously accommodated by "having errands to run" or some other excuse to be out of the house for at least a few hours after Walt's arrival. The July furlough and spousal reunion had been quite passionate and lustful, so much so, that Betty, having cast caution (and efforts toward contraception) to the wind, had become pregnant and was now anxious to give Walt the news but didn't want to include it in a letter, preferring to tell him in person. She was due toward the end of April, so she waited as long as she could, hoping he'd get leave soon, but obviously couldn't wait too long and surprise him with a big "belly bump" by the time he got home. That would have made for a rather anticlimactic, de facto announcement! She was now working in the Maternity Ward of Danbury Hospital and was getting excellent care and moral support from her friends and co-workers. As a Registered Nurse, she knew the drill anyway and planned to work right up until the time of delivery. She also had developed a great circle of supportive friends aside from work, many of whom were also military wives and fellow nurses, not to the mention strong family ties. It couldn't get any more convenient or reassuring.

She worked hard, but thoroughly enjoyed her job, and the cooperative living set-up provided an opportunity to save a small nest egg that would come in handy when the war was over and they were ready to establish a home of their own and start raising a family.

While wartime rationing was in effect, and caused some degree of hardship for many families, her personal arrangement helped avoid much of the inconvenience.

There was rationing on various items needed for the war effort, like red meat, butter, coffee, gasoline and other commodities; and Rudy, like many other Americans, planted a 'Victory Garden' to supply the majority of the family's produce. (Actually, by 1945, there were 20 million 'Victory Gardens' supplying approximately 40% of all vegetables -fresh and preserved- consumed by Americans). The Brett household on Fairfield Avenue also had a large communal garden that the entire family (still living at home) tended and they shared with extended family frequently.

If there happened to be severe shortages of things like red

meat, citizens with the wherewithal and financial capability could always find a purveyor within the illegal meat trade willing to satisfy the demand. There was also a lot of bartering for rationing stamps going on. There were also collection drives for scrap metal, aluminum cans and rubber; and even cooking oil and bacon grease was saved and donated toward the war effort.

With automobile production completely stopped during the war, ingenuity had to be exercised and as a corollary, many Blue Collar individuals learned basic auto mechanics as a necessity, just to keep the old jalopy running.

Generally though, the economy was very good, and after the great depression, and some

wartime related shortages of particular goods, and the slightly uncomfortable deprivation resulting from the rationing, materialism was on the rise, and ironically, this was a time of substantial growth of the middle class. There was an increase in job opportunities, marriages and patriotism, and many (but not all) were moderately prospering.

Cook and Bertie were doing well too, and purchased a circa 1895 farm house at #15 Joe's Hill Road. They had been trying to have children, but were unable. They never disclosed to other family members, even Mary, the cause of the infertility. All they would say is; "The doctor says it's reproductive problems", apparently in an effort to avoid providing personal specifics and disclosure of the partner having difficulty, and thereby mitigating the level of individual sadness, embarrassment and angst. It was easy to see though, that there was a profound disappointment and sorrow, but they put on a good face and claimed, with a dismissive chuckle, to "still be working on it". They had obviously purchased the large home with the intention of raising a family there, but if their continued child bearing efforts were unable to come to fruition, it will have proven to be an ill advised investment. With that said, conception issues aside, they seemed to be content with their lives together and were clearly very much in love with each other. Being childless presented a financial upside though. Bertie, being unencumbered and without responsibility for raising kids, was able to engage in full time employment and worked at Genung's Department Store (the downtown Danbury location) as a department manager, while Cook was thriving professionally as a master steam fitter for the Riggs Disier Company. From an economic perspective, they were prospering well for a Blue Collar, middle class family.

But the one achieving the most remarkable success and prosperity was Henry.

He had worked hard to grow his Insurance Agency, that he had purchased from Rose, after William's death (It had been founded by T. William McAllister). In so doing, Henry had serendipitously found the perfect profession for himself and was well suited for sales and sales management. He used the power of networking to build social contacts, even threw in a little crony capitalism and became a full time student of sales-manship. He practiced and perfected his sales pitch, looking for new and innovative ways to present and promote his prod-ucts and ways to create added value, and was a master at find-ing prospects and identifying qualified leads.

He was gaining social prominence, popularity and noto-riety and employed social interaction as a tool and vehicle to successfully land new business, perfecting his technique to an art form. He read and re-read Dale Carnegie's 'How to Win Friends and Influence People' (and some other of his writings) and carefully observed and learned from other suc-cessful people with whom he hobnobbed, mingled and frater-nized. He obtained training films from Prudential, Chevrolet, Kelvinator Appliance and Emerson Radio and watched them over and over. Henry was a "natural".

He was finally ready to start contemplating leaving the family home, settling down, and starting a family of his own. His financial situation was certainly adequate to continue helping support his mother, while building his future family.

With Cook, slightly older and married, and Walt, seven years younger, and already married, he began to think that it was about time that he settled down as well. He had been dating a delightfully attractive, somewhat sophisticated, well educated woman exuding class and charm, named Betty Riley, whom he not only considered to be a perfect candidate for a wife, but a great partner and ambassador for the business as well (he was always focused on building his business, success, and creating wealth- to the point that it impacted ALL the choices and decisions, including non-business, that he faced). She would certainly enhance the agency's image if she became a part of it, and could be a superb helpmate, even if only part time after children entered the picture and responsibilities of child rearing began to temporarily monopolize her time.

Astute, practical and pragmatic- driven and with high energy, were traits; -no; attributes, if you will, that Elizabeth Riley found irresistible and highly attractive in a man. J. Henry was becoming powerful and socially prominent, not to mention prosperous, all contributing, in her mind, to elevated status as a most eligible bachelor.

It had become a foregone conclusion that she would accept his proposal, when and if it were offered, and sure enough, they were soon engaged and set a wedding date to coincide with Walt's next leave.

The planets must have aligned because not only was Walt able to secure leave, and return the favor of acting as Henry's best man (as Henry had done for him), Leona was able to get home as well.

The mood was ebullient and joyful, with the announcement that Walt and Betty would soon be giving birth to their first child adding to the festive atmosphere, and Mary's great pleasure of having all of her children, including Shelly (without father Guy) assembled before her; all seemingly well and happy.

While Henry and Betty hadn't wanted the wedding to be too large, the planning and invitation list got somewhat out of hand and the affair took on a life of its own. Henry had lots of friends and business associates that needed to be invited, Betty Riley was socially well connected and popular as well, and the family was growing rapidly, with new spouses and their extended families added to the list. The McAllister clan was growing rapidly as well, with four of the seven into, or very near, adulthood (Ruth, working as a dress shop clerk, was 26, Evelyn was 24, and Colin, who had just started working as a police and fire reporter at the News-Times, was 23, while Bettie, at 21, was looking for work). That left Nancy, Robert and Paul still in their teenage years (Paul was the youngest at 14). Both Mary and Rose were very proud of the children, having shared the parenting duties, collaborating daily on child rearing direction and challenges, and considering the circumstances, with the early demise of William leaving them somewhat income deprived and without a father's leadership, they did a commendable job and had every right to be proud.

The years of hardships, sacrifice, the tragic and heartbreaking loss of John and perhaps the worry and stress of caring for such a large family (not to mention her advancing years- she was in her mid sixties), had started to take its toll though.

Mary was beginning to experience health problems and was relieved that, with most of the children now out of the house, she could finally cut back on her work load and relax a bit, and take better care of herself for a change. Also, with her own mortality being on her mind lately, she was thrilled to have so many of the family gathered together for this event. She couldn't be sure that she would get to see so many of them assembled together in one place again; but it would, never the less, be a bittersweet experience. She so wished that John could have been there for the ceremony and festivities too. Even after all these years, she missed him terribly and her heart ached for him as she shed a silent tear. But she was convinced that he would be there in spirit to add his joyous presence and loving oversight. She hadn't been this excited or happy in years.

The wedding was what many would call a typical Irish wedding- A formal, reserved Sacrament of Matrimony followed by a lively and boisterous, and slightly raucous reception with lots of drinking, food, song, dance and laughter; with a few minor arguments, quick reconciliation, hugs, kissing and a few ribald jokes thrown in for good measure. Betty and Henry exchanged Claddagh rings, as a nod to tradition and to John and Mary, who had done the same at their marriage so many years earlier.

After the festivities, the couple took and short honeymoon trip to Florida and obviously wasted no time acting upon their desire to start a family, because Betty discovered within two months of their return from the honeymoon that she too was pregnant.

Walt and Betty M had some excitement too. On April 21st, 1943, a son, Walter Charles Brett, Junior, (they immediately started calling him "Charlie") was born while Walt was on duty in Newfoundland. Then, later that same year, a son, James Henry Brett, Junior, (whom they called "Jimmy") was born to Henry and Betty R. The next generation of Brett men had arrived and the families felt that God had smiled down upon them and they were blessed.

22

A BROKEN HEART, CATHARSIS, A GROWING FAMILY AND BRIGHT HORIZONS

During Henry and Betty's wedding celebrations, there was one family member who didn't appear to be quite as ebullient, joyful and animated as the rest. Quite the contrary, she was uncharacteristically reserved and quiet; bordering on taciturn and reticent, and she avoided any in depth conversation regarding her experiences serving in the Navy. Leona's unusual demeanor was adequately camouflaged by all the manic activity, and her somber, withdrawn presence went relatively undetected and unnoticed by all except Rose. During Leona's upbringing, Rose acted as much like Leona's mother as Mary did (especially after John passed away), and a unique bond was formed. After the subsequent passing of William, the dynamic intensified, with Mary and Rose functioning as the matriarchal co-head of house. The role Rose played as Leona's sister, yielded to her new role as head of the house (and along with Mary, head of family). Leona loved Mary and Rose equally, but felt a closer connection with Rose due to the fact that they were closer in age (although there was still an almost

twenty year gap) and because of the uniqueness of a relationship where Leona could confide in Rose as a sister would,
but respected her as she would her biological mother. Also,
Rose was more emotive, warm and non-judgmental, whereas Mary was stern and direct and disliked shows of emotion.
Therefore, it comes as no surprise that Rose quickly recognized that something was weighing heavily on Leona's mind,
even if others didn't, and took her aside for a candid conversation the day before Leona was scheduled to return to her post.
Leona dismissed any assertion that she was acting differently
and blew it off, saying that it must just be the effect of serving
in the military and how the experience can change one's personality. In spite of Leona's nonchalant dismissal, Rose knew
the truth would be to the contrary, but didn't press it. Leona's
leave ended without ever having the talk that Rose had hoped
for. It weighed heavily on her mind, especially when she could
subsequently detect some of the same distracted and despondent tone in Leona's letters and during the occasional phone
call home.

By the time of Leona's next leave, little had changed and
she exhibited some of the same differences in personality that
Rose had noticed during the wedding of Henry and Betty. She
was determined to have a heart to heart talk with Leona before she next returned to her post and rather than wait until
the end of her leave, and risk and repeat of the previous attempt, she took her aside on the third day of her furlough.

Most important, sensitive or intimate discussions in the
Brett household took place in the kitchen. When two or more
family members were seated around the table, usually with
a cup of coffee or tea, and another person entered the room,
they could immediately detect that privacy was expected, because conversation would stop and the uncomfortable silence
would raise a red flag indicating the one had just inadvertently
intruded. By now, everyone knew the drill and the unspoken
protocol and respected it. On the flip side, if someone were

to be asked to join either Mary or Rose in the kitchen "for a talk", they would immediately know that they were about to be thrust into a serious conversation, be chastised for something, be interrogated or be asked for valued advice, like it or not.

That could have the effect of causing defensiveness and tension, but because it was Rose and not Mary who had requested the private time, Leona was less on guard.

Rose quickly got to the point, saying that she had noticed Leona's more quiet than normal demeanor and that she seemed troubled and distracted. "Is something wrong?"; she asked.

Initially, Leona said that everything was fine, but Rose had good intuition and pressed the issue, sensing that Leona really had something she wanted to get off her chest. Needing a catharsis of sorts, Leona didn't resist too much longer before disclosing the cause of her anguish. She spoke of Ruby, the close friendship that had developed, and shared some of their mutual exploits, holding nothing back regarding some uncharacteristic behavior for the more typically straight laced Leona. She shared some anecdotes regarding Ruby's sexually uninhibited behavior and how Ruby encouraged her to become more liberated and enjoy the time they were spending in the military by "making some new friends"; a euphemism for dating around.

Leona admitted that she had been slightly influenced, but that alone certainly hadn't been responsible for the grave error in judgement she had made. She then took the conversation back to the time of the dance mixer where Ruby had left with another officer, awkwardly leaving Leona alone with his companion. She methodically outlined the development of their relationship, reciting verbatim his words during that first phone call the next day, their next get together, his gentlemanly conduct, the infatuation with him she experienced and the admiration she had for him. His name was Jack. He was a Junior Grade Lieutenant working as an instructor in the Navy's V-5 (Aviation cadet) Program in Annapolis. He would travel from Annapolis, MD to D.C. to visit her as often as he could and while innocent and platonic on the surface, after the first couple of dates, she became highly infatuated by his charm, self confidence, rugged good looks and wit. When both were given a Sunday afternoon off, Jack decided to take advantage of the unseasonably warm mid-Atlantic spring weather, and pick Leona up for a drive in the country. He would surprise her when he arrived in a 1937 Chevrolet Cabriolet (convertible) that he had borrowed from a close friend. She had packed a picnic basket and two bottles of wine, and after taking a leisurely drive, top down, across the Potomac into northern Virginia, and then west into some rural Virginia countryside, they located a secluded roadside park.

They enjoyed the nice weather, the intimate conversation, a delightful picnic lunch; then thinking that some brief exercise might help reduce the glow they were both feeling from the wine consumption, they decided to take a short hike into the adjacent woods on a well cleared meandering path. When they returned to the picnic area and the car, they loaded the items into the trunk and upon discovering that the already secluded area had now completely cleared out, sat in the vehicle for another 20 to 30 minutes engaging in what Leona described as "a very passionate and intense necking and petting session". She didn't want to fall head over heels in love with him, but she was now getting dangerously close to the point of no return. It had been a wonderful day. She was virtually giddy from the wine, but more so from the glow of this growing love affair. When he dropped her at the housing facility, kissed her passionately and said good bye, she waved as he drove away then almost sprinted into the quarters, anxious to tell Ruby all about her day.

From sun up to sun down, she thought of nothing but him and eagerly awaited their next time together. Ruby could easily see that Leona was becoming seriously infatuated far too quickly and in her naivete, could become vulnerable, so she strongly cautioned her against losing control and suggested that she slow down and get to know him better before making such an emotional commitment. Ruby was far more experienced in matters of the heart, and had a somewhat cynical and distrustful attitude toward men in general, but military men even more so. Leona's reaction to the warning was basically to acknowledge and ignore and proceed with the whirlwind romance.

Due to the unique nature of the communal living arrangements in the WAVES branch of the military, intimacy in one's bedroom was exceedingly difficult, if not impossible. Leona had actually never visited Jack- he always traveled to her- so she really wasn't sure, but Jack did indicate that he had shared quarters as well, implying that it would be it awkward, difficult and impractical for her to visit him. She also had no access to a car and he did. When they both became fortunate enough to mutually secure an entire weekend off, they planned the next visit to include a getaway trip to the scenic Blue Ridge Mountain area of Virginia, and because it would extend through Saturday and Sunday, Leona wasn't shocked or offended when Jack tactfully implied that they should spend Saturday night in a motel, and after briefly pausing, as if waiting to check her reaction, continued by adding; "in separate rooms, of course". She smiled coyly, but in all honesty, she was ready to take it to the next level and longed for that ultimate stage of intimacy.

She had anxiously anticipated their weekend rendezvous all week and it began exactly as she had hoped. It was romantic, fun and flirtatious and the most enjoyable time she had spent with him to date. At the end of a delightful day, when he stopped at a roadside motel to check in, she said; "I think one room will be enough". He smiled, paused and said; "are you sure?" She simply responded by saying; "positive".

At this point, Rose was beginning to become a little uncomfortable hearing about such intimate details of Leona's love life, and was hesitant to respond, unsure weather to express happiness over the new romance, or wait for the conclusion and "the other shoe to drop". She chose to say nothing and listen without judging or criticizing. As Leona continued, she was glad she took that course.

Leona proceeded with her story, indicating that they had been intimate on numerous occasions during the month following the weekend trip. As she was rapidly falling in love with her new flame, Ruby, now becoming more curious about Jack and instinctively protective of Leona, began trying to find out more about him. Jack's friend, with whom Ruby had a brief fling after their meeting at the dance social back in the early part of the spring season, either couldn't or wouldn't offer much information, causing Ruby's suspicion to increase. While working at her post late one evening, and taking advantage of her related duties, she took a chance and surreptitiously gained access to files containing personal information and carefully searched for ones pertaining to Jack. It was a dangerous thing to do and could have subjected her to severe discipline, but she was fearless and kept looking until she found it. What she discovered was beyond unsettling: Leona's "boyfriend", Jack, was from California, where his wife of three years currently resided.

It was at that point in the recitation that Rose gasped in shock. Now Rose was beginning to understand the cause of Leona's change in demeanor, and recent sullen attitude.

While Leona continued, Rose learned that apparently, Ruby had encouraged Leona to angrily confront him and threaten to expose his rotten behavior, but Leona refused. She felt chagrin, embarrassment, remorse and shame, but not rage. Annoyance and irritation perhaps, but not anger. Immediately after being provided with the discovery, her affection and, dare she say, "love" for him, turned to disdain and disgust. Confrontation was not part of her agenda; completely removing him from her life was. The letter she sent to him was succinct and concise and right to the point. Eloquently terse, she simply wrote; "You're a despicable piece of shit who has taken advantage of my naivete while betraying your wife". " Never contact me again". Perhaps due to a fear of exposure, impact on career and marriage, he complied. Hearing third hand, through Ruby who had conversed with her old flame and Jack's long time friend, he allegedly expressed sorrow for his actions, added some trite excuses and played up the stress of wartime scenario; while claiming that he had deep feelings for her and that he had been conflicted regarding his relationship with his wife. In truth, Ruby suspected that he was pleased to have gotten away with the affair for as long as he did and relieved that there had been little consequence.

When Leona had completed relating her experience, Rose could sense that it had been cathartic for her. She seemed relieved to have shared the traumatic episode with someone in the family and while Rose hugged her, consoled her and offered some sisterly and motherly advice, Leona appeared to take on an air of confidence and resolve, pledging to never let herself become a victim of such emotionally reckless behavior again.

After her leave, Rose sensed that Leona was returning to base a wiser, emotionally stronger and more self confident individual, albeit, more cynical and judgmental.

As Leona returned to her base in DC, Walt was embarking on sea duty, heading toward The Canal Zone for maintenance and repair duties at Toro Point (Fort Sherman). After having acclimated to New Foundland weather, going to the heat and humidity of Panama was quite a shock to his system. He had spent his entire upbringing in Danbury, with its frequently harsh winters and mild, albeit humid, summers; and then stationed in cold, or cooler, climates during previous deployments, and therefore never had the opportunity to acclimate to tropical weather. He was miserable. Working in the tropics seemed to weaken him and the Panama experience wasn't high on his list of favorites. With that said, he and a close group of friends, frequented some in town bars when off duty and often enjoyed too many rum cocktails, and sometimes opportunistic young women, who often considered these enlisted "Yankees and Gringos" as wealthy by their standards, and ready, willing and able to take advantage of their loneliness and state of inebriation for their personal gain. Like many others, Walt had taken solace and comfort in the company of an occasional Latin beauty. That's not to say the Panamanian citizens were impoverished. Quite the contrary; they were enjoying a fairly good economy and after the Fascist leaning President Arias was replaced (with the help of the American government) by President de la Guardia, many American enterprises were established in Panama, creating a fondness for Americans (or at least American dollars).

But with the exception of these occasional diversions, life, for the most part, was tedious, oppressively hot and humid, mind numbingly routine, and in spite of the fact that they were always on guard due to the importance of the canal to the war effort and to American economy, and cognizant of the danger presented by being in such a valuable facility, he was bored and unhappy.

Earlier that year, the U.S.S Concord had sailed in to Balboa for repairs after a severe gasoline fire that killed 24 men, including her Executive Officer. Because of his steam fitting expertise, Walt and a few other Seabees were assigned to work on the repair project. Toward the completion of the assignment, Walt was working in the engine room and while on a scaffold, slipped on some spilled engine oil and broke his wrist. That left him incapacitated for a while and during his recovery, he contracted malaria. He was sent to the United States Naval Convalescent Hospital in Santa Cruz, CA for treatment and rehabilitation. While there, in December of 1944, he received news of the arrival of his and Betty's second child, Shelagh. With that news, his longing for home and to be with his young family became intense. He was ready to leave the Seabees and petitioned for a medical discharge. After brief stays in San Diego and in Corpus Christi, TX, he was honorably discharged in the spring of 1945.

23

THE "FABULOUS FIFTIES"

It is commonly accepted that the 1950's were a time of innocence, general contentedness, social conservatism, comfort
in conformity, a newfound materialism and vigorous growth
of the middle class. Perhaps a bit of hyperbole exists in that
description, but to a large extent, there is a distinct element
of truth. After a relatively short post war economic recession,
running from the latter quarter of 1948 through the first quarter of 1950, a strong economy (with the exception of some high
inflation during the earliest part of the decade) contributed to
unprecedented prosperity and a rapidly growing middle class.
Returning military men and women were focused on starting
families and successfully gaining employment, many of them
moving to the suburbs, buying freshly constructed new tract
homes, epitomized by the Levittown Communities now being
built at breakneck speed in parts of New Jersey, Long Island,
NY and Pennsylvania. It was a fulfillment of their dream of
the idyllic modern home with the proverbial white picket
fence, friendly neighbors and a safe and nurturing environment for their kids. The "Baby Boom" had officially begun in
1946, but by the early 50's, birth rates had skyrocketed. Some
of the more snarky social analysts would refer to Levittown
styled communities as "Rabbit Hutches". The Brett family was

no exception: Henry and Betty R. had a second child, named William (called Billy) in late 1945 and Walt and Betty M. had their third child, Named Patricia Ann, in April of 1946. In 1949, Cook and Bertie seemed to come to terms with the fact that they would remain childless and sold their house on Joe's Hill Road to Walt and Betty and moved to a smaller home in the Neversink District. All of the Brett men were doing well; Henry successful and prosperous as an owner/ executive in the Insurance Industry (The J. Henry Brett Insurance Agency, that had been founded by his Brother-In-Law, William, which he had purchased from Rose after William's death) and Walt and Cook as Steam fitters. Henry was clearly becoming the most affluent, but Blue Collar Tradesmen like Cook and Walt were doing nicely too. If Henry's family favored the one de-picted on the 50's TV show 'Ozzie and Harriet' or 'Leave it to Beaver', then Walt's was a little more "working man", like 'The Life Of Riley' or 'The Real McCoy's. Ironically, as it would turn out, Henry's boys even resembled the Nelson boys, David and Ricky, from that 'Ozzie and Harriet' television program (especially Billy, who many classmates claimed looked like youngest son, Ricky Nelson). While Henry's home was large, relatively new, slightly extravagant, with beautiful appoint-ments and furniture, manicured grounds and a closer to downtown Danbury address, it wasn't ostentatious. Cook and Bertie's new home was a cute, well kept Cape Cod, common (along with Ranch Style homes) in mid century subdivisions, with a large yard and pleasant landscaping.

Walt and Betty's home was a quaintly rustic, turn of the century colonial, built around the time that John and Mary had arrived in the United States, featuring a huge wrap around front porch, and was situated close to the street on a two acre lot, the majority of which was unfortunately straight up a very steep hill with a flat landing at the base, where the home had been constructed. It had a dug well that would sometimes go dry during extended drought spells in the summer months and even an old outhouse located about 20 yards up the hill. There was also a detached cinder block, single car garage with a convenient workshop at the rear, built into the steep embankment directly off their Joe's Hill Rd. location. Walt wasn't particularly fond of yard maintenance but never the less kept the yard mowed and presentable. Henry, on the other hand, paid someone to maintain the grounds surrounding his home.

The early decade was a serenely harmonious and prosperous time for the family. Mary and Rose continued the tradition of sheltering and nurturing grandchildren, when Rose's daughter Nancy married Jack Estes and moved in, quickly starting a family of their own. Henry, Cook and Walt continued to contribute to Mary's support, and now the communal effort was augmented by the addition of the Estes contribution, as well as some grown members of the McAllister clan providing intermittent support. John would have been very pleased to know that his children and grandchildren never faltered in their dedication to, and support of, Mary.

While cities peaked in growth, suburban migration spurred enormous growth in surrounding towns, but relatively few subdivisions resembling Levittown sprung up in the Danbury area. Most subdivisions, per se, were more custom in nature, partially due to "Yankee sensibilities" and partially due to the fact that Fairfield County was close enough for commuters to travel relatively easily to NYC, ultimately assigning the area with the designation 'Connecticut's Gold Coast' due to the influx of affluent commuter families seeking country serenity, safety, nurturing communities, larger lots and a more bucolic environment. Communities like Candlewood Shores (and similar lakeside communities), Brookfield, New Fairfield and Sherman all experienced rapid growth, inspired in no small degree by the desire to live near Candlewood Lake. As a matter of fact, Leona, who had returned to teaching after leaving the Navy, purchased a home in New Milford, right on the lake, where she would frequently entertain friends and family in her meticulously landscaped backyard prominently featuring a large boat dock, primarily used for diving, sunbathing and lounging. During summer swim parties, many, if not most, of her friends and guests tended to be very conservative, usually lounging lakeside in modest one piece bathing suits and donning latex bathing caps if they actually went into the water, but virtually all, in contrast, were anything but conservative with their drinking and smoking habits. It was well known among neighbors as "the party house".

Shelly was still thriving on Long Island, albeit without Father Guy. Their lives just seemed to go off in different directions and the relationship seemed to die a natural death, but they still communicated and saw each other on occasion for usually brief meetings. They would, however, remain lifelong friends.

With all the economic expansion and growth of the middle class, Danbury remained for the most part, a Blue Collar town; and that's the way Cook and Walt preferred it. As working class men, in the Steam fitter trade, they were conservative democrats, members and strong supporters of their union, and intensely patriotic. They were both living a good life, enjoying the fruits of their labor and quite content. Cook was in a very loving relationship with Bertie, and being childless, they had considerably more disposable income than Walt. Walt, on the other hand, was the "King of his Castle" and was clearly treated as such by his family. Betty worked nights as a nurse in the maternity ward at Danbury Hospital, bringing in a nice supplemental income.

She didn't get much sleep though; at least before the kids became enrolled in school. She'd take care of them during the day and then grab three or four hours of sleep after Walt returned home from work. But, their combined income provided many material things that they wouldn't have dreamed about acquiring 10 years earlier. Walt had purchased a used 1950 Chevrolet pick-up truck for work and they had a new

1952 Chevrolet Bel Air sedan as a family car. They had a new television and Walt ditched the rabbit ears and mounted a large antenna on the roof, which brought in stations from New York and Hartford. They switched from a party line telephone service to a private line (with party lines, one would share the line with 3 or 4 other families, and if someone else was using the line when you wanted to make a call, you simply had to wait until it was freed up), which was considered a luxury for most people. They took vacations to Cape Cod, day trips to Manhattan, Sherwood Isle, The Catskill Game Farm or drove the Merritt Parkway to the Long Island Beaches. Toward the middle to later part of the decade, they even took occasional trips to Florida. Shelly visited them often and frequently took Walt and Betty's eldest child, Charlie, to Ball Games in New York, at Ebbets Field to watch the Brooklyn Dodgers play.

In 1956, Shelly and Leona took a 10 day Caribbean Cruise, which was considered an upper class adventure, beyond the reach of most middle class people.

Walt and Henry's families were close, visiting frequently, and Charlie, Shelagh and Patricia enjoyed playing with cousins Jimmy and Billy. With that said, Charlie, Shelagh and Patricia DID NOT enjoy spending time in Henry and Betty R's home, because everything was in its place and the house was kept fastidiously neat and clean, with some rooms being designated as off limits. Obviously, that could make young children uncomfortable. Walt and Henry's families were clearly living different lifestyles. Jimmy and Billy were coddled and pampered and given anything they wanted. Henry's somewhat nouveau riche status altered his perspective on child rearing and he wanted his children to enjoy his success by surrounding them with material possessions. Walt's parental style was more disciplined and slightly austere, but that's not to say that the kids were deprived in any way. Walt, like his father, John, deferred serious discipline, assigning that responsibility to Betty. He would chastise and scold when behavior was improper or when conduct was inappropriate, especially with Charlie, but it was Betty who would deal with the more serious behavioral infractions.

Betty was reserved and somewhat stoic, seldom willing to show emotion. Her disciplinary style was direct and analytical, while calm and measured. It was quite effective.

Betty was determined and had enormous work ethic and stamina. She ran her household like a well oiled machine, balancing nursing with responsibilities as a wife and mother. Walt and Betty's relationship wasn't by any stretch of the imagination passionate, but it was comfortable and harmonious. As I had said, Walt was the king of his castle and lived life exactly how he wanted. He was a huge sports fan, watching as many games as possible on TV, he played poker a few nights per week with some buddies (many of whom were from work or fellow union members), typically consumed 4 to 6 beers per evening after returning from work, smoked cigars constantly, and a pipe occasionally, and often caroused with buddies at local bars or pubs. Unlike Cook and Henry, who smoked cigarettes heavily, Walt only smoked cigars or occasionally, his pipe.

Not the expensive, hand rolled variety of cigars, but rather the cheap 'White Owl' or 'Dutch Masters' brands. When the cigar wasn't actually burning, he would chew on it, getting the effect from not only the smoke, but the tobacco juice as well.

Even though they were not all that rural, and the Mill Plain section of town was fairly well developed, all three of Walt and Betty's children started school in a quaint little one room school house near the intersection of Joe's Hill Road, Aunt Hack Rd. and Mill Plain Road. After kindergarten and first grade, Charlie and Shelagh went to Main Street School and Patricia, being younger, went to Park Avenue School and then to Mill Ridge school. The kids were very different in personality, and to some extent even physical appearance. Although all were below average in height (not surprising, considering that Walt was only 5' 7" and Betty was only 5' 2"- not sure if Betty's short stature was a genetic predisposition or resulting from the depravation endured as a young child growing up in the old Czechoslovakia before emigrating to the U.S.), they tended to differ in physical stature, Charlie being wiry and active, Shelagh having a tendency toward weight gain and obesity and was relatively sedentary and introverted and Patricia had a more average and typical body type and was fairly active and very social. While Charlie enjoyed the status of first born male and "heir apparent", Patricia was clearly the favorite (at least with Walt). She was extremely cute and cheerful, outgoing and personable and relished her dad's attention. On Saturdays he would take her into town for shopping trips or to run errands, have lunch and sometimes to Rogers Park where he would chat with some friends while she played.

They were a religious family and children were raised Catholic, although Betty was Lutheran and continued attending her family's church, St. Paul's, on Spring Street. The Catholic Church experience for the kids was pre-Vatican II and therefore unlike today's services. The girls wore veil caps, mass was in Latin and Charlie wore a suit. After mass, they would sometimes go to the New York Bake Shop to buy Hard Rolls or during the warmer months they would stop at Moffa's Roadside for hot dogs or grinders (after 1955 when they opened). About one Sunday per month they would have dinner at the El Dorado Italian Restaurant or perhaps the Ho Yen Chinese restaurant, frequently meeting Henry's family there or on occasion Sue and Rudy.

In spite of the war in Korea, which seemed to be ignored by many citizens (probably a result of the psychological exhaustion from World War Two), it seemed a peaceful time, a quieter time, a simpler time, a better time for families and a good time for American exceptionalism and prosperity. It was a slower time and a friendlier time. Milk and bread and even Charles (potato) Chips were delivered to your door, phones needed to be dialed and public phones were coin operated, it was a time of The Mickey Mouse Club, Dick Clark's American Bandstand, the 'Lassie' television series, AM car radios, Kool Aid, Viewmasters, candy cigarettes, bronzed baby shoes, Good Humor and Mr. Softee ice cream trucks; a time of shoe skates; hula hoops, polio pioneers, BB Guns and all of the other iconic remembrances of the decade. During the summer months, Betty would take them to the Danbury Town Park at Lake Candlewood, Lake Kenosia Park or Roger's Park Pool; and sometimes during summer evenings, they would load the kids in the car, dressed in their pajamas, and go to a movie at the Drive-in Theater, and after school was back in session in the early fall, the highly anticipated event of the season, The Great Danbury State Fair, took place over ten days in October.

For the times, it was like a small version of Disney World combined with a huge state fair. They all attended as a family early in the 1950's but as the kids got older, they generally each went with a separate group of friends. Charlie liked school, Patty (a name she grew to hate, much preferring Patricia) loved school and Shelagh, while a good student academically, didn't like the social aspects of it. Henry and Betty R's kids, Jimmy and Billy, tended to both be spoiled brats but exhibited very different personalities. Jimmy was a good student and went to private schools (and as a teenager, to a Military Academy and Marionapolis Preparatory School in Thompson, CT where he graduated with honors) and Billy tended to be a fair to poor student, with a rebellious streak and a slightly sarcastic persona. For him, play and self indulgence were by far more important than studying. Both were basically granted their every wish. Charlie too, was somewhat spoiled, but not materialistically. He was a good kid; obedient, compliant, good natured and seldom, if ever, got into trouble. He enjoyed riding his bike with friends, playing sports (although he wasn't very athletic), and hanging out

with the other boys his age in the neighborhood. He also enjoyed watching sports with Walt, either on television or live.
If Walt was the "king of his castle", Charlie was the "prince".
Even though Walt and Henry's families were close, and the
kids saw each other regularly, they didn't associate with the
same circle of friends; the socio-economic factor and geo-
graphic location being primarily responsible. It was a good
time for kids to be kids. Their diet was simple and wholesome, they had lots of friends, played outside in the fresh air
getting good exercise and they were shielded from many of
the harsh realities of life by being treated more like children
than kids of today. In the summer months they would ride
bikes, play sports, play board games, play jacks or marbles,
hopscotch, or jump rope. The boys would play "Cowboys and
Indians" or "War" which have become decidedly politically
incorrect today.

They knew nothing of social ills like alcoholism, adultery,
pedophilia, organized crime activity, racial bigotry and bias,
etc. because parents, teachers and other adults with whom
they came in contact wouldn't openly discuss those topics in
the presence of children.

For good or bad, they were protected and blissfully ignorant. Even televised or radio news broadcasts were much more
reserved, discrete and conservative-some might say more socially responsible, using nuance and suggestive language that
was beyond the grasp of most kids.

The Christmas season was unapologetically religious,
while simultaneously a materialistic mercantile pageant, but
a truly joyous and magical time for the kids. The extended
family gathered multiple times during the holiday, rotat-
ing from the Brett side, with myriad cousins, siblings, aunts
and uncles, then to the Manacek side, being especially close
to Charlie, Shelagh and Patty's Aunt Sue and Uncle Rudy
(Betty's sister and husband). All in all, the 1950's was a great
time to be a child, to grow up, to get an amazing education

and to form lifelong friendships. There was a pervasive innocence and simplicity of lifestyle and contentment; at least for the children.

Ostensibly, life was very good, but the idyllic sounding existence subtly shrouded a reality that was lurking quietly beneath the surface.

24

THE COLD LIGHT
OF HARSH REALITY

Some things were quietly occurring on a social and political level that would begin to set the tone for more radical changes during the 1960's. Greater acceptance of religious minorities was made manifest when, in 1950, Abe Ribicoff became the first non WASP, a Jew, to be elected Governor of Connecticut, then later became a United States Senator. The war in Korea had ended indecisively with a cease fire declared and the 38th parallel established as the border between North and South Korea. While never a declared war, the "Police Action" was costly in lives and treasure. Tensions between Communist China and the USA, and The Communist USSR and the USA, were increasing exponentially, precipitating the Cold War and nuclear weapons tests were conducted on both sides. This would create a huge growth in the construction of nuclear weapons and the concept of mutually assured destruction, meaning that a nuclear war would virtually annihilate both (or all) warring countries, was frequently addressed by politicians, world leaders and within the media. A Civil Defense Warning System was developed and Fall Out Shelters were clearly identified in most cities. Some people even constructed Bomb Shelters in their backyards, often times keeping them secret from their neighbors. While Civil Defense officials were speaking confidently of group shelters that could protect and accommodate up to 50 million people, anxiety ridden citizens in the suburban communities were taking matters into their own hands, spending from $100.00 to $5,000.00 on their own basic shelter, ranging to the extreme level of underground suites, having toilet facilities, food and medical supplies and telephone. Millions of comic books were distributed to school children, featuring a cartoon character named; 'Bert the Turtle' that coached them on how to "Duck and Cover" in the event of a nuclear blast. Newspapers carried daily radiation readings along with the weather report. This could all be terrifying to children and a fatalistic attitude could easily become the by-product.

During the early 50's, Pop Charts were dominated by remnants of Big Band Era vocalists like Frank Sinatra, Frankie Lane, Nat King Cole, Doris day and Rosemary Clooney. The R&B Charts were distinctly different and generally featured African-American artists performing music directed toward Black listeners in the urban centers and in the south. A Cleveland area DJ, named Alan Freed, became an exception with his 'Moondog Show' which played up tempo R&B mixed in to play lists, creating a fusion of musical styles such as Boogie Woogie, Jazz, Gospel, Country, Electric Blues and R&B vocals which morphed into the genre called "Rock and Roll". In 1953, Bill Haley and his Comets hit number 12 on the Pop charts with 'Crazy Man Crazy' and the Doo Wop group, 'The Orioles', had crossover success on the Pop charts with 'Crying In The Chapel'.

In 1955, Rock and Roll had it's first number one hit with Bill Haley and the Comets, 'Rock Around The Clock'. When RCA records buys out the contract of Memphis singer, Elvis Presley from SUN records, he hits number one with his first effort called 'Heartbreak Hotel'.

The elder Brett's, like many parents of the time, believed that Rock and Roll music was obscene and raucous and vigorously discouraged their kids from listening and felt quite chagrined when they were completely ignored. It had revolutionized music and there was no turning back. Some of Patty, Shelagh, Charlie, Jimmy and Billy's favorites were Frankie Avalon, Ricky Nelson, Fabian, Dion and the Belmonts, Paul Anka, Buddy Holly, Jerry Lee Lewis, The Platters, Chuck Berry, Fats Domino, The Platters and folk revivalists like The Kingston Trio.

On another entertainment front, the movie industry had been caught off guard and severely impacted by the growth of television and by the expansion of its quality programming. In addition, the senate subcommittee investigating "Un American activities" under the zealous leadership of Senator Joe McCarthy had an additional deleterious effect. Attendance and admissions were dropping nationwide during the early part of the decade, but in Danbury, the Empress and Palace theaters continued to thrive and were still a popular venue for entertainment. Toward the end of the decade, when the Brett children were entering puberty, the theaters were a hub for social congregating among young teenagers, many of whom experimented with their first awkward attempts at romance (a euphemism for necking) in the balcony during Saturday matinees. It became a place to hang out even if one wasn't actually going to the movie.

While most middle class and upper middle class kids were living a happy and almost idyllic existence, they were completely unaware that there was still plenty of evil, immorality, political corruption and deceit going on, usually kept far from their view. From marketers promoting smoking and drinking, to workplace sexual harassment, to homosexuals being ostracized and ridiculed, to racial bigotry, to organized crime activity, to cold war fears and anxiety over the potential for nuclear annihilation, there was plenty that would easily qualify as less than idyllic and certainly anxiety producing had they not been, at least to some extent, isolated from the grim reality; but the general parenting style of the 1950's was to keep children blissfully ignorant of "adult concerns".

One example of organized crime activity taking place near Danbury, and impacting Danbury indirectly, was orchestrated by a guy named Salvatore 'Midge Renault' Annunziato, a New Haven based mafia operative, who was a colorful former boxer who took the Renault part of his name from an older brother, Fortunato, who fought under the stage name, Jack Renault, and "Midge" because he was only 5' 3" tall and just over 100 pounds. "Midge" was proficient at getting kickbacks and bribes and to a large extent controlled trash hauling, much illegal gambling, engaged in loan sharking and labor racketeering. As a "business agent" for the state's only heavy equipment operators local, he made a fortune in kickbacks and bribes from workers and contractors.

He seemed to have relative impunity, but when he did spend time in jail, he didn't suffer the punishment much. Either his wife or local restaurants delivered his meals, he slept in the infirmary instead of a cell and had liquor smuggled in regularly. He would provide gambling for other inmates and sometimes guards would let him out for the night. The "Mob" also burrowed into legitimate businesses like used cars, restaurants, night clubs and produce. Anything that was illegal, seasonal or in short supply was fair game. Fireworks, Easter Flowers, grapes and watermelon all lined the mob's pockets. The 1950's was the heyday for the 'Mob' in Connecticut.

(Info on "Midge Renault" gleaned from a June 1, 2013 article in Connecticut Magazine by Chris Hoffman).

Troubling things on the world and national scene aside, life within the Brett's world was good. Most were successful in their own way and there was an intangible feeling of strength and pride derived from belonging to a large, cohesive, supportive family. John Sr. would have been proud to know that his and Mary's dream for his family had come to fruition. They were now an American family living the "American Dream". In 1955, at almost 80 years of age, Mary's health had been failing for a few years. She had high blood pressure, exacerbated by some weight gain and type two diabetes and severe arthritis. She seldom complained of her ailments but had become somewhat more vocal regarding her frustration over not being able to do the things she once could do. She tired easily and would withdraw into long periods of silence. She spoke of John more than usual, recanting memories of long ago and their early years together. Her adoring children and grandchildren tried to visit her more frequently, but busy lives often got in the way. She had always been there for them and it seemed as though she always would be. When she was hospitalized on May 6th of 1955, the reality that she might not always be there for them became apparent. She had developed great difficulty breathing and standing. Concerned and fearful of the outcome, her children gathered by her side. In the early morning hours of may 8th, she peacefully passed away. The matriarch who had guided, nurtured and supported her now large family, was gone. The courageous, steadfast, disciplined woman of wisdom and resolve, with an abiding love for her husband and family had gone to reunite with John. The soft weeping, gentle tears and quietly spoken prayers of those assembled at her side melded together to create a quiet mournful dirge, expressing admiration, affection and respect as much as sadness. It was a deeply emotional time and profoundly difficult for some to accept. The world of the Brett family had changed and the void would be difficult, if not impossible to fill.

Tragically, three months later, before anyone could recover from the loss of Mary, John and Mary's second daughter, Ann Crowley, who lived in Torrington, CT with husband, Christopher, passed away unexpectedly at 59 years of age. As families age and generations change, loss is to be expected, but Ann's passing came far too soon.

Life can throw curve balls and sadness; tragedy and loss can occur at any time. There are no guarantees.

Cook and Bertie had an exceptional relationship, perhaps made even stronger by the disappointment and sadness related to their inability to have children. The love that they might have invested in kids, seemed to have sublimated into a greater and more intense affection for each other. They were closest to Walt and Betty, but well admired and respected by the entire family. Cook was diversifying financially by investing in a Package Store, which is the term used for liquor store in Connecticut. He was also putting on a small addition to his home and spending a lot of time "sprucing it up", as he was fond of saying. He had been permanently employed by Kimberly-Stevens Corporation in New Milford as Head of Maintenance and would oversee installation of new infrastructure, which was a good use of his pipe fitting skills. The shift work provided daytime opportunities for his other projects.

Like most of the males in the family, he was a heavy smoker (as were many within society at the time) and although the connection between smoking and lung disease had been made, the marketing efforts of tobacco companies tried to convince consumers otherwise, and for the most part, it had been successful- either that or consumers were in denial and too weak to break the habit/ addiction once developed.

Compounding the problem was that some people apparently had the genetic makeup that somewhat inhibited the development of disease while others were highly susceptible. Shamelessly, those individuals having a greater resistance were used as examples for the purpose of disputing studies showing cause and effect. And ironically, many smokers themselves cited those very same examples. Rationalization at its finest. Unfortunately for Cook, he fell within the later category and was diagnosed with lung cancer in 1958. It was particularly virulent and taking a rapid toll on him. Knowing that he had received a death sentence, he didn't want his beloved Bertie to be subjected to the difficulties caring for him when be became debilitated and didn't want her to witness his deterioration. He instead wanted to be remembered as he was then; strong, vigorous and handsome. In June of that year, while in his prime of life, and while Bertie had gone shopping, he walked out into his backyard, sat on a wooded bench surrounded by recently planted flowers, and with difficulty, breathed in the crisp spring air and took in the beauty of his world. He regretted that Bertie would be traumatized by his actions, but when compared to the alternative, he felt that this would be best for her- and from a more selfish perspective, best for him. He said a brief prayer, bent over slightly, placing the stock of his 12 Ga. shotgun against the ground and the barrel in his mouth, stretched his arm, extending his reach to the trigger, paused, saying; "Forgive me Dear Lord and forgive me Bertie" and pulled the trigger.

Cook had hoped to spare Bertie from the horrors of watching him succumb to the disease, and the months of anguish by just getting it over with. It had quite the opposite effect. Not only was she severely traumatized by the discovery, she resented not being able to spend his final days caring for him. She became clinically depressed, profoundly despondent and after the conclusion of the funeral and interment, refused to eat, couldn't sleep and withdrew into the confines of her home. Not wanting to go on without him, her own health deteriorated rapidly and she died a mere two months after Cook's passing. The cause of death was undetermined and referred to as ambiguous.

Walt was devastated, as was the rest of the family. Cook had been a role model and stalwart. But for Walt, Cook was a father figure too. He was only 8 years old when John, Sr. had died. As the eldest son, John, Jr. (Cook) had stepped in, along with William, to act as surrogate Dad and he paid special attention to Walt. There were mixed emotions regarding the suicide but never the less, there was a somber, dark, gloomy and sorrowful mood and tenor pervading family gatherings for quite some time. But healing comes with the progression of time, and by the turn of the next decade, the family had re-grouped and was moving forward.

25

REMEMBRANCE AND BENEDICTION

With the heartbreaking and tragic loss of Mary, Ann Crowley, Cook and Bertie a number of years behind them, the family was gradually able to create a new normal, hopeful that the 1960's would be a better decade for the Brett family. With Rose McAllister and a few members of that part of the clan still residing at the family home on Fairfield Avenue, along with Rose's daughter Nancy, recently married to husband Jack, and their young and growing family, Henry and Walt felt that their unofficial inferred (or assumed) obligation to assist in the support of Mary and the family household had been fulfilled. That became a de facto raise in income, which was obviously more important to Walt than to Henry. With Charlie set to enter college in 1961, and Shelagh and Patty both now in high school, with plans of also entering college upon their graduation in 1963 and 1964 respectively, the extra money would come in handy.

Henry's kids, Jimmy and Billy, would also be graduating in '63 and '64, as well, but son Jimmy, although presenting good grades in Prep School, had decided that he would join the Air Force prior to making any decision, so that, in his words, "he would have the opportunity to travel and experience some adventure" before settling down to college life. Billy, on the other hand, was a wild card, and seldom thought that far in advance. For him, partying and procrastination was his life-style and his somewhat rebellious nature was obvious.

Charlie entered Danbury State College (which had recently changed the name from Danbury State Teacher's College and later to Western Connecticut State College in '67, then to Western Connecticut State University in 1983) seeking a degree in education. He was ambitious and traditional, while enigmatic. He was relatively popular during pre-puberty years, with a lot of male friends and play companions, but when those very same friends changed focus upon reaching puberty from outdoor activity and sports, bike riding and tree houses, frog catching and rock skimming, rather abruptly to members of the opposite sex, creating a macho and "cool" image, and developing an obsession with automobiles, Charlie seemed to suffer slightly from arrested development. He maintained friendships with them, but it was a more casual and less intimate friendship, seemingly having difficulty relating to their newly developed persona. The female friendships he had during high school were strictly platonic and he never had a high school sweetheart.

As he matured, he spent a great deal of time bowling at the Brewster Lanes, played poker frequently, hung out drinking beer and smoking cigarettes with his buddies and worked a part time job as a shoe salesman at Markoff Shoes. By mid Junior year, he had become quite bored with the college experience and the specific curriculum and decided to drop out at the end of the last semester. He commuted from home and never lived on campus, which tended to minimize social interactions, and worked as many hours as feasible which both added to the loss in interest. He was anxious to work full time and make more money. He went to full time status at Markoff's and actually seemed to like his work and the interaction with the public. One of the things he did with his new found independence was buy his own car; a new 1963 Corvair- a vehicle that Ralph Nader would later claim (in his 1965 book) to be "Unsafe at Any Speed".

Shelagh would have an average high school experience, gaining reasonably good grades, having some very close female friendships and a few "steady" boyfriends. Like Charlie, she was plagued with vision problems (although not nearly as bad as Charlie, who was profoundly near sighted) and wore Cat Eye shaped glasses. That, combined with a tendency toward weight gain, created a bit of a nerdy countenance but her friendly personality and dry sense of humor and sharp wit compensated and contributed toward her popularity. Upon graduation in 1962 she also enrolled at Danbury State College for the 1963 semester, and like Charlie, she chose a Major in Elementary Education. She too, commuted from home, but unlike Charlie she enjoyed it and followed through to receive a degree.

Patty was a good student and very popular. Puberty was kind to her and she matured to be sexy and attractive with a very active social life. She was short, at only 5 feet tall, and had a very attractive figure, weighing only 98 pounds. A bit of an iconoclast, she rejected the notion of cheerleading and sororities and marched to the beat of "her own drum". She was confident and self assured and seemed to be in complete control of her life. Many claimed that if one had an interest in becoming her boyfriend, he would need to get on a waiting list.

In 1962, Jimmy was completing his Senior year and Billy was in his Sophomore year at Danbury High School. Patty and Billy were in the same home room and shared some of the same classes.

The Brett family seemed happy, finally able to "move on" after the tragic losses of family members, were relatively prosperous and as closely knit as a family can be. They shared holiday celebrations, child rearing experiences, church, and even professional sports affiliations. Shelly would frequently visit from New York, often taking Walt's kids, especially Charlie, whom she tended to favor, to sporting events, to dinner in Manhattan or to plays. She would often come for Thanksgiving and Christmas holidays as well. Shelly had become quite out-spoken and opinionated and could sometimes ruffle feathers but she knew when to invoke the common sense adage, "dis-cretion is the better part of valor" and at worst she could be considered a temporary minor irritation. Some family mem-bers who had suspected the affair with Father Guy whispered the suggestion that her personality became a bit more harsh, with a slightly caustic edge, after the relationship had cooled and for all intents and purposes, ended, compounded by her increasing age and spinster status, as the cause and effect.

Minor irritations aside, the only time on record that she really pissed off Walt was when she had the (in Walt's words) "audacity to bring that damn dog with her" on one Thanksgiving holiday. She owned a Standard Poodle that she coddled and pampered and on that specific Thanksgiving, she was unable to find a kennel with a vacancy. Walt didn't like dogs and certainly wouldn't allow one in his house, and here she comes with a big, black, curly haired dog in tow. Even the many cats that they cared for were kept outside year round and never allowed in the house, come hell or high water. Shelly claimed that the dog was well behaved and would simply lay on the living room carpet, but Walt would have none of it and insisted that "the animal" be kept outside tied to a tree. When it barked incessantly, Walt became furious and abruptly got up from his easy chair, just before the turkey has finished roasting and exclaimed; "I can't take this anymore- I'm going to the El Dorado for dinner!" And that's exactly what he did- alone. It took months for her to be forgiven for that faux pas.

While Leona didn't visit Walt or Henry very much, she spent a good deal of time with Rose, the rest of the McAllister's, the Estes', and the Crowley's; but during the summer months,

Walt and Henry and their respective families frequently visited her at the lake. The kids loved Lake Candlewood and
the adults enjoyed Leona's hospitality. While the youngsters
were enjoying swimming, diving, canoeing and sunbathing,
the adults were enjoying Leona's bartending skill and cocktail recipe acumen. Leona had a distinct fondness for Martinis
but during the warm summers at her lake home, preferred
beer. Even though she was a frequent drinker, she wasn't
an alcoholic, or if she technically was, she was a highly functional one, and her drinking never interfered with her life in a
negative way. As a matter of fact, it might have provided ben-
eficial emotional and psychological relief from a past heart-
ache. She was a very well respected teacher and projected
a strongly conservative, straight laced persona at work but
during leisure time she enjoyed the company of intellectual
acquaintances, most of whom very successful and all shared
her enjoyment of adult beverages. She entertained frequently
and even with her diverse circle of friends, she never became
attached romantically to any of the single males within that
circle. While she was successful, financially secure and well
liked, and seemed content with her life, there always seemed
to be a hint of sadness and melancholy. One might easily conclude that the broken love affair back during her time in the
WAVES had traumatized her more profoundly than anyone
(including Leona herself) suspected and jaded her opinion of
men to the point where she was never able to find someone
whom she was able to trust or emotionally invest.

Like Shelly, she too became rather direct, opinionated and
slightly arrogant as she aged. Never the less, the family all
tolerated each other's imperfections and got along extremely
well.

Part Three

Choices, Pathways
and Transitions

"The bond that links your true family is not one of blood, but of respect and joy in each other's lives".

Richard Bach

25 (A):

A NECESSARY DIGRESSION

In September of 1961 I, the humble author of this narrative, entered the scene and became an integral part of the Brett family story. It was a defining moment in my life and would set the stage for a remarkable journey. I ask your indulgence as I continue to chronicle the life and times of the Brett family, with an abrupt change to more of a first person narrative style, at times seeming to shift to an autobiographical perspective. Having lived through the events right alongside the family since 1961, and after having had first hand experience, emotional connection and factual accuracy are intensified and improved. It is at the point where this bifurcation of perspective begins, that I felt it necessary to designate a Part Three of the saga. My story undeniably becomes an important part of their story. I'll begin by providing some personal background to provide perspective.

The history of my family was quite different from that of the Brett family. Like virtually all Americans, other than the native indigenous inhabitants of what we now call The United States of America, my family were immigrants. However, unlike more recent immigrants like the Brett's, my family tree has been traced back to one of the original Mayflower Pilgrims. On the paternal side, my grandmother was Irish and

English and had descended from a somewhat prominent family. She was a direct descendant of John Dickens, who was a Methodist Preacher serving as a "circuit rider", between the 1760's and 1770's, traveling on horseback in Northern North Carolina and Southern Virginia preaching the gospel in small town chapels and meeting houses. He later became close friends with Francis Asbury and actually named his first son, Asbury Dickens, after him. When he became too old to endure the sacrifice and challenges of traveling preacher, he was transferred from Halifax County, NC and assigned as pastor to a New York City Methodist Episcopal Church with his wife, Elizabeth (nee: Yancy). In 1789 he was moved to St. George's Methodist Episcopal Church in Philadelphia where he completed his career and is buried there, in the yard adjacent to the church. Their son, Asbury Dickens, became a publisher and bookseller, then, in 1836, became Secretary of the United States Senate until just prior to his death in 1861.

My grandfather was of French decent, and he too had been born into a somewhat noteworthy family. One of four sons (Max, Robert, Edgar and my grandfather, George), he was born in Connecticut and, like his siblings, raised by nannies, domestics and paid child caregivers. His mother was one of the earliest licensed female physicians in the state and when not actually practicing medicine, lectured extensively.

Their father was more focused on his business than family and wasn't at home any more than his wife. Upon coming of age, Max served as an officer in the Army Cavalry during World War One and later became a professor at the University of Illinois at Chicago. Robert became an early Vice President of AT&T and Edgar (called Ted) was a Certified Public Account and Stock Trader.

Grandfather George, however, was considerably less successful and tended to be hedonistic, a bit of a braggart and a unmitigated bull shit artist. He made his living selling insurance and had a fondness for liquor and women.

He and my grandmother married relatively young and lived in Manhattan, NY. He was thin, wiry and could be scrappy and pugnacious, and she was attractive and small of stature, while voluptuous, and often referred to as Black Irish due to her jet black hair, olive skin tone and dark colored eyes. They soon had two sons, my father being the eldest and his sibling, George, Jr., 3 years younger. My grandmother was stricken with Polio while the boys were still toddlers, and although it didn't prove fatal, it left her disfigured and semi-paralyzed on her left side.

The arm was twisted and incapable of being held straight and lacked dexterity and her leg turned inward and was slightly shorter than the other, which resulted in a limp with a pronounced dragging of her foot. Sounds somewhat grotesque but she was never the less, able to carry herself with dignity, and dare I say, grace, in spite of the disability. Fortunately, she was fully ambulatory and could get around reasonably well, considering the physical consequence of the disease, but climbing stairs and walking for long periods were out of the question. But, with that said, she felt blessed to be alive; many polio victims died. Unfortunately, her world came crashing down, not as a result of the disease, but due to marital collapse. My grandfather abandoned her and the two boys and ran off with the proverbial other woman while the boys were still toddlers. Unfortunately for her, she wasn't qualified for meaningful, gainful employment for a combination of reasons: obviously, her disability was physically limiting, but even more importantly, due to her early marriage, she hadn't attended college or developed any marketable skills. There were no social aid programs designed to assist women in her position, so in desperation, she identified the one thing that she could do well and market- she became a Nanny for wealthy New York families residing in the exclusive Upper East Side, many of whom expressing sympathy and empathy regarding her condition and generously hired her regardless of any potential physical limitations. Most, if not all, required a live in Nanny, which wouldn't provide accommodation for additional children. Therefore, my father's Uncle Ted (Edgar) and his wife Kate, graciously offered to become surrogate parents for the two boys. As young as the boys were, they were still considerably traumatized by the whole affair. They possessed a fair amount of affection for Uncle Ted and Aunt Kate, but being removed from their biological parents and moving to another home placed them under great stress. But, they adjusted reasonably quickly, and grew up in a nurturing but disciplined home.

Ted had his office on Wall St. and was the proverbial work-aholic, while Kate was a stay at home mother. For her, this was a dream come true (albeit, under less than desirable ini-tial circumstances), because of her desire for motherhood and her inability to bear children. She was well educated, well read and well traveled and played the piano beautifully and used her talents to provide a stimulating, well rounded childhood experience for the boys.

My father was brilliant, and during the years that he at-tended school, bright kids often would skip a grade to keep them challenged and prevent boredom. As a result, my father graduated High School at the age of 16. He attended CCNY (City College of New York) and selected a major in Economics and Accounting. He participated with a rowing team and played basketball.

When he wasn't on the Hudson River practicing rowing or on the court playing basketball, he was active with a Junior Masonic fraternity, called DeMolay. He also worked part time apprenticing at Uncle Ted's office gaining practical training. The DeMolay basketball team occasionally traveled for match-es, and during one such trip to the Catskill Mountain area of Upstate New York, he met my mother. She and a friend were in the crowd of spectators and she made a point of seeking him out during the post game social. He was immediately at-tracted to her and recognizing his interest, she turned on the flirtatious charm, while projecting an image of coy innocence. She was relatively tall, about 5'9", which was only an inch or two shorter than him, thin but shapely, blonde haired and blue eyed.

There must have been an attraction of opposites, considering that he closely resembled his mother's "Black Irish" features; curly black hair, dark skin tone, square jawed, but ironically, the blue eyes of his father. After the mutually intriguing, brief introductory meeting, he expressed an interest in seeing her again and she quickly agreed. It had been a fateful meeting, both parties desperately searching for some nebulous and not clearly defined solution to improving their personal situation. She was the product of a broken family, with three female siblings, raised primarily by her mother. Her father was a ne'er do well, who was an habitual gambler, part time house painter and for a time, owner of a bar/ roadhouse. He would come in and out of the girls lives frequently, but only for periods of short duration.

Now, having just turned 18 years of age, she was ready to escape the dead end life path of small town, Upstate New York, and was seeking a White Knight to ride in and whisk her away to the excitement, bright lights and sophistication of the big city. She began strategizing and contemplating ways to facilitate her escape and that strategy now included him.

He, on the other hand, was seeking a helpmate and partner who could not only provide the stable family environment he so badly wanted, but also to support him in his ambition. He had left the home that Ted and Kate provided, wanting, as most 18 year olds do, independence and freedom. He rented a furnished room near midtown and continued to work at Ted's office, commuting via subway, and attended college part time. He had been very focused and busy and had little time for a social life and was therefore suffering from a slight case of loneliness.

In their impetuous naivete, they identified each other as

the solution they had been seeking. They were wrong.

Their romantic relationship proceeded very quickly; uncommonly fast actually, considering that he had to commute from NYC to Catskill in order to date her, usually taking a bus or occasionally borrowing Ted's car. Her sense of urgency took over, and as she formulated her plan to escape the boredom and tedious monotony of Catskill, the strategy certainly didn't rule out pregnancy as a tactic to facilitate a rapid formalizing of a long term commitment, and sure enough, that first unplanned pregnancy moved the relationship to the marriage point with breakneck speed!

My oldest brother, Bob, was born in October of 1930, followed by brother Gene, in October of 1932. Raising children in Manhattan, especially during the Great Depression, was difficult and she became disillusioned with big city life, his inattentiveness and the demands of motherhood. She felt as though she had been beguiled by his flowery language when, during courtship conversations, he extolled the virtues and benefits of city living and she ultimately indicted him for taking advantage of her innocence. In actuality though, her mental image of big city life had been formed long before she met him. If he were guilty of anything, it was that he tended to validate her unrealistic, fantasy impression. But, assigning at least some degree of truth to her assertions, he was, after all, a young, virile male with raging hormones striving to impress this comely young woman he had just met.

But never the less, she heard what she wanted to hear and interpreted in a way to fit her personal needs. Exacerbating the problem was her growing bipolar disorder, punctuated with bouts of psychosis and hypochondria. She could become melancholy, passively angry and homesick, finally demanding a change in lifestyle. Within a few short years, they simply were not getting along well at all. She also tended to sublimate the negativity, frustration and mental angst by gaining comfort, pleasure and gratification from food, manifesting in weight gain and as a result, it deepened her bouts with depression. The once thin, yet curvaceous and sexually attractive woman he had married began gaining weight immediately after child birth and an episode of postpartum depression. While he never criticized, and for that matter, never found it unappealing, she personally let it negatively impact her self image and sense of self worth.

They argued frequently sometimes over trivial things, sometimes money, sometimes child rearing and sometimes simply because they were frustrated that the respective spouse turned out to be nothing like what they had wanted or expected, and before long they clearly didn't like each other very much. It then became a relationship fraught with hostility and resentment and existed only "for the sake of the kids"; which as justification for continuation, was an obvious red herring and clearly fallacious. They actually would feed off the constant conflict, and she especially, enjoyed playing the role of martyr. His opinion was that he could somehow change her.

Finally, as the boys were approaching puberty, and parents were hoping for an improvement in their relationship, they mutually decided to move to the suburbs and escape the rat race of Manhattan. They rented an older colonial styled farm house in Sommers, NY, complete with a large yard and even an outhouse (albeit, indoor plumbing had been installed and was fully functional) and he commuted to the city via train. The commute extended his day even more and he wasn't spending much quality time with the family. He was a very strict disciplinarian and Bob and Gene were just as glad that he now spent longer hours working.

Contrary to common belief, the move to the suburbs wasn't the panacea that they had hoped for and the relationship continued to qualify as a dysfunctional one, growing more so with the passage of time.

She began to become convinced that once the boys were grown and out of the house, an event that was obviously on the near horizon, he would divorce her and leave.

As bad as the relationship was perceived by her, it was all she had known for the past 15 years and it was better than being alone in her mid thirties, without means of support and no opportunities available. Her irrational thoughts put her in a panic mode and she ultimately came to the conclusion that another pregnancy would become a binding contract for securing a continuation of the relationship, at least for another 16 to 18 years. In addition, she wanted a daughter- (a girl through whom she might vicariously live her life over?)

When she made the announcement that she had become pregnant, he was surprised but took it in stride, also thinking that it might be good to have another chance at raising a child, perhaps doing it somewhat differently now that he had the experience. And interestingly enough, their relationship actually did improve during her pregnancy.

In late summer of 1946, I was born. My father was elated, my mother, not so much. She had desired a girl so much that she became pregnant again within a few months of having given birth. Eleven months after I was born, just over a month before my first birthday, she once again delivered a baby- correction; two babies! She delivered twins; a girl and a boy. They were delivered prematurely and therefore very small. The boy, named Michael, did not survive and passed away within a few days. My sister, Catherine, not only survived but thrived and grew to be a content, healthy child. Early summer of 1947 marked the "coda", concluding the first phase of the relationship, yet bringing it back to an earlier point for a new beginning. Sadly, that new beginning didn't start well and a confluence of unfortunate and tragic events precipitated life altering changes.

Her father (my grandfather) passed away at an early age (in his mid fifties) from an unknown stomach ailment. She wasn't close to him and really had only seen him sporadically during the previous 18 years, but never the less took it hard. When they traveled to Saugerties, in Ulster County, NY for the funeral, she was overcome with grief, using my father's words; "Coming unglued during the service", leaving him shocked by her over reaction.

The next loss heavily impacted my father. His Uncle Ted passed away from lung cancer. He was a only moderate smoker and yet it took his life prematurely.

During his illness, he took on fewer and fewer clients and handed over his largest account, National Baking Company, to my father. He would travel frequently to their various locations conducting audits and other various and sundry accounting tasks, fully expecting to turn it back over to Ted, hopeful that his health could be miraculously restored. An unrealistic expectation to say the least, but being the perennial optimist and in denial, didn't contribute to getting a grasp on reality. Ted, while not his biological father, was certainly his father figure and being his biological father's brother, shared the same DNA. With Ted's passing, Kate would sell the practice and my father could either work for the new owners or seek alternate employment. The choice would become easy however, when after suffering from chronic bronchitis for an extended period of time, he visited the doctor for a remedy and was told the obvious: Stop smoking (like Uncle Ted, he smoked moderately) and look for work out of an office environment, where you can be outside in the fresh air.

Clearly, Ted's death had been the result of smoking, even though many at that time wouldn't admit to it, so that part of the advice was a no brainer.

The other part wouldn't be so easily accepted. He was trained as a CPA and that's all he knew. He struggled with that part of the equation until the other shoe dropped and the third piece of the puzzle fell into place.

My mother had been working part time at the post office in town. She claimed that she needed to get out of the house for a while and the job would help her earn some of her own money.

My grandmother had moved in on a temporary basis in order to help out with the child rearing. According to my father's rendition of the story, some Federal Investigators approached him to inform him that there had been some pilfering of mail going on and that they had been doing an investigation for quite some time; perhaps years. Some mail appeared to have been opened and resealed, other mail had items of value removed and still other mail just disappeared.

They tactfully suggested that motivation might have been theft or it might have just been uncontrolled curiosity, snooping and being very nosey. They then indicated that the primary suspect was my mother. He was shocked. He knew full well that she was undisciplined in character and irrational in thought, but this was beyond the pale. He was incredulous, but deep down inside he knew that there might be some truth in the allegation. To make a long story short, he ended up cutting a deal whereby full restitution was made along with loss of her job, in return for not litigating.

Based upon this trifecta of life altering events, he made the decision to leave small town Sommers, where the rumor mill was running rampant, reinvent himself with a new job and move to far upstate New York where the air was fresh (except for the smell of cow manure) and the people where friendly and not judgmental. The work situation left him in a bit of a quandary but he had a eureka moment when it came to him that he could approach his old friends at National Baking Company to see what they might have to offer- calling in a marker, if you will.

They responded by saying that the only opportunity available was that of a route driver, delivering baked goods to stores and restaurants as well as door to door home delivery, which was common in those days. Before long, we were reestablished in Johnsonville, NY renting a half of a farmhouse that had been converted into a duplex. Bob and Gene hated it there and soon Bob enlisted in the Marine Corps. Unfortunately, the Korean War was getting under way and after Basic training, that's where he would end up. Gene wasn't far behind and as soon as he was of legal age, joined the Navy. Having her sons in the military didn't help my mother's emotional state at all, and she expressed her anxiety by lashing out at my father, blaming his parenting style and the move for their desire to enlist as soon as of legal age. The bickering and fighting continued with renewed vigor. My sister and I shared a bedroom upstairs that was heated only through an open vent above the kitchen. The heat from the lower level, combined with the heat generated in the kitchen from cooking and baking would convect upward through the open vent, providing a little warmth for the room. We would frequently spy through the vent and could easily see the goings on downstairs, especially at the kitchen table. But our clandestine spying did little more than cause stress and anxiety due to exposure to their constant arguing, many times while seated at the table- starting as a discussion but always degenerating into full blown argument.

My father worked extremely long hours leaving very early in the morning to go to the distribution center and load his truck, then drive his route to arrive at the stores and restaurants before opening time, then segue into the door to door portion of his route. Then he'd drive back to the distribution center, clean out the truck and reconcile his books, often not returning home until well after dark. During one of those long days during the dead of winter, he stopped to buy groceries on his way home. My mother didn't drive, and even if she did, we had no car at home for her to use, so he would be responsible for shopping the majority of the time. He also didn't trust her with money so if she did go shopping, he was with her. That infuriated her as much as anything. After purchasing groceries from her list, he returned to the truck (it was a Chevrolet panel delivery) and headed home.

Not only were the roads icy, but he was exhausted from a

very long day and beginning to doze off, catching himself before actually falling asleep at the wheel. The combination of an ice patch and one of those head nodding episodes caused him to veer off the road, climb an embankment and flip the truck over. A State Trooper brought him home none the worse for wear, showing only bruises and some small lacerations and a damaged ego. My mother seemed more concerned for the loss of the groceries than for his well being and the following morning I accompanied him back to the crash site to help retrieve the salvageable canned goods. Even though he was in a somber and solemn mood, I was having fun, as though it was a treasure hunt. I had visions of discovering some wonderful baked goods from the product that he sold. Maybe a box of cookies or a chocolate cake, but no such luck. He had been to the distribution center first, cleaned out all the "day old" items for sale at the thrift store, and had gone shopping with an empty truck. Bummer!

All I was finding was canned goods. But four year olds have a way of turning something like that into a game and each time I would discover a can that had been scattered among the tall grass, brush and brambles, I would exclaim: "Got one"! Expecting a congratulatory "atta boy" that never came.

A few months after the "great grocery scattering episode" my sister and I were awakened very early one Monday morning by my mother. It was still very dark but I could vaguely hear my father's truck driving off in the distance, so I'm guessing it must have been around four-thirty in the morning. He tended to leave earlier on Mondays in order to take care of some additional preparation for the week ahead. My mother immediately made the announcement that "we were taking a trip". She followed that confusing and rather surprising statement by instructing us not to make any noise and be as quiet as a church mouse, indicating that we certainly didn't want to awaken the neighbors in the unit next door. She normally wasn't an early riser and in retrospect, I'm sure she didn't want to arouse suspicion and alert the neighbors to the un-characteristic and unusual goings on. Remaining somewhat groggy and sleep deprived from what seemed to us a middle of the night awakening, we moved pretty slowly, frustrating her and causing her to become irritable and testy. We eventually got dressed, Cathy taking much longer than I, and she had us help her pack a few clothes in a tattered old suitcase and some additional items in a large shopping bag.

We went to the kitchen and had a full breakfast, which again, in hindsight, seems strange being that she was obvious-ly functioning with a sense of urgency. We didn't understand it at the time, but I assume she was making sure we would be well fed for the long trip. When we finally finished breakfast, she tossed a few snack items and bananas into the shopping bag and quickly ushered us to the back door. She was getting more tense by the minute and kept looking at her watch and glancing at a folded piece of paper, which I'm guessing was a bus schedule. Leaving the dishes on the kitchen table exactly where they sat, without so much as placing a single item in the sink, she hustled us out the back door reminding us to be very quiet and not speak a word until she said it was okay.

Exiting the rear entrance, we rounded the side of the house opposite the neighbors, hastily walked down the dirt driveway to the gravel road adjacent to the house, then after walking about an 8th of a mile, to a paved county road where we walked another, much longer distance to the bus stop. To me, it seemed like an interminable hike, mainly due to the fact that I had to carry the satchel with our clothes while she carried Cathy, now whimpering and complaining, part of the way. I was relieved to have arrived at the bus stop and even more pleased that the early spring sun was beginning to rise. We waited in the silence of the cool fog and misty morning air for quite a long time, which to a four or five year old, seemed like an eternity. By now, the sun was fully above the horizon, dew was glistening off the surface of the moist grass and weed patches, causing steam vapor to rise from the surface of the ground; while the silence was occasionally interrupted by the sounds of chirping birds, rustling of squirrels, foraging wood-chucks or some other undefined critter slowly making its way through the bulrushes growing in a soggy hollow across the street, all becoming active and welcoming the day.

There peaceful sounds were intermittently punctuated by the faint "hiss" or "whoosh" of a passing car off in the dis-tance on an intersecting highway or by Cathy's occasional soft whimpering and crying. I'm not sure if it was due to be-ing awakened so early or because she was frightened by the strange proceedings. It was about twenty minutes later that I could detect the unique and unfamiliar sound of the diesel engine powering the bus, faint at first, but intensifying to a roar as it approached, becoming a cacophonous crescendo as the air brake engaged with a loud hiss bringing the monstrous Greyhound 'Silverside' coach to an abrupt stop.

Frightened by it all, I thought of a dream, a nightmare ac-tually, wherein a monster, (who probably resided under my bed) made similar frightening sounds while trying to decide if I would become its next meal. I clearly remember the graphic image of the racing Greyhound emblazoned on the side of the massive passenger conveyance, which pleased me and helped mitigate the anxiety slightly.

The bi-fold door opened and we hesitantly followed our mother's lead, stepping into the mouth of the beast, as would be lambs following a Judas goat. Exacerbating the palpable fear level were the passengers. Some dozed, heads propped against small pillows resting against windows or tilted rear-ward against the seat backs, while others stared blankly out the windows, trance like and appearing semi conscious, as though hypnotized by the rhythmic sound and motion and the inner thoughts produced by feeling alone while surrounded by other people, and finally, the most intimidating were those staring straight ahead, zombie like, fixing their penetrating gaze upon us.

I didn't like them or being stared at and felt very uncomfortable and wondered if they were going to the same place we were going or if any of them even knew where we were going. Then, the anxiety and fear became tempered by a flush of excitement as the door closed, sealing us from the cold and dampness in this giant womb like capsule, enclosed where it was quiet and warm, and then with a hissing release of the brake, the bus jerked and lurched ahead. As Cathy and I settled into our shared seat, our mother took a small blanket out of the bag and covered us, attempting to make us comfortable and relaxed, and I began to imagine some really nice, surprise destinations were we might end up- like the beach or an amusement park or the big city, but then I grew very tired and fell into a deep sleep; and memory fades. I think I slept all the way to our destination point, four hours away.

I never did figure out how we landed in Danbury, Connecticut, in a run down duplex apartment on a dead end street called Chichester Place, but it sure was a disappointment- clearly nothing like the big city, an amusement park or the beach! The bottom line is that we were there simply because she wanted to finally leave our father, and facilitated this poorly planned departure without giving adequate thought to a means of support once she made her exit. We lived next to a family named Flynn and they were extremely welcoming and friendly considering that we had just showed up out of the clear blue, so I suspect that there's much more to the story than I'll ever know, but they took us under their wing and were helpful and supportive from day one.

About two months in, the adventure took a freaky turn. My mother, in her inimitable style, assembled the host family, along with Cathy and I, for an announcement of grave importance. She sat in a large upholstered chair, with the Flynn family seated around her on the sofa and side chairs, Cathy and I seated on the floor in front of her, and quite dramatically and emotionally, with her theatrical flair, disclosed that a lump had been discovered....a "tumor" that would likely take her life. Without disclosing where, or how the discovery had been made, the impact of the announcement had elicited the shock reaction that she had desired and all were visibly distraught. Personally, I wasn't quite sure exactly what she was saying other than she would probably leave us as orphans. Pretty scary stuff. In reality, she was fine, but she thrived on this kind of attention and the drama she created and this first, of many similar incidents, only signifies the first occasion that I can remember but the pattern would repeat itself over the next 35 years. I'm no psychoanalyst but I came to the conclusion that she could only feel loved if she were perceived to be sick. I'm convinced that it is the result of her childhood experience and rearing, when her father would only come to visit when one of the children were sick, and during those visits she would be given special attention, affection and treats and it had been a conditioned part of her personality since she was very young. Later, as an adult, she would in some cases find a medical professional who would be complicit, and she had numerous surgeries and operations, the necessity of some of which I now question. If it could come out, she wanted it out. Appendix, gall bladder, uterus, ovaries, tonsils, adenoids, benign growths, you name it! For as long as I could remember she presented herself as being not well, demanding pity and sympathy, implying that she could die at any moment. As time went on, she got better and better at playing the part, proclaiming her imminent demise.

In fact, she wasn't well but her sickness was more mental than physical. She enjoyed playing the tragic heroine, analyzing the shock effect her "spells", as she called them, would have on her audience, performing as though she were starring in some 'B' grade film or TV soap opera, frenetically working on the emotions of all who would listen or observe, then forget the episode and move on to the next health crisis creating the next chapter in her victim narrative. It got pretty crazy from that point and by the time Cathy and I were preteens, labeling the family as dysfunctional would be a gross understatement.

I could write a book on the experience growing up in that severely dysfunctional household and how I was able to overcome the negative impact, get my life's trajectory on track and achieve success in spite of it all- and as a matter of fact, I did. My first book was a memoir outlining the experience, learning ways to change life's direction, figure out ways in which to extract benefit from adversity and redirect as necessary to create a life of value and meaning. I have digressed from the narrative of the Brett family solely to provide important perspective, the need for which will become evident as I continue in future chapters.

Once my mother had frightened the crap out of Cathy and me with her swan song, she totally ignored it and acted as though it was never said. Ironically, I believe that she realized a few months after her departure from Johnsonville that she had screwed up and became desperate to reconcile. I'm not sure whether my father tracked us down or if someone contacted him providing our where about's, but he showed up a week or two after the Sawn Song announcement and the next thing I knew, we were living in a small, top floor apartment on Moss Avenue adjacent to Londa's mattress factory. That's where I lived when I started school and walked to Balmforth Avenue to attend kindergarten and First grade. I hated it. Being the new kid, I became the object of bullying and got beat up regularly on my way home. I befriended two brothers, named "Johnny Boy" and Larry, both of whom had a proclivity toward trouble making. When I began to mirror their behavior my parents became concerned and began looking for a better environment to raise kids. When "Johnny Boy" and I stole some matches and decided to play with them while hiding under some evergreen trees along side the front entrance to the building, and ended up igniting them causing a fire that could have potentially burned the building down, they got more serious about making a move. When my father left Upstate New York to reunite with us, his was able to quickly find another route delivery job, this time for a Bridgeport based baking company called Bork and Stevens. He was doing well with the job but their marital relationship sank to an even lower level. His frustration with her escalated to a point where he could no longer control his emotions very well and became physically abusive. During one highly animated argument he picked up a steak knife and threatened her with it, causing Cathy and me to scream in terror. Johnny Boy's father overheard the commotion, entered the apartment through the partially opened front door and disarmed him. He left the house in a fit of anger, and returned two days later. Upon his return, they cast a nasty look at each other but neither spoke a word and life continued as though nothing had happened.

I had overheard them talk of moving and wished with all my being that it would happen soon. The summer after first grade was miserable. After the fire starting incident, and another where we placed a cat in an abandoned ice box that had been discarded in the back yard, inadvertently suffocating it, I wasn't allowed to play with the neighbor kids and spent a lot of time inside.

I recall one particularly unpleasant evening, sitting on the living room floor sweating and whining about the heat, playing with some coins that I had been given to keep me quiet and temporarily amused. As little kids will sometimes do, and for no logical reason, I placed a penny in my mouth and accidentally swallowed it. Frightened, I let out a yelp. My father quickly grabbed me by the ankles, turned me upside down and shook. As I think back, it seemed like a pretty lame reaction but miraculously it worked, and the penny fell out. Relieved, I must have chuckled about it for 15 minutes. Everyone else was pretty amused too.

But on most days, the unpleasantness of the oppressive

heat created by poor interior ventilation, the noise from the incessantly barking dogs and sometimes drunken neighbors, the bickering, tension and anger between my parents and the squalor of the surroundings made for a really bad summer. During some of those hot, sultry summer afternoons, I would sometimes lay on my bed directly in front of one of the humming fans, listening to the street noise through the open window, enjoying the breeze on my sweat dampened body, contemplating the white noise silence created by the harmonious blended drone of the combined street noise, running appliances, TV background sounds, and distant chatter of occupants of other apartments; occasionally punctuated by manufacturing sounds emanating from the mattress factory. The frustration was mounting and I wanted out in the worst way.

26

THE BLESSED RELIEF OF A CATHARTIC MOVE

When I learned of our plans to relocate to a bucolic little neighboring town called Brookfield, I was elated. During the week prior to the move, we all piled into our 1949 used and abused Kaiser- Frazer four door sedan to drive up to the country to view our next home. It was a very cute Cape Cod styled house with a large yard, knotty pine paneled walls in the living room, nice large brick fireplace, an arched entry way into the small dining room, a galley kitchen, two bedrooms and one bath, unfinished attic and basement. My parents created a bedroom in the attic, leaving a bedroom for Cathy and one for me downstairs. Even at the tender young age of seven, I could perceive, or at least become hopeful, that this might usher in a period of at least some semblance of normalcy for the family. We moved what meager furniture and possessions we owned into the house very quickly and in September, Cathy entered first grade, I entered second, at Brookfield Consolidated School. I loved it. I quickly made friends with the many boys in my neighborhood, while Cathy remained a homebody and became even more introverted. From all outward appearances, we projected the image of an average middle class American family, albeit my father, being a city boy and unaccustomed to home maintenance or yard work, allowed the house to deteriorate and seldom mowed the grass or trimmed shrubs or hedges, causing more than a little irritation among neighbors, most of whom were home owners, not renters. In addition, in my father's defense, he worked very long hours, including Saturdays, and had little free time for yard care.

Because my mother didn't drive, she remained homebound and seldom ventured out except when my father would drive her to the grocery store each Friday evening after work. That represented her outing for the week. They never dined out, socialized, participated in any recreational activities, other than the once or twice per month Sunday afternoon ride in the country. Our father would faithfully take us to church each Sunday, but our mother, being of a different religion, and frankly not at all motivated to attend, never went. After church, he would come home, read the paper (The Herald Tribune), drink coffee (he was a coffee addict, drinking it with every meal and consuming up to 6 to 8 cups per day) and listen to classical music on the phonograph, while she prepared Sunday dinner, which was usually served around 2:00 PM.

She strongly disliked his Sunday leisure time routine, for reasons I could never figure out or understand. There was a minimum of conversation, which was usually a blessing due to the strong likelihood that it would degenerate into an argument. I disliked Sundays and hoped they would pass as quickly as possible, hoping that the day would end without a fight. But, I was able to cope the same way I coped with my mother's crazy behavior during the week; I escaped by going outside, playing with friends or playing in the nearby woods. Out of sight, out of mind.

Unfortunately, for all the outward appearance of relative normalcy, my mother was sinking deeper and deeper into depression and Bi-Polar Paranoid Schizophrenia. Her weight gain had reached morbid obesity levels, reaching well over 300 pounds. She became obsessed with daytime soap operas, watching one after another. I would often come in from the yard to get a drink or a snack and find her weeping over a dramatic scene, or shouting at the villain as though she were present on the set. Other times I would discover her self mutilating, making small cuts on her arms or legs or pricking herself with darning needles. Sometimes after viewing certain tragic events on "her shows", she would try acting them out in her own life, especially if they included some sort of illness. But on the positive side, she would be able to remove herself from that dark place from time to time, and would seem to be on the mend and making progress, unfortunately only to slide back a while later. In retrospect, I can't help but wonder if the mental state was directly caused by the relationship or whether it was more organic and biological in nature. Either way, it was unpleasant and I coped by becoming cynical and sarcastic, and proficient in avoidance techniques. I became skillful in detecting the imminent arrival of one of her crazy episodes and developed ways to escape before the onset, thereby depriving her of an audience member. Poor Cathy was subjected to virtually every one. And because these bouts with her demons would ebb and flow with predictable regularity, by the time 1960 came around, avoidance became second nature to me. I clearly recall an hour in the winter of '60, when the rising tension was palpable and my internal Richter Scale was indicating that a quake followed by an emotional tsunami was probable and imminent. It seemed that I had two options: Either gird my loins, do some deep breathing exercises, engage in some transcendental meditation and psychologically prepare for an almost certain onslaught, or somehow facilitate another clandestine escape from the harsh reality of the chaos that would soon come to pass within the confines of our dysfunctional home. As usual, I chose the later. With the well practiced stealth and sharply honed avoidance technique of a veteran Cold War Soviet Spy, I rather adroitly, if I do say so myself, secured my winter coat, balled it up tightly, surreptitiously stashing it under my arm, and slipped out the rear entrance of our modest little home. The house was located on a meandering little country road called 'Rabbit lane' and about a mile from one of my favorite locations-A secluded place where I could often find blessed relief from the difficult to comprehend and patently irrational behavior that would periodically engulf our home like a dark, cold and ominous fog.

Once outside, I discovered a partly sunny day, just slightly overcast, with the long afternoon shadows of a mid-winter January thaw and diffused sunlight casting an ethereal glow upon my welcoming outdoor world of delicious freedom; the sun's warming rays were comforting enough to almost eliminate the need for my winter coat. I walked rapidly down our lane and as I turned left at the intersection of the wider, yet sparsely traveled state road, I eased the pace slightly and began to relax, thinking that my escape had once again been successfully executed.

After walking about a half mile, I turned right onto another country road that had recently been bustling with construction activity resulting from the new found popularity of our quaint little town. I was quite disturbed by it all, fearing that it would eliminate the seclusion and pastoral privacy, and it would soon be taking over my refuge. But for now, ample acreage from this abandoned grazing land remained, largely due to its close proximity to fairly steep and very rocky terrain, rendering it difficult to excavate in preparation for housing construction, and also due to some adjacent high voltage power lines and tower grids. Still safe from progress and development and still, for the time being, my personal oasis. I walked past the first of two subdivisions, which were still separated by this private retreat, or what I liked to call my meditation zone, turned the corner and came upon my favorite meadow. It was a long grassy incline, and while the grass was brown and dry from seasonal dormancy, it was high and there were numerous rock clusters, apparently stacked by farmers who might have moved them to improve grazing. A few saplings had also sprung up due to the recent discontinuation of grazing and from neglect; with the unknown owner probably assuming that it would only be a matter of time before some over zealous builder would make them an offer to purchase that they couldn't refuse anyway, so why bother keeping it cleared? A well worn path extended from the bottom of the meadow to the top in a semi-circuitous arch, then turned sharply left, continuing through some thicket and brambles toward the home of a friend. The path was used regularly by both him and me when traveling to and from each other's house, which contributed to the well trodden appearance. At the top was a flat, dense forest area, which had seemingly evolved half way between the pine- oak cycle, and therefore having an almost equal mix of balsam pines, hemlocks and spruce on the coniferous side of the equation and young oaks and maples on the deciduous side. The co-mingled scents of the pungently fragrant evergreens and the decaying leaves from the deciduous trees were in delightful juxtaposition and had a distinctly relaxing, therapeutic effect. Approximately half way up the meadow were some hollowed out areas where it appeared that some mysterious digging had taken place many years prior. Now they were grass covered with a thick layer of pine needles deposited within the hollows by the breeze, with the pine needles lining the bottom like cushions. A few years earlier, I would play war with some of my friends, using these hollows as pretend foxholes, hunkering down and firing our toy guns at each other. Now, however, I would use their safety and protection from a more real threat to my psyche that only this obscurity could provide.

I loved sitting in them for long periods of time, reclining against the south facing slope, contemplating and enjoying the silence. I was somewhat protected from the cool, albeit unseasonably moderate breeze for January, yet could hear it moving, gently caressing the tall blades of grass, as the winter rye, perennial fescue and tall wheat grass would sigh and whisper, as though faintly singing with pleasured gratitude, happy to have been gracefully animated with dance like movement, and indebted to the wind for the motion assist. It had been one of those unusual, relatively snowless winters thus far, so the grasses were still standing erect and tall, reaching worshipfully toward the unseasonably warm winter sun.

I would remain here as long as possible, enjoying the measured solitude, the sounds of nature, , the delightful scents of pine, grass and leaves, while suppressing my fear of the crazy behavior on exhibit at home and planning my permanent escape in the not too distant future. But for now the gauntlet remained, and it was already time to return to the house, hopeful that I had timed my disappearance accurately enough to have avoided the full fury of the storm and would return to witness only the aftermath.

My escape and avoidance techniques, along with my self imposed emotional isolation worked well enough to create a reasonably happy life while I lived on Rabbit lane. I liked my friends, liked school, got decent grades, enjoyed scouting, camping and playing sports. Pretty much a normal childhood, in spite of the severely dysfunctional family life. My father was in denial and kept believing that things would magically change. He continued working long hours, probably as much to stay away from home as to get ahead financially. But getting ahead financially wasn't in the cards. My mother had very poor discipline and even though she didn't drive, she was able to connect with a few friends with similar "issues" who did drive and was able to get out a little more frequently and shop, spending money that we didn't have. She was also a mail order shopper, sometimes compulsively. Of course when bills arrived that she couldn't intercept or hide, and when my father discovered that she had incurred large debt, more arguing and fighting ensued. In spite of it all, I tried to remain oblivious and was a pretty contented kid.

That began to change at the end of 1960 when we again moved; this time to an old farmhouse with acreage called 'Long Lane Farm'. My father decided that he could put the land to good use by raising chickens, creating a route for selling the eggs, raising a few head of cattle and planting a large garden, none of which he knew how to do. I hated the place. It was run down, isolated, near the foul smelling and highly polluted Still River and the kind of place where I didn't want to bring friends. I felt ostracized, resentful and angry. Feeling the full effects of puberty didn't help either. I wanted a social life and instead got chores around the "farm", primarily being completely responsible for tending the 100 plus chickens, two steers and half acre of vegetables. In addition, on two days per week during the summer, I would work with my father on his egg route. By 1961 I had become rebellious, sullen and a general wise ass. My mother's mission in life was to get her children to hate our father and she had great success playing me against him. When we spoke at all it was terse and sarcastic.

When I obtained my driver's license things got worse. I would leave the house for days at a time, hang with friends who were almost as troubled as me; smoking, drinking alcohol and creating mischief.

During that summer I stopped taking care of farm chores, so as a result, he butchered the steers and killed off the chickens and let the garden go to seed, creating more resentment and animus. I spent the majority of the summer with friends at the lake and during the winter I hung with friends who had cars, some of which were bona fide Hot Rods and most of whom had a fondness for trips "over the line" to New York State bars and getting inebriated; and minor trouble making was usually part of the itinerary.

By the fall of 1961, starting the '61- '62 school year, the kids from Brookfield were bussed to Danbury. Brookfield had yet to grow large enough to warrant its own High School. Brookfield's Longmeadow Junior High included 7th, 8th and 9th grade only, and for Sophomore year we attended DHS. It was quite a culture shock, going from a Brookfield Freshman Class of about 34 to a DHS Sophomore Class of hundreds. By this time I had been labeled a miscreant by many authority figures and had perfected my 'rebel without a cause' persona to an art form. I must admit that I had a pretty bad attitude. On the first day of school, my father drove me in his VW Microbus because I had missed the school bus. I searched around the unfamiliar building, clearly lost and at a disadvantage compared to the students who had completed their Freshman year there, until I located my home room and arrived there a few minutes late, which clearly irritated my home room teacher and didn't make a stellar first impression. She handed out some paperwork and forms to be filled out, and I asked her for a pencil. Apparently that wasn't wise thing to do because she severely chastised me for coming to school on the first day without, in her words, so much as a pencil, notebook or the amount of sense that God gave to a goldfish. After glaring at me for a minute or so, she announced to the class that "Mr. Lack of Preparation" had come to class without a writing implement and could anyone kindly lend him something so he can get the paperwork filled out before we adjourn and head to first class?"

My digression can now loop around to an earlier point in this narrative, hopeful that the relevance of that digression, which was primarily intended to add perspective and explain the Brett family's reluctance to offer acceptance to yours truly, will later be understood.

Patricia Brett raised her hand and said; "I'd be happy to lend him a pencil". She was seated diagonally behind me and when I turned to see who was connected to that sweet voice, I was simultaneously intrigued and pleased. My mind's eye perspective of the ideal female had just offered me a pencil! I still remember what she was wearing, her sexy walk, her coy and alluring smile and her confident demeanor. I thought to myself; "that's the cutest girl I have ever seen". She was short and perky, wearing a white blouse with a Peter Pan Collar, pink culottes that accented her perfect little ass and what was then called a "virgin pin" affixed to her collar.

I can only assume that it was called such, either simply because it was intended as an arbitrary declaration of virginity or because it resembled a hymen in shape. Apparently, if it were worn on the left side, it indicated that the wearer hadn't yet done the deed, and if switched to the right side, or removed completely, it signified that virginity had been lost. In those days no one was bold enough or honest enough to wear it on the right side! Discretion was more common. But for most, it was just a simple piece of popular jewelry and the wearer attached no particular meaning other than to get the boys wondering about the veracity of the implied declaration. Either way, I suspect that it wouldn't be very popular today. Her hair was cut medium short and had wavy curls and her eyes were intensely green. If there is such a thing as love at first sight, I was completely stricken. Throughout that entire school year, I would make a point of striking up brief conversations during the home room period and in the halls during change of classes, but as friendly as she was, I could plainly tell that she was just being cordial and flirty by nature, and was attached to a steady boyfriend. But, I wasn't prepared to give up.

We didn't share any of the same classes, so I seldom saw her any other times, except when I would observe her riding with her close friend, Shirley, who owned a little Nash Metropolitan (the Lois Lane car) as she would arrive to school in the mornings. The morning ritual consisted of being dropped off a block from the campus so that no one would see me arriving in something a nerdy as a VW bus (it wasn't until much later in the sixties that it would become a "cool" hippy icon of counter culture transportation- if ya see me rockin', don't come a knockin'), I'd exit the vehicle without saying so much as "see ya later" to my father, knowing that he'd be glaring at me with his ever so ineffective "you better get your shit together and stop wasting your life look" while I adroitly ignored his presence. From there I'd walk down to a little cafe called 'The Spa', for a cup of coffee and a buttered round of Syrian bread to go, then walk two blocks back to the corner of White Street and 5th Avenue to stand on the corner adjacent to the high school building with fellow loitering malcontents, talking trash, smoking cigarettes, drinking coffee and watching with envy as students privileged enough to have hot cars and obscenely nice rides rumbled by. My car at the time was a 1954 Buick that wasn't dependable enough to use as steady transport, so I continued to rely on the unpleasant VW Van ride to school with my lecturing father. But the routine would usually extend from early September until the snow started flying and it became too uncomfortable to stand outside for thirty minutes before class. My primary motivation, aside from making myself envious of the privileged pricks driving cars I could only dream about, hanging with other miscreants, getting my caffeine and nicotine fix before the class room imposed abstinence began, and expressing my displeasure regarding the structure and discipline associated with student life, was to catch a glimpse of Patricia as she and Shirley would arrive. Like some dyed in the wool stalker, I would immediately bolt toward the rear entrance, which was used by those entering from the parking lot, hopeful to intercept them before they got inside and wishing for a few minutes of conversation before the bell would ring. My success rate ran about 25%.

One particular individual who contributed to my envious automobile lust was Patricia's cousin Billy. Henry and Betty R would bestow lavish gifts on both Billy and Jimmy, and on Billy's sixteenth birthday, they provided him with a red 1960 Oldsmobile convertible.

It was gorgeous and I was so damn jealous! Billy was in

the same class as Patricia and I, but was almost a year older. Unlike his more studious and serious brother, Jimmy, he was a bit rebellious and iconoclastic. He neglected his studies, wanted to party constantly, thoroughly enjoyed drinking and hung out with friends of generally a lower socio-economic class. He was a class clown and cut up in school and could be slightly disrespectful of teachers. He had many black friends during a time when it was less common for close inter-racial friendships. And they weren't the popular athletes, scholarly types or children of doctors or lawyers either, they were the black kids coming from the less privileged neighborhoods. But for whatever reason, they seemed to relate well and develop genuine friendships. Henry and Betty were permissive and tolerant of his overall behavior and seldom provided stern discipline, nor did they chastise severely for his lack luster grades.

He was very popular in High School and friendly to everyone. He was handsome, well dressed and well liked, even by teachers, in spite of the fact that they knew that he was lazy and could do better academically. He wasn't brilliant, but he wasn't stupid either and should have been a 'B' student not a 'C' student. But Billy was witty, charming and deep and had an "old soul" that shined through like a charismatic glow, and it was that charisma that was responsible for his popularity. Billy and I never became friends during high school, simply because there was little opportunity for it, but rather, casual acquaintances, who would talk and joke in the halls, share a contraband cigarette in the boys room, and have lewd conversations about "fast girls" within the Sophomore Class.

It was in January of 1962 that I clearly remember sitting in homeroom, dreading another boring and tedious day, doodling 'Rat Fink' cartoon cars on my note pad, when the principal entered the room with a serious and solemn look on his face, and as he approached our homeroom teacher, he bent over, whispering in her ear. She too, then took on a very serious and emotionally tense look, nodded her head in understanding and motioned for Billy to approach her desk. Billy's desk was front row, diagonally to the right of the teacher, while mine was almost the last row, to the left, so I could overhear very little of what was spoken. All I could make out were the words "father" and "Sorry" and as Billy was led by the principal from the classroom, I noticed that tears had welled up in his eyes and that he was shaking. As curiosity was getting the best of us, many of his fellow classmates were intending to ask Patty if she knew what was happening once the bell rang indicating that it was time for us to adjourn for the first class. But before anyone was able to approach her she exited without pausing for any questions and headed directly to the principal's office. Being family, she obviously knew more of the story. Henry had been diagnosed with lung cancer just a few months earlier and the disease had taken him quickly. His heart had given out before the actual disease could claim him, which might have been a blessing. Never the less, family always hopes for the best and optimistically prays for a cure, or perhaps even a miracle, so it came as a shock when Henry passed so quickly.

James Henry (J. Henry) Brett was a well known and respected business man, worked with the volunteer firemen's groups and the Knights of Columbus and a member of the Elks Lodge. He was a beloved father and husband and the loss had a devastating effect on Jimmy and Billy. Rose, Shelly, Leona and Walt were also terribly grief stricken by the loss, and it would have a profound effect on the family dynamic moving forward.

John Brett's legacy was to have raised a quintessential American family, inspired by his optimism, his quest for the proverbial American Dream, his ambition, his work ethic and by his determination and courage. Rose, Anna, Shelly and Leona were the embodiment of his legacy; strong willed, proud, confident and ambitious, as were his sons, Cook, Henry and Walt. With two of John and Mary's sons and a daughter now gone, the "torch of his legacy" was being metaphorically handed off to the boys who carried the Brett name; Jimmy, Billy and Charlie, and it would be difficult to fill the shoes of their fathers and grandfather. But most importantly, if the lineage, including the Brett name, were to be passed on, it would be up to these three boys to do it.

27

BOOMERS COMING OF AGE

Henry's wake and visitation was well attended with extended family, including the Crowley and McAllister wing of the Brett family, and Manacek and Engles family, along with many local dignitaries stopping by to pay respects. The funeral itself, however, was kept small, intimate and private, and Charlie and Colin McAllister were among the pallbearers. Betty was composed and stoic, well in control of her emotions, in spite of the devastating loss of her husband, and Jimmy and Billy were somewhat withdrawn and reserved, accepting expressions of sympathy and condolences with simply a nod and faint, appreciative smile. Close family assembled for a post funeral reception, which was considerably more somber than typical Irish, post funeral gatherings. Refreshments were served and alcohol flowed liberally and as more alcohol was consumed, more tears began to flow. Henry's siblings shared anecdotes of childhood experiences and others praised Henry's achievement and accomplishment. By the time of Henry's death, Charlie had graduated from high school and had entered Danbury State College and continued to work part time at Markoff Shoe Store and was therefore able to purchase his own car. Jimmy would turn 18 within a few months and would graduate that year and Billy was a Sophomore.

Shelagh and Patty were in their Junior and Sophomore years, respectively. When Charlie suggested to Jimmy and Billy that they "get out of the house and take a ride for a while", Pat and Shelagh weren't included. Charlie had assumed that a diversion might help distract them and temporarily get their mind off of the tragic loss of their father and the anxiety associated with the uncertainty of what a future without him would bring. A favorite hang out of theirs was a sleazy bar across the state line, in New York, called 'The Hunt Club'. It was popular with area teens because their fake ID's were less than scrupulously examined and getting served alcohol was all but assured if one's bogus identification was at least reasonably authentic looking. At the time, the legal drinking age in NY State was 18, while in Connecticut it was 21. Charlie was of legal drinking age, but ironically, he was the only one of the threesome that wasn't a big drinker. Jimmy and Billy, in spite of being under age, frequented many of the bars and nightclubs in Brewster and Putnam Lake. Jimmy's ID was quite convincing and he was just shy of legal age anyway. Billy seldom needed to produce an ID because he could generally get served based upon his charismatic personality and convincing gift of persuasion alone and because he patronized those places so frequently, they all knew him.

The brief excursion worked well and before long they were all pretty drunk and fraternizing with other miscreants, shooting pool and flirting with tawdry young women. Jimmy and Billy were in their element, but Charlie was out of place. He was awkward and naive when it came to women and didn't have the ability to approach and strike up a conversation, or have a "pick up line" memorized to break the ice. He seldom dated, and if he did, it wasn't for more than a single date or two. He was clearly more comfortable in male company and even his recreational pursuits were exclusively male, or at least male dominated.

As Jimmy and Billy each latched on to a couple of willing

and slightly inebriated young female patrons, and the conversation become more and more suggestive, Charlie was feeling very out of place and suggested that they had been there long enough and indicated, much to the chagrin of his cousins, that it was time to leave. Being that Charlie was their ride, they had no choice but to acquiesce after a brief protestation, and pile into the car feeling that a night that had just begun had been brought to an abrupt end. When Charlie, Jimmy and Billy were younger, the cousins got along well and enjoyed frequent interaction, as did Shelagh and Patty. But now, as they were maturing and becoming young adults, they had less in common, other than being blood relatives, and Charlie was drifting away from them. For one thing, he didn't have the same libido as they did and wasn't as preoccupied with girls. Being somewhat narcissistic, he was perfectly content to limit his social interactions to only those things that gave him personal pleasure without including anyone who might require attention or special consideration. He enjoyed working at the shoe store because it provided him with money to spend on himself, and he didn't want to spend any of it on someone else, be that a casual date or a romantic interest. He played poker with a close group of buddies a few times per week and bowled in a league. He was very fond of other forms of gambling as well and wagered wisely and actually usually came out ahead. He was an avid sports fan and a highly analytical statistician, following teams and players closely, which certainly helped promote success with sports betting. He was never very athletically talented when playing sports as a child but learned the strategy well and understood the nuances of various games thoroughly. That's not to say that he wasn't always playing baseball, football and basketball with his buddies when he was a kid; he was. But due to his physical stature, he never got very good at the games. He wasn't a geek, but he wasn't a star player either- just a shade off average. He was fairly short and not particularly muscular, even though he was active. For that reason his love of sports segued into becoming a dedicated spectator, and translated into following closely as an avid fan and wagering on the games. Walt was never much for athletics either, although he did play softball with a work team for a while. But Walt preferred to be a spectator too, watching sports from the comfort of his living room or a stadium where he could relax, smoke cigars and drink beer. His job was very physical and demanding and when not working, physical exercise was the last thing on his mind. He never took Charlie fishing or hunting and seldom, if ever, went outside to toss around a baseball or football with him.

The one exception was bowling. Walt bowled in a league and took Charlie with him when he went to practice. For all his physical limitations, Charlie was a natural when it came to bowling. Walt taught him the fundamentals well and Charlie took it from there. He too, joined a league and within a few years was carrying an average of around 220 to 230. He joined multiple leagues and the Brewster Lanes became his second home.

By September of 1962, Shelagh and Jimmy had graduated from high school, Patty and Billy were entering Junior year and Charlie was heading back to Danbury State College, which he didn't like very much and was considering dropping out. The thought of becoming a teacher depressed him and he really wasn't sure whether or not to transfer to another school and switch majors or to just enter the work force. Shelagh, on the other hand, very much liked the concept of becoming a teacher and had also enrolled in Danbury State.

Jimmy wasn't ready to immediately jump into college, especially after the structured and disciplined education he had experienced at Military Academy and Private School. Instead, he decided to enlist in the Air Force, which ironically would obviously be every bit as disciplined as his schooling. Jimmy longed for excitement and travel and also wanted to "do his part" to serve his country with the war in Vietnam heating up.

While he wanted to do his part, he didn't want his part to be a boots on the ground deployment, if it actually escalated to that level, and he was aware that the draft might ultimately make that decision for him. After careful thought and deliberation he concluded that the Air Force would be a good compromise where he could serve, but with a reduced likelihood of being placed in harm's way.

Jimmy and Billy's mom, Betty Riley Brett, had, with the assistance of a trusted and talented high level employee, taken over running the insurance business after Henry's passing and was doing a commendable job of it.

Shelly had moved into Manhattan and Leona was happy teaching.

Like the previous year, I shared home room with Patty and Billy, and like the year before, I continued with my fascination over Patty. Once again, we had no classes in common, so I was unable to engage in much meaningful conversation with her, and when I shared my fixation on her with a couple of my friends from my hometown of Brookfield, they responded by saying; "don't waste your time. She has an older, steady boyfriend who drives an Impala convertible and you don't have a snowball's chance in hell". They made the point and it was just as well. I had many other things on my mind anyway. I had romantic entanglements of my own, albeit none lasted very long. It seemed that I always had her in the back of my mind though, and others didn't seem to measure up.

I had gotten my driver's license that summer and spent the majority of my time trying to come up with a car that was cheap enough for me to afford. It was my top priority and represented mobility, freedom and an escape from my severely dysfunctional home. Finally, my big brother, Bob, having sympathy for my plight, located a police car at an auction that had been taken out of service, and won the bid at $50.00.

I had $40.00 saved up and reimbursed him with that and my old Mossberg 16 gauge shotgun to cover the balance. It was a 1953 Ford with a flathead V-8, police spotlight on the front fender and a big blood stain on the back seat. I spent all my free time trying (usually unsuccessfully) to get it to run and to clean it up. However, it lacked dependability and I spent a lot of time hanging out with a couple of close friends from Bethel, one of whom had a bona fide hot rod in the form of a 1956 Ford, complete with an 'Interceptor' 312 cubic inch V-8, four barrel carburetor and dual exhaust . Both were a couple of years older which made access to alcohol easier during those weekend trips "over the line", which was a euphemism for binge drinking and rowdy behavior in various New York State bars.

Most of the time we followed a specific ritual. Bill, the friend with the car, would pick up Bob, who also lived in Bethel, and then drive to my house to pick me up. From there we would drive to 'The Lark' drive in, where a car hop would take an order for some cheap, greasy food which would be accompanied by some contraband beer, discretely hidden in the back seat. We would linger as long as the mood allowed, checking out "the action", watching street rods, modified hot rods and daily drivers come and go, revving engines and squealing tires. It was as close to a scene from the movie 'American Graffiti' as you'll find. Occasionally we would follow the same routine at a drive in restaurant in Bethel called the Sycamore, but The Lark was more popular simply because it was closer to NY State. After spending an hour or longer at The Lark, we'd head over to Brewster for some bar hopping. Occasionally there would be fights at some of the more rowdy bars but we stayed out of them for the most part, and on those rare occasions that we actually did get sucked in, no one got seriously injured.

When I wasn't hanging out with Bill and Bob, I spent my time with a couple of friends from Brookfield who were for the most part, as rebellious and anti social as I was. We got into a fair amount of trouble and I was developing a reputation of being a delinquent with severe behavioral problems. My grades

in school were dropping precipitously, my father wrote me off
as a lost cause and my mother ignored me and my behavior
and I pretty much would come and go as I pleased. Sometimes
I would go for weeks without speaking to them.

My sister, Cathy, had a steady boyfriend and their relationship was getting very serious, which kept my mother focused
on them.

My Junior year was pretty much a lost year. My grades
were so bad that I was told that I would have to attend summer school in order to advance into Senior year with the rest
of my class, my parents were fighting more than ever, making
me want to stay away from home as much as possible, cutting
class and skipping school were common occurrences and my
behavior was getting more and more reckless by the week. As
the school year was winding down and would soon come to a
close, I was entering an intense state of confusion and anxiety.
I would turn 17 in July of the upcoming summer and had no
direction.

I hated being anywhere around my family, obviously I
wasn't headed for college unless some miraculous turn around
occurred during Senior year, and if the war in Vietnam continued to escalate, there was a strong likelihood that I would be
drafted and sent to that Asian shit hole and get shot at, plus,
I suspected that I'd get thrown out of the house at 18 because
my parents didn't like me any more than I liked them. My rebellious and antisocial behavior had made enemies of virtually every member of the teaching staff at school, not to mention
the local Brookfield law enforcement authorities, and it also
had the unintended consequence of limiting my circle of
friends to a select few fellow miscreants. If there was a ray of
sunshine at all, it was a job I had taken in late February, working for a newspaper delivery company driving a small panel
truck loaded with bundles of 'The Danbury News Times', to be
delivered to drop off locations for kids who had paper routes.
In addition, I would do door to door delivery of the Sunday

paper to residences surrounding the lake and the northern parts of town.

The owner of the business provided the truck for use strictly as a business vehicle but it was kept in my possession at all times for safe keeping. I thought it was pretty cool to have access to an almost new, albeit very basic and austere appearing truck. I was permitted to drive it to school, which was another major perk, because I would drive directly from the DHS campus to the News Times loading dock after classes were completed at 12:20 PM. The high school was severely overcrowded at that time, requiring split sessions, with the Sophomore, Junior and Senior class sessions running from 7:00 AM until 12:20 PM and the Freshman Class running from 12:30 to 5:00 PM. After picking up the bundles of papers, I would deliver to drop off sites around town and usually finish by 3:30, leaving the rest of the afternoon free. I actually enjoyed it and certainly enjoyed making some spending money. What I did not like, however, was getting up at 4:00 AM on Sunday mornings to make deliveries of the Sunday paper to all the residences. Apparently my boss felt it important that the paper be delivered BEFORE the subscriber had awakened and gotten out of bed. Makes sense. Most people like to read the paper with their morning coffee. But personally, I felt that it was a real hardship getting up that early after partying late on Saturday evenings, and it was especially arduous on those Sunday mornings after snow or ice accumulation.

On one spring morning in late March, I parked the truck in the student parking lot, then followed my ritual of: walk to the 'Spa', buy a cup of coffee, stroll two blocks back to the corner of White St. and 5th Avenue adjacent to the campus, light up a Lucky Strike cigarette, watch the student vehicles cruise by, and trash talk with other loitering malcontents. It was an unseasonably warm day, remaining piles of the dirty remnants of previous snow storms finally beginning to melt and the sun shining brightly. Like the other street corner apostles of hedonism assembled there that morning, I expressed my joy and pleasure associated with the now almost certain early arrival of spring, after a particularly long and cold winter.

Knowing the uncertainty of the very fickle reality regarding Connecticut weather in the springtime, it was obviously an overly optimistic prognostication, but yielded the desired effect of placing us in a good, if not conflicted, mood. Conflicted, because no matter how delightful the weather that day promised to be, we had to spend the time in class, facing boredom, monotony, tedium and torturous structure; all creating a contrasting mood which was in direct conflict with the one we were currently experiencing. A solution needed to be found and a choice had to be made. Either we would grin and bear it, dutifully show up on time in home room, and waste this God given respite from the miserable winter (and dare I say, reject this "invitation" to follow more hedonistic pursuits), or we could skip classes that day. I frequently skipped single classes, especially the ones I hated, but seldom skipped the entire day. This day, however, was way too good for just an hour here or an hour there. I decided to roll the dice and throw caution to the wind and loudly exclaimed; "fuck it, guys, I'm skipping school today and I'm using the truck as my "freedom ship!", intending to create an early sixties, Redneck, White Trash version of Ferris Bueller's Day Off.

Within seconds, I had three cohorts request permission to come aboard the "freedom ship" and join me in a day of reckless abandon and revelry. As was frequently the case with my decision making process in those days, the choice was ill advised and things didn't work out well. As luck would have it, we headed toward Durkin's Diner to regroup and develop a plan for our day of truancy, teenage debauchery and general misbehaving, but crossed paths with my boss on the way. Here I was, truck filled with hyperactive delinquents, two of whom were seated on bundles of left over, outdated, undelivered newspapers due to the lack of seating accommodation, clearly speeding, cigarette smoke billowing from the open windows like an industrial fire in a textile factory, headed in the opposite direction of the school. He sounded his horn and motioned for me to pull over but I acted as though I never saw him. I took a quick turn on Triangle St. heading for a more isolated and obscure section of town, losing him before he could turn around, then ultimately ended up at Roger's Park. I knew I was in deep shit but we held to our plan of skipping school that day anyway and had as much fun as possible, while the knowledge of impending doom occupied the back of my mind. Sure enough, when I got to the News Times loading dock later that afternoon, he was waiting for me and I was unceremoniously fired before I could make any effort to explain, or come up with some bogus justification. Before I could say two words, he said; "don't give me any bullshit, just give me the keys". Without acting contrite, showing any remorse or regret, I simply tossed him the key and said; "Fine. See ya around".

I had no other transportation so my only recourse was to hitch-hike the 25 miles home. It took three separate rides and I arrived home fairly late. I assumed that my boss would make it a point to call my father (he knew him from some social interaction or another, perhaps the Masonic Fraternity) to explain what had happened, and the assumption was correct. Expecting the worst, I was surprised when all he did was call me an idiot and shake his head while giving me his most disgusted look, and then just walked away without saying another word.

Losing that job certainly had an impact on my wallet, so out of desperation I spent a couple of days per week during that following summer working for my father on his egg route. It was made more tolerable by getting to work one of those two days by myself. He had purchased a 1958 Ford, 'Country Squire' station wagon for the explicit purpose of using it to deliver eggs, and whatever other produce he had decided to sell on a whim, and I figured that I might be able, if I was discrete and patronizing enough, to commandeer said vehicle for my own personal use, especially if I surreptitiously had a second key made. Friday was my work alone day and Wednesday was the day we would work together, delivering from his VW Microbus. Wednesdays seemed intolerably long. When there was conversation at all, it seemed to be him lecturing and preaching, and me simply responding with an ummhmm while staring blankly out the passenger window. I call it a conversation but it was more like him engaging in a soliloquy while my mind wandered.

On the days I didn't work delivering, I did some routine chores around our generally dormant "mini farm" as quickly as possible (generally half assed), and then I would spend the balance of my time at Lake Candlewood hanging out with some Candlewood Shores friends, hanging out with friends Bill and Bob (who were also DeMolay Fraternity Brothers of mine), or with Brookfield friends, Paul and Dave; or working on my own dilapidated car, knowing that the effort was pretty much a waste of time. Because my old Police Car was a lost cause and beyond my limited ability to repair, I therefore maintained civility between my father and me as much as possible for the simple reason that the '58 Country Squire Wagon was my only real potential means of dependable transportation. I wasn't aware of it at the time, but this would be my last summer of freedom from much responsibility or accountability.

As the start of the next semester was looming large, merely weeks away, the thought of having to take the bus, or be driven to school by my father was profoundly depressing. I not only needed the freedom and convenience of my own transportation, I craved the autonomy it would provide. My car was clearly beyond my ability to repair and my personal finances wouldn't permit putting enough money into it to get it running dependably, so that left but one option: get virtually full time access to the Ford wagon. In spite of the fact that it was a 'station wagon', I liked it. It was grey in color with that fake wood grain paneling on the side quarter panels. It had a large 8 cylinder engine (a 352 cubic inch Interceptor V-8) with a four barrel carburetor pushing out around 300 horsepower. The interior was red vinyl and although it certainly wasn't a "chick magnet", it ran well in spite of its high mileage reading on the odometer.

At the tender age of 17, I already realized that I had an innate sales talent, so I strategized that while working Fridays, on the door to door delivery route, I would take the initiative and dedicate some time to canvassing homes adjacent to existing customers to see if I could build the account base.

My approach was almost comical: I projected the image of "the farmer's kid" trying to help dear ol' dad establish an outlet for our increasingly bountiful harvest of ultra fresh eggs from the pristine, bucolic and pastoral farmland in nearby Brookfield where our contented and happy chickens laid eggs with a smile on their beaks. In realty, my father typically purchased approximately 65+ cases of eggs, at 30 dozen to a case, per week. That's almost 2,000 dozen per week. He purchased wholesale from corporate egg farmers in Litchfield County and retailed door to door. Starting his business one day per week (he was a Teamster Union Member while working on the bread route and Teamsters always had Wednesday off) he was able to build the business so well that his Wednesday supplemental income endeavor overflowed into late afternoons and evenings of every other work day until he finally quit the baking company and went full time on his egg route. Credit where credit is due- It's remarkable that he was able to create his own business doing something as simple as developing an egg route and earn considerably more than he did at the baking company.

Anyway, my effort not only worked well by increasing the customer list significantly, so significantly in fact, that many of them had to be added to a Saturday route because there wasn't enough time to call on them all on Friday; it worked equally well by ingratiating myself with my father, thereby resulting in his acquiescence on the full time use of the car issue. By the time the semester started, the car was mine to use.

The semester started off on a down note. I had been assigned to a Junior class home room, mainly because I hadn't made up quite enough credits during summer school to qualify for Senior status, and secondly, I suspect, to invoke the humiliation factor as a subtle wake up call in a last ditch effort to get my attention. It didn't work. I felt ostracized, disconnected and somewhat embarrassed, and most importantly, angry and resentful. Unfortunately, this placement, along with being required to repeat one of my Junior classes, had a profoundly demoralizing effect and I attended classes in body, but not in mind and spirit. It seemed as though life was just a process of going through the motions. I attended classes but my mind was elsewhere; I continued working part time for my father, I avoided my fractious family as best as I could, and continued hanging out with my rebellious friends, smoking, drinking and getting involved in general mischief and borderline mayhem. The high point of my day was intercepting Patty and her friend Shirley as they walked together from the student parking lot to the rear entrance of the school building. Shirley usually drove her little "Lois Lane" car, the two seater, Nash Metropolitan, but sometimes an old, beat up 1950 Plymouth station wagon that smelled of horse manure from being pressed into service as a work vehicle on their small horse ranch, and sometimes had bales of hay in the rear compartment. Either way, they were easy to spot within the parade of student commuters. Now that I no longer had home room contact with her, this early, before class interaction took on greater significance. I would still catch a minute or two between classes to talk and ask how her morning was going, but this early pre-class socializing was my primary opportunity to get to know both of them better.

Shirley actually took a liking to me, in a platonic way, and became my de facto ally, providing reconnaissance, keeping me posted regarding Patty's state of attachment, encouraging me to ask her out, and would give her positive input regarding my potential as a boyfriend. As a matchmaker, Shirley was my advocate. As September came to an end, and October brought on cooler weather, there was an inversely proportional warming of our casual relationship. We spent longer time chatting than we should, making all three parties late for home room, and I eventually began walking Patty to her home room so we could continue our conversation right up until the bell rang. Shirley would split off, being in a different home room, leaving private time for Patricia and me. Once the bell rang, she would enter her home room and I would need to quickly go to my own home room on a different floor, resulting in a tardy arrival every day. It became an expectation and my home room teacher eventually discontinued the chastising comments and finally just resorted to shaking her head, giving me her most stern, threatening, dirty look as I entered late, sometimes disrupting her announcements and comments.

Halloween came and went and November ushered in much colder weather. Due to the discomfort of the chilly temps, we wouldn't linger very long outside, so I began using my stalker techniques once again, sitting in my Ford wagon with the engine idling and heat on, and as I saw them pull into the parking lot, I'd move my car to a spot near, or directly adjacent to them, so we could sit in the car and chat for a few minutes and then walk with them from the lot to the building. On the morning of Friday, November 22nd, they seemed to be in a very jovial mood, maybe because the cold spell had broken and it had warmed to more tolerable levels or maybe because the Thanksgiving Holiday was less than a week away and there would be a long weekend and holiday festivities. On this particular morning, I intercepted them as they exited Shirley's car, and as we approached the entrance at a much slower than normal pace, and I commented about

Thanksgiving being so close, and for that matter, Christmas was just around the corner! Making small talk, I inquired if they had started their Christmas shopping yet, and both responded with an emphatic; "No, but we better get started soon"! To that I replied; "no better time to start than now". "Let's just skip school today and drive down to Bridgeport and do some shopping at Korvette's" (Korvette's was a popular department store). "Besides"; I said, "we won't get many more nice days like today to enjoy before winter officially sets in". After a pregnant pause, they looked at each other for an indication of mutual agreement, smiled and said; "Okay; let's do it". Now remember, Patricia was a good student and never skipped classes, let alone school for the entire day. I then said; "Okay, then, let's get out of here before we're spotted". On our way back to my car, Shirley abruptly said; "Oh shit! I can't go with you." I have to make up a missed test during study period". I suspect that her assertion was totally bogus, but she realized that she would be the third wheel and opted out because her matchmaker agenda kicked in. With Shirley opting out, I suspected that Patty too, would rethink her decision and back out. To my surprise, she simply said to Shirley, "okay, I'll call you this afternoon".

To say I was pleased would be an understatement. This was uniquely uncharacteristic behavior for her. For better or worse, I guess I was having an influence on her and she was apparently willing to take a risk in order to spend the day together.

So off we went, on yet another impromptu version of Ferris Bueller's day off, only this one, I had hoped, would go much better than the previous debacle with the newspaper truck and my miscreant posse. I pulled up the car in front of the Spa while Patty ran in for two cups of coffee to go and we headed southeast to Bridgeport, taking back roads out of Danbury in order to remain as stealthy as possible. With our truancy conspiracy now fully engaged, we both felt slightly anxious and perhaps just a little awkward, anticipating a full five hours of uninterrupted private time to converse and relate in a more intimate way than ever before. There's nothing like spending five hours together in the confinement of an automobile to get to know someone better. The conversation started off in a reserved, somewhat cautious manner, but the longer we talked and the better we got to know each other, the deeper and more personal the discussion became.

She told me about her family; her mom being a nurse and dad a steam fitter, about her cousins, sister and brother, her ambition to become a Radiologist after attending college or Community College, and finally about her ex-boyfriend, with whom she had recently broken up. I interpreted that as a declaration that she was available.

Upon arriving at Korvette's Department store, we parked and sat in the car for at least another half hour, car idling to keep the heater on and 'Musicradio 77 WABC' (our mutual favorite) AM radio playing music in the background. We finally went in, browsed for a while, then decided it would be unwise to actually buy something, recognizing that bringing a package or two into the house after school, from Korvette's no less, might require some serious explaining. The pretense of Christmas shopping was clearly a ruse, and neither of us had any intention of actually shopping. We did buy a small box of chocolate truffles though, which we enjoyed on the return trip. We continued our conversation in a more lighthearted manner, joking and laughing, mocking some unpopular teachers, social conventions, boorish, arrogant and conceited fellow students, then turned more serious again, expressing confusion and anxiety regarding life after completing school and living in an adult world.

What had started years before as a lustful attraction was quickly evolving into much more. What could have been classified as lust at first sight, back on that first day of my Sophomore semester, when Patty Brett loaned me a pencil, was morphing into love at first meaningful dialog. I was decidedly smitten. She was awesome; bright, articulate, cheerful and optimistic, cute and sexy, confident and most of all, caring. She had a depth of soul that I found uncommon and irresistibly appealing. Obviously, I couldn't have known it at the time, but she possessed much of the traits that made her grandparents, John and Mary Brett, so unique and special.

Our morning together flew by and not wanting it to end, I took a long, circuitous route back to her home. The plan was to drop her off a few houses away so her mother wouldn't realize that it was me and not Shirley who had driven her home. I knew the area where she lived fairly well, due to its close proximity to the New York State line. I was quite familiar with a seldom traveled, very remote dirt road, just across the border in NY where my buddies and I would often spend late evenings when there was nothing to do, drinking copious amounts of beer or Seagram's Seven shots, telling stories, jokes or just outright braggadocios lies. It can be considerably difficult finding a secluded, private, quiet place to park during daytime hours but this was perfect. We had about 45 minutes until she had to be home, so I suggested this spot to kill the time. After parking, I indicated that I hadn't used the restroom since before departing this morning on our romantic sojourn, needed relief, and excused myself as I ventured off about 20 yards into some thicket and bushes to pee. When I returned to the car, I noticed that she had slid over into the center of the seat. Hey; my momma didn't raise no fool! It was all the invitation I needed and we ended up enjoying a half hour long make out session that was the high point of my young life!

When it became way too heated for propriety, she gently pushed me away and with a coy smile said; "it's getting late, we have already been here too long and I really need to get home". I took a deep breath, tried to get my head to stop spinning and nodded in agreement. I dropped her off within 15 minutes, gave her a kiss and said that I'd call her that evening.

In my delightfully manic state, I drove back to Brookfield, re-living the day's events in my mind, looking forward to the next time we would get together. After noticing that the car was, as usual, running on empty, I stopped at the local Esso service station at the corner of Rt. 7 and White Turkey Road to refuel. As the tank was filling and attendant was cleaning my wind-shield, he leaned over toward my open window and asked if I had heard the news. I replied that I had been in classes all morning (not sure why I felt it necessary to lie to him) and hadn't heard anything since around 7:00 AM. He responded solemnly and in a hushed tone; "President Kennedy has been shot". My mind was so filled with thoughts of my incredible day that it took a few minutes for that to sink in. Incredulous, I could only respond with; "what?...Seriously?" He said that it had just happened in Dallas, then; "musta been some crazy bastard" or something to that effect, then took payment for the gas and walked back to the station shaking his head. I immediately turned on the car radio to hear the latest news reports and obviously it was being discussed non stop on broadcast news on every station. When I arrived back home I immediately called Patricia to hear her thoughts. By that time JKF had died. Like many Americans, she was in shock. Her family deified Kennedy as an icon of the Irish-American com-munity and felt a distinct pride and commonality with this president. Like the Brett family, the Fitzgerald and Kennedy families emigrated from Ireland to escape an impoverished existence and to seek greater opportunity in "the new world" and to pursue the American Dream.

The Kennedy's success in that pursuit is legendary. In ad-dition to their Irish roots, they shared the Catholic religion and were lifelong democrats. While not overtly political, both Walt and Henry identified as conservative democrats, with J. Henry, much more than Walt, somewhat involved in local pol-itics. The term conservative democrat might sound a bit like an oxymoron today, but in 1963 it could easily apply.

During our phone conversation, Patricia said that she was very pleased that we had finally gotten a chance to get to know each other better and that she really enjoyed our impromptu and totally unstructured "date", but almost felt guilty that we had chosen such a tragic and meaningful day in history. We continued talking for almost an hour, until her mother finally told her that she needed to use the phone and emphatically told her that it was time to hang up.

We didn't see each other that weekend, due to some family commitments on her end, but we spoke on the phone multiple times both days. On Monday, the next scheduled school day, it (the assassination) was all anyone talked about. Our Friday truancy and dalliance had gone virtually unnoticed by the normally vigilant "buzz kill inducing" class advisors due to the gravity of the news of the assassination and what would have normally resulted in yet another probable bust and subsequent detention time went largely undetected.

Much to Shirley's chagrin, I began driving Patty home from school that Monday so we could spend at least some time together each day. She and Shirley would frequently hang out together after school and this new protocol threw a wrench in the works, but be that as it may, the drive from White Street to Joe's Hill road became the much anticipated high point of my day.

Thanksgiving was spent with our respective families, but we planned to meet up early that evening after dinner, and spend some private time with together just riding around in the station wagon, which had become, for all intents and purposes, my car. I no longer had to even ask to use it or explain where I was going. At the top of Joe's Hill Road, near the New York State line is a small lake; a pond actually. There was a pull off area next to it, that I assume was created by sightseers wanting to enjoy the lakeside scenery, or perhaps fishermen parking there before walking along the shoreline to their favorite spot. Due to the remote location and extremely low traffic volume in that area, it also took on the "lover's lane" designation, and in reality, was used for the latter purpose considerably more than the former. When Patty immediately suggested that we just drive up there an park for a while so we could talk, to say I was elated would be an understatement. We talked, joked, listened to music on the radio and necked for a couple hours. By the time I drove her back home, it was clear that we both intended to have an exclusive relationship and we would date each other steadily from that day forward. We saw each other almost daily and the romantic intensity of our love affair continued to grow.

As our deepening relationship became intensely passionate, I must admit that I was obsessed with her. I thought of nothing else but her and anticipation of our next time together. We were quickly becoming very serious and it had a profound effect on my outlook on life. I began to believe that there was truth in the assertion that we each have a "soul mate" and was convinced that I had found mine. When with her, I was uncharacteristically happy and optimistic, and in my youthful naivete and rather clouded view of reality, I began, at the tender young age of 17, to have thoughts of wanting to spend the rest of my life with her. She too, might have been thinking along those lines, but for her, the leap would seem less logical, have greater consequence and certainly be more disruptive. We were in lust and in love, having great fun together and enjoying the time we spent with each other immensely, but she had other plans. As a high school Senior, she had direction and had established goals before we began dating, whereas, I was living day to day without direction. A continued long term relationship with me could throw her life into chaos. With her good grades and great family support, it would have been an easy transition from high school to college, seeking a career as a Radiologist (with encouragement and prodding from her mother, the Registered Nurse). I suspect that her mother had visions of her working in a medical environment and perhaps meeting a single doctor or another medical professional, ultimately getting married, and living an idyllic life of affluence, social prominence and prestige. And, because she was socially active, self confident and popular, she certainly wasn't ready to settle down at 18 years of age.

If we were to make a lifelong commitment, it would ideally need to be deferred until other plans and goals had been accomplished and met. But we were both caught up in the moment and seldom spoke of the future other than to say that we would marry "some day".

The potential of a future together, where we could build a loving, nurturing and harmonious family, seemed to me to be a pathway to correcting the dysfunctional family environment I had experienced throughout my childhood and adolescence and a way to make the world right. It would be a ticket away from the wreckage of my past. I believed that I had journeyed through an oppressively dense jungle of anxiety, resentment, anger and frustration to have emerged into a bright clearing of fresh air and brilliant light. In a mere five weeks from that devil may care day of truancy, we had very quickly developed an intense relationship and were ready to spend our first Christmas together. Because we were already so close, it would be appropriate to exchange gifts, and my selection would portend, in a subliminal way, the uncertainty of the future of this relationship I so badly wanted to go on indefinitely. I purchased a sterling silver charm bracelet and included a single charm; A silver heart with a question mark engraved upon it. When she opened the gift, she thanked me and chuckled saying; "I love it but what's with the question mark?" "Don't you know that my heart belongs to you?" I was hopeful, but in truth, questions remained.

28

A TECTONIC SHIFT

My father had pretty much given up parenting my sister, Cathy. There were two fundamental reasons: One, my mother wanted complete control of her and when he tried to get involved, she reacted like a mother bear protecting a threatened cub. It always got ugly. The second was that he was incapable of effectively parenting, or at least so clueless regarding the upbringing of a female child that he felt intimidated by the prospect and therefore simply ignored her. It was for that reason, when my mother announced that Cathy and her boyfriend, Jim, had decided to get married, he didn't object. Remarkably, she was only 16 years of age, so he should have risked the wrath of "Momma Bear" and demanded that they wait until a more appropriate age, but he was so disconnected that he acquiesced immediately and went along with the program. That, and the distinct possibility that another tie that had bound him to my mother had been broken and removed. Cathy's betrothed was actually the brother of my friend Bill. To complicate matters even more, our older brother Gene, had married the sister of Jim and Bill a year or two earlier. Gene was a career Navy man, and the respective mothers had played matchmaker and had set them up on a blind date during one of his furloughs and the rest, as they say, is history.

Cathy and Jim were married in January of 1964 at St. John's Episcopal Church in Sandy Hook, Connecticut. I was one of the Ushers and Bill, if I recall correctly, was the Best Man. There was a small reception in the basement of the church but Patricia and I only stayed for about an hour. I guess the ceremony must have put us in a romantic mood because our favorite parking spot at the top of Joe's Hill Road, which I had renamed "Pat's Lake", was beckoning.

Toward the end of February my father disclosed that he had gotten into "a situation" with the IRS and apparently owed a considerable amount in back taxes on the business. As a former CPA he felt comfortable enough to handle the audit and hearing solo and without representation, but it wasn't something he could talk his way out of so virtually the entire amount initially assessed had to be paid. That simply caused more stress and strife between my parents and exacerbated the level of dysfunction within the household. It was about that same time that something came up that would require him to be away from Brookfield for an entire Sunday, which was the day that he dedicated to traveling to Litchfield County to procure product for the next week's egg deliveries.

For some unknown reason, it was necessary for my mother to accompany him, but I have completely forgotten the where and the why of it all. Obviously, this presented an extreme hardship and something needed to be put in place to ensure that he would be able to have product to deliver on Monday morning. I was called into service and told that I needed to drive the VW bus to Sharon, CT and pick up a 35 case quantity from the wholesaler. The Ford wagon wasn't large enough to handle the volume so the VW was the only option. Therefore, he would drive the Ford to his engagement and I would drive the VW bus, which had a heater that was virtually useless, on one of the most frigid days yet, of an abnormally cold February.

I couldn't bear the thought of being required to spend the day without seeing Patricia, so I called her and asked if she would be willing to join me on this little frostbitten adventure and she enthusiastically agreed. Having experienced winter travel in this ice box of an automobile before, I loaded up some lap blankets and a thermos of hot chocolate and we hit the road. It actually turned out to be enjoyable. The winter scenery was beautiful, with some fresh snow covering the ground, gaining depth as we ventured north on Rt 7, passing by some partially frozen streams and areas of dense conifer forests, with an occasional ray of sun glistening off some adjacent ice covered rock formations from which the roadway had been carved. After loading and making payment, the sun broke through the clouds, providing some relief from the single digit temperatures. We took a leisurely drive back home (there was no other way than leisurely to drive the grossly under powered microbus) and joked and laughed a lot, fantasized about the future and spoke of our affection for each other. Once back in Brookfield, we stopped at Val's Drive-in restaurant for some cheap hamburgers before heading back to the house to unload. It was now getting dark and more frigid but she stood with me as I unloaded the truck, refusing my offer for her to go inside and warm up. She even offered to help unload the cases but, weighing in at just under 30 pounds per case, it was beyond what I would have expected her to comfortably lift. I completed the task relatively quickly and, chilled to the bone, we rushed inside for the first real warmth in hours. After getting comfortably seated on our huge overstuffed sofa (the upholstered cushions were actually down filled and to this day I have never found a couch that comfortable) I went into the music room, located to the immediate right of the living room, which is where the thermostat was located and cranked it up another couple of degrees. We called that room the music room because our piano was in there, in addition to our HiFi phonograph and a small love seat where my father would sometimes bring the Sunday paper, The Herald Tribune, and listen to classical music or opera recordings while sipping his typically strong black coffee. It was his escape and coping mechanism and it would usually piss off my mother for some unknown reason, and she'd stomp by the french door entry to the room grumbling something under her breath, but loud enough to signal her bad mood and displeasure with him enjoying some solitary pleasure.

After jacking up the thermostat, I placed one of my favorite R&B/ Jazz albums on the turntable, 'Bill Black's Combo- Greatest Hits' and went back to join Patricia on the couch. Taking full advantage of the mood and surroundings, we engaged in our most passionate "make out session" to date; but this time, when we reached a point where it became way too heated for propriety, she didn't push me away. Our love making was slightly awkward, but gentle and filled with loving emotion. The climax was quick but we remained in an embrace for at least 20 minutes after. The memory of this first time for us remains indelibly stamped upon my brain as though it happened yesterday. I had experienced an epiphany and if I had been crazy about her before, this put me over the edge.

We got ourselves together and prepared to drive back to her house just as my parents were arriving home. As we crossed paths on the entry sidewalk, I acknowledged them with a cursory wave and Patricia politely said hello, then I immediately interrupted with a succinct explanation, stating that I needed to get her home right away due to some unfinished homework assignment that needed attention.

She sat next to me with her head on my shoulder and we said very little during the drive to her house. Our relationship had just crossed a point of intimacy where we no longer needed conversation to communicate. Love making became a part of most of our dates from that point forward.

By March, our relationship was intense, passionate and fully committed. Unfortunately, my influence on Patty was having a negative effect on her grades, or perhaps it was simply that we were spending so much time together that she was distracted and didn't concentrate as much on academics as she had previously. It wasn't terrible though. Her A's and B+'s might have dropped to B's and B-'s, but it was a tangible drop never the less. I suppose that grade drop, combined with my less than stellar reputation, caused Walt, and to a lesser extent, Betty, to encourage Patty to see less of me. It got so bad that, on those evenings when she just wanted to keep peace and not argue with them about going out with me, she would fake fatigue to justify retiring early for bed, then dress and climb out of her bedroom window onto the porch roof, jump off the roof onto a snow bank deliberately piled up near her exit path (or sometimes leaves, depending on recent snowfall levels), then walk a block or two down the road where I would be waiting at our preordained meeting place. She would return late enough that both parents would be sleeping, albeit tiptoeing directly through their bedroom was the only access to the stairs leading to her upstairs bedroom. On those nights when Betty was working the night shift at the maternity ward, it was easier because Walt was a sound sleeper. Miraculously, she was never caught. That was made more remarkable because some of our rendezvous included drives "over the line" where adult beverage consumption (her drink of preference at the time was a Sloe Gin Fizz) would be part of the agenda, making those clandestine reentries reach a difficulty level of 9.5 or higher. So, the bottom line was that I was generally disliked by them.

Not a visceral hatred, mind you, but simply a "you can do better than that" mindset. However, we were undeterred and simply became more creative in designing ways to meet.

At my home, I met no resistance because I was pretty much ignored. The marriage of Cathy certainly didn't help to improve the level of marital discord between my parents; it somehow exacerbated it. That boiled over, and further deteriorated the already strained and adversarial relationship between my father and me, and the anger and frustration caused him to verbally express extreme dissatisfaction with my behavior and the way my life was heading and our dialog became snarky, sarcastic and caustic. Even through he had become violent with my mother on many occasions, and her with him, he never physically abused Cathy or me. There was plenty of verbal abuse, but not physical. I suspect, but can't be sure, because brothers Bob and Gene were out of the house and in the military by the time I was two or three, that he might have been physically abusive to them.

As a matter of fact, I did witness an altercation between him and Bob a couple years earlier that presented a strong indication that there was indeed the probability that physical violence might have been part of the dynamic. Bob had returned home to live with us until he got his life back in order after some personal difficulties. I'm not exactly sure what those specific difficulties might have been; whether it be financial, relationship, or drinking related; but all were, at the time, distinct possibilities. Being charismatic and charming, intelligent, hard working and handsome, he would usually excel at his job and gain the admiration and favor of his employer.....when he was sober. Unfortunately, sobriety was an intermittent state, and during that phase of his life he would fall off the wagon at regular intervals. It was a "Jekyll and Hyde" scenario and the damage done during his binge drinking episodes could be severe and relationships were broken, cars were wrecked, arrests were made and jobs lost. He could go for months at a time without drinking, but then disappear for days on end, only to be discovered in some seedy hotel, a police station, wrecked vehicle or perhaps even a hospital. Years earlier, while in the Marine Corps, serving in Korea during the "armed, police action conflict" (a euphemism of the day for war) he was badly wounded during the battle of the Chosin Reservoir. The Korean War was short but extremely bloody and the United States military suffered over 100,000 wounded and over 33,00 battle deaths. In the 1950's, PTSD wasn't a term used, or even a recognized diagnosis assigned to discharged military personal suffering the after effects of battlefield trauma, so those afflicted with that disorder were on their own to sort out the manifestations. In Bob's case, it was made manifest through alcoholism.

During the time he had returned home, he was working at a company called Barden Bearings and was doing very well. Indications were that he might have his demons under control and our mother, who absolutely adored him, was optimistic that he might be experiencing a miracle recovery.

However, he and our father never had a very good relationship, and in spite of him showing signs of getting on the straight and narrow path toward a more productive life, there was still tension and mutual distrust. While seated at the breakfast table, something triggered an argument; with them it could be just one sarcastic word or comment, and all hell broke loose. Intrigued and fascinated, I entered the kitchen from the living room just as Bob grabbed dear old dad under the arms and around his chest and picked him up like a Rag Doll and heaved him across the room. Bob was a powerful man with a short temper which can be a dangerous combination. Airborne for about 6 feet, our father came to a landing on his butt and slid another foot or so into an old cast iron range/ oven, making a deafening thud. Dazed, he just stared straight ahead without speaking a word as Bob stomped out of the house, got into his car and drove away.

With that memory still clear in my mind, I considered the prospect of pissing off my father to the point of physical altercation to be a very real possibility, and I decided that discretion was the better part of valor and tried to curtail the snark and sarcasm somewhat and speak in more measured terms.

However, my temper wasn't much more disciplined than Bob's and when he started to come down on me for the amount of time I was away from home (usually with Patricia) I lost it and said, in no uncertain terms, "mind your own

BY PLUCK AND BY FAITH

fucking business". In 1963 one didn't say fuck to one's parents, or anyone else for that matter, except when hanging out with male buddies. When he reached up his hand to slap me silly, I blocked it with my arm and shoved him with my other. He immediately shoved back, and I staggered rearward a few steps. We then just stared at each other for a few seconds, then turned and walked away. It was the low point of our relationship. I really loved my father and had sympathy and empathy for him and the level of frustration and disappointment he must have been feeling at the time. Try as he might, the relationship between my mother and him was failed and poisonous almost from the start, and yet he continued to hope for improvement that was impossible to gain. At 51 years of age his life was still miserable, with little hope for better times in future years. As his last vestige of hope- hope that I would see the light and start to focus on making a success of my life, and make him proud of my accomplishment- I had thrown it in his face with a patently disrespectful use of words and a shove. For the next five days, not a word was spoken.

On that following Monday morning he was gone. Even though he usually left the house early to load his truck and begin his route, my mother would get up early too, and prepare breakfast for him. As bad as their relationship was, she always ensured that he was well fed. Most of the time there wasn't much conversation though. Just a dutiful going through the ritual and even a simple goodbye was seldom uttered. I always found that ironic and almost downright weird that after a heated war of words the night before, she would make breakfast, serve it to him, then they would sit together at the table while he ate as she watched, drinking coffee and saying not a word.

On this particular Monday, he awakened very early and quietly left without disturbing anyone. When my mother arose, she found a terse note on the kitchen table. It read: "I'm done". "Going to Mexico for a divorce". "Sold the business to Bobby" (an employee of his). "I'm not coming back to Connecticut".

Incredibly, she didn't see it coming. They had been tolerating the misery for so many years, she just thought it was a way of life and would continue indefinitely. Now, with him gone, the wake up call had arrived and it wasn't going to be a good day. The income stream had instantly dried up and we were on our own.

29

THE VALUE OF CHAOS

Like a punch drunk boxer, my mother was stunned and had difficulty making sense of what had happened. She began calling her few friends to tell them what a bastard he was, as though it were just another conversation about an argument, her long suffering victimhood, and how she had become a martyr for her children. It was as though she fully expected that he was bullshitting her and that he would stroll in the door that evening. After a few days passed, reality sunk in, she began to regain her composure, and desperately started to strategize her survival plan. She actually became resourceful. She called her closest friend, a foul mouthed, boorish and somewhat masculine woman named Glenda, who had connections at an electronics and transformer factory in Brookfield, near the Danbury town line, told her again about her plight and asked if she could "call in a marker" and pull the appropriate strings to get me a part time job. Obviously, with my father in parts unknown, I no longer had the obligation to work on the route, and with the split session structure at school, with dismissal at 12:20 PM, I would have afternoons available to work and contribute to her support. Glenda agreed, partly because she thrived on the stories of other's suffering generously offered up by my mother and seemed to gain some abstract pleasure hearing of others misfortune. I guess it made her feel better about her own life. Second, she had a visceral hatred of my father and wanted to help my mother prove that she could be independent and didn't need him. I reluctantly agreed, hesitant that it would severely curtail my leisure time pursuits (specifically, spending time with Patty), but well aware that I had no option. Clearly, minimum wage at a part time job wouldn't adequately support my mother and me, so she applied for some government assistance programs. I really wasn't paying much attention so I'm not sure which one she was able to access; it might have been social security disability due to her many "health conditions" or perhaps welfare, but ultimately she was able to secure some sort of monthly check.

We were able to survive, albeit, even though I was working, I had considerably less spending money than before. But the lack of personal funds really didn't present a hardship, in that I spent all my free time with Patty and we didn't spend money on much more than gasoline for my car (my father left with the VW bus and left the Ford behind), occasional trips to Brewster for pizza and a few beers or an occasional movie. She had use of her parents car at times as well. They were fans of the Chevrolet Corvair and owned two of them. She also worked part time after school at W.T. Grants department store, saving the majority of her earnings for college.

I would generally pick her up after work so that we could spend an hour or so together each night she worked.

Once in a routine, I barely noticed my father's absence. The job at Rapid Electric Co. was tolerable and I actually started to learn discipline and some skills. I began as a "gofer" in the stock room, but advanced to the silver plating department, plating electrical components.

At school, little had changed. Patty and I skipped classes on occasion and often times skipped the entire day, frequently including Shirley and her new boyfriend, who just happened to be one of my best friends from Brookfield. Most times we would drive to Kent Falls Park or one of the other area parks to "make out" or just ride around town spending the day in each other's company. Graduation was only 6 weeks away and it would soon be time to come to grips with reality and make some decisions regarding the future and put these halcyon days of carefree freedom behind us. Patty celebrated her 18th birthday in April, and we commemorated the event by creating a small party of intimate friends at Nick's Pizzeria in Putnam Lake, New York. She was one of the few in the group who could order alcohol, now that she was considered legally an adult. After breaking off with the group, we enjoyed a private celebration at "Pat's Lake", listening to music on the AM radio, which was now dominated by a new style of rock and roll initiated by a band called 'The Beatles', as well as other bands emanating from the UK. As much as we should have been having a serious conversation about our future, we didn't. We simply joked, laughed and teased, and frequently fantasized about a vine covered cottage with the white picket fence, perhaps located up near one of our favorite parks.

Reality of reckless behavior: One can not engage in a conjugal sort of interaction multiple times per week without the piper ultimately demanding payment. I picked her up at her home on the Saturday following her birthday, planning to take a drive north on Rt. 7 to enjoy in the scenery and the spring blossoms now in full bloom. Before we had gotten to the intersection of Joe's Hill Rd. and Aunt Hack Rd. less than a mile from her house, she confided that she had missed a couple of periods and suspected that she was pregnant. That news brought me to an intersection too- the intersection of panic and elation. I was concerned, yet thrilled and ecstatic. To me, it secured our relationship and I assumed that it would fulfill my dream of us being together for the rest of our lives. But I could tell by the tone of her voice that for her, it wasn't so clear. What would happen to her goals and ambitions? Was she ready for this? She wasn't so sure. It was a very difficult time for her and as we got closer to graduation, and she would likely appear to be pregnant, how would she handle the controversy and gossiping? No matter how much she tried to hide it, she would ultimately have to come to a point where a critical, life altering decision would have to be made. While we frequently talked of marriage, and I came to believe that it would ultimately happen, I don't believe she was as resolute until she gave the issue more serious contemplation and soul searching. Although she seemed to have honest intentions, I think she paid lip service to the concept, while leaving other options open. We would need time to come to a meeting of the minds.

As an indication of the significant stress she had been enduring, in mid May she experienced a fainting spell between classes and was taken to the school nurse. After resting for a short time, she was given the third degree by the nurse and was as evasive as possible, but we were both concerned that the nurse suspected what her condition might be. Interestingly enough, the guidance counselor called her into her office the following day for "a talk", and again Patricia said nothing. I'm convinced that her blackout was as much caused by mental and emotional stress as it was a result of pregnancy related physical implications.

May and June were a roller coaster, with emotional highs and lows. There were two distinctly different paths for her to take, both having a lifelong impact. She must have felt as though she were in a barrel floating rapidly down the river towards Niagara Falls and had to decide between traversing the falls, risking the long shot of a successful landing at the bottom; or seeking to alter the course of her confinement vessel, beach it on the shoreline and facilitate an expeditious escape. She waffled back and forth with indecision but ultimately postponed coming to a final decision until after graduation was behind us. It was a very difficult time for me as well. I couldn't have a direction until her decision was made. She had options. She could, as gently as possible, break off our relationship.

She could then think of ways to deal with the pregnancy as discretely as possible and place her life back on her predetermined track. Abortion wasn't legal at the time, but even if it were, she definitely wouldn't have chosen that direction, but there was an abundance of adoption agencies available, the most prominent being run by the Catholic Church.

After graduation, she became even more distant and asked for "space". Fearing the worst, I decided to do what I do best and work with words. She was avoiding my phone calls so I wrote a letter, speaking from the heart, clearly expressing my sincere desire to commit my life to her and our baby, that I would do all within my power to make her happy and secure and with her trust and support, would ultimately become a husband of whom she would be proud and would love with all her heart. I guess it struck a responsive chord. She called me immediately after receiving it and said that she was deeply moved by it and decided to proceed with plans to be married. We chose a date in August, after my birthday. She was of legal marrying age but I was not. In New York State, however, I too could marry at 18 with a parent's consent. If my mother didn't know already (I think she strongly suspected it), it was time to tell her.

Patricia saw something in me that few others saw (perhaps aided by an inherited risk taking gene passed down from her grandfather, John?), and I promised her that I would do all within my power to provide a good life for her and my family. July was a whirlwind month, with me going on full time employment at work, seeking appropriate housing, looking for bargain basement furniture, locating a church in Brewster willing to perform the ceremony, planning a very small wedding- no reception, no honeymoon; and breaking the news to friends and relatives.

We secured a small, three room, upstairs apartment in Brookfield Center in an old colonial house across from St. Paul's Episcopal Church. Between my mother and Patricia's relatives on her mother's side, we obtained enough additional hand me down furniture to set up housekeeping.

We met with the pastor of the Brewster Presbyterian Church who had agreed to perform the ceremony. By the time we met with him Patricia was clearly showing as pregnant but he was very accepting and nonjudgmental, and we confirmed the August date at that meeting.

Walt was angry about the entire situation and took on an "I told you so attitude" with Patricia's mother and he, as well as Charlie, refused to attend the wedding. My brother Bob was my Best Man and Patty's sister, Shelagh, was Maid of Honor. Patty's mother and aunt were there and my good friends Paul and Dave from Brookfield, as Ushers. In total, there were less than 15 attendees. It was the best day of my life, and whether Walt liked it or not, I was now part of the Brett family and Patricia was part of mine.

We had a comfortable little home, anxiously awaiting the arrival of our first born child and started to build a life together. Work was going okay and even though the salary was less than $75.00 per week, without overtime, we were making ends meet. My mother moved from the house at Long Lane farm to an apartment in Sandy Hook, near Newtown, CT, and she too, was doing okay. Interestingly enough, she actually seemed less "crazy" without my father around and had mellowed out considerably, which leads me to believe that the root cause of their problem was each other. Patricia and I visited her almost every weekend and we became closer than we had ever been.

Because I had gone on full time status, I was required to became a union member, which was kind of a joke because the union, as it were, was run by management, a bit of a sham, and did little for the employees. The IBEW (International Brotherhood of Electrical Workers) attempted to work its way in but met with stiff resistance. For the first time, I attended union meetings and got to see the corruption and politics involved. A vote was taken and the IBEW failed to gain control of the "shop union" but they weren't finished and planned another try in mid winter of 1965. There was talk of a Wildcat Strike as a way to crush the opposition, which caused me great concern. I certainly couldn't afford to be out of work for any length of time.

The end of November was a glorious time as we welcomed our beautiful baby daughter into the world. She was perfect and bore an equal resemblance to her mom and dad. That Christmas was wonderful, with our first tree, a shiny metallic one that was horrendously tacky by tasteful standards, and some simple and practical gifts, and visits from lots of family; with the exception of Walt, who was still sullen, resentful and angry that his plans for his favorite daughter went somehow awry.

By February, the Wildcat Strike did, in fact, materialize. Part of the work force remained at work and were called Scabs and threatened, and part joined in with the strikers, hoping for better benefits and better representation and maybe even better wages. There was the implied promise of some strike pay from the union to help us weather the storm but it never materialized. In my naivete, I recklessly joined the strikers, but after a few weeks of walking the picket lines without an income, I became desperate.

My marriage to Patricia provided an opportunity to compensate for the debacle that was my dysfunctional family. My mission was to create a more perfect family and better life; to create a loving, prosperous, nurturing and harmonious environment where children could be raised with proper support, encouragement, direction and caring guidance. Being on strike, essentially out of work and without income, didn't fit into my plans. It presented a troubling obstacle that would need to be rectified as soon as possible. By the beginning of March, after a few weeks of walking picket lines and hoping for the best, I was ready to throw in the towel. Some good fortune arrived by way of, none other than Walt. His paternal instinct must have kicked in and he finally accompanied Betty on a visit to our apartment to see the baby.

He was immediately smitten by his first grandchild and seemed to relish grandfather status. He and I spoke very little but at least there wasn't any overt hostility. And apparently, he had reached a point of acceptance without clearly broadcasting it, because less than two days after that visit, he provided a new job lead.

He knew a guy named Jack Bray, who was a top executive at a firm called Kimberly-Stevens, in New Milford. Cook had worked there years before, and Walt had done a short stint there as well, doing contract steam fitting work. It was during that time that he became friendly with Jack. Kimberly-Stevens produced non woven fabrics for items like bra padding, pool table covering, clothing liners, filters, etc. It was, as the marketing B. S. of the time said; "A glorious collaboration between Kimberly Clark and J. P. Stevens". They were quite busy and had openings, so when Walt approached Jack and asked if he could do him a favor and schedule an interview for me, he agreed, without making any promises. The interview went well and I was offered a job at entry level, driving a fork lift and doing odd jobs in the warehouse. Needless to say, it was a lifeline and I grabbed it. It was a 24 hour, 5 day, three shift operation and I was placed on the night shift, working from 11:00 PM to 7:00 AM. That worked well for me. I had a voracious appetite for learning and with those hours I could devote time to educating myself. I studied text books given to me by Charlie and Shelagh after they had completed courses at Danbury State College, took individual courses there myself when time permitted (Most related to those taken by students majoring in English), and even took correspondence courses in Commercial Art and Design, thinking that marketing might be a worthy pursuit. As I gained tenure at Kimberly-Stevens, and gained respect and credibility after demonstrating my work ethic, ambition and dedication, I was promoted to a position in the Quality Control/ Quality Assurance department. After learning the techniques and procedures, and demonstrating proficiency, I was selected to accompany the department manager to take QC Engineering courses offered by Yale University. Somewhat boring but I earned brownie points with management. My goal was to learn as much about as many things as possible, in the shortest time possible.

Business was brisk, requiring an increase to 12 hour shifts and I was assigned to the 7:00 PM to 7:00 AM shift. That created a temporary hiatus in my educational pursuits and quest for knowledge but the overtime certainly helped our financial situation.

In addition, many of the night shift employees (not all, but many) tended to be quite a motley crew, some having migrated from West Virginia or the areas of various upstate's along the border with Canada. Many were just weird, some were anti-social misfits, a few were parolees and ex-convicts, some were young, returning veterans of Vietnam, many of whom appeared to be suffering from PTSD, and others "functional" alcoholics. It was an interesting mix of some southern "Rednecks", attracted and recruited from the J. P. Stevens textile mills side of the collaboration, based down in "Dixieland", northern white "trailer trash" attracted and recruited from upstate New York, Pennsylvania and Maine, from the Kimberly Clark Paper mills side of the equation, and a few West Virginia "hillbillies", profoundly ignorant and displaying some pretty weird sexual obsessions and fetishes (think 'Dueling Banjos').

I have to say that some of the ubiquitous West Virginia jokes seemed to hold some validity and I suspected more than a little incest and inbreeding. As evidence, I submit the individual who was "married" to his aunt (his momma's sister!). I'll admit that I was rather entertained and amused by my arm's length observations and would come to consider the experience a unique observational, real life, grassroots study in demographics and sociology. For the most part, many were lower middle class laborers, not well educated and struggling to survive while dealing with some behavioral issues. By contrast, upper management were well educated, well to do and rather aloof and would seldom venture down from their posh second floor offices into the grime, noise and grit of the production floor. I often wondered if I would be doomed to a life constantly struggling within that lower tier, or if there would be some way that I could ever bust through into that upper echelon. After frequent contemplation, I became determined to find a way.

In all honesty, it is completely unfair for me to paint that group of night shift employees with such a wide brush. There were many fine, upstanding, moral and righteous individuals within the group as well; the majority, as a matter of fact; but I was much more intrigued by the unique and seedy characters and as a result, I was fraternizing with some low class, troubled individuals simply due to daily exposure, a fascination with the odd behavioral traits and not much time for after work social life, and I must admit it had a negative influence on me, the most obvious of which was heavy drinking. If I had tried to maintain an "arm's length" relationship with co-workers, it became a very short arm. I could go on for many pages re-telling the stories of the craziness that took place during that time but I'll refrain.

The drive to New Milford was a fairly long commute and my current vehicle was beginning to experience mechanical problems, so we upgraded to a new 1965 Mustang. It was exciting buying our first new car but it probably wasn't the most practical family transportation. Never the less, it made for some entertaining drives on weekends.

A serendipitous event also took place that year just as the lease on our tiny apartment was about to expire. A small, very cute two bedroom log sided home, right across the street from Walt and Betty became available. It had a beautiful ceiling high stone fireplace with a massive hearth, hardwood floors, knotty pine walls, multiple levels and a nice screened patio with a built in barbeque and the garage had been converted to a recreational room.

It was quaint and rustic, albeit small. Although it was more expensive than the apartment, it was directly across the street from Patricia's childhood home (down a long driveway and somewhat behind another home) so it would offer easy access to babysitting by her parents and provide an opportunity for Walt and Betty to see much more of their grandchild. It also had a very nice yard for our child to play. It was a "no brainer" and we jumped at the opportunity. It also marks the time when I gained full acceptance from Walt.

The downside of the move was that it created an extremely long commute to work. We traded the Mustang on a 1966 Chevelle SS, which certainly made the commute more comfortable; and faster too, if I ignored the speed limits with my new fire breathing monster of a vehicle.

In late August of that year we ushered in the arrival of our second beautiful daughter and Patricia decided that the 12 hour shifts combined with the long commute were placing a strain on the family time and could become threatening to meaningful quality interaction with the kids. While not actively seeking a new place of employment, I kept my eyes open and in March of 1968 I discovered that a small optical coating laboratory called Laser Optics, Inc. was seeking a technician who could learn aspects of thin film engineering. It was at 98 Mill Plain Rd. about a mile and a half from our house. Dropping my commute time down from hours to minutes was very appealing and I immediately applied. It was a fortuitous moment in my life and was my introduction to the optical industry, within which, in various forms, I would make my lifelong career.

We traded the SS Chevelle, due to the high mileage logged during those long commutes, and went with another Super

Sport; this time a Camaro. I had developed a casual interest in Drag Racing while working at Kimberly-Stevens and occasionally raced the car in its stock form. Now, with the Camaro, I took a greater interest and began to make performance modifications and Drag Racing became a frequent Sunday pastime.

It was around that time that we learned of another event that took place a few years earlier, that didn't have much impact upon Patricia and I, but certainly had an impact on Shelagh and Walt and Betty. During the time Patricia and I were dating and not yet married, Shelagh was involved with a serious boyfriend as well. I knew him but not well. We had actually double dated one time and ended up finishing the evening by visiting the unoccupied home of a friend of his located on Lake Lillinonah, near Bridgewater, Connecticut. After a few cocktails, quiet music and some brief conversation, we adjourned to a couple of bedrooms, respectively, and enjoyed some intimate time prior to heading home. Shelagh and her boyfriend broke up shortly after that but the consequence of that dalliance would remain.

For most of her life, Shelagh had a bit of a problem with weight gain and to some extent, self esteem, but that, however, didn't interfere with her social life. She had a good personality, a good sense of humor and was attractive; and being socially active, she had numerous boyfriends; some casual relationships, some more serious.

After the breakup with her boyfriend who participated in the double date and romantic interlude at Lake Lillinonah, she became quite despondent, leading us to believe that she cared more for him than we initially thought. Her reticence and log periods of silence and confinement to her room we attributed to the heartbreak of lost love and we all though that it would pass. Shelagh herself, wasn't completely sure why she felt so blue. She cared greatly for her ex-boyfriend, but wasn't what one would call head over heals in love with him. When she experienced a disruption in her menstrual cycle, she attributed it to emotional distress. As the months progressed, she either went into denial or irrational avoidance mode and never disclosed the issue to her mother or anyone else.

And, because she was somewhat overweight, her pregnancy didn't show. Everything came to a head when, on a Sunday evening after watching some television with the family and then retiring early to bed, she felt some uncomfortable pressure and, thinking that she needed to use the bathroom posthaste, quickly descended the stairs and almost running past the family still seated in the living room in front of the TV, she entered the bathroom and slammed the door. Concerned, Betty approached the door and asked if she was okay, and based upon the response, she knew that Shelagh was in great distress. She entered to check on her just as Shelagh was having a miscarriage at about 5 months into gestation. Either she knew that she was pregnant and didn't tell anyone, postponing the announcement until a later date, or she was in extreme denial and sincerely didn't know. Either way, it was a traumatic experience for not only Shelagh, but for Walt and Betty too. As a maternity ward nurse, Betty knew how to provide the necessary immediate care, then drove Shelagh to the hospital.

Walt didn't take it well. It seemed a rapid succession of emotional "hits" for him over the past few years. It all began with the loss of Walt's sister, Ann, then his mentor, father figure and beloved brother Cook had become ill and ultimately committed suicide, then, more recently, the loss of Henry. Charlie dropping out of college was another disappointment, then Patty's hasty marriage and Shelagh's pregnancy and miscarriage. Combine all the emotional strife, with the heavy cigar smoking, physically exhausting job, considerable beer consumption and a diet that was fairly typical for the time, which is to say, not the most healthy, and you have a surefire formula for health issues. The specific health issue became heart disease. Walt suffered a serious heart attack a short time after Shelagh's miscarriage and was hospitalized for a considerable amount of time. It also marked the end of his career. He discontinued working and began drawing compensation from the union and social security. Fortunately, Betty was a skilled nurse and provided not only an ongoing income, she provided excellent care at home for Walt. He became a different man from that point forward- more tolerant, slightly less opinionated, more laid back and easy going, and doted on our daughters. He adjusted well to the forced retirement and he and Betty traveled more, and actually seemed closer than before. She enjoyed the feeling of being needed by him more than she ever had been before.

30

THE HEIR APPARENT

When J. Henry Brett passed away in his prime of life, his wife Betty (Riley) summoned up the strength and courage to do what was necessary to protect his business legacy and ensure that the agency would continue to remain strong and successful, not only to continue to support her and the boys, Jimmy and Billy, but to even gain strength in preparation for inclusion of the sons in the business, and ultimately to hand it off to them completely. Jimmy, who was the eldest, the more intellectual and slightly more serious of the two, was looked upon as the most likely candidate to head up the agency once he completed his time in the Air Force and hopefully, after that, some time in college studying business administration. Billy, being more reckless, hedonistic and fun loving, had some growing up to do before he would be ready to assume the responsibilities of the business, but she was hopeful that he too would eventually join. Meanwhile, between her, and her trusted employee as her immediate assistant, she would run it to the best of her abilities. As it would turn out, her abilities were extensive and she was profoundly qualified. She had been an integral part of the day to day operation of the business while Henry was alive and learned more, and had been responsible for more, than anyone knew. Her distraction however, would be the boys. Jimmy was stationed in Alaska at Campion Air Force Station and Billy had enlisted in the Army after high school and was a paratrooper deployed to Vietnam. She feared greatly for Billy's safety and agonized about the danger he faced. By early 1966, fighting had escalated significantly and evening news broadcasts spoke of the increased intensity of the fighting and the substantial losses suffered, which exacerbated the fears that were keeping her awake at night. She received a letter from him in February where he told of his involvement in 'Operation Marauder' in the Plain of Reeds, Mekong Delta, graphically describing the battle and casualties. He was part of the 173rd Airborne Brigade Combat Team. To Betty's dismay, the horrors described by Billy were written about very matter of factly and she was becoming concerned about his psychological state. He seemed more agitated and distraught about an air drop of warm beer, most of which missing the mark, than to the exposure to horrific loss of life.

Jimmy, on the other hand, was, for all intents and purposes, out of harm's way and seemed to be greatly enjoying his time in the service. His deployment to Campion Air Force Station wasn't a cake walk though. It was located on the Yukon River in a very remote part of Alaska with the nearest town, Galena, being 7 miles away via a dirt road and Fairbanks was 240 miles due east. The average winter temperature was 20 degrees below zero, and there was only 2 to 3 hours of sunlight. It was a small Continental Defense Radar Station constructed during the 1950's to provide early warning should there ever be a Soviet attack, and the Korean War made its presence even more necessary.

The personnel were generally confined to the heated buildings (which were connected by heated hallways and tunnels), during the extremely harsh winter months and due to the psychological strain and physical hardships, tours of duty were limited to just one year.

Jimmy had just been sent there after enjoying a Christmas leave at home, so he would be deployed elsewhere toward the end of that year (1966) or beginning of 1967. Coincidentally, Billy too, had been lucky enough to be home at Christmas and Patricia and I visited them and Betty during the holiday. I had only met Jimmy once, and that was during June of 1964, shortly after he had enlisted in the Air Force, and a few months prior to our wedding. Patricia and I were seated outside in an area where their barbecue grill was located, on a couple of those stereotypical 50's and 60's metal outdoor chairs with the tubular arms, and Jimmy drove up in Billy's convertible and, for some unknown reason, was in uniform. Patricia introduced me to him but based upon his cool and slightly arrogant response, I suspected that he had already heard plenty about me and had developed some preconceived notions about me that were slightly negative. He didn't stay long, but it was long enough for me to get the impression that he and I wouldn't be getting along very well unless I made an effort to change his opinion. Interestingly enough, even though Patricia and I were now a married couple during that second meeting over the Christmas holiday, our respective opinions of each other didn't improve much. Patricia's mom and Aunt Betty had taken our baby daughter into another room where they could have an adult conversation of their own, leaving Billy, Jimmy, Patty and I in the family room where we had a fairly light hearted and jocular conversation, mutually poking fun and teasing, exchanged a few trivial gifts and drank quite a few 7&7's (Seagram's 7 Crown blended whiskey and 7-up). The more we drank, the more antagonistic Jimmy and I became toward each other and before long a heated argument was raging. Thankfully, Patty and Billy interceded and calmed things down before it got out of hand, because I still tended to be persona non grata with some of her family members anyway and a full blown feud with Jimmy would not have been a wise idea. In truth, I liked Jimmy and admired his willingness to push back when I became obnoxious. I think, based on the similarity of our personalities, it was merely a game that we both enjoyed. Anyway, at the end of the evening, with a hand shake, we wished each other a Merry Christmas.

While Jimmy and Billy were home during that Christmas, Aunt Betty took advantage of the opportunity and tried to brief them on what was happening with the business and even took them to the office on a couple of occasions, I assume trying to get them more interested, and in a subliminal way, attempting to slowly and gradually prepare them for what she hoped would be their future. Both had other things on their young minds though, and when they both returned to their respective military deployments, Aunt Betty recognized that it would be a "long row to hoe".

By June of '66, Jimmy had endured a particularly long, dark, tedious six months and was beginning to see some light at the end of the proverbial tunnel. Even though there were recreational opportunities available at Campion, like ping pong, pool tables, a few bowling lanes, a gym for basketball and volley ball, as well as horse shoes, skating and even skiing, Jimmy and his friends were suffering from a wicked case of cabin fever.

He was assigned to radar maintenance, which kept him relatively busy, but never the less, boredom had set in and many of the personnel were ready to spend some time outside in the lengthening hours of sunlight and relatively warmer temps. The ice break up on the Yukon had begun somewhat late that year but by June it had been complete for about a month. On that Monday, the 13th of June, Jimmy and two of his closest friends, John, from Snohomish, Washington, and Ray, from Portland, Maine, all Airmen 2.C., pooled their disposable spending money together and decided to rent a 16 foot long, flat bottomed river boat and do some fishing and sightseeing on the Yukon River. In spite of the water being cloudy from the glacial runoff, the fishing was good, with reports of nice catches of Northern Pike, Grayling and Chum Salmon common. In addition, the daylight hours were almost 21 hours long, with the sun rising just after 3:00 AM and not setting until after midnight. That meant that their excursion could last well into the evening without concern of darkness. In addition, the weather had been abnormally warm lately, with lows in the mid 40's and highs in the low 70's. After a quick trip to the NCO Open Mess/ Club for three six packs of Carling Black Label beer, they headed out on their adventure about 1:00 PM in the afternoon. With some borrowed fishing equipment and their cameras and snack foods in their back-pack, and beer on ice, they headed down river, enjoying the Alaska scenery, the fresh air, sun on their face, the cold beer and music playing on a portable AM radio. They caught quite a few fish, but only kept a few, and even those, they intended to give to some locals. After a couple of hours, they made a 'U-turn" and started heading back up river. They vowed to make an encore trip as soon as possible, only next time buy-ing more beer for the outing-Their cooler was now empty for the return voyage! Squalls and quick moving storms are leg-endary on the Yukon, and they had been warned to pay strict attention to any weather changes, but today was uncommonly tranquil and although the current flow was strong this time of year, and the boat worked harder going up river than it had going down, all was going smoothly. It was a delightful day and seemed to revitalize and invigorate all three of them after a long, difficult winter in the confines of Campion.

The water was getting a little choppy from some increased wind and the small craft was porpoising a bit and slapping the waves creating a hollow "thud" sound. This made them anx-ious to get back on land and their fuel supply was adequate enough to allow for some open throttle navigation. When 'Paint It, Black' by The Rolling Stones (the number one song at the time) came on the radio, they cranked the volume up all the way, leaned back in their respective seats and enjoyed the music, keeping the craft directed straight ahead, paying little attention for potential hazards.

And there was indeed, a very treacherous hazard that went unnoticed. A large, water logged tree trunk, the majority of which was floating just beneath the surface, was directly in their path. John, who was at the controls, spotted it first, yelled; "Oh shit!!" and cut the boat sharply toward the port side attempting to avoid it. Had it only been the exposed portion, they would have easily missed it, but because the majority was slightly submerged, they had no way of knowing that the boat had been guided directly into the main part of the huge log.

They hit with such force that the vessel capsized, throwing all three of them into the water. Fortunately, they were all wearing life vests and quickly surfaced, swimming to the capsized boat to hang on. The water temperature in the Yukon seldom goes above 50 degrees Fahrenheit during June and this year was no exception. As a matter of fact, due to the late ice break up, it was colder than normal. As they hung to the boat, contemplating their serious, life threatening dilemma and considered various options for dealing with their plight, the surprise turned to panic, then to blame. "If you're in charge of the controls!", Jimmy shouted, "you should be paying attention!" "None of us were paying attention, Jim", said Ray. "Shut up and let's come to a decision on what to do". With that, they all became more calm and began strategizing. "We can try to swim to that island over there and wait for rescue"; Ray said. John replied; "It's too far and the current is too fast". Jimmy agreed; "I'm not the world's strongest swimmer either and I doubt that I could make it that far". They weighed options for about 45 minutes but by then were starting to feel the effects of hypothermia setting in and Ray said; "I'm going for it before we drift any farther away". Both Jimmy and John tried to discourage him but he pushed off from the boat, leaving the two of them behind. They continued to drift, losing sight of Ray as he was swimming toward the tiny island. John and Jimmy drifted for another 10 minutes and by then, exhaustion had made it impossible to attempt a swim to shore or an island, if there had even been one within distance. They simply hung on for as long as they could, hoping against all odds, that rescue would arrive. John lost consciousness, released his grip on the boat and began to float away. Jimmy attempted to reach for him but was too weak. He too felt consciousness slipping away and an inexplicable peace and warmth came over him. He let go, and floating on his back, gazed up at the early evening cloud formations, convinced that the images of his father, and of his grandparents, John and Mary, that he saw in those formations were not hallucinations, but rather his loving family welcoming him home. Oddly, he recognized John as his grandfather, even though he had passed away long before he was born. It was a remarkable awareness and connection that he had never known, and provided great comfort. He smiled and thought to himself, I'm glad we now meet. I have so much to ask you. He closed his eyes and took the first step through the portal to eternity.

31

A CULTURAL SHIFT

It took weeks to find and recover the bodies of Jimmy and his friend John. Ray, who had decided to attempt a swim to that distant island surprisingly succeeded and survived. There were a series of communications from the Air Force, first alerting Jimmy's mother of his status as missing after the accident, followed by an update communication that said "presumed dead" and finally the one informing her that his body had been recovered, expressing condolences and sympathy for the tragic loss.

When the loss of a child occurs, even a child who has just entered adulthood, it would be easy to become overwhelmed by the dark fog of grief and gut wrenching emotional sadness. It's an unfathomable loss that was compounded by the untimely loss of a spouse a mere four years earlier. At only 22 years of age, Jimmy, her beloved son and hope for the future, was gone. But Patricia's Aunt Betty showed remarkable strength and composure. When a reporter from The Danbury News Times interviewed her, Betty mechanically passed the telegram to her and stoically commented that; "the one I didn't worry about was gone" and all she had to hope for now was that 20 year old Billy would be released from Vietnam. She continued; "I have asked The Red Cross to make an appeal".

The appeal was granted and Billy got an emergency leave to attend the funeral and was later released with an honorable discharge.

The services took place at the Cornelius Delury Memorial and St. Peter's Catholic Church. A requiem high mass was offered by a cousin, the Reverend Robert Shanley, pastor of St. Joseph's Church in Poquonock. There was an official escort representing the Air Force there and once again, Charlie served as one of the pallbearers at a funeral of a close relative.

Once home, Billy had some difficulty readjusting to civilian life. While not officially diagnosed as PTSD at that time, it was claimed that he might be suffering from "Battle Fatigue" and the V.A. prescribed some temporary medication.

But Billy self medicated with alcohol to a much greater extent. He worked off and on at the insurance agency, bought a new Corvette and tried as best as he could to emulate the "The Playboy lifestyle". He drank, partied, gambled and caroused and flip flopped between cheerful, outgoing, highly social and almost manic states, to pensive, introverted, quite melancholy and meditative.

After I began working at Laser Optics, Inc. on Mill Plain Road, a few of my work friends and I would frequent a bar and grill called the Oasis, on Lake Avenue, fondly called "The Big O" by regulars. It became an after work hang out on at least a couple of days per week and we would often times run into Billy there. He was a much more frequent patron than we were and I suspect that it was due to its close proximity to his childhood home, where he was then living (with Aunt Betty). I never knew which Billy I would run into, but if it was the cheerful, outgoing, joking and story telling Billy, he would be fun to be around. If not, and I could always immediately tell by the way he was sitting at the bar, we would just say hello and keep our distance.

If I were to go there alone and run into him while he was in one of those solemn moods, I would sit at an adjacent stool indicating that I was prepared to listen if he wanted to talk. He seldom did. There were times that I detected what could almost be classified as a subliminal guilt, having survived when Jimmy did not. He spent a lot of time in New York State bars as well, frequenting many that were popular watering holes during our high school escapades. Following one night of bar hopping, a few years later, he struck and killed a pedestrian while driving his Corvette, allegedly somewhat intoxicated and traveling above the speed limit, but because the pedestrian was walking on the wrong side of the road, wearing dark clothing and somewhat inebriated as well, Billy got off without any charges being filed. The unusual and rather irrational behavior extended into his love life as well and although he dated many women, he began dating a cousin. She was very cute and fun loving, but it just seemed weird. For all we knew, it might have been just platonic, but for a while, they were always together and we suspected that it had gone beyond that point but obviously couldn't be sure.

By early 1968, Patricia and I got an opportunity to purchase our first home. We loved being right across the street from her mom and dad, but when the lease expired on our little rental, and the owners, a decidedly unfriendly lesbian couple, refused to consider selling it to us rather than rent, we began shopping. We were financially ready to make a down payment and my job was going well and I felt adequately secure enough to make a commitment. We would miss being in such close proximity to her parents; their support and child rearing guidance were priceless, but Patricia was instinctively a great mother and seemed to have a natural ability to know the best way to raise and nurture the kids and while the close support and guidance were appreciated, it had become largely unnecessary. Besides, they would be just a phone call away. She was a stay at home mom at the time and completely devoted to them.

She actually had them doing basic reading, writing and

mathematics before they entered school, and provided the perfect mix of gentle discipline, challenging playtime, caring engagement with games and activities and became the balancing yin to my yang parenting style of strict disciplinarian and my "Drill Sergeant" approach. We located a house for sale on a short little cul-de-sac where there had been construction space for a mere three homes, and the one for sale was at the very end, providing a quiet environment and safety for the children. Apparently, there was just enough available space between two existing homes on High Street, which is what the larger, through traffic street was named, to cut in a road and provide access to lots located behind their houses. Either that, or a contractor purchased a small amount directly from them; just enough to construct the road and provide access to the rear lots. The three homes on High St. Extension were actually at right angles to the ones on High Street and our side yards bordered their back yards. It was located on the south end of town, off South St. and near Shelter Rock Rd, and named High Street Extension. "High Street"--What an appropriate name for a potential residence during the cultural changes taking place during the late 60's and early 70's!

The house was small, having just two bedrooms, one of which the girls would need to share, but a nice, flat 1/3 acre lot, a screened back patio, radiant heating in the tiled, cement slab floor, that ensured warm feet during long, cold Connecticut winters, even for little kiddies who avoided shoes, a large wood burning fireplace and in the 1950's tradition (it was constructed in 1952) it had knotty pine paneled walls in the living room. The exterior was sided in what was called "First Cut" or "Half Lap" which was the first cut of timber when it arrived at the mill. It left a live edge that presented a very rustic and quaint appearance while providing excellent insulation qualities due to the thickness.

I was also pleased to have a garage for my car, which we didn't have at the previous house. When we bought the house, it was painted barn red with white trim and an exceedingly tacky black and white checkerboard pattern on the garage door. One of the first things on my agenda was to repaint it a more subdued, colonial inspired grey-green color which a lighter celery green trim. And best of all, it was far enough from Walt and Betty that it would discourage frequent visits, promoting a greater feeling of independence.

We settled in quickly and became very happy there. We were extremely busy raising our young family; I was working hard, enjoying the fruits of my labors by purchasing a motorcycle, remodeling the house as necessary and had a large in ground swimming pool installed. We had a great circle of friends, some from work, some from our old high school days and some with whom we became acquainted through my sister, Cathy, and her hubby. But on the other hand, we had completely lost touch with my old childhood friends from Brookfield, and with my old friends from Bethel, Bill and Bob. After serving in the Air Force, Bill had moved out of state and Bob had become a teacher in either Vermont or New Hampshire. And, for some undefined reason, we lost touch with cousin Billy, except for some anecdotal info coming from Walt or Betty.

As my primary form of recreation, I became heavily involved in weekend drag racing, frequenting drag strips in Wingdale, NY (Dover Drag Strip) and others on Long Island or upstate New York. Even Patricia and the kids enjoyed going to the strip to watch dad race. Other than that, yard beautification, a small garden, weekend hikes with the kids and lounging by our pool filled the available leisure family time.

I'm not sure if it qualified specifically as a suburban lifestyle, urban lifestyle or in a nebulous area in between, but whatever it was, we were quite pleasantly engaged in it and quite content. So content in fact, that we hardly noticed the dramatic cultural changes taking place in America, even though we were obviously directly and indirectly exposed to them.

One couldn't help seeing evening news broadcasts of Vietnam War protests, hippies, a rise in Feminism, assassinations of Dr. Martin Luther King and Bobby Kennedy; and of Lyndon Johnson's decision not to seek re-election due to the war and civil unrest, Watergate, Black Power Movement and more. But for us at the time, it was peripheral. By 1969 Hippies were commonplace, "head shops" were springing up, friends were trying to introduce us to marijuana, peace signs and tie dyed shirts were commonplace and eventually, we began to become aware of, and to some limited extent, embraced the counter culture movement; at least as much as we felt comfortable doing. We were after all, responsible parents, trying to remain upwardly mobile professionally, but more than anything else, we were deeply saddened by what appeared to be the senseless loss of life in Vietnam, some of those lost were high school friends, and the futility of the war effort, with so many Americans and the media obviously dead set against it.

Had my life taken a different track, there was a strong likelihood that I would be there and that was a troubling and very personal realization. Risking my life in that Asian shit hole for a war that I personally believed at the time, was completely unnecessary was sobering. My draft status when I registered was I-A, which meant that there would be little likelihood that I could avoid being drafted into military service, then fortuitously, after marriage and the birth of our first child, changed to III-A. I didn't give it much thought at the time, but it was obviously a serendipitous stroke of good fortune and that change in status offered the opportunity to focus on my new family without fear of being taken from them on short notice.

But the reality was that this now ubiquitous counterculture movement had migrated to grassroots communities from places on the west coast, like Haight Ashbury in San Francisco and Los Angeles and other large mid-western cities, and many participants were expressing the ethos and aspirational desires of our generation, and it had arrived with a full head of steam to Connecticut cities and conservative suburbia and even good old Danbury. The 'Summer of Love' and Woodstock made it mainstream and if the decade of the sixties was referred to as "The Cultural Decade", for us, as late adopters, it was more like 1965 to 1975 as the years of cultural change (or at least our awareness of it).

Remembering that many young people of our age had yet to settle down and start families and careers, while we were living a lifestyle of people ten years older, easily explains why we didn't have the luxury of full engagement in the counter culture movement, as had been done by many of our peers.

I must admit though, that I embraced the movement much more than Patricia. Thank goodness! She was the rock that kept me from straying too far off path. Some of our (mostly my) friends were borderline radicals, and I became influenced by their commitment and dedication to help initiate social change. I took on the look of hippie myself, more as a bow to fashion de rigueur than as a statement against social convention or customs. I let my hair grow to shoulder length and grew a bushy beard, wore tie dyed clothing and bellbottom jeans and smoked weed somewhat regularly. I even participated in an anti-war protest at the Federal Correctional Institution in Danbury, organized by Activists Fathers Daniel and Phillip Barrigan (as I recall, organized from their respective prison cells, as a result of an earlier incarceration). But in truth, I never really fully embraced the contention that society was fatally flawed and needed to be reconstructed from the ground up. I was just playing a role, seeking only temporary distraction and diversion from what had become the rather mundane and tedious routine of work a day existence. Basically mimicking the iconoclastic behavior and paying lip service to the concept as a way to capture a sense of freedom and identify with a cause without honestly believing in it; and soon the reality of my responsibilities as a husband and father easily over shadowed and took precedence over the limited enjoyment I derived from playing the irresponsible, pot smoking hippie game. Besides, I was playing the game alone, in that, Patricia never joined in (other than accepting some of the fashion trends), and certainly never smoked weed (or anything else, for that matter- She was the ONLY ONE in her family to never smoke cigarettes). She tolerated my inappropriate behavior and my iconoclastic demeanor as a mother would sometimes tolerate the minor, mischievous actions of her hyperactive child; and shaking her head, casting a condescending and patronizing glance and occasionally offer a sarcastic comment, somehow, in her wisdom, knowing that this phase would soon pass.

Even our kids were embarrassed when "hippie Dad" would attend PTA meetings and some of their friends would appear shocked, stare and whisper, commenting about my rather radical sartorial and grooming direction when compared to their own fathers. Interestingly enough though, both daughters really liked my left of center friends, unique fashion statements, bushy beards, long hair and all, and would always stop playing and join with the group that had gathered, just to hang out with them too, and listen to the music and conversation and get exposure to unorthodox views; and the kids were readily accepted by most of them as "cool, bright and personable kids", and they all welcomed having them engage with us, even at their young age.

In addition, not to sound defensive, I was a good eight to ten years younger, on average, than most of their friend's dads, which might qualify as another extenuating factor. Or not.

But before long, the hippie diversion was little more than a distant reflection in the rear view mirror of a vehicle called better judgement. My focus soon returned to creating a better life for my family and I gradually shifted back toward the middle.

By the late sixties, Shelagh had fallen in love with a guy

named Eddie, who had been recently divorced, had children by that marriage, but obviously had no compunction or mis-givings about moving to Florida with Shelagh and leaving them behind. I also believe that there was an ongoing dispute regarding child support that also added to the attractiveness of moving to Florida where he wouldn't face extradition. They ended up in Miami where they started their life together and were married on June 18th. Before long, their family started to take shape with the arrival of their first child, a daughter, then a second daughter close behind and finally a few years later, a son. Eddie made a living as a short run truck driver, mostly picking up scraps and waste grease from restaurants and food processing plants to be processed by the soap manu-facturing company for whom he worked. As his kids got older, they would tease him, calling him "Ol' Fat and Bones", making a joking reference to the primary material he would pick up and his chosen type of employment. But he was a good guy, hard working and good natured, and they seemed happy and well adjusted in their small, modest stucco home in the land of sunshine.

Due to the separation distance, and the fact that Shelagh was preoccupied with raising her young family, as were we, Patricia and Shelagh didn't communicate very much. It was a time before email and cell phones, so long distance phone calls and "snail mail" were the only options for communica-tion which also explained the lack of frequent contact.

But as her family grew and started enjoying life experi-ences, Shelagh would include photographs in her correspon-dence, and Patricia would do the same. Some were every day family photos, others were taken at various holidays, and some were the rites of passage sort, like first holy communion, first day of kindergarten, etc., the net effect of which was to create a longing in Patricia for an occasion to visit Shelagh and her new family in person, and she became anxious for a trip to Miami. I think that a trip to the south Florida beaches and warm, sunny weather might have been a contributing factor as well.

Finally, I think it was around 1972 or 73, we decided to embark upon what seemed to us at the time to be a great adventure, and piled the kids into the car and embarked on the long road trip of our sojourn to Miami for a combined family visit and brief vacation. Patricia had traveled to Florida previously on family vacations , both as a child and as a teenager, but I had personally never traveled south of the Mason-Dixon line. At the time, the cost of airfare for flying a family of four to Miami was out of reach, so a twenty-four hour drive was the only option. It was actually quite enjoyable and I got to see places and things that I had never seen before, and more importantly, the kids were well behaved and enjoyed seeing the sights and new experiences as well, intermittently napping, playing games and doing some good natured bickering and teasing.

After our arrival in Miami, we checked in to a budget priced motel, did some sightseeing and tourist stuff, before meeting up with Shelagh and Eddie and their kids. We met them at an upscale Chinese Restaurant the first night, then went to their home for a visit the following day. Then a few days of beach visits and attraction visits while Eddie was at work and before we knew it, the time to face the long return drive home had arrived. We had enjoyed a very nice visit and by the time it concluded, Patricia and I were completely infatuated with Florida. In spite of the fact that the trip had taken place in mid summer (the only time I could get vacation days off), we loved the climate, loved the easy access to the beach, were impressed with the casual and very active lifestyle and the glamour of the city. In addition, we were surprised with the relatively low cost of living, once out of the metropolitan area. The seed had been planted, and we began to fantasize and consider "what if scenarios" which would ultimately come to fruition and precipitate a major change in our lives. But for now, it was back to the grindstone and to life as usual in Connecticut.

The sixties had ended with a flourish. Social and cultural changes were settling in, technology was advancing, as evidenced by the Apollo mission, manned by Astronauts, Armstrong, Collins and Aldrin, and Neil Armstrong's lunar walk on July 20th, 1969. An in your face manifestation of the hippie counterculture movement occurred that year as well, with the Woodstock Music Festival on August 15-18th, which set the tone for the direction of music for the first half of the next decade. Patricia and I had secured the services of her mom to watch the kids for a couple of days so we could attend, but when we encountered jammed traffic on the New York Thruway, my irritation and impatience kicked in and we aborted and returned home without ever even getting close. In hindsight, it was just as well.

For us, the seventies began with a much more traditional and conventional approach to life and family rearing. When our kids entered school (Called Shelter Rock School), Patricia decided to seek employment, claiming that she would suffer from acute boredom with the girls at school and being responsible only for housewife duties in such a small home. She was offered a part time job at Howland's Department Store that accommodated her need to be home when the kids arrived home from school. Being very personable, outgoing, charismatic and assertive, she made an excellent salesperson and as the girls got a little older, went on full time status.

I was doing well at work too, learning the technical end of the optical business, specifically vacuum deposited, thin film coating applications on laser lenses and other precision lenses, reticles, optical filters and mirrors (one of which ended up in a reflector device and placed on the surface of the moon during a later lunar landing). We discontinued seeing many of our old friends, simply because we outgrew them and had much different priorities. Our circle was smaller, but we had more in common and we were genuinely closer to them than we had previously been with the old group. Life was generally good.

We hadn't seen Billy since we moved from our old address on Joe's Hill Rd. to High Street Extension but kept abreast of his exploits via family gossip, anecdotes and rumor.

And like Billy, Charlie didn't come around much either, with him being fairly self absorbed and egocentric, and spending most of his time when not working at Markoff Shoes, practice bowling or league bowling, watching sports, reading detective novels and murder mysteries, playing poker or hanging out with buddies. But we did see him when visiting Walt and Betty, and he always seemed genuinely pleased to see his nieces and they were quite affectionate toward him. Walt and Betty visited us at our house at least once or twice per week and were doing a masterful job of spoiling the girls. During those spontaneous visits to Patricia's mom and dad's house, if Charlie was in fact there, he seldom carried on much of a conversation with us, so we knew little of his social life other than what we heard indirectly from Walt and Betty. So, one can imagine the surprise when we learned of his intention to get married.

32

AN UNLIKELY UNION
OF HEARTS

We were so disconnected from Charlie that we never knew he was seriously dating someone, let alone planning to take the leap into marriage. As Brother's-in-law, we had little in common, other than the family ties, and it seemed that we lived in a parallel universe. In truth, I never really liked him, but certainly didn't dislike him either. I was ambivalent toward him, as he was toward me, and we simply never made much of an effort to become more friendly. I found him to be a bit of an enigma anyway, never quite sure if he was gay and "in the closet" (as many gay people were during that time), heterosexual but with little libido, or perhaps hetero but super inhibited or even impotent, or just too self absorbed to be willing to share his time, treasure, psyche or an emotional connection with a girlfriend or spouse.

Now, with the announcement of his imminent wedding, I assumed that we might develop a closer bond due to the increase in commonality. He was soon to become a husband, and because she had kids from a previous marriage, a father, and we would at least have that in common. His fiancee was quite nice; attractive, of Italian decent and from a prosperous family. I'm not sure how they actually met; perhaps it was through an introduction by a mutual friend who worked at the local Chevrolet dealership in Brewster, NY, or a serendipitous encounter at his favorite hang out, the Brewster Lanes bowling alley, another bar, or something else, but either way, the date had been set for December 1st of 1973 and Patricia and I were excited for him. As stated, she had been previously married and had two sons, one approaching teenager, who really didn't accept Charlie well and by all appearances, didn't like him very much, and another around 7 or 8 who seemed to get along with him well, or at least tolerate him well.

The wedding was quite large and absolutely gorgeous, the bride looked lovely, the wedding dress was stunning, and the reception was over the top. It was held at the Fountainhead in New Rochelle, NY and the celebration extended into the wee hours of the morning. Massive ice sculptures, champagne fountains, a great live band, excellent gourmet food and top shelf wines and liquor all helped define the affair as elite and fashionable. Everything was executed flawlessly and it was the most upscale event that Patricia and I had attended to that date. Ironically though, Charlie seemed distracted and acted as though he were more a guest than the groom, taking direction rather than offering any, and was uncharacteristically reticent. He took little part in the planning, other than the Vegas honeymoon, and basically appeared to be along for the ride- his words, offered jokingly but clearly containing some degree of truth.

After the wedding, they went to Las Vegas for a lavish honeymoon, and upon returning, moved in at a ski resort, in the Patterson, NY area, owned by her parents, and where she worked helping to manage the facility. In addition to skiing facilities, there was an upscale restaurant and catering business. It seemed to me that Charlie would be in his element, but unfortunately, it just wasn't meant to be and within months, she was seeking an annulment and it was granted without question or opposition.

Charlie claimed that she refused to use the Brett surname, which angered him to the point where he decided to bail, but I suspect that there is more to the story than that. As a matter of fact, the wedding reception program and menu introduced them as Mr. and Mrs. Walter C. Brett, Jr. and she showed no indication that she would balk at the concept of becoming Mrs. Charles Brett. I know for sure that he quickly regretted having married based upon his sullen and depressed mood during the months that followed but he never articulated the cause.

There were few reasons accepted for granting an annulment by the Catholic Church at the time, and I don't think that refusal to use the husband's surname rather than maiden name is among them, but I guess it's not relevant. The net result was that he was living back home within a few months of the wedding. With that union virtually stillborn and officially classified by an annulment as having never happened, another was on the horizon that would hopefully have better outcome and greater longevity.

A mere 3 months later, the wedding of Billy and his fiancee, Gail, was scheduled. Once again, as with Charlie, we had virtually lost contact with Billy and had received no indication that he had become that serious with someone. We had settled down into a family lifestyle, busily trying to raise children, advance careers and avoid frivolous spending, whereas Billy was living the carefree, bachelor (or as some relatives would say; "playboy") lifestyle and we simply no longer had much, other than being family, in common. When we received the news of the wedding and received the invitation, we were as surprised and incredulous as we were when receiving Charlie's announcement, but for entirely different reasons. Although Billy was working at the insurance agency with his mom; primarily as a salesman; he wasn't fond of keeping regular hours and concentrated more on partying than work. Still suffering the effects of PTSD associated with his experience in Vietnam, still drinking heavily, gambling, still bar hopping in New York State and at local watering holes like The Big 'O', The Brass Rail, Dave's Old Six, The Red Rooster and others, still driving fast cars and dressing in expensive clothes and, still living at home; he seemed to us to be the least likely candidate for marriage. Never the less, the date had been set for February 16th of '74 at the First Congregational Church, In Ridgefield, CT with a reception following at the Red Lion Restaurant, also in Ridgefield.

While far less extravagant than Charlie's, and considerably smaller, it was a nice affair, with lots of family in attendance and a good number of friends from both sides. As Irish weddings often do, this one became slightly raucous, with copious amounts of alcohol consumed, lots of joking and laughter.

I must admit that Patricia and I did more than our share of drinking as well and were enjoying a significant buzz by the time we headed home. Fortunately, we had ridden with Walt and Betty, probably anticipating some degree of incapacity related to my sobriety level, potentially impacting safe and proper motor vehicle operation; further, assuming that Walt, who by now had endured three heart attacks, would be at least somewhat prudent and judicious with his imbibing. Wrong assumption. Although we didn't realize it at the time, by the conclusion of the festivities, Walt, whom had clearly been having a good time, socializing, telling jokes and drinking Irish Whiskey mixed with ginger ale, was "three sheets to the wind" and feeling no pain.

With Walt behind the wheel, we slowly made it back, without incident, to their house, where our car was parked, although much to Walt's chagrin, Betty kept offering some subtle driving coaching and an ongoing critique. Just as we thought all was well and we could collectively breathe a sigh of relief, Walt pulls into the driveway, only about a car length long, and on the approach to the garage entrance, plowed into the side of the opening, breaking the left front headlight, dent-ing the fender and grill and destroying the garage door mold-ing, the track and knocking out one of the rollers. The door consequently tilted about six inches left rendering it inoper-able, and while laughing, Walt exclaimed; "To hell with it. It's no big deal. I'll fix it tomorrow. I'm taking a nap!" One would have to know Walt to have appreciated this but wisely, no one ever mentioned it again.

Regarding Billy and Gail's marriage, we heard very little about it after the fact, but assumed (and hoped, for the good of the relationship) that Billy had altered his behavior and that they were doing okay. She had a good job as an accountant working as a Profit Analyst at Benrus Corporation and he con-tinued as a salesman at the family business. Quickly, we once again lost touch.

33

A LEAP OF FAITH

In the spring of 1974, after Billy and Gail's wedding, Patricia and I took another family trip to Florida to visit Shelagh and her growing young family. She had been writing to Patricia regularly and they exchanged photos of the respective kids with most of the correspondence, which served to intensify our desire to visit them again. As with previous trips, our infatuation with Florida grew and we began to explore fantasy scenarios where we would relocate and enjoy a vastly improved lifestyle in the land of sun and surf. I don't really believe that Patricia took it very seriously, but I was beginning to put thoughts into potential actions. It wasn't that I was completely unhappy at my job or that I disliked Connecticut that much, but the high taxes and cost of living, the sometimes brutal winters and relatively short summers were beginning to take a toll. Combine that with the realization that my Optical Coating Technician job at Laser Optics would ultimately provide little opportunity for advancement or true financial success, not to mention that I was exposed daily to dangerous chemicals in the film application process, some of which were radioactive, provided the impetus to create change. I began researching Optical Coating Laboratories located in Florida in various trade journals and discovered one in the Tampa Bay area. After doing my research and due diligence, I learned that it was a small "mom and pop" operation involved more in the manufacture and creation of mirrors, reticles and precision coatings for industrial substrates, while devoting a lesser effort and concentration on state of the art laser lenses. I immediately drafted a current resume and sent it off, highlighting my design knowledge and application acumen specifically in the one area where they were weakest. I was elated when I received a positive response requesting a meeting and informal telephone interview.

My solicitation was conducted without Patricia's knowledge, primarily because I didn't want to get her excited and/or nervous without reason, not being all that confident that I'd receive a response. When I brought her up to speed regarding canvassing for related jobs in Florida and the progress I had made, she became slightly conflicted; pensive and somewhat anxious and apprehensive, juxtaposed with excited and joyful at the prospect of a positive lifestyle change.

But, she could be a procrastinator at times, and needed some prodding and cajoling and assurance that it would go well before she would completely embrace the concept. After an encouraging and positive telephone conversation with the prospective employer, we set up a face to face meeting time for further discussion. I could only get a couple days off so, embarking on a Friday evening after work, we did a marathon overnight drive, sharing the driving duties while the other napped, and got there in 20 hours. We checked in to a modest bay side motel in Dunedin, FL and, thinking positively and optimistically, spent Sunday checking out the area, the available homes, schools and restaurants, and of course the beaches. Afterward, we drove to Safety Harbor where the facility was located, and while surprised at the small size of the operation facility, located in a store front on the main drag through town, it appeared a good deal larger as we peaked into the windows and saw the equipment. The more we looked, the more we fell in love with the area.

On Sunday evening we met with the owner and his wife, as well as his son, who also worked there. I learned during the meeting and interview that the son had previously worked for a company that was a leader in the industry and based near Santa Barbara, California, and the owner himself had worked for an industry icon (B&L) for many years before retiring and starting his own business, which obviously provided credibility and an assurance that this wasn't a fly by night operation. Their primary interest was to capture the plethora of proprietary, state of the art designs that I tucked nicely away in the recesses of my brain during the 7 years I had worked in the industry, and while they weren't actively seeking to hire someone when I first made my approach, I was able to peak their interest enough that they were prepared to offer a position. My strong desire to make a lifestyle change and to escape the tedium and monotony of my current position, as well as our infatuation with the Gulf Coast of Florida, combined with the high cost of living in Connecticut, especially when compared to Florida at the time, clouded my judgement. After many discussions and conversations over the phone during the next few weeks following the interview, I accepted offer of a position with a lot less money than I had expected. The saving grace was that they implied that at some point, after integrating the designs and gaining additional business as a result, I would be offered a small percentage of the business as compensation. In my naivete, I got nothing in writing.

Patricia was excited yet apprehensive. Conservative by nature, she became hesitant and balked at walking away from a secure job (two actually, when adding her department manager position at Howland's Department Store into the mix), taking the kids from a school that they really liked and where they were doing well scholastically, leaving our comfortable, albeit very small, home with a relatively new in-ground swimming pool, our close circle of friends and most of all, leaving

Walt and Betty and extended family behind. Walt wasn't in very good health after his multiple heart attacks and Betty and Walt were both of enormous help with child care, perpetually available and providing a strong, positive influence for the kids as well as a home that they found very enjoyable to visit and to be entertained.

Obviously, that stacked up on the negative side of the equation, but the excitement of the proposed change of day to day life, and the prospect of professional advancement, not to mention warm sunny days, sandy beaches and crystal clear Gulf Waters, all weighed heavily on the positive side and before long, she was enthusiastically supportive and fully engaged in the process.

I asked for a private meeting with the company president to make a proposal. My plan was a long shot, but due to being held in high esteem, my work respected and appreciated, and the cordial, friendly and family-like work environment, I didn't think it unreasonable.

I began by thanking him for the opportunity provided 7 years earlier, for the education they provided through job training and for the casual and fun work atmosphere they had created. I thanked them for the fond memories, all the holiday parties and company picnics, their willingness and financial support to allow me to create an Industrial Softball League team and the occasional bonus check. Then I asked to be laid off! Boom! Shocked and perplexed, the initial response was; "WHAT?!" I explained that I had been wanting to make a move to Florida for quite some time, I realized that there was only so far I could go at this current job, considering their perception of me as a technician and not manager, and without going into detail, told of securing another position. I also stated that the move and related preparations would take over a month and that a 30 day lapse in income would create a hardship, and rather than simply quit, and therefore be without a money stream for 4 weeks, to be "laid off" would provide access to unemployment insurance and greatly assist in the transition. Finally, I said that I knew that I was asking a lot but to analyze my contribution to the company over my tenure there and if he felt it worthy, I would be very appreciative. He graciously agreed.

Things were falling into place and we would soon be off on our great adventure.

The house sold quickly By Owner and it had fortunately appreciated nicely during the time we were there. Granted, we had made some nice improvements and the country had been experiencing severe inflation during much of that time but it had almost doubled in value which, based upon equity received at sale, provided a significant down payment on our new home in Florida.

We purchased in a new section called 'Countryside' which was composed subdivisions of various price points, convenient shopping, medical care, restaurants and entertainment. It was a typical Florida cement block construction with applied stucco, open and bright, small yard and screened lanai. We rented a transition home in Hudson while construction on our home in Dunedin (Countryside) was being completed and I commuted for about 6 weeks before actually moving in at a subdivision called 'Woodgate'.

Patricia and the children adapted quickly and loved living there. The kids adjusted rapidly to their new school and made friends quickly. Patricia was decorating the house and learning the area. We frequently went to the beaches, purchased a used ski boat and visited many of the attractions.

It was as though we had incorporated a vacation with every day life. After a while though, Patricia became restless and decided to go back to work. She secured a position in a privately owned, single location, upscale women's dress shop as a sales person and quickly became the manager. It was conveniently located in Countryside Mall, a mere .8 miles from our home. Her outgoing personality, gregarious nature and charismatic presence all contributed to her rapid success. The owners, a retired Air Force Lieutenant Colonel and his wife, became very fond of her and before long, started treating her like family.

I, on the other hand, hadn't adjusted very well to my new job. There existed a dramatic conflict of personalities between the owner and his son and me, and the resulting work dynamic was, to say the least, tense. I've never been known to repress my thoughts or emotions and I express frustration in a very direct manner. In addition, it became quite evident that they had never intended to provide part ownership as a component of my compensation. Without that, the salary simply wasn't enough, and as my awareness of that fact increased, so did my anger and hostility level. I held my tongue for as long as I could, but a relatively insignificant event occurred (I can't even remember specifically what it was now) that became the proverbial straw the broke the camel's back and I erupted in a fusillade of epithets, accusations and claims of fraudulent hiring practices which abruptly ended with an emphatic; "fuck you; I quit". Not a smart move. Emotion and frustration got the best of me and I had spontaneously created a big problem. When I arrived home at mid day, Patricia gave me a "what the hell is going on" look, suspecting the worst based upon prior disclosures of my frustration level and anecdotes of profoundly irritating office occurrences. When I confided that I had just dug a pretty deep hole by resigning and that we needed to strategize a plan 'B', she didn't panic and didn't cast aspersion. She was completely supportive and said; "Don't worry". We'll figure something out". What we figured out ultimately became a disaster.

The following day I returned to finalize the terms of my departure. As expected, they were probably as happy to see me go and I was to leave and offered no resistance. However, they stated that they would withhold my final paycheck and a two week severance check until I provided documents containing various written design formula for the substrate coatings. Unfortunately, no such document existed, in that all designs were taken from memory and calculated guess work. This issue became a major bone of contention and it took many weeks for me to jot something down that they deemed acceptable, but they ultimately provided the final compensation. We parted ways amicably, and in retrospect, it eventually worked out for the best, but not until a dramatic life lesson would take place that would place our marriage in dire straights. Finding employment in the general area, in my chosen field, would be nearly impossible due to the specialized and esoteric nature of the optical coatings industry. Searching outside my particular discipline would require virtually starting over learning a new skill and working up through the ranks before I could match my previous income.

I had too many obligations to make that practical but searched anyway, hoping for the best.

Walt and Betty missed the kids greatly and longed for the family gatherings that we had all enjoyed so much while in Connecticut. Patricia missed her mom and dad too, and frequently suggested that they get a small second home near us in Florida. It was about this time that they decided to take her advice and start shopping for that second home where they could spend the winters and reconnect with their grandchildren and with Patricia. We accompanied them on their home shopping excursions while they stayed at a motel near downtown Dunedin, FL. Within a short period of time we discovered a very nice mobile home community (there are many in Florida) within a few miles of our house and they purchased it immediately.

Being out of work was a double edged sword. On the plus side, Patricia and I had time to show Walt and Betty around the area, take in some attractions, go with them and the kids to the numerous beaches and parks and enjoy a lot of late lunches and happy hours at beach side restaurants and bars.

Shelagh and Eddie and their children also traveled up from Miami to visit and we had ample time to entertain them. We boated in the Gulf and water skied at Lake Tarpon, played tennis at the community courts and worked in our yard. The bad news was that we were going broke! By six months in I was entering panic mode. In desperation, I began going back to the trade journals to see what employment opportunities might be offered there. Before long, I discovered an optical coating laboratory in Huntingdon Valley, PA that was seeking a person with my skills. After a long heart to heart discussion with Patricia, she agreed that we had no other option except to fan out and seek employment where ever it might be. If hired, it could be a stop gap measure; or, if it worked out very well, perhaps a permanent move. I could rent an apartment on a six month basis, rent furniture and test the waters while she maintained the home front. I would try to travel home as often as possible and would send her my paycheck every two weeks to maintain the home and pay the bills. She assured me that she would be fine, having her parents and her new employers, with whom she had become very friendly, there for her emotional support.

I applied, they responded positively, an interview was set up, for which I drove to the Philly area, and after the interview, I was immediately offered the position. I accepted and headed to the Philadelphia area the next week.

34

THE BEST-LAID PLANS
OFTEN GO AWRY

Patricia had more traits in common with John and Mary Brett than she realized at the time. It was as though it was part of the DNA passed down from paternal grandparents, one of whom she never met and the other she only knew when Mary was elderly and in failing health. She was optimistic, strong and strong-willed, a romantic like John and a pragmatist like Mary. She valued family, both near and extended, and shared their desire to create a comfortable, secure life for her children. She cared about others and enjoyed serving and doing things for them. She was amiable and extremely likable and had a charm and charismatic presence that was unmistakable. She also needed to feel loved.

I was a thousand miles from home, focusing my entire concentration on rebuilding my career, while covering my expenses with as little cash outlay as possible so the bulk of my income could be sent home. Food, lodging and transportation expense was kept to a minimum-

Exhibit 'A' was my apartment in a small Philly suburb called Crydon. I took the place sight unseen, with absolutely no preliminary investigation, simply because it seemed like a good value, but quickly discovered that I had made a mistake. It wasn't in the best area would be an understatement, made worse by a neighbor in the adjacent unit who was confined by friends in an effort to resolve her drug addiction and get her off heroin. The sounds of her agony going through withdrawal easily penetrated the paper thin walls of my apartment, keeping me awake for many hours during virtually sleepless nights. Another part of my cost saving effort was to reject the notion of having a phone installed, opting to simply use the phone booth located in front of the WAWA Convenience store directly in front of my complex. These were before the days of cell phones and email, so communication wasn't nearly as convenient or easy. I would write letters to be included with pay checks mailed home and call from the lab if I worked on a Saturday or sometimes when staying late after most of the other employees had left. Needless to say, not a good system.

I liked the job reasonably well and after the initial six months, began to think in terms of making it permanent. I took a few days off to drive home and discuss it with Patricia.

She agreed to arrange for Walt and Betty to watch the kids while she would drive up to the area the following week, and together, we would view available homes and towns that might be acceptable. Our realtor took us to view multiple houses in various suburban towns within commuting distance and the more we looked, the more Patricia hated it. The housing costs in that area were considerably more expensive than in Florida, she didn't like the style of the majority of homes, and didn't like the traffic, the noise and the "rat race" lifestyle. She returned home less than enthusiastic about leaving Florida for that area. Discouraged but not ready to throw in the towel, I leased another apartment, this time in Hatboro, for a twelve month term, basically just kicking the can down the road.

As time progressed, the demands of the job prevented taking long weekends to travel home to spend time with my family and I was feeling more and more isolated and disconnected every day. The home visits were decreasing to one every couple of months and when I did get to come home I felt like a guest in my own house. I knew that something needed to change quickly or the negative impact of the separation would ultimately destroy our marriage. We continued going through the motions, primarily due to inertia and monetary need until a wake up call occurred one Saturday morning. It was a literal wake up call for Patricia and a figurative wake up call for me. I had gone to the office early that Saturday, mainly because I had nothing of a personal nature planned and thought that it might be a way to fend off the typical weekend boredom and blues. I arrived before anyone else and decided to take advantage of some private time to call home. It was then about 8:30 AM, so if she had decided to sleep a little late that morning, I would provide a wake up call and get in a brief conversation before she got involved in weekend chores, shopping or transporting the kids to some destination or event. When she answered, I said; "Good morning sweetheart". "How's your day going so far?" She responded; "It's good, Honey". "How about you?" I replied; "The weather is cool and rainy and I thought that it would be a good idea to come in to work for a few hours this morning". There was a long pregnant pause followed by; "Who is this?" An odd question considering how I had begun the conversation. Incredulous, I said; "What the hell do you mean, who is this?!" She said; "Oh, I'm sorry. Your voice sounded different. It must be that office phone". My thought was, "Houston, we have a problem", but we briefly continued a rather awkward conversation, both anxious to have it conclude so we could mutually analyze what had just transpired. It didn't take a rocket scientist to determine that we had reached a critical point and that if I wanted to save our marriage, immediate action needed to take place. On Sunday I packed my clothes and some personal items into my car, wrote a resignation letter, took it, along with the key to the laboratory entrance, and left them on my boss's desk and headed home. I concluded the resignation letter with the following words: My decision is irrevocable. Please don't call me.

Her faux pas was obviously unintentional, but I believed that she subconsciously wanted to broadcast that a crucial point had been reached and if we didn't take immediate action, we would soon reach a point of no return.

I had failed my family and I had failed my wife. My responsibility was to not only supply an income and adequate cash flow, but to provide emotional support, companionship, love and leadership as well. She was conflicted. For the first time in her adult life she was experiencing being virtually single, due to the thousand mile separation, and enjoying the associated freedom and excitement. On the other hand, she enjoyed being part of a nuclear family, nurturing her children and creating a comfortable, harmonious home. Things had gotten out of control because I had abdicated many of my responsibilities as a husband and father and it was long past time to come to a meeting of minds so that we could map a path forward.

My return home was a difficult time. There was shouting and arguing, there were accusations, tears, finger pointing, assignment of blame and ugly things said to each other. But in the end, we mutually decided that we had something far too valuable to allow it to be destroyed. A new plan and strategy must be created. She was still convinced that we could succeed while remaining in Florida. Her mom and dad were now living just a few miles away, having moved to Florida to be close to their grandchildren and to us, she loved the casual Florida lifestyle, the weather and her job. Her mom and dad also loved it and were actually spending ten months of the year there and only spending the hottest months of July and August at their Connecticut home. As a matter of fact, they spent so little time in Connecticut that they signed over the deed to the house to Charlie. When they traveled home they were technically visiting him. Walt thoroughly enjoyed hanging out with buddies, playing shuffleboard, mini-golf, cards and all the other stereotypical trappings of retired life in Florida. Betty also had a close circle of friends, some of whom were also retired nurses, and a good social life. To move and leave them behind after they had fairly recently moved, just to be close to us, seemed unthinkable to her. I eventually acquiesced and we spent the better part of the next few months formulating a potential plan.

When in crisis mode, one should draw from strengths, but also acknowledge weaknesses attempting to minimize exposure to them. Our eventual plan did the former but ignored the latter. But, it sounded like a good plan at the time and serendipity provided a few missing pieces of the puzzle. Patricia liked the business of fine ladies apparel and had wanted to someday open her own store. When a new, upscale shopping center was built in Dunedin, both she and her employer at the time, were very impressed with the concept. It was rustic yet hip, sophisticated yet welcoming and beautifully landscaped. The siding was raw cedar that was sanded to a smooth finish and stained in a beach weathered tone and accented with individual planter boxes at each store front. Colorful nautical theme canvass awnings over each store location and meandering walkways with benches, pergolas and trellis' invited shoppers to linger. It was anchored by a popular grocery store and a trendy restaurant to ensure traffic. While engaging in casual conversation with her employers, Chris and Robin, she mentioned that if she ever had the where with all to open her own store, it would be in a center like that.

"What a coincidence"; they replied. "We had taken notice of that center too and were thinking of opening a second location there!" One thing led to another and before long they had come to conclusion that Patricia should open the store as her own, and they would function as silent partners. It was a mutually practical solution, in that, they would have difficulty getting approval from the powers that be at Countryside Mall for a satellite location, under the same name, to be opened so close to their existing store (it was only a couple of miles away). Patricia and I had some savings to invest in the business, but not much due to maintaining two households while I was in Philly and most of my income going to meet expenses.

Chris and Robin would act as advisors and consultants, Patricia would manage, sell and do product procurement and I would build the interior, the dressing rooms and assemble racks and handle bookkeeping, accounting, cleaning and maintenance, advertising and promotion. Done deal! Seemed like a win/ win for both parties. We decorated to project an upscale, sophisticated image, targeting the middle aged to mature woman with a fair amount of disposable income. The carpets were steel grey with flagstone tile walkways, chrome fixtures, including waterfall racks and rounders, chrome and mirrored etageres and navy blue canvass awnings over the wall racks to tie in with the exterior theme. It launched well and in spite of the fact that it was our first attempt to run our own business, most knowledgeable people and self proclaimed experts we knew said that we "were doing everything right".

Unfortunately, as I has alluded to earlier, we ignored our weaknesses when we planned to open the business. The first weakness, at least it was a weakness in this case, was that I am a very direct, assertive, take charge individual and ended up rubbing our partner the wrong way. Chris and I didn't get along very well and he, as the one with experience, expected that I would contribute my part and then basically disappear until needed. That didn't happen. I wanted control. Eventually, he was the one to chalk it up as a lesson learned and disappear and remained a partner in name only. The other weakness that we hadn't adequately considered was that we were, like many who start their first business, under capitalized. The store was covering expenses and showing a slight profit, but certainly not enough to live on. To compound the problem, my previous dilemma, which was having no job opportunities in the immediate area where I could secure employment and thereby supplement our cash flow, still hadn't changed.

Finally, we had befriended a couple who had opened a sporting goods store only three stores down from ours, and when they confided that they were having difficulty getting their store profitable, I offered to help.

He was working for an oil company based in Houston, and had little to do with the store due to his hectic schedule and extensive travel requirements.

She was basically left to fend for herself and do as best as she could with their new business. Having teenage kids at home intensified the pressure on her and she was getting burned out very quickly. I figured that I was there anyway and could split my time between the two stores. I would help her with the sales, giving her some much needed time at home, do some of the product purchasing, management duties and advertising direction. In return, I would get a portion of the business. Once again, ego and ambition clouded my vision.

We kept at it, hoping for a dramatic, albeit premature, spike in business, not knowing that it typically takes at least two to three years before one can start drawing a significant income from a start up business. We were slowly sinking.

35

TO EVERY THING THERE IS A SEASON, AND A TIME TO EVERY PURPOSE UNDER HEAVEN

The summer of 1978 was a particularly difficult one. I was busy at the sporting goods store, organizing softball games, 5k and 10K running events, racquetball tournaments and tennis matches, hoping to gain some peripheral business, but saw little result from the effort other than participating in enough of the activities and events myself to get in really good shape. In addition, I was doing a lot of service work like stringing tennis racquets, re-lacing old baseball gloves and heat pressing soccer and other team jerseys- anything I could think of to bring in extra revenue. Patricia's business had slowed considerably as well, with the "snowbirds" back up north in the cooler climates. The days were hot, steamy and sultry but the demands of the business kept us from getting much enjoyment from the beaches. We had also sold our boat and therefore had no opportunity to going skiing at lake Tarpon. Recreation pretty much consisted of dining out or hanging out at a downscale little sports bar that had recently opened in the shopping center. Patricia and the girls also missed Walt and Betty and were anxious for their return from Connecticut.

During Patricia's conversations with Betty she learned that Billy and Gail had divorced after only a couple of years of marriage and that Billy was living back home with his mother and still selling insurance. I can't say that we were surprised. She also brought her up to date on all the other family gossip and mentioned that she and Walt would be heading back to Florida in September and suggested, as a way to celebrate their return, perhaps bringing the kids to Disney the week after they arrived, as well as going to the Kapok Tree Restaurant, which we thought of as a tourist trap but they liked. Even though the kids were reaching the age were Disney World didn't hold the same allure for them as it did when they were younger, they still liked to go, but we suspected that they'd want to bring a friend along to enhance the enjoyment level. Betty also mentioned that Charlie would be coming down shortly after September, mainly to go to the tracks (horse and greyhound racing) and Jai Alai matches to gamble.

By the time September arrived we were looking forward to the prospect of cooler weather, although that never really happened until November during most years, and the return of the "Snowbirds", hopeful that they would arrive with pockets and purses full of money and a strong desire to replace items in their wardrobes with some of the beautiful, new, stylish apparel that we purchased and hung seductively throughout the store in anticipation of their arrival. The store was called: 'Patricia A. Bergeron- Fine Ladies Apparel' and we had planned to launch a radio campaign and print media ads to coincide with the influx of visitors and winter residents. However, September was primarily a month for anxious anticipation, with relatively few of our target audience arriving before the end of the month, and many more later in October and November.

It was no surprise then, as the afternoon of Friday September 8th was upon us, that we had seen virtually no increase in business yet. I had returned back to the dress shop after my partner in the Sports Center had returned from picking her children up from school. We were preparing for an appointment with a blouse rep who was scheduled to bring some winter items for preview. It was her best selling line of ladies tops so she didn't refuse the appointment, although she discouraged vendors to show up during business hours. The phone rang, and thinking that it may be her rep, named Lee, either canceling or running late, she immediately answered. I overheard the voice on the other end and it sounded like it might be her mother. After Patricia cheerfully greeted her, a long protracted silence occurred, followed by a look of shock, then with a broken voice saying; "Oh my God, no!" She appeared weak and had to sit at her desk to continue. Concerned and somewhat frightened, I said; "What's wrong", but she just shook her head and turned away, continuing the conversation in hushed tones.

The conversation was short and when she hung up the phone she turned to me with tears welled up in her eyes and in a broken voice informed me that Walt had passed away on their way back to Florida, in a town in Virginia called Staunton, while behind the wheel of their car. Betty said that they were traveling on Interstate 81 headed south, traveling at about 65 miles per hour, casually conversing and enjoying the scenery, and in the middle of a sentence, Walt gasped and bent over, dying immediately. She had the presence of mind to grab the steering wheel and guide the vehicle to the shoulder. Fortunately, his foot disengaged from the accelerator and they coasted to a stop. Shaking and hyperventilating, but maintaining composure, she checked him for a pulse and as a registered nurse, knew immediately that he was gone. Some Good Samaritans had stopped to offer assistance but nothing could be done but wait for the ambulance. After being pronounced dead, he was taken to a funeral home and Betty drove to a hotel and checked in for the night. I held Patricia tightly for a few minutes while she wept, then quickly gaining composure, she immediately got on the phone and attempted to book a one way flight from Tampa to Staunton and finally found one on Ozark Airlines.

She was clearly shaken and devastated over the loss of her father, and surprisingly after weeping for only a few additional minutes, regained her composure once again and made contact with her mother to provide the details of the flight and inform her that she would be accompanying her on the remainder of the drive back to Dunedin. I greatly admired her strength and inner fortitude as she took control and laid out the plan. She adored her dad and was closer to him than were any of her siblings, but she was also strong and knew that she needed to remain so, to support and comfort her mother. She contacted one of her part time employees to fill in during the time she would be transporting her mom back to Dunedin, then we went home to tell our daughters the terrible news.

Walt was only 70 when he passed away, but in truth, it was longer than many of us expected due to his series of heart attacks. He was a fighter and he was strong and kept, for the most part, a positive attitude and a lust for life. He was the last of John and Mary's sons to pass away, and with Jimmy gone, the torch would now be handed to Billy and Charlie; the last two male descendants carrying the Brett surname.

Walt had some remarkable experiences, served his country well and his family well. He had a good marriage with Betty, and although they weren't the most romantic couple, they suited each other well and clearly shared a strong mutual fondness, even if outward displays of affection were rare.

He was at times opinionated and demanding but tolerant as well. He never achieved notoriety or fortune but he was a good man, provided excellent paternal nurturing, care and support for his family, and loved his children, especially "Patty", above all else. And, after he had gotten over his initial disdain for me, we bonded and got reasonably close. As with John and Mary, his legacy was in his children and in the values that he had instilled in them. He had at times, been disappointed in them, but he was also proud of them. He had done his best and the ball was now in their court.

He was cremated at the mortuary in Staunton, Virginia and his cremains were sent to the Dunedin, Florida post office, where I picked them up a week after his demise. There is something quite sobering about holding a box containing the remains of a loved one. We intended to travel back to Danbury, Connecticut to have a short, private service and arrange for interment at the family plot, at St. Peter's Cemetery. Fittingly, he would be buried next to John and Mary's grave and the Navy would be providing a headstone. (Henry had purchased another family plot on the opposite side of the cemetery, where he and Jimmy were buried).

By this time, Shelly had retired and moved back to Danbury, living in a retirement home near Deer Hill Avenue, but Leona, who had also retired, had moved to Ormand Beach, Florida, so coordination of the service would be somewhat difficult if we wanted them to be included. Leona had a car, a white Chevrolet Impala, but never actually drove it and it sat unprotected in a designated, covered, but open air, parking space under her condominium.

As a result, the salt air (she lived right on the beach) wreaked havoc with the paint and chrome, yet the interior was as new. I'm not sure that she had remained capable of driving anyway, so if she were to attend a service in Danbury, another mode of transportation would need to be considered. She had become slightly eccentric in her old age but Patricia and I visited her on a few occasions and always enjoyed the time spent with her. She was an intellectual and sophisticated woman and I loved talking politics, world affairs, literature and theater with her and after she consumed a few martinis, and the subsequent glow from the alcohol took effect, she would invariably get animated and boisterous. As I recall, her daily ritual included a minimum of two to three martinis and she loved the way I made them (with virtually no more than a drop of vermouth and another drop of olive brine) and I enjoyed the challenge of keeping up with her. She had developed a "white fetish" made manifest in her choice of clothing (always white with only sparse pop of color from a strategically placed accessory) and all her furnishings (white upholstered couches and chairs, white painted wooden furniture, white carpeting, white themed paintings, such as snowy winter scenes, and white themed wall hangings and curio pieces), and finally, white walls, curtains, draperies, cabinets and appliances, which all coalesced to cause some degree of trepidation when we visited with our two kids. In spite of the fact that she spent many years teaching, she had by this time, seemed to have developed an intolerance for children, not only because they could disrupt the serenity of her rather isolated idyllic, pristine, protected little cocoon, but also due to the potential they had for disturbing the order of her carefully placed items and for soiling her ubiquitous whiteness. She had always been fair complected and blonde haired, but by that age she required hair coloring to keep it from showing grey, and sure enough, she chose a color of blonde that was almost white.

When we visited, she would typically chat with us for a while, while savoring her martinis, then offer to take us to her favorite steakhouse, an upscale eatery just a short one mile drive from her condo, where we would sit for an hour or so, continuing to enjoy a few additional martinis before finally ordering. She was quite opinionated and really didn't care who would overhear her political diatribes and had little concern whether or not someone took offense. Quite candidly, I encouraged it by introducing a topic that would get her started, just for the entertainment value. She was feisty and self confident and I really liked her.

As it turned out, it would be many months before we could get back to Danbury for the interment, and ultimately, Shelly and Leona didn't make it to the graveside service; just Patricia and I, her mother, Charlie, Patricia's Aunt Sue and Cousin Jane (on her mother's side) and Aunt Betty attended. Walt was laid to rest in the Brett family plot, near John and Mary, "Cook" and Bertie and other family members.

There were sites designated for Leona, Shelly, Charlie and Betty (Walt's wife) as well, assuring that at some point in the (hopefully distant) future, most of the original family members would be at rest together in perpetuity. The family plot was located at the south end of the cemetery adjacent to Kenosia Avenue and near Lake Kenosia. It was sublimely peaceful and tranquil with a wooded area farther south and a small section nearby designated for still born children or children who had died shortly after birth. The cemetery was also very near the home where Walt and Betty had raised their children and where many happy memories were created, which I'm sure, made Walt's spirit happy.

36

ANOTHER QUANTUM SHIFT IN DIRECTION

Walt's passing had deeply affected Patricia, and although her behavioral and attitudinal changes were subtle at first, which would obviously be expected while one is grieving, the effect became more pronounced as time went on. She was quieter and slightly withdrawn, her language was more caustic and sarcastic, and she seemed disengaged, distracted and, as far as our relationship was concerned, disconnected. That, combined with the difficulties generating enough profit from the businesses to adequately support our family, created a very strained and tense dynamic. We frankly weren't getting along very well. It was a time for her to reevaluate her life and I don't think she really knew what she wanted from it. I, on the other hand, knew exactly what I wanted: professional success and prosperity, but was struggling with finding the correct pathway. I wanted nothing more than to make my family proud and to support them well. I had taken risks to move outside my comfort zone and achieve my goal, but had failed thus far. I wanted my children to be well provided for and happy, and I think that they were reasonably content at the time, but the future was uncertain and in jeopardy, which troubled me greatly. I adored them, although they probably didn't realize it at the time due to my decidedly autocratic and strict, authoritarian, Drill Instructor approach to parenting, and worried that a collapse of the business would cause undue hardship.

If only we had more time and better liquidity, I thought, we might be able to make a success of the stores. In desperation, we sold our home to gain access to the equity, and rented another to replace it, also in the Countryside section, but this time across US 19 near the mall in a subdivision called Cypress Bend. That had the effect of generating enough funds to last us for another year. It did not, however, improve the circumstances of our odyssey together as a couple. Troubling and uncertain times indeed.

Charlie was profoundly affected as well. Although he showed little emotion, Walt's passing provided the impetus for a somewhat dramatic, life altering move on his part. More accurately, I should term it a maneuver. With Walt no longer around to offer advice, direction, critique, chastisement or to castigate for reckless acts of self indulgence, Charlie decided to sell the family home, turning the equity (100% of the value) into a de facto inheritance, and at least to some extent, support his proclivity toward sports betting and gambling. His intention was to relocate to Florida, moving in at 'Lark Haven Manor' mobile home park with Betty, his mother.

There was a guest bedroom available in the double wide and she would cook, clean and do laundry, just as she had done when he was a kid. In his eyes, it was the perfect lifestyle. He took a job doing what he had always done- selling shoes. On the upside, he began investing in the stock market, but approached it as just another method of gambling. He did fairly well for a while but not for long. Too many high risk, high return investments that became more risk than return. He dined out a lot, he frequented horse tracks, dog tracks, Jai Alai matches, sporting events and had a regular poker group with whom he became very friendly. He was working hard on pissing away his "inheritance".

Prior to Charlie's arrival in Florida, Betty had asked me to come over to help move a few things around in preparation for his move in, to take some of Walt's old tools from the shed (some were old enough to be considered antiques, but I loved them and really appreciated her giving them to me- It was a neat way to remember him), and to help her clean up the Pontiac Sunbird, which hadn't been cleaned since they left Connecticut on their fateful journey south. During my process of detailing the car, I ran into a problem cleaning off the windshield. There was an area about the diameter of a basketball in the center of the driver's half of the glass that appeared to have been etched or frosted, but oddly, it was on both, interior and exterior sides and no matter what cleaning solvent I tried, I simply could not remove it. Betty claimed that she hadn't noticed it before leaving Connecticut, or during the trip south, but when she returned to the driver's seat after the ambulance had left the scene, she noticed it then. While driving to the motel where she would spend the night, her mind was racing, she was overwhelmed with grief and she paid little attention to what she believed to be a large smudge, or perhaps some condensation on the windshield, and there was no time for musing in regard to the source of the cloudiness. However, the following morning she returned to retrieve some items, and noticing it again, she got a moistened bath towel and attempted to clean it. After trying with no success, she began contemplating and came to the conclusion that when Walt died instantly, his soul left the imperfection in the glass as it passed through the windshield. When she related the hypothesis, my first reaction was that it was just her private way to help cope with the traumatic occurrence and that the theory was patently ridiculous. However, I never discovered the cause nor did I ever have any success in removing it. As preposterous as her assertion sounded, I can't help but wonder.

We eventually had to replace the windshield.

By the start of 1980 we had reached another crisis point. Once again running out of funds, and the business still unable to support us, we were channeling our frustration toward each other and it was having a deleterious effect on our relationship. Compounding the harshness of unbridled reality was receiving some very sad news from Danbury. We learned that Billy had unexpectedly passed away on January 13th, at a mere 33 years of age.

The circumstances surrounding his demise were murky and Betty (Betty R., his mother) simply said that he had become ill and quickly passed and would discuss it no further. We heard other rumors though, some suspecting suicide, or suicide by alcohol (Cirrhosis), one indicating that he had gotten into a dispute that resulted in an altercation which caused internal organ damage from repeated blows to his midsection and another suggesting that it had been pneumonia complicated by heart disease and despondency. Whatever the cause, it was a shock. One can't imagine the profound sadness, grief and despair that Betty R. had endured, losing her husband, then both sons at such an early age.

And coincidentally, Charlie, much to his chagrin, was now the last living descendant of John and Mary Brett capable of carrying forward the family name; not that he personally assigned any importance to that.

Billy was the same age as Patricia and I, and not only was he her cousin, but a classmate and friend as well. Losing someone your own age tends to put life into perspective and sometimes create a sense of urgency in getting one's own life on track; especially when that person who had passed was the young age of 33.

It drove home the fact the something radical needed to be done to correct our off target trajectory and increasingly tenuous marital harmony. Early that summer I decided to take a drive to Catskill, NY where my mother had relocated with her partner, George. It would provide time for me to clear my head, get my thoughts together and ponder our next move. When my mother had left Brookfield, she moved into a modest duplex in Sandy Hook, Connecticut. Years earlier, she and my father had met and become somewhat friendly with a Newtown couple named George and Grace. George was a cabinet maker and carpenter by profession and she was a nurse. They divorced about the same time that my father had left for "parts unknown". As luck would have it, George ended up moving to the other side of the duplex where my mother lived and they soon developed a friendship that evolved into a romantic attachment. They shared the commonality of a broken long term marriage and a past casual friendship, which jump started the relationship. Oddly enough, she seemed happy with him and much better adjusted and mentally balanced than she was with my father. He eventually moved in with her in order to cut expenses but they obviously never married due to the impact that would have on her government assistance income. As she aged, and her health began to further deteriorate, she pined for her old home town and convinced George that Catskill was a worthy destination for retirement. It didn't take much convincing, in that, George didn't work steadily and when he did, he charged exorbitant rates and took a very long time to complete a project. That tended to severely limit the number of available jobs but he did have a loyal following of generally quite affluent customers wanting ultra custom work and willing to pay top dollar for it.

And, with all that said, he performed masterful craftsmanship and created beautiful pieces, sometimes approaching works of art, and probably well worth what he charged. I had worked for him part time on a few projects while he was living in Sandy Hook, and I must say that I learned a lot from him. Our children liked visiting them when she and George were in Sandy Hook, before we moved to Florida; and for that matter, we did too. My mother would always prepare a feast, special occasion or not, George was a music lover, so he and I would play guitars or just listen to music on their phonograph, we would talk philosophy or world affairs as he would whip up batches of his favorite cocktail; Stingers- (cognac and Rumplemintz). He was a proud Swede and somewhat arrogant, getting more so with the consumption of a few Stingers, but our spirited conversations were always mutually enjoyable.

Now, in early 1980, as her health was getting worse and she was in her 70's, and as I was having personal difficulties, I felt that it would be a good time to get some "windshield time" to engage in some deep contemplation and planning on my way to New York, and well as accomplishing a long past due visit with them. Fortuitously, I stopped at a service station/ convenience store to refuel, stretch my legs and purchase a soft drink before proceeding north. After filling the tank, I pulled up and parked in front of the store to pay (that was before 'pay at the pump' or 'pay first' was initiated), walked inside, browsed the soft drink cooler for a minute or two, then decided on a selection from the chest type cooler with cold (somewhat dirty) water surrounding the bottles of soda.

I chose one called 'Cheerwine' simply because I had never heard of it, and the young lady at the checkout counter informed me that it was produced right there in North Carolina, in a small town called Salisbury, a few hours west of our location on Interstate 95. She followed by saying; "Y'all are a long way from home". "I seen your Florida plates!". I replied in the affirmative, while indicating that I wasn't sure how long I would remain in residence there though. She said; "I get it; I used to live in Florida for a while too, and it's nice, but I found it to be much nicer up here in North Carolina". I asked what was nicer about it and she said; "Well, just about everything- the people, the cost of living, the climate, the beauty of the land, the changing seasons, easy access to the beaches and the mountains, you name it!" She then asked where I intended to move and I responded; "To the state of Confusion", the facetious nature of which apparently took a minute to register. She then said; "Well, you should consider North Carolina for yourself. It's beautiful and growing fast". "I like it in Raleigh, where I live, but if you moved to Charlotte, you'd probably like it better and you'd be only a couple hours to the beach and a couple hours to the mountains, and have all that big city convenience right there in your backyard". Unbeknownst to her, she had planted a seed that would quickly take root.

After a brief visit with my mother and George, I decided to take a different route back to Florida.

I would travel south on Interstate 81 to I-77 south, then proceed to Charlotte, on the NC and SC border, stopping for the night there to investigate. I had been thinking about the words of the young lady at the gas stop for a few days, and considered it to be some form of divine providence, or at least a fortuitously delivered conceptual idea during a chance meeting that would provide a topic for some mental masturbation on the long drive home. I liked what I saw, and by the time I returned home, I decided to retake control of my life and Charlotte would be the place to do it. I didn't yet know what I would do for employment, where we would live or even if Patricia would agree to the plan, but I felt inexorably drawn to it and had great resolve to make it happen. I instinctively knew that remaining in Florida would destroy our relationship and if she chose not to accompany me to North Carolina, it would simply be the acceleration of the inevitable.

She was at first hesitant and undecided but wasn't willing to toss 15 plus years of marriage, and soon agreed that she would, once again, support my seemingly poor judgement and reckless folly and join in with the new adventure. She still saw something in me that few others did, and while not very enthusiastic about the prospect of starting over, she expressed continued trust and commitment. I suspect that the spirit of her grandparents, John and Mary, and perhaps even Walt, were looking down upon her, and having a view of the future unavailable to mere mortals, guided her in that decision.

We placed the store (actually stores- she had open a second location in a new shopping center in Oldsmar, FL by then, for reasons not worthy of explanation within this missive) on the market, priced for a quick sale.

I had continued at the sporting goods store during the transition, making it clear to the owners that it would only last for a few weeks longer. It was during that transition time that a sunglass salesman entered the store to pitch his product and to outline the profit potential that it would offer the store. We had never carried optical sunwear previously and the margins were extremely attractive.

I resisted at first, but when he offered to place the first 12 piece display in on consignment, as a test to demonstrate the ease with which they would sell and the extra profit that they would generate, I agreed. We placed the mirrored display at the checkout counter, thinking that it would, in spite of the fact that these were an upscale, moderately priced accessory, create impulse purchases and point of sale activity. He was right. I sold eleven of the twelve before he returned at the end of the month.

I was very impressed, not only with the product, but with him. He exuded success and exhibited the trappings of a guy who enjoyed an affluent lifestyle. He drove a new white Mercedes, wore expensive clothing and jewelry, owned a Miami Vice style Cigarette Boat, talked about vacations to the Caribbean Islands and had a nice condo on the beach. He surfed in the summer and went on ski vacations in the winter. He was blonde haired, tanned and confident and at a young age, he had seemed to have "made it".

Frankly, I was envious. We ended up expanding the collection to 48 pieces and the sell through was good enough to place a selection in Patricia's dress shop as well. He had fashion forward items suitable for her clientele as well as the sports oriented products that targeted cyclists, boaters, runners, tennis players, hunters, surfers and just plain old beach bums. My foray into retail sunglasses was brief, but something that would set the stage for future involvement that would prove very lucrative and this preliminary experience would be highly valuable.

By the fall of 1980, the Florida experience (read that, debacle) was behind us and we were in Charlotte ready to begin the first day of the rest of our life.

37

THE NEW BEGINNING

As bad as the Florida experience was, it was also cathartic and educational. We were both down but not out; had lost some battles but not the war. Being without money and without direction was actually a double edged sword. The negative side is obvious, but on the plus side was the ability to chart an entirely new direction, unencumbered by preconceived notions of what we must do and where we must do it. We were broke but had no outstanding debts either. The house we rented was in east Charlotte, at the time a reasonably good section, but not so much now. It served the purpose while we became adjusted to the area and got oriented to our surroundings and would be a launch pad for future moves. We got the girls registered in school in time for the start of the first semester. They seemed okay with the move but I knew that in truth, they were very unhappy with it. But they were both very outgoing and made new friends quickly. Patricia was the first to score a job. She took a position as the manager of a ladies clothing store called Stuart's in Freedom Mall, out toward the airport. It was still a viable mall back then but has since all but disappeared. It was a bit of a commute but it provided a much needed income while I was still investigating opportunities. And investigate I did. I gravitated toward sales and applied at a car dealership, audio store and a Biotech Company, and for various reasons, rejected them all. Then, about six weeks after we had settled in, a serendipitous event occurred that would change my (and our) life forever and place me on the road to success that would surpass my wildest dreams and expectations. I'm now fond of saying that if one wants to achieve great success in life, one must first discover and identify what it is that they are truly and inherently good at, then embrace it with full gusto. You have to absolutely love it. Many career decisions are made at the tender young age of eighteen or twenty-one and the path of one's career is established as a result of parental pressure or expectation, teacher "guidance" or even societal pressures, with the mind's eye creating a glorified image of a particular vocation that is unrealistic and the result of inadequately informed naivete. Once that path is established and the journey begins, it's exceedingly difficult to alter course and embark upon an entirely new direction. I ask; "from which eighteen year old would you take career advice?" The simple answer is very few, if any. It takes time to mature and discover what one's true strengths are and to identify which have grown during the first dozen years or so out of the formal education system and exactly which job would best suit their specific skill set.

For me, this was a time when the planets aligned, cards fell into place, good fortune shined down and gods of serendipity magically appeared, and I was offered an opportunity that suited my skills better than anything ever presented previously. I'm not sure if it was actually serendipity, or another case of divine providence sent to intersect and meld with the other divine providence message blithely delivered by the checkout girl at the service station on I-95, months earlier; but I heard it loud and clear, and it changed everything. It was the rebirth and fresh start that I had hoped for.....no, had committed to discover.

While pursuing the help wanted ads, I discovered something

of interest under the listings for Trades and Technical, that was headlined: Optical Sales Representative. My assumption was, based upon the location in the classified section, that it was soliciting for a position calling on the optical manufacturing industry, promoting the sales of precision optics. Suspecting that it would require a degree in engineering, which I didn't possess, and having no outside sales experience, I almost passed it over, but something told me that I had nothing to lose, and interviewing experience to gain by simply applying. I rolled the dice and called. After all, I thought, I have a good working knowledge of lens manufacture and thin film application, so why not? My only concern was that, if by some fluke I were to be awarded the position, I would be so far over my head that I would crash and burn immediately. Never the less, I called the number listed and connected directly to the East Coast Regional Manager, who was staying at the Radisson Hotel in uptown Charlotte. He said that he was nearing the completion of his interviewing process but, due to a cancellation, had a slot open in the morning just prior to the departure of his return flight to New York's La Guardia airport.

Fortunately, I arrived early for the interview because the Radisson parking garage was full and uptown Charlotte parking can be a nightmare. I called when I entered the lobby and he said that he had a suite on the 9th floor and the door was propped open, so just come on up. The guy who had canceled actually called him back and showed up for an interview after all, but it had been a short meeting and he had just left. To say he was an interesting guy would be an understatement. He was quite short, perhaps 5'5" or 5'6" but clearly exhibited the physique of a bodybuilder. After introductions, I jokingly said; "Does the job require heavy lifting? If so, it would appear that you have been doing it for quite some time". He chuckled, then indicated that he had been seriously involved in the sport of body building for quite a while and had competed in the 'Mr. New York' Bodybuilding Contest previously and placed in the top three, twice. He was born and raised in Queens, NY and the accent made it quite obvious. Some of my relatives were from Queens and I recognized the accent at once. He had a great sense of humor and easy going, while aggressive, personality. His selection of attire surprised me though. I had expected a buttoned down, conservative executive in a three piece suit, but to the contrary, he was wearing cowboy boots, designer jeans, white dress shirt with a turquoise and silver bolo tie and what appeared to be an expensive sharkskin sport jacket.

There was also a large cowboy hat sitting on the dresser. It was around the time when a very popular and successful movie, starring John Travolta and Debra Winger, called Urban Cowboy, had created a strong social influence and both men and women were embracing "the look", and western apparel was somewhat commonly seen, to some degree or another, on even the most unlikely people (like middle management executives from New York representing an industry dominated by Jewish entrepreneurs!) When I somewhat disingenuously complemented his western garb, he replied that in sales, and more specifically, sales of a fashion product, one needed to be aware of fashion trends, stay on the leading edge of changes, and project an image of design awareness. When I returned a quizzical look, he quickly said; "you might be under a slight misunderstanding".

He continued by stating that the position available was for an outside sales representative to call on what he called "the three 'O's", selling eyeglass frames for their dispensary. The three 'O's were Opticians, Optometrists and Ophthalmologists, primarily in independent practice. That was a bit of an epiphany. I wasn't sure whether I should be relieved or disappointed and apprehensive.

He then continued further to say that in a highly competitive field, one needed to stand out in the crowd and with a multitude of salespeople competing for limited frame board display space within the dispensary, it's helpful to make a memorable first impression and to be easily remembered when you make your follow up call six to eight weeks later. As a side bar comment, he said that Representatives have an account load of approximately 250 customers, some more, some less, both active and potential and that the Rep. calls on the same accounts on an eight week cycle. Further, he said that most successful representatives are charismatic and "can entertain". He had adopted the western look as part of his shtick. I was beginning to understand.

We discovered some commonality, not only having a similar sense of humor, but also because I was Born in Westchester County New York and both of us were the offspring of New York City natives. We hit it off well right from the start. In spite of that, I thought it would be a long shot. I had no real fashion experience and he made it clear that although it was certainly a medical device, it was for most people, especially women, more a fashion accessory. I would have a lot to learn. Finally he said that the compensation was straight commission and that I would be working as an Independent Contractor, taking a draw against commission. I knew that would not make Patricia happy. She desperately wanted me to secure a steady, dependable income that could provide security at once.

But that would return me to prior situations where we were simply spinning our wheels and not truly prospering. However, I had yet to be offered the position and he indicated that he had conducted a total of nine interviews with some highly qualified candidates, so it was a moot point.

Much to my surprise, he called early the following morning and, initially assuming that it was just a courtesy call to thank me for my time and to inform me that another of the candidates had been selected, I didn't get too excited about it. But after exchanging a few pleasantries, he said; "I'm going outside the box on this one and I'm willing to take a chance on you. I have a gut feeling that you have the drive and charisma necessary to become a great success in this field. If, after our interview, you still believe that this is what you want to do with the rest of your life, I'm prepared to offer you the position". I had mixed emotions. I was excited and anxious to get started, and actually thought back to the sunglass representative I had met at the sporting goods store, and although this new position didn't include sunglasses at the time, the product and sales concept were similar enough to cast a glow of optimism and a promise of prosperity. But I also felt some trepidation. This would be an entirely new direction and there was a small amount of uncertainty. Conflicting emotions aside, I immediately accepted.

I said that I was unencumbered by other work commitments and would like to get started as soon as possible, so he agreed to meet for training the following week. Training was brief (only two and a half days) but intensive. We spent day one in the hotel room, going over product, history of the industry, history of the company, organization of an itinerary, techniques for controlling travel costs and insight into the needs of "the three 'O's.

On day two, we cold called, with him doing the approach and the product presentations while I observed. On day three, I did presentations, with him chiming in as necessary and offering critique in the car after the call. On day four, I was on my own. Somewhat nervous about going solo so soon, I asked; "Is that it?" "Don't you think I can use a little more training before being turned loose?" His response was great. He said that in his mind, sales is an art form and each successful salesperson is therefore an artist. He followed by saying that if one were to hang a Picasso and Van Gogh masterpiece side by side on a gallery wall, one would immediately recognize them as brilliant works of art. But if you asked Picasso to create a painting that looked exactly like that Van Gogh next to it, you'd get nothing like it. The same applies to van Gogh. He could not create a painting that looked exactly like the one created by Picasso. Each artist had his own style and must be true to it. Therefore, if sales too is an art form, you, as an artist, need to discover your own style. I don't want you trying to imitate or emulate my style, I want you to find your own. I'll be back in thirty days and we'll analyze what you have learned and the style you have developed. That was exactly what I needed to hear.

I could write another book on the experiences within the industry and the juggernaut that my career became, but suffice it to say, I quickly achieved great success. Within the first year, I became one of the top three salespeople nationwide. In year two, I was at the number one spot. I was building a reputation quickly and my competitors were frequently intimidated when entering an office and seeing the amount of my product occupying the client's frame boards. After having just turned thirty-four years of age, Patricia and I discovered a serendipitous path to professional success. I say "Patricia and I" because it was as though she had taken the job as well. She offered constant encouragement, support, planning assistance and motivational advice. We were in it together. I traveled weekly, leaving early on Monday mornings to reach my first appointment by the time the office opened, or sometimes, if it was at the farthest reaches of my territory, leaving on Sunday evening in order to start my week without delay. Many times I wouldn't return home until late Friday evening. She never complained and took on almost the entire responsibility of parenting. Thirty-Four was late to be starting an entirely new career so I felt a sense of urgency, wanting to advance my career faster than would be normally expected. When a competitor, who had been considered one of the industry leaders, was prepared to launch a new division, I was recruited. It was for a line of product that would be classified as "high end" and "high quality" compared to the budget priced line of product that I was currently carrying. My current collection was comprised of copies and knock offs of old standards, like items based upon iconic styles from industry stalwarts like Artcraft, American Optical, Bausch and Lomb, but also items copied from designers like Diane Von Furstenberg and 'Playboy' (which was one of the first to license their brand name for eyewear) by a company named Optyl. Sunglasses were now becoming a major component of my product line. Switching to the new, more upscale product line would mean targeting a different demographic of quality minded patients and more upscale dispensaries. I threw caution to the wind, dropped my current line, accepted the new offer and as it turned out, the transition was easy, and the new line provided even greater success.

We moved from Charlotte to a smaller but more centrally located town, from a territory perspective, called Salisbury, within a year of starting in the business. The house was a new, expansive ranch style home on a full acre of property, located just outside the city limits, providing a rural, country atmosphere, yet with easy access to town. We later installed a large in-ground swimming pool and made numerous improvements during our time there.

Once again, even as a "rookie", I was ranked within the top salespeople in the company, consistently within the top five, frequently within the top three, and was able to do so without the luxury of a chain store located within my territory and with a smaller sized account load than the other top finishers. The number one Rep each year happened to have a store called 'Precision Lenscrafters" located in his territory, which bought product for a multitude of stores, many of which were located within other states and sales territories, giving him a huge advantage.

They bought in that territory and shipped to other locations outside the territory. Never the less, credit where credit is due; he landed that account in the first place which certainly benefited our entire company, and with those profits generated, contributed to the benefit of all, through new product innovations and ultimately through acquisitions.

While this narrative is the saga of the Brett family, and not intended to be my story, I became an integral part of it when Patricia and I married. She and I became one and the synergy between us created my career, which I usually categorize as "our career". I will continue to outline how it developed, specifically because it impacted not only Patricia and I, and our own family, but later, other members of the Brett family as well. In addition, the dreams John and Mary Brett had for their family and descendants were realized more by Patricia than any other and for that reason, I'm including it in the odyssey of the family, while glossing over many of the minor career details and focusing upon only the most salient.

By 1986 the new company division had experienced tremendous growth, necessitating dedicated management. Previously, the regional managers from the original company division were managing both the flagship lines and the new division, but now it was time to promote a team of managers from the ranks of the new division. Based upon my performance and my interactions with upper management, I was one of the individuals selected for the pool of candidates. We all applied for the position by offering a thesis outlining 'What we would do with the company if we were the owner'- (ie; changes to product, changes in direction, changes in management style, etc.), and then going through a subsequent interview process. I must have said the right things because I was one of the candidates selected. I was given two options: Behind door number one, I could manage the Southeast Region, which was already the highest performing region in the country, remain in Salisbury, "cherry pick" a few of my top accounts to retain for my own sales effort, and with little disruption, segue into the position gracefully. Behind door number two, was lurking a potential monster. I was offered the opportunity to assume leadership of the South Central Region. It, unlike the southeast, was at the bottom of the list in terms of performance. It would require intensive care and complete attention.

I would need to relocate to Texas and cover the states ranging from the Mexican border to the Canadian border cutting a swath through the central part of the nation. I would be traveling constantly, I would actually take a cut in income, I would leave my family behind for the first year while I rebuilt the region and only get to travel home about once per month, and then only for a couple of days at a time. Patricia would be allowed to take over approximately 25 of my top accounts for one year while I was getting organized and rebuilding but after that they would go to my replacement salesperson (whom I was personally able to select). What choice made the most sense for me? I found it obvious. As previously stated, having started somewhat late, I wanted to fast track my career. I didn't want to level out at the position of Regional Manager.

As the company continued to grow, I wanted to continue to grow with it. Making the easy choice wouldn't adequately test my management skills, nor would it get me noticed by the powers that be in corporate. If I could turn around the debacle that the south central had become, I would certainly get noticed, but also have the potential of making a lot more money from the sheer weight of numbers and accounts. I could demonstrate my talents and position myself for even greater challenges. There would be risk involved, but without risk, there is seldom significant gain. Patricia and I discussed it for hours and we mutually agreed that door number two was right for us. She knew that it create hardship for her, having me remotely located, but in the spirit of unwavering support of my ambition, she committed to helping me make it work.

Once again, whether it be divine providence or simple timing and luck, we made the correct decision. After basically cleaning house and firing the vast majority of existing sales Reps and replacing them with energetic, focused, ambitious people, we quickly became the top region in increase and total sales dollars nationwide. In many respects, they were uniquely talented but not the typical, normally sought after candidate. With my mind on the opportunity I had been given when I was an unqualified applicant hoping to break into the industry years before, and having enjoyed the benefit of a manager willing to think outside the box and take a chance on me, I intended to pay it forward. I hired a former chef who had been in business with his father and closed the restaurant, a former, aging NFL Cheerleader, a former Baptist Preacher who had questioned his faith and wanted to "take a break from religion", a couple of opticians who wanted to redirect their optical knowledge to outside sales, a safety advisor for the trucking industry, a former small town, west Texas sheriff who had been shot at and decided that he no longer wanted the risk, a beer truck delivery driver, and a long list of others who didn't fit the mold but seemed to share my enthusiasm and a desire to reinvent themselves and desperately needed a fresh start. My "rag-tag group of irregulars", as my boss used to call them, took good advantage of the opportunity and launched the region to top ranked status. I had trained them well, coached them through the formative months and motivated them with continuous positive input, praise where appropriate and caring correction when necessary. After spending the majority of year one in Fort Worth, I shopped around the thirteen state swath through the center of the country for a better location from which to manage my region and soon discovered what I believed to be the optimal location.

We moved to Tulsa, Oklahoma, once again to be centrally located within my new region, and enjoyed continued success and prosperity there. We also made some of the best friends of our lives there. The most difficult aspect of that move was leaving our daughters, who had recently married and were starting a life of their own, behind. We had a home built on the south end of town, on a relatively high bluff overlooking the small neighboring town of Broken Arrow.

It was a California Contemporary with a split cedar shingle

roof, a wooden catwalk bridge entrance, natural stone and cypress siding and massive arched windows. The expansive upper floor interior had a large, open family room and dining area, separated by a huge double sided natural, native stone fireplace open to both rooms and a state of the art kitchen. The entire rear side of that level had four large sliding glass doors facing east toward Broken Arrow, providing outstanding views. Adjacent to the massive fireplace was a wet bar, a mere two steps from the deck, which offered excellent entertaining possibilities. A large deck, built on stilts, extended the entire length of the house on both levels. On the lower level were the bedrooms separated centrally by another family room and the lower deck. The back yard was terraced and beautifully landscaped. We loved it there but with my travel schedule, I wasn't able to spend very much time at home to fully enjoy it.

In 1988 the company signed an exclusive license with one of the world's top designers at that time; Giorgio Armani, and launched another division for that new product line.

While maintaining my full responsibilities for regional management (the thirteen state region), and my personal account load of approximately 50 accounts spread throughout the entire region, I was also selected to simultaneously become a Co-National Sales Manager for that new division. Within the next few years, the success of the new designer division became legendary within the industry. The styling was revolutionary, Armani having drawn design inspiration from small, round, vintage eyewear from the twenties and thirties, using unique and striking materials artistically presented in juxtaposition to state of the art technology. Consumers were ready for a change, elevating a mundane medical device to a haute couture fashion statement status. It became a marketing driven, highly profitable category.

Shortly after the creation of the new designer division another new division launched, positioned between the mainstream and designer lines, with lesser known, somewhat edgy and esoteric designers along with some trendy generic product intended to fill the void and target younger consumers. Patricia was interviewed for that position, covering eastern Oklahoma, northwestern Arkansas and a small section of northeastern Texas.

She too became a top performer very quickly and enjoyed the opportunity to become even more involved.

Life was good. We were prospering nicely, taking lavish European vacations, driving really nice cars, wearing designer clothing and bought a weekend condo on one of the nearby lakes.

I was also designated, without much fanfare, as a National Sales Manager for my division, offering yet another source of income, which required interacting even more frequently with upper management.

I reported directly to an individual who had earned my greatest respect and admiration, and although he was a few years younger, he became my mentor and role model. He was brilliant and the quintessential salesman and manager. He had an innate ability to understand exactly what motivated customers to want to buy, and what motivated salespeople to want to sell.

He had grown up in the business, having a father who had worked for the company when it was very young, prior to him joining. During summer vacations from school (Penn State as a Criminology Major) he would sell frames from the trunk of an older Cadillac to make spending money and help with tuition and upon graduation, simply continued and discovered that he was a natural, instinctively knowing the intricacies and nuance of salesmanship and people management. He gained a respect for my work too, and became a major advocate, assisting in my upward mobility.

Those were exciting days, partly for the ability to succeed and prosper, but also for the satisfaction of contributing to the remarkable growth of an outstanding company. The Tulsa experience was one of the happiest times of our lives, marred by two frightening and sad experiences. One afternoon, while working the Oklahoma City area of her territory, Patricia's BMW was broad sided on the passenger side by a speeding driver and struck with such force that the car skidded sideways for about eight feet before spinning ninety degrees, front end violently striking a concrete abutment. While the paramedics had her strapped on the gurney, preparing to take her to the hospital for examination, she refused to leave without her sales samples (valued in the tens of thousands of dollars) and she was making quite a scene when another sales representative from one of our sister divisions coincidentally approached the scene of the crash, and saved the day by offering to take her samples back to Tulsa for her. Finally, she agreed to go to the emergency room with the medics. The car was totaled and Patricia suffered from hip and back problems from that day forward. The second incident occurred after a regional meeting that I had organized in Hot Springs, Arkansas. It had been a great meeting that combined the sales team from her fledgling division with my larger flagship division. It had been highly productive, but also included a lot of entertainment and activities. I had actually towed my boat to the meeting so we could take advantage of the resort's Lake Hamilton access and do some water skiing. One of my salespeople was a former Mississippi State Slalom Champion and he offered to put on a show. After a busy weekend of work and play, we headed back to Tulsa. On the way home, Patricia started to experience some bleeding and assuming that it was simply a long overdue menstrual period, thought little of it. She had started experiencing frequent irregularity of her menstrual cycle and attributed it to the aging process. This time she had gone over three months without it and seemed relieved that it had finally arrived. By the time we got about half way home, the bleeding had gotten profuse, but she still wasn't too concerned, thinking that it was abnormally heavy because of the length of time between periods. She changed pads multiple times on the way, finally running out and because we had gotten close, just used a beach towel between her and the car seat until we got home. By the time we arrived home we were both getting very concerned and somewhat frightened and when I walked her into the house, she passed out from loss of blood.

My next door neighbor and I rushed her to the hospital where she was examined and found to have suffered a miscarriage. We were shocked. It never dawned on us that she could have been pregnant. At forty-three years of age, we felt that the likelihood was small.

Her blood loss was significant and we were told that she would have died if we had waited any longer. After undergoing a D&C procedure and spending a day in the hospital she returned home for a couple of weeks of recovery. She had refused a blood transfusion and it would take a while for her body to naturally replenish her supply. That was a very frightening experience that caused us to pause and take a careful introspective look and perform an analysis of the break neck pace of our lives. Ironically, it didn't cause us to slow down our intensity, but rather, had an opposite effect. It created greater urgency to attain further success and financial security and we weren't willing to get into an easy rhythm and plateau at the middle management level just yet. And, as fate would have it, the company saw greater potential in me as well.

By 1990 the company had grown by leaps and bounds, and with a sales team of representatives numbering in the mid one hundreds, they found a need for the addition of the new position of 'Vice President of Sales'. Apparently, my strategizing when considering the Regional Manager Position, and the selection made, as well as my jockeying for the National Manager positions for the designer division and the flagship lines, helped define me as an ideal person for selection when company growth required someone to assume greater responsibility and challenge. I was delighted and ecstatic to have been chosen and thrilled to advance to a top management, executive level position.

Two of us were selected, both with the official title of V.P. of Sales; I would be managing the managers and my associate, a fellow named Gene Stevens, would be jokingly called "The Company Priest" answering to the needs and misdeeds of the individual salespeople. There was great symbiosis, and we functioned well as a team, although I must admit that, being rather assertive by nature, I insinuated myself as the lead person of the duo. The compensation offered was generous. My current income, for all the positions simultaneously held, including the income derived from personal sales to my key accounts, and adding in the income from Patricia's personal sales was matched, plus, a fifteen percent increase was added to the total as an incentive to accept the offer. To simply match it would have been treading water. They also created a bonus program related to sales increase. To top it all off, a substantial relocation package was provided. We had just entered the much maligned and frequently vilified ranks of the top one percent of income earners in the country. But, that wasn't even the best part. The excitement, pure pleasure derived from witnessing the rewarding growth and success of what we had created, the joy of watching our salespeople succeed and prosper and the inspiring camaraderie and esprit de corps shared by the top management team rounded out the package to categorically qualify as a dream job. The company founder had sent his son, directly from Italy, to manage the United States distribution arm of the company when he acquired full control of the U.S. branch. He had a vision of complete vertical integration and this was the next logical step in the process.

And, while his son was very young (early twenties) and inexperienced, he was profoundly intuitive and innately talented and his business acumen grew exponentially and after a couple of years he was as qualified as anyone out there to run an up and coming young company destined for greatness.

The transition from 'hired gun" and "road warrior" to in house executive wasn't easy and being confined to an office from 8:00 AM to 7:00 PM required an adjustment, to be sure, but I loved the casual atmosphere and close bond developed between myself and the President/ CEO and the other top executives and fairly quickly got into the routine. The slightly awkward transition was further mitigated by the beautiful North Shore of Long Island location, my posh office- one full glass wall facing the sound, grey flannel wall covering, navy blue carpet and a wet bar, and the friendships quickly formed. Patricia didn't work, rightly assuming that it would be nothing more than a distraction, and that the income would be diminished to the point of useless endeavor due to our tax bracket. Instead, she got involved in community activities, became President of the area Newcomers Club and learned golf. She formed a very close relationships with a group of women in similar situations, and together they enjoyed all that Long Island had to offer. Gene and I moved to the area about six months prior to our wives, to seek out appropriate housing and to quickly dive into the tasks at hand at work, while Patricia and Mary Ann (Gene's wife's name) attended to wrapping up affairs back at our respective homes. Gene and I shared a rental condo in Huntington, NY for six months while we were house shopping. He ultimately bought in Northport, directly on the Long Island Sound, and Patricia and I bought in the Dix Hills area. Our house was only about 75% complete when we discovered it. The builder had constructed seven homes on the end of an existing cul de sac and the final two were incomplete when he filed for bankruptcy. Ours was well on the way to completion but the seventh only had a foundation. We contracted a builder and had it completed to our specifications and it turned our beautifully. It was contemporary, about 4,600 square feet with soaring cathedral ceilings, a full wall white stone fireplace, Nanny or Maid quarters, three car garage and an acre plus of beautifully treed and landscaped property, which is uncommon on Long Island. Patricia loved the house and loved the lifestyle. I took up mountain biking, jet skiing and running for weekend recreation, when I wasn't busy at conventions or off site meetings, and when we had the opportunity, we traveled. Business travel was as enjoyable, or perhaps even more enjoyable, than personal, with trips to Italy for factory visits being the highlight. When there, we would extend our time and travel from the Italian Alps, in Northern Italy, where the factory was located, to Positano, Capri, Sorrento; or to Rome, Florence, Milan or Venice.

On a business level, the growth would make a normal person's head spin. It was during my time there that we launched a major vertical integration campaign, first acquiring U.S. Shoe, the parent company for Lenscrafters, then spinning off the apparel and shoe entities (Nine West, Petite Sophisticate, August Max, Casual Corner) and focusing on the retail optical portion.

From there is was "Katy, bar the door" as the company went full gonzo in acquisition mode. Ray Ban, Pearle Vision, Oakley, a plethora of designer licenses, development of their own managed vision care plan, creation of office management software all followed, making the company the largest optical company in the world; by far! We were having the time of our life, until at six years in, another wake up call arrived.

38

A "ONE EIGHTY"

The year 1996 was one of reflection and contemplation. Betty (R) Brett had passed away in 1988. She survived for eight years after Billy's death, living a relatively solitary existence and never stopped grieving for Henry, Jimmy or Billy. In 1991 Shelly had passed, having lived well into her nineties. She had taken up residence in an assisted living retirement home in Danbury. Leona had passed away peacefully at her home in Ormond Beach in '92, That same year, Betty (M), Patricia's mom, became terminally ill and when Charlie could no longer care for her, they moved her to Miami, where Shelagh cared for her until she passed. Her ashes were buried next to Walt's in St. Peter's Cemetery. Leona and Shelly are there too. My parents died in the mid eighties, my mother was buried in Saugerties, NY and my father was buried near Baltimore, Maryland.

Charlie remained in Florida for a few years after betty died, but eventually moved to Las Vegas, taking a job as a dealer in the Poker Room at the Las Vegas Hilton. Patricia and Shelagh had little contact with him other than the occasional phone call. We did look him up when we took business or pleasure trips to Vegas, usually to take him to dinner or to hang out with him while making the rounds at various casinos. It was actually kind of nice having an insider to guide us around and provide tips on which casinos were giving higher slot pay outs at that particular time. On one occasion we took him with us to 'Bonnie Springs Ranch' out near Red Rock Canyon which was an old west replica town with a bar, small hotel, game farm and horseback riding. After a few beers, we convinced him to get on a horse and go riding with us. It was his first time, and a real hoot, watching him hang on for dear life.

Our hectic schedule made return trips to North Carolina to visit the kids, and now young grandchildren, difficult, but we tried to make it on major holidays. But, in reality, we were essentially missing our grandchildren growing up, and that pained us greatly. Seeing them so seldom certainly didn't offer much opportunity to bond, and when we visited during Christmas of '95, and greeted them, they shied away, recoiling from lack of familiarity, as if they didn't know us. We then realized that we might be sacrificing more than we were willing by being so far removed from them. It was then that we began thinking that a return to North Carolina and re-bonding with our family might be in order and prudently necessary for maintaining good emotional health. After agonizing over it for months, we decided to submit my resignation and implement as graceful an exit as possible, intending to reunite with our family. My resignation was not fully accepted. Rather, an optional solution was offered. I would be able to resign as V.P. of Sales, return to North Carolina, assume the position of Regional manager for North Carolina, Virginia and Florida and pick up some personal accounts for our sunglass lines of Persol, Briko (ski goggles and cycling sport sunglasses), Moschino and a few other designer sunglass lines. Perfect! I could both leave and stay.

We moved into a rental home in Matthews, NC toward the end of 1996 and contracted a builder to construct a home in Harrisburg, close to where the kids lived. Shortly after moving into the Harrisburg home in March of 1997, we got a condo in

Melbourne, Florida to use as a base of operation when working field visits with Florida salespeople.

In spite of the drastic cut in income, it was a great move.
The joys of being involved with family, celebrating holidays together, milestones with grandchildren, extra leisure time and
participating in the rearing of our three grand kids far out-
weighed the monetary loss. Once again, we felt very blessed
and exactly where we wanted to be in life.

But after three solid years, I was approached with an offer
that I couldn't refuse. It would create yet another disruption,
but by this time, disruption was something to which we had
become accustomed. And, truth be told, I missed the stimula-
tion and action of steering a company and providing overall
leadership and guidance. We were happy, and I was professionally satisfied, to some extent, but still felt that I had many
more years of leadership and talent to provide, and secretly
pined for the old days, making a difference and being a person of higher value to a company. And candidly, my ego had
taken a hit, and functioning as a Regional Manager wasn't
as professionally gratifying as being a Vice President, even
though we had a much better relationship with our children
and grandchildren.

While attending one of the biggest trade shows of the year
in Las Vegas, a fall show called Vision Expo West (the top
show was Vision Expo East, held in the spring of the year at
the Jacob Javits Center, in New York), I was approached by a
Japanese Company looking for someone to take over the Vice
President's position, and assist them in, as they described it,
reaching the next level. They were in the number four position
for optical companies in the United States and had stagnated
there for a number of years. Their sales were in the range of
60 to 70 million, a mere drop in the bucket when compared
to my current company, but they were anxious to reach that
mythical point of 100 million in yearly sales, believing that
once that threshold was crossed, and trajectory established,

there would be nothing to prevent them from emulating good old numero uno, my current employer. Unfortunately for them they were in a quandary regarding just how to attain the goal. Their "ambassador" and my liaison, was a gentleman whom I had previously hired as a salesperson to carry the Giorgio Armani line in the Long Island territory. He had done very well, but felt as though he had little opportunity to advance into management there, expressly suffering from the proverbial Catch 22 syndrome- ie; he was reaching very high sales and growth numbers, and therefore someone who might be looked upon for advancement, but advancement was unlikely due to the negative impact removing him from his territory would have on sales and profits. For that reason, he took a management position elsewhere and eventually moved to this Japanese company as the leader of their high fashion designer division.

My interest was piqued and I expressed a desire to meet directly with the "powers that be" from the headquarters in Japan.

I learned that the President of the United States branch was a very charismatic individual, well loved by the employees, but needed help in correcting the dysfunction that had developed. Essentially, the inmates were running the asylum and it was a pretty undisciplined team. There was inter departmental infighting and regional sales management dissension.

They needed a strong leader; a figure head who could instill a sense of common purpose, motivate (especially during speeches at national sales meetings, publication of a company newsletter, individual attention to poor performing regional managers and getting into the field with specific sales reps to coach, mentor and encourage), launch an initiative to acquire more chain store accounts and offer advice for the marketing effort. That sounded intriguing and quite appealing but the piece de resistance of the offer was the salary. It would essentially double what I was currently earning, and although still only about half of my total compensation while functioning in my former position as V.P. of sales, it would be a welcome way to augment retirement saving accounts while I still could.

Once again, Patricia and I had a meeting of the minds. Decisions of this magnitude always required lengthy discussions and careful analysis before coming to a decision. This would require a move to New Jersey and once again, cause me to be away from home for extended periods of time. While not disclosing the time frame of three to five years, mutually agreed upon by Patricia and I, the position was accepted. Patricia and I set the arbitrary cap of five years, hoping that I might be able to extricate myself prior to that. This time we would help mitigate the impact on our relationship by agreeing to meet at least monthly at various locations mid way between New Jersey and Harrisburg, NC, at Bed and Breakfast Inns or quaint motels at scenic locations, and when I was too busy to drive all the way home for an extended weekend, she would drive to New Jersey for a few days. I purchased a condominium in Cedar Knolls, very close to our main office (I could actually walk to work during nice days in the spring, summer and autumn) that was quite nice and very comfortable and Patricia always said that it was like a mini vacation when she came up to visit. The arrangement worked out well and although we missed each other greatly while apart, knowing that we had placed a definite limit on the time frame, helped keep spirits high. In addition, Patricia had taken a position working in the optometry practice office of a friend to keep her active and amused while I was away. She apprenticed as an optician, dispensing glasses to patients and assumed responsibility for buying product. As it turned out, she absolutely loved it and decided that she would make it the focus of the balance of her working career.

I felt somewhat guilty not providing full disclosure to the company and allowing them to infer that I was working toward relocating and making it a permanent commitment, but never intentionally implied that, and rationalized that within the allotted time, the improvement realized would more than compensate for any unintentional deception.

I began in the fall of 2000 and by September of 2001, we were on track to set an all time sales record. Both the company and I were very pleased with the early result and were quite optimistic based on all the changes that I had implemented.

On the morning of September 11th, I awoke early and seeing that the weather was nice, I walked to the office. I had arrived at approximately 8:25, went to the break room and made myself an espresso, grabbed a left over granola bar from a bowl that had been set out for a meeting scheduled for 10:00 AM and headed to my office to prepare for the day. At around 8:50, my Administrative Assistant abruptly entered my office.

I immediately sensed that something was wrong. The color had drained from her face and she was visibly shaking. She said; "You're not going to believe this!" A plane has just flown into the World Trade Center!" She had gotten the info from a live news feed on her computer. Thinking that it must have been a small, private plane, I said; "What an idiot". "Seems like someone should have taken more flying lessons before applying for a license". She responded; "NO!" "You don't get it"- "It was a large passenger plane!". It took a minute for that to register. Without saying anything else, I got up and walked with her to her computer. As other employees arrived, they too gathered around computers throughout the office. Some had heard it on their car radio on their way in, others didn't learn of it until they arrived. There was an unnatural silence, everyone awestruck and glued to the computer screens, trying desperately to make sense of it. As more details became available, some started to panic. Many had close friends, family or relatives who worked in or around the WTC buildings and the concern was reaching a fever pitch. Some began weeping, others ran for telephones and still others asked to return home to wait for news. While most were watching the live news broadcasts, a few of us walked outside to gaze east. We were only 35 miles west of Manhattan and could clearly see the smoke rising and dust clouds forming. By noon we decided to close shop and send everyone home. Nothing could be done at the office during the midst of this tragedy. By 1:00 PM a policeman arrived and told the few of us that remained at the office that we were sequestered there until further notice. They weren't sure yet that the attacks were over and wanted to keep roads clear for emergency vehicles should the need arise. By 3:00 PM we received the "all's clear". I was finally able to get through on the overloaded phone lines and reach Patricia who was attending a lens seminar at one of the Uptown Charlotte Hotels. After telling her that I was safe and sound, I returned to my office to ponder the day's events, not yet contemplating the effect that it might have on business. As I sat there in deep thought, I realized that I had dodged a bullet. I remembered that one of our designer Reps had requested that I join him on an early morning call (9:00 AM) to the Lenscrafter's Store located on the bottom floor of the WTC. Most of their stores bought product at their central location in Ohio, but the few stores located in very upscale, or high fashion districts, were allowed to do some purchasing on site, due to the unique nature of their demanding and sophisticated clientele. Because I had a close relationship with them through my association with my former employer (their parent company) he thought I might be of assistance during the call. For some reason, they contacted him on Thursday, the week earlier, to cancel and reschedule. Had they not, we would have been there at the time of the event. A very sobering realization indeed.

The events of September 11th had an immediate effect on business, or at least how business was conducted, but the effect on sales figures was delayed. The major convention scheduled for later that month in Las Vegas was canceled, in the short term, flights were curtailed, rental cars were hard to come by and people were more nervous when traveling, and in the longer term, increased security measures made flying more difficult. But, sales continued unabated and we finished the year by breaking a record in total sales. The year 2002 was a bit more difficult, with the fabric and culture of our country having changed as a result of the attacks, but regardless, another consecutive record was set for sales that year.

During the next couple of years we took full advantage of that 180 degree turnabout in employment status, and the associated spike in cash flow, to invest in some rental real estate. We considered properties ranging from newly constructed town homes and condos, to small, inexpensive Mill Houses (Shotgun homes) and eventually decided on a mix of each.

In the spring of 2005, as Patricia and I were quickly closing in on the Big Six Oh!, and realizing that we were entering the autumn of our lives, we decided to invoke our mutual promise and adhere to the time frame we had established when I accepted the position at the company. It had been a good run; we had consistently set sales records for the duration of my tenure and I got to travel to the factories in Mainland China, Hong Kong and Japan numerous times, not to mention calls on key accounts overseas, but Patricia and I needed to spend more time together before we ultimately rode off into the sunset. I handed in my resignation, accepted a very nice severance package, sold the condo in Jersey (for a nice profit) and returned home. My intention was to do some part time consulting when the mood struck, in order to remain involved in the business, and to get my home and yard back in order after my long absence.

It was also around that time that Eddie, Shelagh's husband, passed away. He hadn't left her with much, so she sold her house and moved into a small apartment in North Miami Beach with her son Walter, who was disabled after surgery performed when he was a young teenager to remove a malignant brain tumor. Her daughters had both moved out, married and were living on their own. After a year of trying to make ends meet on basically social security and the few dollars realized from the sale of the home, she decided to relocate to North Carolina with Walter, where the cost of living would be lower; and after finding a very modest mill house for rent about an hour and fifteen minutes west of our house, made the move. Interestingly enough, her youngest daughter relocated from Florida to North Carolina about that time as well, but I'm not sure that her mother's decision had any relevance in the thought process.

After about six months off, I secured a consulting job with an Arizona based optical company looking to create an outside salesforce and to make the jump from providing low end, private label product to chain stores, to facilitating direct sales to Eyecare Providers. I was tasked with recruiting and training the new sales force. Then, I accepted a short term gig with a small Florida Optical Company run by a Cuban Expatriate.

Again, to expand the sales force and to train and motivate. They distributed various licensed collections from lesser known, 'B' list designers. While those adventures were somewhat challenging and fun, neither organization had much vision, drive or real commitment to grow, and when my contract was over, I was relieved and glad to see it end.

Patricia remained in her position as a dispenser of eyewear and actually took a similar position in a much more dynamic, progressive and busy multiple office operation. She grew to like that office even better and thoroughly enjoyed the work and the interaction with patients. We began to truly relax for the first time in our lives and "semi retirement" was everything we had hoped it would be.

39

TROUBLE IN VEGAS

During the last year of my run with the Japanese Company, Patricia and I traveled together to that autumn trade show in Las Vegas that had been canceled after the September 11th of '01 tragedy. That year it was held at the Venetian Hotel and as always, it was extremely busy and great fun. Patricia frequently joined me, mainly to view new products and to do some buying for her office and to catch up with old friends that we had made during our long involvement in the industry. It was work, but also a four day long party. Rather than return to the office at the conclusion of the show, Patricia and I stayed for a few extra days to enjoy Vegas and to visit with Charlie. We took him to the Rosewood Grill, on Las Vegas Blvd. (the "strip"), one of his favorites, for lobsters and martinis, then did some casino hopping. He was more quiet than usual, seeming pensive and distracted, and his health didn't seem to be very good. He was still smoking a pack of unfiltered Camels per day and was breathing second hand smoke in the casino for his entire work shift. His COPD was getting worse and starting to slow him down. He vaguely alluded to some big wins while gambling but also told of a few really big losses. Never the less, he claimed to be "almost breaking even" and having a good time living the Vegas lifestyle. He had a small, unkempt apartment in a not so nice part of town and his only social life was remaining at the casino after his shift, hanging out with some co-workers, gambling solo (with a heavy emphasis on sports betting), or on those rare occasions when he was winning big, blowing his winnings on fine dining at five star restaurants and taking in one of the many available shows, with a casual friend or two. We had a good visit and it was nice to see him after a rather long hiatus. Coincidentally, he began calling Patricia more frequently, mainly because he seemed to be lonely and enjoyed talking to her and getting some moral support. At times he seemed lost without his mother, who had pampered and coddled him all his life, and now, at this later stage in life, Patricia was, to some extent, filling the void. As a matter of fact, he never called Shelagh and seemed to have no interest in speaking with her. I'm really not sure why, other than the fact that Patricia had the uncanny ability to make everyone feel important and cared for, which in turn fostered closer relationships. I've never known anyone who didn't like her, and her magnetic personality drew people in like moths to a streetlight.

Sometimes she and Charlie would talk for an hour or more; him talking about a recent book that he had read (he was an avid reader, loving detective stories or murder mysteries) or sharing melancholy reminiscences of good old days in Connecticut, and her attentively listening. He and I never spoke but if I was around to overhear the conversation I would always ask; "So, how's Charlie doing". The answer was usually the same; "Oh, he's okay". But she didn't sound very convincing.

Then a break in the routine occurred and there was over a three week gap between calls. She was becoming concerned to the point where she was prepared to initiate the call herself, something she seldom did, not knowing his work schedule, or play schedule either, for that matter. Then late one Friday evening he called obviously upset. He said that he didn't want to burden her with his problems but he had gotten into serious financial trouble and was close to being evicted from his apartment. He was essentially broke and deeply in debt and couldn't see how he would get himself out of it. Not only did he owe on credit cards and back rent, but he owed the IRS a lot of money in unpaid taxes as well. He was convinced that he would soon be homeless and living on the street. But that wasn't the worst of it. He also owed money from gambling debts and the people owed were dangerous. It had gone beyond threats and a confrontation had occurred after work on the way to his car. He had completed his shift in the poker room, strolled over to the casino bar area for a martini before heading home, then left the building and walked to the designated employee parking section of the hotel garage. It was on the second level but there was a walkway from the casino that entered on level two, so he really didn't have far to walk once he had entered the garage. He was approximately twelve rows away from his vehicle and as he got halfway there he reached into his pocket for his keys. That minor distraction left him unaware of his surroundings, so he was slightly surprised and taken back when an individual appearing to be one of the many indigent vagrants, essentially living on the strip, sleeping on benches and panhandling to survive, seemed to appear out of nowhere, stepping out from between the parked cars. Initially, he thought that he was simply going to be asked for a hand out or charitable donation. Panhandling had become very common and most of the time he just blew the solicitors off, knowing that on most occasions an immediate rejection was enough to send the derelict beggars on their way without incident. Relatively few became aggressive or hostile other than a few epithets or nasty comments being grumbled as the street dwellers turned and left empty handed. And in truth, Charlie wasn't capable of offering a handout to someone anyway. In his mind, he might join their ranks at any time. Slightly irritated at the inconvenience of having to deal with this leech, he gazed at him and started shaking his head to indicate "no!" Undeterred, the guy kept coming and stopped his approach directly in front of Charlie causing him to halt nervously. As Charlie got a better look at the guy he recognized that he had been mistaken. Although the individual was dressed to appear to be a street person, perhaps to be ignored and blend into his surrounding, he was large and burly, had a confident demeanor and a very aggressive "edge".

As he stepped directly in front of Charlie he said; "Stop right there. I have a message for you". He then took a loose cigarette from the pocket of his tattered shirt, lit it, took a long drag and exhaled smoke as he spoke the following words; "You own my friends some money". "It seems like you have no intention of paying your debt, and that could be a very painful mistake". He then paused briefly, as if waiting for Charlie to respond, but Charlie was beginning to panic by this point and couldn't have responded if he wanted, and the stranger finally said; "You DO NOT want to see me again". "You have one week to make good on your obligation". He then flipped the freshly lit cigarette away and said; "Do you understand?"

Knowing that this was probably a discretion is the better part of valor scenario, and realizing that to offer any extenuating circumstances or to plead for a time extension would be futile, Charlie simply nodded, and the guy turned as if to leave, then spinning around 180 degrees, landed a blow against the left side of Charlie's head, in the area of his temple. Charlie was reeling from the blow as the guy landed another, this time against his right jaw. His knees buckled and he dropped to the ground. The guy then kicked him in the midsection, repeating his last statement more emphatically; "You DO NOT want to see me again", then slowly walked to the exit stairs and disappeared as Charlie writhed in pain on the floor of the parking garage. If he had already known that he had gotten himself into some trouble, this certainly drove home the fact that it was SERIOUS trouble. He began to panic. His life was in chaos and it had reached a critical point. He spent the next few days confined to his apartment, contemplating his dilemma as he recovered from the bruising and soreness of the beating. He had called in sick, using a few vacation days to cover his absence. Finally, having reached no conclusion and not knowing what course to take, he called Patricia. During the course of an hour long conversation, he provided all the sordid details, finally asking for advice. It was not only a request for advice but also a veiled plea for help.

She tried to put his mind at ease and told him she would discuss the situation with me and call him back in the morning. After listening to all the lurid details, culminating with the assault and battery, then seeing how upset and concerned that Patricia had become, my initial response reaction was rather foolhardy and knee jerk: I would pack my 357 magnum into my luggage, with enough ammunition to get us out of any potential altercation, drive across the country, ride into Vegas like some White Knight and save Charlie's sorry ass from the bad guys. I would make it an adventure, enjoying the excitement of it all, I thought to myself. We would rent a Uhaul trailer and transport his torn and tattered furniture back here to North Carolina and get him on the way to a new life. Fortunately, her cooler head and higher level of common sense prevailed and she promptly shot down the idea with an appropriately chastising; "Don't be a dumb ass!" Admittedly, her idea was more practical, prudent, mature and better thought out, to say the least. Her observation, after having recently visited Charlie's dump of an apartment, was spot on when she said that he owned nothing worthy of hauling back to NC.

Her idea was to just simply pack his clothes and important papers into his car in the wee hours of mid morning, using the stealth of a cat burglar, trying to remain as unnoticed as possible, and telling absolutely no one of his intention, and leaving no forwarding address, then ride off into the sunset; or in this case, sunrise, to never be seen again. She aptly said that he had nothing worth moving and his mission, should he chose to accept it, was to simply get the hell out of Dodge while he still could. She told him to; "get some sleep before leaving, preferably intend to leave between 2:00 AM and 4:00 AM, and keep driving for as long as you can before stopping to rest. As far as anyone would know, you just silently folded your tent and stole away into the desert and disappeared into oblivion. Plan accepted. He headed east two days later and never looked back.

We found an apartment for him in Concord, NC and scavenged some used furniture from flea markets, second hand stores and no longer needed stored items from the condo in Melbourne that we had sold. He went back into his old stand-by job of shoe salesman, securing a position at Rack Room Shoes. After the initial period in the modest apartment, he moved into our daughter and son-in-law's basement apartment nearby and then, within another short period of time we were able to place him in one of our rental properties, a shotgun style bungalow in Kannapolis, NC where he quickly settled in to an almost reclusive and hermit-like existence, seeing few people other than immediate family. When purchasing the rental bungalow where he would be living, we serendipitously acquired another parcel of property, directly adjacent, that conveyed with it. We had no idea of the windfall until closing, with the agent casually dismissing it as virtually useless due to the local energy company exercising right of way to construct power line towers on it. With me rapidly approaching full retirement, and seeking projects to remain active during that time, I decided to plant grape vines there. While the towers might have been unsightly, and the land was rendered useless for building, there was nothing to prevent me from creating a vineyard in the location. My intention was never to commercially produce wine, but rather to sell my crop to local wineries for supplemental use in their product. I planted Viognier, Petite Verdot and Cabernet grapes along with some varieties of table grapes. That would not only keep me busy tending vines, I could combine necessary maintenance of the rental unit at the same time. In addition, we were seeking property for the creation of a Bed and Breakfast Inn and located a great spot in the Yadkin River Valley (The Wine Region Of NC) that would make the perfect candidate. To round out the retirement itinerary and investment portfolio, we acquired a rental townhouse in a new complex in Harrisburg, NC.

Charlie seemed content, eventually paid off his back taxes and his whereabouts were never discovered by the more nefarious associates of his past. His health, however, began deteriorating fairly quickly and his COPD forced his full retirement.

Coughing spells caused blackouts so he had to stop driving and he spent his time watching sports on television and reading. His adult life had always been sedentary but now it reached the extreme, further exacerbating his poor health. Never the less, he seemed relatively happy and Patricia frequently helped him out financially as well as providing moral support and we visited regularly, providing companionship. He got to be included in some family events and at holiday gatherings and was able to form a closer bond with our daughters (his nieces) and grandchildren. But, he was admittedly despondent and melancholy on frequent occasions, so we attempted to ramp up the frequency of visits and would convince him to dine out with us when we could get him motivated. I built a large deck extending the entire length of the rear of his house, purchased a barbecue grill for him and he enjoyed grilling during nice weather. I also designated a somewhat large space for a vegetable garden in his backyard, that provided him with surplus produce. He wasn't living a luxurious retirement but it sure beat the alternative of trying to survive on the streets in Vegas!

40

THE SWAN SONG

I had become more than slightly frustrated with the limitations and lack of control that were associated with functioning as an independent, outside consultant. It was, to some extent, enjoyable but didn't provide the satisfaction and sense of accomplishment that being an integral part of an organization could provide. After targeting sixty-five as my firm, full retirement date, I now came to the realization that five more years of consulting wouldn't work well for my psyche. I still had a good five additional years to give and wanted to single out a prospective organization where they might glean substantial benefit from my involvement, and I might derive an appropriate crescendo to an accomplished career and a platform to create my "magnum opus". I put out some feelers and sent a curriculum vitae to a few select companies that intrigued me and decided that Patricia and I would attend the major trade show of the year, held in March at the Jacob Javits center in NY, to follow up with anyone expressing an interest in bringing on someone with my skill set and talent. At the very least, we could look up old friends, enjoy Manhattan, and she could do some buying for her office and attend some interesting seminars. As always, our time in The Big Apple was a blast; fine dining, staying in a great Midtown hotel, Broadway plays, trendy bars and nightclubs, socializing with friends, attending the ancillary events and cocktail parties. But from a business perspective, I was a little conflicted and perplexed. The companies expressing an interest in my services and potential involvement were the peripheral players that I had previously placed in my cross hairs as minor competitors, either to be defeated offhand if they became a nuisance, or ignored as an inconvenient distraction, generally capturing only a minuscule amount of market share and therefore unworthy of full bore frontal attack like those launched against the largest competitors. After having enjoyed top executive positions at the largest companies in the industry, it would seem an anticlimactic swan song of the nth degree to wrap up my career with one of those minor players. Not at all the blaze of glory exit that I desired.

Ironically, I had gotten a call from a lens manufacturer (Israel based with a distribution and sales base in San Diego, CA) a week or so before the convention, that had heard I was in the job market and wanted to set up an interview at the show. My first reaction was that I probably wouldn't be interested, knowing that they had nothing to do with frames or the fashion end of the optical industry and were specifically involved with the manufacture, distribution and direct sale of state of the art Progressive Lenses to the Eye Care Providers. Never the less, I returned their call and had a lengthy conversation with their Director of Human Resources, who was delightfully engaging, charming, informative and encouraging, ultimately convincing me to schedule an interview for the final day of the show.

We weren't returning to North Carolina until Wednesday anyway, and we had little else on our schedule, so there was nothing to lose other than an hour or two of my open time.

During the week that ensued, between the call and the trade show, I spent a great deal of time considering the opportunity and became quite enamored with the concept of completing my career doing something very different; something that would require further educating myself and learning a new type of product at this very late career stage, and that had some genuine appeal. And, the more I thought about it, the more intrigued I became. I understood that even though it was a departure from the fashion aspect of the industry, sales is sales, management is management and motivating salespeople is motivating salespeople. It really wouldn't be much of a leap from frames to lenses and a Vice President of Sales position would be essentially the same in any segment of the industry. With that said, I was willing, and even anxious, to meet them for an interview to at the very least hear what they had to say. It would be as much me interviewing them as them interviewing me. In addition, she (the HR Director) had indicated that they had a few interviews scheduled with some other candidates that same morning, tactfully disclosing that they had experience in the lens arena, or in an optical laboratory environment, so the competition would be intense.

The night preceding the interview was filled with a skosh too much revelry and we didn't return to our hotel until quite late, which didn't help contribute to me being on the top of my game for the interview, nor did it contribute much to a sartorial propriety, when I dressed for the occasion. I chose to wear a grey flannel Hugo Boss suit, a white silk Giorgio Armani shirt, worn open collared, black, lizard skin cowboy boots, carried a hand tooled, western patterned black leather briefcase and sported a full beard, having recently turned more grey than brown. I was later told that their first reaction was "who the hell is THIS guy" and "We might have been mistaken to think that a frame guy could be appropriate for lenses". However, they also later disclosed that "the minute he opened his mouth and spoke, we knew that he was our guy". In all honesty, if I had impressed them, they impressed me more. The interview was enjoyable, inspiring and exciting, listening to their synopsis of that end of the business, their history and their vision for the future stimulated my desire to get involved. I felt an immediate affinity and admiration and was affected by their enthusiasm. The only downside was that the salary wasn't anywhere near what I had become accustomed to, but I really didn't care; I wanted in! I met with Patricia for lunch after the interview and surprised her when I said I really wanted the position. All I could do then was to wait a few days for an up or down call.

When I was offered the position later that week, I immediately accepted without hesitation. The learning curve was brief and I was able to segue into the V.P. position with ease, ultimately during my tenure, advancing to the position of Senior Vice President. I restructured, brought in some former friends and associates from the frame arena to fill Regional Manager spots and open sales positions, learned the new account base quickly (wholesale laboratories and lens distributors more than eyecare providers) and rapidly enjoyed nice sales increases.

I rapidly bonded well with our Marketing V.P. and the CEO. As a matter of fact, the CEO was a unique, talented, dynamic and energetic individual who had been raised in Israel and we quickly became good friends.

The company is based in Israel, on the western slopes of the Golan Heights in the Upper Galilee area near the Lebanese and Syrian borders. It is actually a kibbutz and one of the most successful and prosperous kibbutzim in Israel. They do research and development, manufacture and distribution of progressive lenses (many eyecare professionals claiming that the product is the best available today), they manufacture non-woven fabrics and have a large apiary producing honey. For me, it seemed a perfect way to finish my career, having started my working life in a non-woven textile mill and now to finish in a segment of the optical industry in which I had yet to become engaged, and to top it all off, they were moving into the thin film optical coating arena, which provided an opportunity for me to offer my experience in that area as well. I got to travel to Israel and visit most of the important sites there, even climbing to the peak of Masada before dawn to watch the sunrise over the Dead Sea. I thoroughly enjoyed motivating the sales team, the public speaking, the interaction with laboratory executives and traveling the entire United States to conduct meetings and create seminars and relished the challenge and excitement of building a young company again, but when my predetermined time frame converged with the acquisition of our company by the dominant player in the lens industry, precisely at the intersection my personal disappointment, and the strong desire to embark on retirement "projects", I decided to resign. I had no desire to work for the merged company and to be honest, the commute from Charlotte, NC to San Diego, CA was wearing me down. They graciously provided a retirement party in conjunction with a National Sales Meeting replete with thoughtful gifts and kind words. It had been the culmination of a fantastic career and I couldn't have been happier to have it end on such a high note. But there were things to do during retirement that were calling and I was completely ready to make a graceful exit and embark on the next phase of our lives.

41

THE LAST BRETT STANDING

While it has been frequently stated that many people, especially formerly busy executives, find the transition into retirement difficult, I have to say that's not the case with me. Patricia decided that she wanted to remain engaged in her optician duties and continue working, eventually going on a part time schedule, while I pursued a long list of activities: investment property management and remodeling, cultivating a garden and vineyard, antique auto restoration and Corvette Club involvement, writing a book, entertaining great grandchildren, mentoring and much more.

Shelagh got by very modestly on social security and Walter's disability and kept occupied with her grandchildren who lived within a few miles of her. The brain tumor that had caused Walter's disability, and had allegedly been completely removed many years earlier, reappeared after years of remission and he deteriorated quickly, passing away at forty-four years of age in December of 2014. Shelagh was devastated and lost without him to care for.

Charlie's health also quickly went down hill starting around the end of 2013. He was plagued with reoccurring kidney stones and severe breathing difficulties. Stomach problems followed and when we were unable to reach him via the phone, we drove to his house to find him unconscious on the floor. We called the ambulance and had him taken to the hospital where he was diagnosed with pancreatic cancer. He refused surgery, after being told that his survival chances were only about 30 percent and post surgery life span would be short. He was placed in hospice but after almost three weeks without any degradation of condition, they released him. He returned to his house where he survived surprisingly well until another episode in February of 2015 occurred. Virtually the same scenario, but this time in addition to finding him unconscious in his reclining chair, he was bleeding profusely. Once again, he was admitted to the hospital, told that there was little that could be done, and he was subsequently admitted to the same hospice facility where he was over a year earlier. We visited daily, and our daughters and granddaughter and grandson came to see him when possible as well. Our youngest daughter even drove four hours plus, from Atlanta, GA to Kannapolis, NC, to see him on multiple occasions. He seemed relatively comfortable, as the nurses and attendants provided medication to ease his pain. On March 18th of 2015 he peacefully passed away. We had just left the facility a few hours prior, so sadly, he passed alone. But that seemed to me to be somewhat fitting, in that, it was the way he had lived his life. My initial thought was, what a tragic waste of a life.

He had accomplished nothing of significance, had virtually no possessions, had formed no lasting relationships with anyone other than Patricia and died penniless. He had been intelligent, been given a good upbringing, given the family home (carelessly squandering the porceeds from the subsequent sale), provided opportunities and did nothing with any of it. In all candor, he was profoundly lazy and narcissistic. It seemed like such a shame and a complete squandering of a life. But, who am I to judge? He made the conscious decision to live life the way he wanted and owed no one an apology. And when death came, he was ready and welcomed it.

Without Walter's disability checks, Shelagh could barely survive. She and her daughter who lived a few miles away mutually decided that she should move in with them. That was a huge mistake. Conflict developed, as it frequently does in those situations, and she finally called Patricia asking for help moving her few meager possessions out of the house and requested that I drive her to Jackson, Mississippi, where her eldest daughter lived. She was a single mother raising two daughters and having a difficult time of it, but never the less invited Shelagh to move in with her. A few days later I packed her belongings into our SUV, took Shelagh to a hotel for the night, then, the following morning She and I drove to Jackson. I unloaded that same evening, wished her well, and immediately started the return trip home. We were relieved to have her there, even though it wasn't the best situation, and hoped that it would work out well. Patricia called her each evening to hear how things were going, and it seemed as though it might have been a good move. Then, within a month, we got a call from Shelagh's daughter stating that Shelagh had gotten ill, and was unable to get out of bed that morning. She had called the ambulance and Shelagh was admitted to the hospital. After initially diagnosing her condition as pneumonia, they later discovered a heart problem that needed immediate surgery. On January 20th 2107, she died either during surgery or shortly after. Shocked would be an understatement.

Charlie's ashes remained at our house from March of '16 until July of that summer when we were finally able to find time to drive to Connecticut. His first wish was to have them spread along the strip in Las Vegas, but bringing ashes on a plane to Vegas, renting a convertible, dropping the top, popping a CD into the player, selecting Kenny Rogers singing 'The Gambler', after cranking up the volume to a level of '9.5', and then letting them fly while cruising the strip, seemed like it might be a poorly thought out plan; not to mention the consternation and public panic that might ensue during these times of potential terrorism. I can see the headline now: North Carolina Redneck couple arrested after suspected release of anthrax on Las Vegas Boulevard. Hummm...might be wise and prudent to go to plan 'B'. We therefore decided to stick with tradition and place his cremains in his designated spot at the family plot in St. Peter's Cemetery. It was, after all, the last grave space in the family plot and his rightful place to be.

He was the last of John and Mary Brett's direct lineal descendants with the surname Brett. With his passing, the Brett name (with a direct line to John and Mary), had died with him.

That afternoon was quite hot and humid; a sultry and hazy thickness hung in the air while tree frogs and locusts, grasshoppers and crickets contributed to the creation of a white noise in the background, especially from the area around Lake Kenosia, located approximately one eighth mile away, diagonally across the street. Typically, while visiting the cemetery, we bring a few gardening tools and implements to be used for cleaning up weeds and overgrown grassy incursions, reaching over the top of the horizontal stones like angry tentacles, nefariously attempting to obscure the memory of the deceased. Even the main vertical stone had some intrusion, grass first covering the flat base, then climbing up the vertical surface an inch or two before turning to the side, seeking to take root elsewhere.

After edging back the trailing grass around the smaller stones with a flat spade, I sprayed some 'Round-Up' along the perimeter to further discourage growth, at least temporarily, then headed over to the large family marker where John and Mary were laid to rest. I knelt quietly for a moment, then Patricia approached from another stone that she had been clearing, and knelt beside me. Deep in contemplation, I had been pondering the significance of the day, and the placement of the final child named Brett to rest alongside the family members who had passed before him, as the date of John's passing caught my attention. Amazingly, it was exactly one hundred years prior to that day. I let that sink in. This day was the 100th anniversary, to the day, of the passing of John Brett; the man whose pluck and faith provided the courage, determination and resolve to leave the only home he had ever known to embark upon a dangerous journey with his new bride and aging mother, to set roots and establish a new life in the United States of America so many years before. What a remarkable coincidence. A full century had passed, lives were lived and stories created, a legacy of courage, faith and hope and a willingness to take risk passed on, along with opportunities for their descendants to make their own life choices, be they right or wrong, in an environment where a spirit of independence and freedom were offered, were nurtured, grew and thrived in this great new country; a country that John and Mary Brett grew to love as their own. Though it sounds paradoxical, the family was exceptional, while quintessentially average American. And the word "average" certainly isn't intended to demean. There is something very noble, free spirited, glorious and distinguishing about being an "average" American family; especially an immigrant American family. They embraced life, perfected the art of possibility, made good decisions and bad, poor choices and good, had weaknesses and profound strengths, loved and laughed, wept and despaired- All the things average families do. But they did it with a gusto and "joie de vivre" that produced a great story, while contributing to the creation of the fabric of American life and the formation of what is oxymoronically described as a "typically unique" American family.

And if there was one set of defining attributes or traits that could be assigned, across the board, as passed along to John and Mary's descendants through the DNA, the bloodline, or the spirit, it's the pluck, courage, willingness to take risk, and resolve to create opportunity for their children, and the strength to face life's difficulties and challenges that will surely come, with the faith that they will persevere and tomorrow will provide new opportunity.

They were optimists and risk takers, those traits made manifest in a myriad of different ways. Some achieved great success, long, productive lives, contentment and a gratifying sense of accomplishment, while others did not; and one can not deny the role that fate plays as life unfolds. But, that's true for any family. I am greatly pleased and honored to have been a part of it; to have been adopted as family, through my marriage with Patricia, and to have had the privilege of weaving my life story into theirs.

My seemingly oblique diversion during the telling of the Brett family story, to include my own personal life experience, with an in depth discussion of my career path and trajectory, might seem incongruous to some, but it clearly had enormous impact on Patricia's life, and as we journeyed together, it became her story as well. And, at risk of sounding profoundly immodest, that journey together, contributed to her living the dream held by John and Mary, greater than any other of their offspring.

In addition, my early life trajectory had elicited a patently negative set of expectations from prognosticators of all sorts with whom I had contact during that time, and to have turned around what seemed potentially like a life fraught with failure and disappointment, to redirect onto a path of enormous success, primarily due to the symbiosis created from my relationship with Patricia, should reinforce the importance of proper selection of an appropriate life partner, as well as inspire a young person who might also have launched on a less than favorable trajectory to redirect and take control of their life, knowing that potential exists, and path changes are possible.

And now, at the end of the century of Brett's in America, with Patricia being the last of John and Mary's lineal descendants remaining (the last to have been born with the surname Brett), this narrative might appear to be a requiem of sorts.

Quite the contrary. The DNA and spirit lives on in names like Moseley, DeBertott, Pethel, Gooden, Cooper, McAllister, Cominsky and others. The "melting pot" that is America is continuing according to tradition, and the contribution of Irish culture and custom, spirit and DNA, courage and resolution in the face of difficulty, defined as "Pluck", the joy of living, eternal optimism and unabiding love of family, God and country, added generously to the mix by the Brett family, has now joined other cultures, ethnicities, nationalities, and stories of other immigrant families, to yield the quintessential American legacy. A legacy that captures the best of differing cultures, traditions, traits and even physical characteristics of previous generations, while continuing to evolve with the creation of new families and new experience. That, in my humble opinion, is what defines America.

EPILOG

Why did I feel compelled to share the odyssey of the Brett family? They were indeed "average" in many ways and achieved nothing particularly noteworthy, at least in terms of a grand accomplishment, to be ultimately recorded as part of their legacy. It could just as easily have been the untold story of many other immigrant families who came to America with a dream, seeking success in ways that only they could define. Collectively, they have all contributed to the creation of the greatest country on earth, and to me that's reason enough, and the Brett family is merely a representative example. I suspect that in many cases, with minor changes, it could be the story of your family.

John Brett left no monetary or financial legacy to be handed down to his offspring. What he did leave however, by having the courage, determination and fortitude to take risk and travel to America, and by creating a nurturing and value based environment within which his family would be raised, and to sacrifice for them on a daily basis, was to expose them to, and prepare them for, the *opportunity and potential* that America had to offer. He placed them in a country where they would be limited only by their ambition, the choices they made, good or poor, and the decisions made, right or wrong, prudent and well analyzed, or impetuous and reckless.

And, as you will have discovered after reading the story of the Brett's in America, by the relevance of that intangible and ambiguous concept of "fate". We are all given potential and opportunity, and good choices and proper judgement, as well as analytical decision making, can lead us in the proper direction, and to some extent, mitigate the effects of fate; but in the end, we simply do our best and await the result, and our destiny, after the capricious, fickle and ever present hand of fate has had its say, can provide a resulting outcome that can potentially astonish and delight, or disappoint, in equal proportion.

Finally, I think that providence and circumstance had placed me in a position to write their story, because if I hadn't, it would have never been told. The names of John and Mary Brett would have been spoken for the final time, signifying the third and final death. And, as importantly, it was worthy of being told; there are life lessons contained within the re-telling of it that are of some potential value, and I'm hopeful that glimpses of the human condition will be entertaining while offering inspiration for contemplative introspection. I know personally, that becoming a part of the family through marriage, and therefore offering my own story as part of the composition, primarily to contribute important context and personal perspective, encouraged my own introspection and ultimately became quite cathartic.

AUTHOR BIOGRAPHY

Lansing Bergeron has aptly been called an authentic Renaissance Man, having been involved in retail apparel, retail sporting goods, highly technical aspects of the manufacture of precision optics and a long and highly successful career as an optical industry sales and marketing executive, leading a team of specialized representatives carrying iconic brands of fashion eyewear and 'state of the art' sunglasses such as Ray Ban and Oakley, and well known licensed designer products of Giorgio Armani, Valentino, Versace, Hugo Boss and many others. An entrepreneurial spirit and multi disciplined background lead to real estate investing and real estate management, construction, public speaking, mentoring, consulting, sales training; and on a leisure time basis, sports car enthusiast, auto racing participant, antique automobile restoration, viticulture and vineyard creation; and now, with the completion of his second book, author. A history of extensive world travel and a keen interest in American history, and in genealogy, combine to present a unique perspective when creating the saga of the three generations of the Brett family. *Lansing Bergeron* lives in North Carolina with his wife, Patricia.

CPSIA information can be obtained
at www.ICGtesting.com
Printed in the USA
BVHW031945041220
594198BV00023B/126/J

9 781977 200228

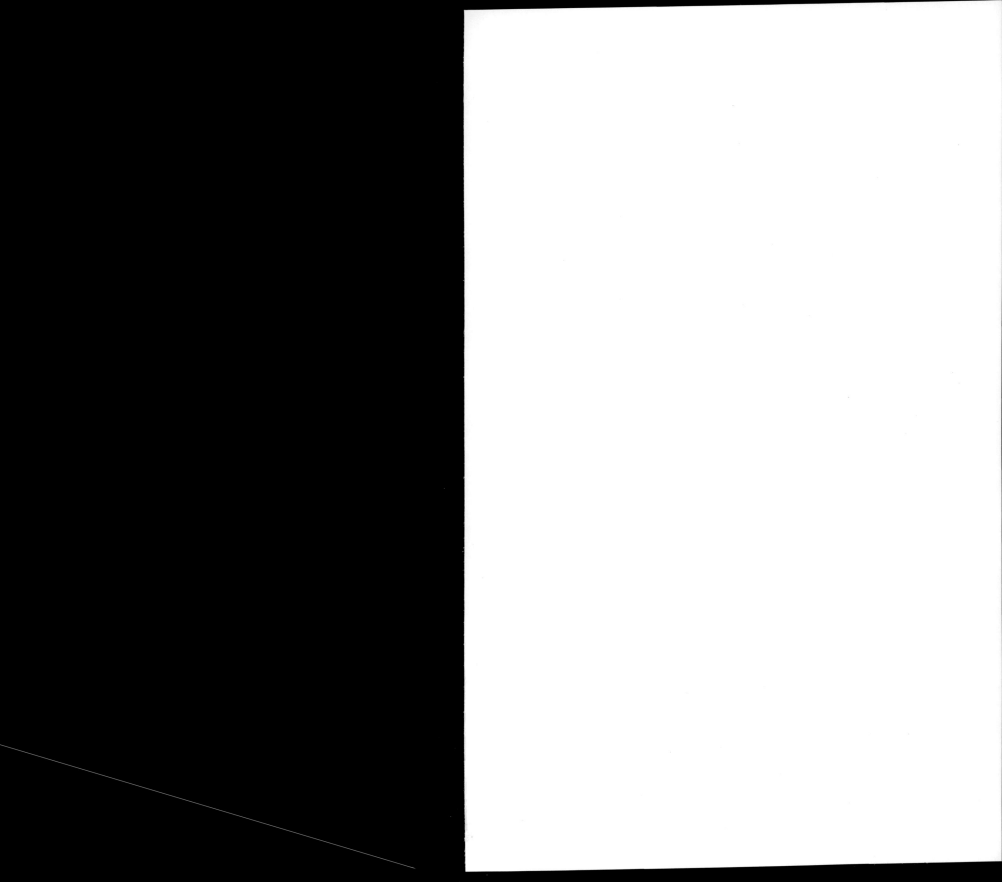